A Place Of Refuge

A Place of Refuge

Brian C. Puckett

A Place of Refuge

Copyright Brian C. Puckett

Cow Trail Publishing / First publication 2018

ISBN 978-0-578-20725-4

For Patty

Chapter One

The Big Island of Hawaii — 1986

The two boys hid their bicycles in a tangle of brush beside the dusty path and scrambled down the hillside toward the shore, where crystal-blue waves rolled in from the Pacific and slapped themselves into foam against black lava rock. They had pedaled to this spot from their homes in the small village of Mokolea, located on Hawaii's southwest coast. Both boys were ten years old, and both were black-haired, brown-skinned descendants of the original Polynesian islanders.

The boys halted a few feet from the water. Here and there the falling tide revealed wet furry patches of brownish algae that filled the air with a musky odor.

The smaller boy took two empty juice cans from a sack. "Wan' sta't ovah deh brah?" he asked, pointing. His English was a rapid flow of words dropping sharply in tone at the end, a pidgin vernacular peculiar to Hawaii.

"Shu," his friend said.

They removed their sneakers and stepped barefooted into the glass-clear water. Wading through the shallow surf to the nearest exposed lava rocks, they

1

crouched down and used short knives to pry *opihi* from the bare areas where they clung tenaciously. The mollusks, which grew shells in the shape of flattish fluted cones a couple of inches across when fully mature, were good eating either steamed or raw.

The smaller boy had gathered nearly half a can of *opihi* when he spied something floating on the waves, bobbing in the water perhaps fifty yards from where he stood. It looked like a bundle of rags.

"Ey," he said, pointing with his knife, "what you tink is?"

His friend stood and shaded his eyes with one hand, squinting and frowning. Careful of his footing, he stepped onto another rock for a better view.

"Look like gobbij," he finally said, shrugging.

"I'm gon see." The smaller boy wedged his can into a crack in the rocks and set off, clambering expertly across the lumpy lava.

The taller boy moved down to the water's edge again. He'd seen drifting garbage before. Plenty of it. Plastic sacks of crap from ships at sea, hunks of busted styrofoam, blobs of crude oil, swarms of plastic bottles, shit-stained Pampers, all kinds of horrible stuff that ended up on Hawaii's shores by the ton.

He had just spotted a patch of five good-sized *opihi* when he heard a shout. He looked over his shoulder and saw his friend hurrying back, moving across the lava like a frantic crab and yelling about something. With a last glance to mark the location of the *opihi* the taller boy climbed a few yards away from the soft slap and hiss of the breakers and shouted, "Ey! What you fine?"

His friend stumbled and fell as he ran but got up immediately and kept coming, ignoring the cuts on his knees as he leaped from one rock to another. He stopped a few yards away, clinging to a lava crag for balance and gasping for breath. His face was strangely blank.

"What?"

"Is a guy, brah!" the small boy blurted out.

"What you mean?"

"Is a guy!" the boy shouted. "Somebody dead in da watah!" Tears sprang from his eyes. He had never seen a dead person before, and this one—even though it was swollen and chewed by fish—looked like someone he knew.

Chapter Two

The '75 Chevy Cheyenne sped south along the Queen Ka'ahumanu Highway, following the coastline. Slouched behind the wheel of the rust-eaten pickup, Neal Tate took off his sunglasses and rubbed his eyes, blinking at the endless azure sprawl of the Pacific Ocean off to his right. He was struggling out of a torpor brought on by sun, heat, and the steady mutter of the engine. The highway itself was sleep-inducing; most of it was as smooth and straight as a runway as it sliced through miles of dry yellow grass and gray-black lava flows of the Kona Coast.

Tate glanced at his watch when the sign for Honokohau Harbor came into view. He was running late.

The truck's balding tires complained as he wheeled into the entrance, followed suddenly by plumes of steam streaming from beneath the truck's buckled hood.

"Ah, hell." Nothing new but always a pain in the ass.

At low speed Tate followed the paved road to a fork, bore right, and bounced across the acre or so of bare ground that served as the harbor's parking lot and dry dock. To his left a forest of masts and towers seemed to sprout from the earth. The harbor wasn't natural; it had been blasted from solid lava and sea level was several feet below the surrounding land.

Tate parked his steaming vehicle near the middle

4

boat ramp, directly above the *Suzy Q*'s slip. He took a plastic jug from the back of the truck and walked down the ramp to the slip.

The *Suzy Q* was gone, which meant that its owner, Tate's friend Big Jim Perkins, was probably out fishing with a client. Tate located the end of Big Jim's cheap vinyl garden hose and cranked open the valve, causing the hose to swell up and hiss like a snake, but a couple of kicks at the twisted heap straightened the kinks and produced a steady flow of water.

As the jug filled Tate caught his reflection in a cracked boat windshield propped against the rock wall of the harbor. He looked a lot better than he had in LA. Tanned. Healthy. The karate and weight lifting were filling out his muscles again. He turned his head, letting the hard light fall across his face. The cheeks weren't as gaunt as before but otherwise his features looked the same as always. Hawkish, Susan said, and he could see it. A heavy brow hooding his eyes, a nose just large and broken enough to suggest a beak. She also said he was cute but he had to take her word for that.

The jug filled with a gurgle and he turned off the faucet and climbed up the ramp to his truck.

A hot geyser spewed upward when he knocked off the truck's radiator cap. He let the steam subside, refilled the radiator, then restarted the truck and rumbled across the parking lot to the far end, where he turned onto a short, unpaved road near the harbor mouth. Parking at the end of the road, he looked across a quarter mile of flat lava shoreline and saw small specks moving on a gleaming crescent of sand. The specks were naked humans. They were throwing Frisbees, smoothing on tanning oil, taking in the sun at what was called, for lack of a better name, the Nude

Beach.

Tate opened the door and propped his foot on the hinge, getting comfortable. Four months ago, when he and Susan first came to the island, he had not been enthusiastic about lying naked on the sand with equally naked strangers only a few yards away. But after a few visits he'd gotten used to it. More or less.

The Nude Beach was one of several good things about Kailua-Kona, but it was fate and not planning that had brought them to this town in Hawaii. Before the state's bureaucracy had tracked him down with notice of George Akoki's bequest, Hawaii had been mostly a mental abstraction for Tate—beaches, palm trees, hotels, tourists. He thought that Honolulu was located on the biggest island before looking at a map, but the state's capital city was actually on the mid-sized island of Oahu. The island called Hawaii—the Big Island—was located some 130 miles southeast of Oahu along the Hawaiian archipelago.

In the last four months Tate's knowledge of the Big Island had grown considerably. In the first place it was indeed big—nearly twice the size of the seven other major islands combined. From above it looked vaguely like a turtle swimming northeast in the middle of the Pacific Ocean, head extended, left foreleg stroking, two webbed rear feet splayed. The turtle's shell had two high humps located approximately in the middle: Mauna Kea and Mauna Loa, volcanic mountains over thirteen and a half thousand feet tall, nearly as high as Colorado's loftiest peaks. In general the turtle's left side—in the lee of the trade winds—was dry and covered with grass or scrub growth at lower elevations, while its right side was wet and covered with jungles and forests.

6

As a whole the island was sparsely populated. The biggest city, Hilo, was located just above the turtle's right rear flipper. With its seaport and airport, Hilo had formerly been the island's uncontested center of activity, but tourists now flocked to Kailua, located directly across from Hilo on the sunny west coast, the Kona Coast. Kailua had its own jetliner airport now, just a little ways up the coast. If not for the advice of the travel agent who sold them their tickets they would have flown into Hilo to await the probate proceedings.

Tate saw Susan coming up the sandy road ahead, identifiable by her khaki shorts and pink tank top. As she got closer he saw sweat shining on her long, tanned legs. Time on the island hadn't hurt her either. Her hair had lengthened and the sun had turned it a streaked auburn that looked good against her caramel skin.

Susan saw him and waved. He lifted a hand in return, watching her approach. He liked looking at her. Especially her face. After ten years and dozens of portraits he could draw her from memory. The strong, straight nose. The wide, gently downturned mouth, lower lip slightly fuller. Her eyebrows, smoothly tapered arcs, black like the heavy lashes that made her hazel eyes seem pale and feline.

As she strolled up to the truck Tate tapped his watch and said, "You're late."

Susan pulled off her sunglasses and arched an eyebrow. "Oh, really? How long have you been waiting?"

"Seems like forever."

Susan rolled her eyes. "I saw you drive up, pal. They don't call you Mr. Late for nothing."

"Are they calling me that again?"

"Among other things." Susan tossed her bag and

beach mat into the truck and got in. The dented pickup belched blue smoke as Tate coaxed it into motion.

When they were on the highway headed for town Susan said, "How did it go?"

"Painting? Great." In fact things had gone remarkably well that morning. He had somehow crossed a hundred yards of sharp *a'a* lava, backpack and all, without a single stumble, and within a few minutes of reaching the isolated cove on the far side he found an excellent vantage point. After setting up, leveling the easel and stool with hunks of lava, tying the umbrella down with nylon cord, and clamping down the canvas, he penciled in the rocks and water, squeezed fat lines of paint onto the palette, and got to work, starting on the sky with quick, short strokes of a one-inch filbert. Two hours later he was working on another view of the cove.

"It seems like you've been working a lot," Susan said. "If you—" A mongoose suddenly scurried across the highway, looking like a stretched-out squirrel on rollers. Susan yelped and stamped on a phantom brake pedal. Tate guided the truck through an easy swerve, watching the animal shoot into the brush. "Those things drive me crazy when they do that," Susan said, exasperated. "I think they wait until you're close on purpose."

Tate grunted. "Could be. No cobras in Hawaii so they do this for kicks."

"I was going to say if you keep this up you'll have enough stuff for a show before long."

"Well, it'll be a while," he said. He had a list of places on the Kona Coast he wanted to paint, compiled during the time they spent in Kailua, and he had about half of them done. Unfortunately a number of the remaining sites were north of town and now that they lived near Mokolea it was a long drive. On the plus side the weather up north was nearly always perfect, they liked to visit Kailua, and they made a lot of side trips to places they hadn't seen before.

Susan shifted her position on the seat and Tate glanced at her. She was leaning out of the window, fluffing her hair in the breeze.

"What?" she said, pulling her head in when he laughed.

"You remind me of a dog with your head out like that."

"That's so sweet."

"A really *cute* dog."

"Keep working on it," she said. She took a brush from her bag and ran it through her hair. "So, what's the plan here?"

Tate hitched himself up in the seat. "Personally, I'd like to hit the Kona Inn and eat a grotesquely large meal."

"Sounds good. I wouldn't mind hanging out in town for a while after that. Sort of wean myself from civilization gradually."

Tate snorted. "I'm still not convinced Los Angeles *is* civilization. Which reminds me—I wanted to stop by the GYRO office."

"Oh? How come?"

He lifted a shoulder. "I thought we'd give 'em a few more bucks."

The brush stopped. "More? Good grief, Neal, we already gave a hundred dollars."

"What they're up against, that's nothing."

"It's not nothing. What brought this on, those trucks?"

Tate shrugged again. "I guess so. I thought we were finally getting away from everything. First there's the launch site madness and now this, right next door. They're probably putting in a fifty-story hotel."

"Not way down there, Neal. I still think they're just fixing up the ranch."

"I hope you're right," Tate said grimly. "I'll flag down one of the trucks and ask when we get back."

He turned down Kaiwi Street into Kailua's industrial area. Four blocks down, after stopping to let a dusty mongrel trot across the driveway, he pulled into a small, half-full parking lot in front of a row of storefront offices.

Susan lifted her sunglasses. "Looks like they're gone."

The sign over the unit that had housed the GYRO Hawaii office was gone and the plate glass windows, now missing their bamboo blinds, were dust-dulled.

Tate got out. "Right back."

He went up to the office door and peered through it with his hands cupped around his eyes. There was nothing inside but bare carpet and a few scattered papers. He stood in the sun a moment, then entered the office next door.

Susan was fanning herself with a magazine when he returned to the truck. "What's the deal?"

"I don't know," he said, looking puzzled. "The people next door say the GYRO office was open last Saturday and empty when they came back Monday. Looks like they moved."

"Maybe they closed down."

"I hope not. Or if they did I hope it's for the right reason. I'll try to track 'em down later."

Tate started the truck and turned it around. As they

pulled into the street Susan said, "Since we're near, you want to stop by Harry's and say hi?"

Tate stuck out his lip. "How about later? Maybe we can get together at *pau-hana* time and have a drink."

They drove down Palani and turned onto Ahi Drive, entering the heart of Kailua. The streets and sidewalks teemed with the first wave of the post-Christmas tourist horde. Tate turned up a narrow street across from the Kona Inn and pulled into the parking lot at the end, where, miraculously, he found an empty space in the shade of a *kiawe* tree.

"Give me a minute," Susan said when he killed the engine. "I want to fix my hair."

Tate slumped against the door, sliding down in the seat enough to ease the pressure on his back, which was tight from sitting in front of the easel. While Susan braided her hair he stared through the truck's cracked windshield. The quiet inside the cab was soothing. His eyelids began, slowly, to droop. Outside, in a world colored amber by his sunglasses, a mynah bird swooped down to the parking lot to peck at a rotten papaya. He moved his eyes; yellow rays sprayed off chrome and glass, dazzling and hypnotic.

Susan touched his shoulder. "Hey," she said in a whisper. "I'm ready. What are you thinking about?"

It took a conscious effort to tear his eyes from the light and turn his head. "I...nothing, really."

"Come on."

"I don't know. I just had this weird feeling. Like this was all a dream, us living here. Like I was going to wake up and..." He shook his head.

Susan leaned across the seat and kissed him. "It's real all right. Look." She tapped the dashboard with a finger. "This truck is proof. Something this bad couldn't exist even in a nightmare."

They got out. "You know," Tate said, shoving his door closed with a creak that sent the mynah bird flapping into the air, "sometimes I get the feeling you don't like my truck. But when the market for iron oxide picks up you'll see how clever I was."

As they strolled down to Ahi Drive Tate absent-mindedly plucked cans, wrappers, and bottles from cracks in the rock wall bordering the sidewalk where slobby tourists and natives had stuffed them. He deposited the trash in a receptacle across the street in the Kona Inn Shopping Village. "Haven't been here in a while," he said. For a tourist trap, the Village—an old resort hotel converted into a tree-shaded, open-air boutique mall—was not unpleasant.

They bought two iced teas at Billy Boy's and took them out to the lawn overlooking Kailua Bay, where a steady breeze stirred the palm fronds overhead.

Settling onto the grass, Susan made a moaning sound of contentment. "Boy, I had a great day doing nothing."

Tate stretched out beside her. "Well, hell, after a three-week vacation a person needs to relax a little."

They sipped their tea, watching a line of sailboats rock at their moorings. The breeze, smelling of salt and chlorophyll, gradually cooled them off. Tate finished his drink first and rolled into a sitting position. "I think I'll try to find out what happened to GYRO," he said. "Want to wait here while I use the phone?"

Susan moaned again. "You couldn't move me. Take your time."

He found the pay phone near the restrooms already in use. A local kid attired in lime-green baggies and orange sandals was tugging at his crotch and shouting angrily into the receiver. "Shit, brah, how you *broke?* Don' broke a boogie wit' one fuckin' *hammah,* brah, shit!"

Tate waited on a bench. When it became evident conversation was just warming up he headed for the coffee shop *cum* bistro farther down the mall.

He paid for a cup of Kona Dark and took it to a table shaded by a small banyan. He dumped a packet of sweetener and two containers of half-and-half into the coffee and stirred it thoughtfully. The sweetener was carcinogenic, the half-and-half was loaded with artery-clogging cholesterol, and the caffeine would disrupt the functioning of various internal organs. As he sipped the steaming toxins he reflected on the fact that, correctly applied, science could suck the joy out of anything.

He was staring into space when a blazing orange aloha shirt appeared in front of him. "Well, well!" a familiar voice bellowed, "Look who's back in town!"

Tate raised a hand to shield his eyes. "Hey, man, you could blind somebody with that shirt!"

James "Big Jim" Perkins bent down and peered from under his shapeless Panama hat. "Wait, now," he said in his plodding tones, "is it Paul Gauguin or...Vincent Van friggin' Gogh?"

"You've been in the sun too long," Tate said. He slapped the bench encircling the banyan tree. "Have a seat."

Perkins circled around the table and lowered himself ponderously onto the shaded bench, which creaked under his weight. Perkins was just over six feet four inches tall and had the massive build of a defensive lineman, which he had been for the Raiders before a neck injury ended his football career. His huge frame was still heavily muscled but carried a noticeable layer of fat, the result of poorly restrained cookie and beer habits.

"So," Perkins said, dragging off his hat and clawing his hair and beard in a feeble attempt at grooming, "how's the paint dabbin' goin'? Used any good...pthalocyanine blue lately?"

Tate felt the first wave of Big Jim symptoms hit him. Perkins' sluggish mode of communication, with long pauses right in the middle of a sentence, seemed to drop people into low gear. It was Tate's theory that Big Jim's very *being* produced relativistic effects in his immediate vicinity. Time, motion, and biological processes actually slowed to a crawl. Remaining in the force field long enough caused important tasks to be shoved aside in favor of eating, drinking, bullshitting, and goofing off.

Tate sighed. "You never cease to amaze me, Large James. First you stun me by knowing Gauguin's full name *and* by making an effort to pronounce it correctly, and then you say 'pthalocyanine'. Who would imagine that a disheveled, semi-literate fisherman could come out with such a word?"

Perkins came precariously close to a laugh but caught himself and covered it with a cough into his hand. "So," he said. "You here to do a little...*plein-air?*"

Tate feigned shock. "There you go again!"

"What is it?" Perkins asked. "You're being more...c*ruel* than usual."

"You think so? As cruel as the guy who gave you that haircut?"

"As a matter of fact," Perkins said, giving his chest a proud pat, "I cut it myself. It's the natural look. Who wants to look like a...TV newsman?"

"I'm fairly positive no one could mistake you for a

TV newsman," Tate reassured him. He eyed the thick hair covering Perkins' arms and chest. "A gorilla, maybe."

"Oh, now that really slays me," Perkins said. "Scrawny little paint-dabber taunts..." He puffed out his chest. "...powerful sea god!"

Perkins checked the clock on the coffee shop wall and grunted. "Gotta cruise, dude. Clients to meet. Beer to drink." He stood up and clapped on his hat. "Glad to see you're back. Be in town awhile?"

Tate shook his head."We've got to get back and do some stuff, like finish unpacking. You want to come down? Take a break from this high-pressure scene here?"

"Can't," Perkins said. "I'm booked for the...next five days. When are you coming back in town?"

"I'm not sure," Tate said. "Two or three days."

Perkins' eyes lit up. "That's New Year's eve. We can party!"

"In that case we'll be here."

"*We* is right." Perkins pointed a finger. "Don't show up without the...*broad*."

Tate looked pained. "It makes me sick to repeat this but she actually said she missed you."

"Of course she did. Hey, when you come...leave a message with the...charter girls." Perkins flashed the *shaka* sign, thumb and little finger extended from his fist. "Aloha, brah." He strode off, his frayed tennis shoes slapping the fake cobblestones.

Tate took his empty cup back to the counter and strolled over to the pay phone.

The telephone directory hung from its wire like a shotgunned fowl, splayed pages soaked with a pink, sticky fluid. Using his fingertips he picked through the soggy mess and found a listing for GYRO—for Get Your Rockets Off—Hawaii.

When he dialed the number a recorded voice explained to him with false sympathy that it had been disconnected or was no longer in service.

Tate stood with the telephone in his hand, trying to remember the name of the woman who directed GYRO. Something with a B. Betty, Bobbi, Barbara, Belinda...

Bernice. Bernice what? Collins came to mind, but that wasn't right. He went back to the directory. He was peeling apart pages in the C's when the name popped into his head: Bernice Hollings.

A husky female voice answered on the third ring. "Aloha and hello-ah."

"Is this Bernice Hollings?"

"It most certainly is. Who has the pleasure of speaking to me?"

"This is Neal Tate. I met you at one of the GYRO meetings a couple of months back."

"Ah, Mr. Tate," Bernice Hollings sighed theatrically. "I've been expecting to hear from you."

*　　*　　*

Susan was reading on the seawall with her legs dangling over the rocks below when he came up behind her. She looked up and smiled and then saw his face. "Neal, what's the matter?"

He sat down beside her. "It's bad."

"What is?"

"I called the woman who runs GYRO. Bernice Hollings, the one who spoke at the meeting we went to." He pressed his fingers into his temples. "Remember the launch site, the thing they were trying

16

to stop? Apparently they didn't stop it."

"Oh. Well—that's bad news, all right."

"Yeah, it is. You know the blasting and all the trucks driving back and forth that started in the valley north of us while we were gone? That's where they're building it."

Susan stared at him. "*What?* Wait, I don't understand. I thought they wanted to build it on the *other* side of the island."

"They changed their plans or something. I don't understand it either."

"My god. Is all this absolutely certain, Neal?"

"Who knows? Bernice seemed to know what she was talking about. I asked her to meet us at the Kona Inn later and explain what the hell's going on." He hit his leg with a fist. "Dammit! I *knew* everything was too good to be true."

Susan set her book aside and slipped her arm around his waist. "Come on. Like you say, no sense getting upset until the facts are in. And you know how these things go. It may never get completed."

"Yeah, let's count on that."

"You never know, Neal. Look, when's the meeting with this woman, Bernice?"

He took a deep breath and let it out. "She's supposed to be there at five thirty."

Susan looked at her watch. "That's almost an hour from now. Why don't we get something to eat? You don't look so good."

"I don't really feel like eating." Tate blew out another long breath. "I wouldn't mind a drink, though."

Chapter Three

Smiling with practiced insincerity, the waitress at the Kona Inn jotted down their orders and left, working her way through tables crowded with tourists and the local *pau-hana* contingent.

Bernice Hollings lit her second cigarette, inhaled deeply, and put her elbows on the table, sending a gold charm bracelet sliding down her arm with a loud jangle. Her pose and her coaster-sized purple sunglasses gave Neal the impression of a praying mantis. A benign, bleached-blonde, late fiftyish praying mantis. "So, to answer your question, hon," she said, her voice foggy with smoke, "we're still trying to find some way of stopping them. But it doesn't look good."

He absorbed this stoically, having suspected it wouldn't look good. "Well, what I really can't understand is how the launch site got pushed through with all the opposition."

"Hon," Bernice said, "it's the same old story. There was some *persuasion* going on."

Susan leaned forward in her chair. "You mean somebody was bribed? Or something else?"

Bernice looked over her sunglasses. "That, and everything else you can imagine," she said evenly. She pushed back her hair with one hand, making the bracelet tinkle. "I could name names, but I don't want to get sued for libel, or slander, whichever the hell it is."

"What sort of things happened?"

"Like I said, it's the usual stuff. Promises for future contracts, campaign contributions, political and business favors."

"How do you know this happened?" Neal asked.

"I have what you'd call reliable sources. People I've known since I came here twenty years ago. They ain't the type to talk out their asses, if you'll pardon the expression." Bernice leaned back in her chair and waved away a fly with a flick of pink enameled fingernails. "Anyway, what they say just confirms what I've seen myself. Like information withheld from GYRO or lost by 'accident', lousy court decisions, discrepancies in procedure."

"Could you give an example?"

"Sure. First, the environmental impact study for the Keanapa Point site—that's the valley north of you— probably holds the world's record for shortest completion *and* acceptance time. Of course South Point was supposed to be CSS's first choice for a site, but when that was nixed and CSS announced that they wanted to put the site at Keone Flat, south of Pahala. So the folks living in Pahala and Na'alehu and the other towns raised holy hell. They've been some of GYRO's biggest supporters."

The waitress appeared with their orders, set them down, and hurried off again. Neal pulled his mud pie closer and prodded it unenthusiastically with a fork. He said, "So what happened with Keone Flat?"

"The answer is—nothing. The Environmental Impact Study had some complications that were bad for them, the natives were hostile, and the big environmental groups were up in arms because a launch site would ruin any plan to extend Volcanoes

National Park down to Keone Flat." Bernice paused for an angry puff on her cigarette. "Then CSS suddenly announces they're going to build the launch site at Keanapa Point, where you are. Lo and behold, the EIS for Keanapa was completed a *year* ago, contrary to what we were told. They hold a couple of quick hearings on it and it's accepted. We didn't have time to prepare. Also lo and behold, CSS has already *surveyed* Keanapa Point and already has *blueprints* for the launch site. It was a *fait accompli*, however the hell you pronounce that. We found out they'd negotiated the details of the land deal almost two years ago." She lifted her beer. "Cheers."

Neal took a sip of his coffee because he couldn't think of anything else to do, but it didn't taste good. Nothing tasted good at the moment. He said, "When did CSS actually announce the plan to build at Keanapa Point?"

"A couple of months ago. I'm surprised you didn't know about it. It's been in the papers quite a bit."

"We've been gone for a while," Susan said. "And we don't read the papers much. We're pretty isolated down there."

The ash on Bernice Hollings' cigarette had grown long enough to droop. She patted it into an ashtray. "That must be pleasant, hon, but I'm afraid you won't be isolated for long. The businessmen and politicians behind CSS are salivating over the money in this thing and they don't give a damn what it'll do to the island. Hell, most of 'em live on Oahu."

Susan frowned. "Is there that much money in it?"

"In the short run, yes, for the various suppliers, construction companies, engineers, shippers, you name it. But for CSS, maybe and maybe not. See, the U.S.

20

used to be the main supplier of launch vehicles, with the Delta and Titan and then the shuttles. But we fell behind in producing unmanned launchers, and of course the *Challenger* accident is going to knock out the space shuttles for at least another year. Maybe more than that, the way NASA works. Suddenly the commercial launch business looked so good that the Chinese and Japanese and Russians jumped in. Of course the French already had their Ariane rockets. A couple of other American companies are getting into it, too."

Bernice paused for another puff on her cigarette. "It looked like a potential glut of launchers," she said, hissing out the smoke, "but CSS figured it could still get a piece of the action. They decided to specialize in LEO launches—that's low earth orbit—and sub-orbital launches. That's why they were able to switch from Keone Flat on the east side of the island and go with Keanapa Point on the west, which fooled us."

"I don't get it," Neal said.

Bernice set her elbows on the table again. "CSS spent a bundle starting up their company and developing their rocket, but when they suddenly had a lot of competition they changed their game plan to doing the LEO and suborbital launches. That meant they could use a west coast site, like Vandenberg in California, for example. They didn't need the full boost from the earth's spin. For that you want ideally a low-latitude site on the east coast of whatever place you're launching from so the rocket flies over an empty ocean when it takes off. That made Keanapa Point look great to CSS and they quietly went to work getting it."

Susan poked thoughtfully at the ice in her tea. "I'm still a little confused. What does that all that mean?"

"It means," Bernice said, "that all this talk about Keone Flat was just CSS farting chaff, pardon the expression. It was a smokescreen to throw us off, so we'd keep our attention and resources focused on that area. And it worked. Basically, we fucked up, pardon the expression. When CSS went with Keanapa our anti-rocket coalition fell apart. We didn't have a legal or environmental or political game plan for Keanapa, and the local population where you live is too small to have any clout. CSS did an end run around us. That's why we closed the offices here and in Pahala. The only GYRO staff left is me and a few other diehards."

They were silent. Neal tried his coffee again. He switched to water.

"I was wondering," Susan said. "Why Hawaii? I mean, aren't there lots of places they could launch from?"

"Not as many as you might think," Bernice said. "First, you want a place that's part of the United States for political stability and investment considerations. Then you want clear weather for work and launch considerations. And you want an unpopulated flight path, like the ocean, so if your rocket goes haywire it lands on fish instead of on Newark or some place. Of course if it did land on Newark you'd be doing everyone a favor, but that's another matter." Bernice drank the last of her beer and patted her mouth with a napkin. "Our lovely island meets all the requirements."

For the last half hour Neal had felt his body growing heavier, as if Bernice's words were an infusion of lead. His gaze wandered across the bay to the town pier. A charter boat had come in, and fishermen were wrestling their catch to the dock. Toward the tip of the dock, passengers disembarked from the day-cruiser

Captain Cook. His eyes moved to the sea wall bordering the lawn of the Kona Inn. Tourists were watching a fisherman in the shallows below, an old man who moved cautiously across the broken lava, his one-toed *tabi* gripping the rocks as he first positioned himself and then spun his net into the water with easy expertise.

"*Neal.*"

He turned to Susan. She was looking at him worriedly. "Bernice was talking to you."

"Oh. Sorry, it's my ear." He touched it. "It rings sometimes."

Bernice lowered her chin, looking at him over her sunglasses. "What happened to your ear, hon?"

"I, uh—injured it. A burst ear drum."

She winced. "How on earth did you do that?"

"Actually, it happened in Vietnam."

Bernice's lips parted in a sudden look of dismay. "Oh. I'm so sorry."

"It's no big deal, but thanks." He managed to smile. "What were you saying?"

She stared at him blankly. "Oh, yes. I was asking about the people who live near you."

"Who? You mean the Kahookes?"

"I believe that's right. Are they gone yet?"

His smile gelled. "No. Why would they be gone?"

"Because CSS is buying their land."

Neal's look turned to one of disbelief. "That's impossible. They wouldn't sell. They love that place. Kawika's grandfather built the house there."

"That may be," Bernice said. "I'm just going by what I was told." She slipped another cigarette from her leather case. "I hope you don't mind the smoke. I can't seem to stop myself today." She lit the cigarette with a

23

well-worn gold Zippo that had an anchor insignia engraved on one side. "All I know," she said, puffing as she snapped the lighter shut, "is that CSS just bought that parcel from a land syndicate, Pacific Investment Corporation."

Neal's eyes narrowed. "Pacific Investment? They've been trying to buy my place ever since I got it."

"Sure," Bernice said, "Your place is part of the land they want for the site. CSS got a deal on the rest of the land at Keanapa Point. It's a little complex, but not too hard to follow. Pacific Investment is a Japanese corporation that owns a venture capital subsidiary that owns a hunk of Concord Space Systems. The truth is CSS itself is a Japanese corporation in all but registration. They have a lot of American engineers and technicians working for them and a few American execs, but all the principal shareholders are Japanese. Anyway, Pacific Investment already owned Keanapa Point and most of the surrounding land, so when CSS went looking for a site they naturally checked out Keanapa. The only hitch was that two parcels of land kept the package from being complete—yours and your neighbor's. Now it's just you, since your neighbor's gone."

"Wait a minute," Neal said. "Are you sure we're talking about the Kahookes? They own the property just below ours."

"That's it."

He sat back in his chair, disturbed. "This is really strange. Kawika or Muriela would have said something."

"We've been gone," Susan reminded him. "We haven't seen them for over three weeks."

Smoke streamed from Bernice Hollings' nostrils in a

double jet. "Well, they should've known about it for at least a couple of months."

The waitress appeared on her rounds. Bernice ordered coffee and Neal ordered a beer.

"You own your land outright, don't you, Neal?" Bernice asked when the waitress was gone. "It's not a long-term lease?"

"No, I own it."

"Well, that's good. If CSS wants it they'll have to pay big." She mashed her half-smoked cigarette into the ashtray. "They haven't contacted you, huh?"

"Not CSS," he said. "Just Pacific Investment."

Bernice smiled grimly. "That was smart, hiding who it was. And since you obviously aren't anxious to sell they'll probably wait until you come to them. There won't be much peace and quiet down there when things get going. People, traffic, the rockets. They won't be launching every day of course, but you'll know it when they do. It's loud. I saw a couple of launches from pretty close range at White Sands."

"White Sands? With the military?"

"The Navy. My husband Jack was in some weapons program at the time, rest his soul."

Hesitating, Susan said, "Your husband is—gone?"

"No, no," Bernice laughed. "That's a little joke. Jack's a rear admiral over in Honolulu. We're separated. We get along better that way."

The waitress returned with the coffee. Bernice blew on her cup and took a tentative sip. She said, "Neal, I'm curious about something. I understand the people who owned your land before you were Hawaiian. At least the name looked Hawaiian to me. Is that right?"

He shifted uneasily in his chair. "Yes. The Akokis."

"Right, Akoki. Well, if it's not being too nosy, I was

25

wondering why they sold you their land. I mean it's pretty strange, with the launch site thing hovering in the background."

"Actually," he said, "I didn't buy it. I inherited it."

Bernice's eyebrows lifted over her sunglasses. "I see. So, you're part Hawaiian?"

He shook his head. "No, I'm pure *haole*. George Akoki left me the land when he died about six months ago.

"Oh. I see. How did he die, hon?"

"Well—they're not sure. A couple of kids found his body floating near the shore. He had a head injury, so they guess he was out fishing and he slipped and hit a rock."

"Oh, that's terrible," Bernice said, shaking her head. "Well, hon, if you don't mind my asking, how come he left the land to you? Are you somehow related?"

"No, I never even met George Akoki. Or his wife. She died about two years ago. He didn't have any other relatives, and their son..."

Susan answered for Neal when she saw him groping for the words. "They had a son," she said. "His name was Dan. Neal helped save his life in Vietnam but he was killed later in the war. When Mrs. Akoki died, Mr. Akoki left the land to Neal since there was no one else."

Bernice Hollings was still for a long moment. She finally nodded, a slight repetitive movement. "That's very sad," she said quietly. Her voice sounded hoarse. "Sad that he died. I'm sorry, I'm sure you don't like to talk about that. With GYRO and everything, I'm afraid I've gotten into the habit of being nosy."

Neal looked away a moment. "Well, it's hard not to think about it since I live in the house. No need to apologize."

They sat in awkward silence. Bernice dabbed delicately at her forehead with a paper napkin. She suddenly looked at her watch. "Oh, gosh! I'm sorry, but I really ought to go. I have to be some place at six thirty." She took her wallet from her purse. "Let me pay for this."

"No way," Neal said. "Go ahead, Bernice. I'll get the tab. I'm the one that dragged you over here anyway."

She seemed flustered. "Well, all right. If I can buy you and Susan a drink some time."

"That'd be great."

Bernice inclined her head. "Listen, you two might be running into some problems with this launch site mess. If I or GYRO can do anything to help, just give me a call. In fact—" She flipped through her purse and found a business card, which she put on the table. "Here's my work number, too."

Neal picked up the black and gold card. *The Treasure Chest*, it read, over an embossed wooden chest overflowing with pearls and coins.

Bernice stood. "Well, it was nice meeting you two, even if the circumstances weren't so pleasant." She squeezed Susan's shoulder. "Call me anytime, hon. 'Bye."

They watched as Bernice Hollings made her way toward the front entrance. When she was a couple of tables away she suddenly stopped. Her shoulders drooped slightly and she turned around and came back.

"Did you forget something?" Susan asked.

Bernice nipped her lower lip. "No." She sat down, perching on the edge of her chair. "I...I had a son. She set a hand lightly on Neal's leg, and her voice quivered slightly. "You remind me of him a lot. He was killed in

Vietnam."

She gave his leg a pat, stood, and hurried off again.

Neal sat still, holding his beer, the low afternoon sun burning one side of his face. The same side that was burned when the rocket tore through the barracks roof and exploded, blowing out his eardrum and blowing Dan into ragged red pieces. A swarm of images hovered at the edge of his mind, ready to invade, but he forced them back. He was good at it after so many years.

Chapter Four

They were quiet on the long drive home. As they climbed from arid brush land to dense forest, the sun settled into the ocean amid a fan of fiery clouds.

When they passed the old lava flow above Ka'u Loa Point Susan suddenly slapped her thigh. "Oh, darn it! We didn't go see Harry."

Neal grunted. "Damn. Well, we can phone him later. I wouldn't have been good company anyway."

"I guess," Susan sighed. "You know, I've been thinking. Things might not turn out so bad after all. If you sold the land you could buy a place somewhere else on the island. Maybe even a better one."

Neal shot her a glance. "I sure as hell doubt it!"

The burst of anger in his words left them hanging in the humming pickup cab like solid objects.

Susan waited long enough for her own anger to subside before continuing. "Oh. Why don't you think so?"

"Because," he said, the heat gone from his voice, "CSS hasn't contacted us themselves and their construction's going ahead. Obviously our place isn't critical to their plans. Even if it is they probably figure we'll take whatever they offer when they get around to it. No one else is going to want it anymore."

"Somebody might."

"Yeah, maybe, if they're blind and deaf. Anyway, the idea of selling it bothers the hell out of me."

Susan reached over and put a hand on his arm. "I understand that, Neal. But *we're* not blind and deaf. Do you want to end up living next to this launch site?"

"I don't know. I can't think right now."

They drove the next few miles without speaking. Neal turned off the highway onto Mokolea Road and they dropped down the flanks of Mauna Loa toward the sea.

"I can't believe this," he said, shaking his head. "Everything was so great."

"It has been great," Susan agreed. "Hawaii's wonderful."

"It's not just that," he said. "I mean look at my life before this, everything except you. Almost forty, I hated living in the city, hated doing commercial art, hated living in a shitty apartment. Now suddenly I've got a house and land. I've got a chance to change my life, do what I want."

He piloted the truck around a tight curve. "When we were flying back I realized I'd started to feel like this is *home* here. I haven't felt like that since I was a kid." He shook his head. "It's funny. When I was little, watching Tarzan and Jungle Jim, I wanted to live in the jungle. And now we live in a place that *has* jungles." He laughed, but there was no humor in it. "A *safe* jungle— no snakes, no leeches. No booby traps. No one trying to shoot you or cut your damn throat."

They were silent again. Ahead, a light showed through the trees.

"I'd like to stop at the store and get a few things," Susan said quietly. "And we need to check the mail."

They pulled into the dirt parking area in front of a small cinder block building with a yellow plywood sign affixed to the front that said *Yamata Store*. The store, run by an elderly Japanese couple, supplied groceries and sundries to the area's scattered residents and, occasionally, to tourists off the beaten path. It also served as the local post office; rows of small lockboxes were set into the building's outside wall beneath a projecting section of roof. Susan fit her key into one and pulled out the items inside.

"Here's something," she said, studying a slip of paper under the yellow bug light. "Says you got a certified letter."

Inside the store, Mrs. Yamata looked up from her sweeping, clawing a loose strand of gray hair into place. "Nee! Soo-san! Goo eenin!"

"Good evening, Mrs. Yamata," Neal said, returning her smile. He held up the slip. "I guess you have something for me.

"Oh, yes! Certify lettah!" Mrs. Yamata set aside her broom and scuttled to the rear of the store.

While she poked around in her post office cubbyhole Neal said, "Mr. Yamata's not out *fishing*, is he?"

"Ahh, yes, yes!" Mrs. Yamata said irately, wagging her head. "Same alway—he pray, I wuk."

This was her standard complaint, one that Neal prankishly exploited on occasion—as now—but it did seem true that Mr. Yamata—a quiet, smiling man who wore white tee shirts and Old Spice—was incredibly inept inside the store, and Mrs. Yamata pounced on his bumbling mistakes with a torrent of heated Japanese. It wasn't clear yet whether the bumbling was due to a dull wit or subtle cleverness.

"Ah! Here is lettah."

Neal examined the sky-blue envelope. One corner was embossed with the logo and Honolulu address of

Concord Space Systems. He signed for it and then accompanied Mrs. Yamata back to the register, where Susan waited with a collection of items. They paid, wished Mrs. Yamata a good evening, and left.

Neal drove down the narrow, bumpy blacktop while Susan opened the letter and held it under the cab light. "Well," she said, "this answers your question about whether they want your land or not."

"What's it say?"

"Reading between the lines, they want to buy, but most of it's blah, blah, blah. Signed by Edward H. Treadway III, Vice-president, Public Affairs. Boy, this guy's into some serious rhetoric. *I am looking forward with pleasure to making your acquaintance and am very anxious to discuss this important matter, which will affect your future, the future of Concord Space Systems, and the future of Hawaii.*" She looked up. "Looks like the course of history is in your hands."

"Pretty humbling. I'm surprised he didn't say the future of the world."

"He's probably saving that." Susan refolded the letter and slid it back into the envelope. "Well—are you going to talk to him?"

Neal grunted. "I don't know if I want to or not. I need to talk to Kawika and Muriela first."

"Sure. But it wouldn't hurt to just see what they're offering."

"I'll tell you what they're offering," he said shortly. "They're offering to screw this place up. Forever."

They slowed and turned off the pavement onto the steep, rutted road toward the house. Shadows bounced among the trees and an earthy smell rose from the rust holes in the cab floor. Pulling into the yard, Neal parked the truck, switched off the engine, and sat back, resting his head against the door. Outside, a few stars danced in the deepening sky.

Susan slid across the torn seat and put her arms around him. "I know you're upset."

"Yeah, you might say that."

"Well, as you say, no sense freaking out until all the facts are in."

"Do I say that? What an idiot."

"But you're *my* idiot. Hey, this'll cheer you up. Guess what I saw at the beach today? You won't believe it."

"No point in telling me then."

"Ho, ho. I'll tell you anyway. I saw a guy cruising around with a paper sack *picking up trash*."

"That's great," Neal said humorlessly. "Now we've got *three* people picking up crap the other five billion are throwing down."

Susan pecked his cheek and pulled away. "I'm sorry about this, Neal, the launch site. I don't want you to be depressed."

He shrugged. "I can't help it. But what about you? You're not?"

"I am, but I think it could turn out all right. If they really want this land they'll pay a good price for it. We can get another place."

"I don't *want* another place," he said, turning toward her. Her features were blurred in the dark. "I want *this* place, leaky old house and all."

"You mean because of Dan?"

He pressed his fingertips against his eyes; blue and green dots swam like fireflies in a black void. "Yeah," he said quietly. "Because of Dan. And his dad. They wanted me to have it. If I sold it I'd feel like a...a traitor or something."

"A traitor? Come on, that's silly."

33

He looked away. "Is it?"

They went inside, Neal carrying the sack of groceries up the worn wooden verandah stairs behind Susan. While she went to take a shower he felt his way through the darkened kitchen to the refrigerator. He put the milk away and pulled a beer from the six-pack at the rear of the rusty shelf. Squatting in the feeble light of the open refrigerator, cool air cascading over his legs and feet, he twisted off the cap and drank. The beer burned as it went down but it tasted clean. He put away most of the bottle in three long swallows, then pushed the refrigerator door shut and sat on the floor in the dark.

It was several minutes before he stirred. He finished the last dregs, then stood and pulled out the rest of the six-pack, shoving the refrigerator door closed with one foot. He could already feel the sly approach of a comfortable, dulling warmth from the beer.

Kawika.

Neal plowed through the house toward the bathroom, banging one shoulder on the corner as he turned into the hallway. It felt good.

Peppermint-scented steam flooded out when he opened the bathroom door. Over the noise of the shower he said, "Susan, I'm going down to Kawika's and ask him about this shit."

"Okay."

"You want to come?"

Her feet squeaked on the bottom of the old clawfoot tub and an elbow batted against the shower curtain. "No, I'm really tired. Say hi for me and I'll see them tomorrow."

"All right."

As he turned to leave the peppermint smell jogged

his thoughts. He reached up and took a bottle of Dr. Bronner's Pure-Castile-Soap off the shelf. Fearing it wouldn't be available on the island Susan had bought a dozen bottles of the stuff before leaving Los Angeles. He let his eye fall at random on the fine print crowding the label.

"76" Alpha Centauras' messenger of God's law, the Messiah, Halley's Comet, teaches Abraham-Israel-Moses-Buddha-Confucius-Hillel-Jesus-Spinoza-Paine-Mohammed, every 76 yrs., 79x76=6004 by '86, 6000 by '82, unite Gentile and Jew! We're All-One or none, as African astronomer Israel teaches since the year One to unite the whole Human race in All-One-God-Faith."

He set the Dr. Bronner's back on the shelf and departed, mystified as usual.

Outside, he made his way down the footpath toward the Kahookes' house, flashlight in one hand and beer in the other. When he came to a break in the trees he stopped and turned off the light. To the north, beyond the intervening ridge, a harsh glow lit up the sky. He could hear the faint sounds of machinery coming from the valley. Thinking of the place they were destroying gave him a stab of anger.

Since moving into the house in late October he and Susan had been to the valley five or six times. It was a beautiful place—green, open, and uninhabited. At some time in the past it had been a ranch; there was an abandoned two-story wooden house at the upper end, along with a broken-down barn and corral. The trees had been thinned from the valley's lower reaches to make a continuous, sprawling meadow, and at the bottom several acres of flat, treeless land jutted into the ocean, forming a small peninsula. The peninsula was a perfect picnic spot but he and Susan hadn't been there since the *KAPU—No Trespassing* signs were posted along the boundary the previous month. Not long after the signs appeared men on horseback started riding the fence line. They looked like *paniolos*, Hawaiian cowboys, which made him think the ranch was being restored to working order, but it was clear now that they had been patrolling the site. It was also clear why, on their past jaunts, they had occasionally come across survey markers.

Thumbing on the flashlight, Neal walked down the footpath until he came to the Kahookes' back yard. Their house was perched on a bluff at the far side of a sloped clearing and was almost as decrepit as his own, but it had its good points. The view of the sea from the second-floor verandah overlooking Muriela's garden was spectacular. Plumeria trees, front and back, sweetened the air with their perennial blossoms. Fat-trunked coconut palms swayed overhead in the breeze and an old fig tree shaded a spool table where the Kahookes sometimes ate. The house itself, even with all the paint peeled off, looked clean. There were no junked cars or garbage in the yard, a typical sight where the island's less-than-wealthy lived.

Neal crossed the yard to the screen door and moment later Kawika's immensity filled the yellow of light.

"Ey! Neal Tah-tay! Ey brah, come in, come in!"

"Ey, Kawika," Neal grinned as they shook hands. "It's been a while." He stepped into the kitchen, blinking from the glare of the bare ceiling bulb. A blast of canned laughter erupted from the TV in the next room. He liked the Kahookes home; the clutter and cooking smells made it feel cozy. "Beer," he said, hefting the six-pack.

"You tink I don' see it?" Kawika laughed, snagging a bottle. "Ey, you jus' in time, brah." He pointed to a bowl of grayish paste on the table. "We got some poi."

"Gee thanks, but I'll have to pass," Neal said. "Maybe I'll come back some time when I'm starving to friggin' death."

Kawika laughed again. He took a tortilla chip from a bowl on the table, scooped up a gob of the mashed taro root, and crammed it into his mouth. "Mmmmm," he said, munching with relish, "dis stuff da kine, brah, make you big and strong."

Neal opened another beer for himself. "This will too. Big, anyway."

"Like me." Kawika patted the paunch that bulged over his Bermuda shorts. The fat on the rest of his body, evenly distributed and covered with smooth brown skin, gave him a look of bovine solidity.

A high-pitched voice called out from the TV room, "Ey, who ees?"

"Neal's back, Muriela," Kawika bellowed. "He bring some beah. Come have wit us."

There was a creak of sofa springs and Muriela Kahooke bustled into the kitchen. "Neal!" she squeaked. She came at him with her *muumuu* billowing like a tent and pulled him against her enormous bosom, giving him a smacking kiss on the cheek. "When you get back?"

"Night before last."

"What?" She held him at arm's length, her plucked eyebrows lifting into thin arches. "An' you don' come see us 'til now?"

"We came by twice yesterday but you guys were gone."

Muriela's smile faded for an instant. "Oh. Right."

She brightened again. "Ey, you have a *mele Kalikimaka*?"

"Yeah, we had a pretty merry Christmas all right. I wish we'd—"

He was cut short by a blood-curdling scream from the television.

"Jus a sec," Muriela said. She disappeared into the other room. Another scream ended abruptly, accompanied by a whine of anguish from Kealoha, their six year old boy. Muriela returned to the kitchen shaking her head. "Nuttin but crap on da TV anymo."

Kawika handed his wife a beer and wrapped a thick arm around her shoulders, pulling her close. "So, howzit, brah?"

"Well, actually," Neal said, "it's not great. I came to see if things were okay with you."

Kawika's smile slowly faded. He looked down at his wife. "Ey, well, you know, tings ain't so good, really."

Neal started to speak but Kealoha wandered into the kitchen with a huge grin on his face, apparently having recovered from the shock of the TV screen going blank. "Look, Neal," he said, holding a stack of comic books over his head like trophies. "Mama buy fa me today."

"All right, Kealoha, the Incredible Hulk. My main man."

"Yeah. Look." Kealoha pulled away the top comic book and showed him the one underneath. "Supahman. An' look, dis one too!"

Casper the Friendly Ghost smiled up bulbously. "That's great, Kealoha," Neal said. "Casper's kind of a wimp, but at least he's friendly."

"Ey, Keke," Muriela said, "we tok to Neal a lil bit, okay?"

Kealoha took the hint and ran out of the kitchen,

making wet gunfire sounds with his mouth.

Neal looked from Kawika to Muriela. "I heard you guys were selling your house. Is that true?"

Kawika seemed to deflate a bit. "Not ezackly. But we leavin', brah."

"You are? Well, hell, why didn't you guys say something before?"

"We gonna tell you, but you been gone."

"You mean all this happened since we left?"

"Not ezackly. But I don' say nuttin befo cuz..." Kawika didn't finish his sentence. He sighed cetaceously, tugging at the goatee that hung from his chin like black moss.

"Cuz we din tink dis gonna happen," Muriela finished. "See, we got da lettah a few week ago, an' we figgah dey some mistake, we can fix it. But den tings happen. Lass week, we see we really have to go."

Neal sat on the edge of the table. "Wait a minute, what letter? How did this start?"

"Ah, shit," Kawika said, sighing again. "My poppa toe me 'bout da lease, don' nevah pay late cause dey can take da lan' away."

"What do you mean? I thought you owned this place, Kawika. You said you were born here."

"Iss true, brah. But we don' own it. My grampa, he got a niney-nine yeah lease. My poppa say if I miss da payment, dey can make us go. I pay right on time always. But a coupla time I pay late a few day, one time maybe a mont', when Kealoha go to da hosbital. I tink, so what, you know? Den I get da lettah bout da lease is cancel. Nex' ting, some guy come an' gimme some papah an' say we gotta be gone by dis time."

Kawika noticed his beer bottle was empty and threw it into a plastic garbage can by the door. "What can I do, ey? I got no money, I can't fight da big people."

"Did you even try talking to a lawyer?" Neal asked.

"Yeah. I fine dis lawyah, he say can't do nuttin. So I call my pop on Oahu. He wan' fa broke my neck. He tok to my bruddah, an' my bruddah have his lawyah look at dis ting."

"And?"

"An' nuttin. He say we can fight dem in coat, but it coss a lot and we gonna lose."

Neal rubbed the toe of his flip-flop over a hole in the linoleum floor, thinking. "When did they say you had to be gone?"

"Right now, we spose ta be outta heah in two week," Muriela said. "Evah'ting."

"Two weeks? What the hell are you gonna do?"

Kawika reached for another beer and twisted the cap off. He took a long swig. "We go to Honolulu," he said, licking his lips. "My bruddah gonna help me get one job. I tink I toe you bout him. Da dentiss."

"Right, the dentist. What kind of a job?"

Kawika tugged glumly on his beard. "Gobbij man."

"A *garbage* man?"

"Yeah, right. My bruddah know da guy who hire 'em."

"That doesn't sound so hot. You're a fisherman, Kawika."

"Ey brah, somebody got to pick up da gobbij. Dey pay good, too."

Muriela suddenly burst into tears. "Dam dis crap!" she wailed, "I don' wanna live in Honolulu. I like it heah." Clumps of mascara slid down her cheeks. "I tink I go lie down fa minute," she sniffed. "I don' fee so good. I talk to you latah, Neal, okay?"

She hurried out of the kitchen.

Kawika reached over and grabbed the six-pack. "Less go, okay? Boddah me when I see Muriela cry."

Outside, he said, "We *holo-holo* down some."

Neal followed him down the path toward the rushing sound of the sea. He was feeling slightly giddy from the beer, as if he were floating in his private envelope of darkness. Halfway to the breaking waves they turned onto a footpath and crunched over the pebbles to an outcropping of smooth *pahoehoe* lava. Kawika climbed onto the rounded mass of rock, grunting with the effort, and sat down. Neal settled near him. Below, the ocean spread out like an unending pane of rippled gray glass.

"This is totally screwed, Kawika," Neal said. "I wish you'd told me when you first got the letter."

"Ey, I tot da lettah muss be one fuckin mistake, brah. Den when all dis stuff happen, you gone to LA"

"Wait, what stuff happened when I was gone?"

Kawika laughed reluctantly. "Lass Satady dis dude from da company drive up an' see if we gonna go. I been drinkin' a lil, an' uh...I broke da windows in da cah."

"You? You're kidding me."

"No." Kawika shifted his rear end. "I kick in da cah doahs."

"You kicked in the doors?"

"Yeah, yeah. Den...I chop all da tiahs up some. Wit one axe."

"Jesus, Kawika. All this happened last weekend?"

"Yeah, lass Satady. I was a lil *lolo*, brah. Da guy lucky I don' pull off da *ule*."

"Hell, I guess. What happened after that?"

Kawika belched. "Scuse me. Ah, I don' remembah too good. Nex' ting I know I'm in jail. Den dis guy from da lease company, da one who own my lan', he come to da jail. He say if I sign dis papah right now an' fahget about dah lawyah dey give me five tousan dollahs. Den dey won' do nuttin 'bout bustin' up da cah."

"And you did it?"

"Shu, brah. If I don' do it I lose da place anyway, I don' have one fuckin ting, an' I gotta pay fa dis cah. I tok to Muriela an' den I sign da ting an' dey let me outta jail."

Kawika took a long pull at his bottle and belched again.

"Scuse me. What else could I do, brah? I got no choice. Day befo yestahday Muriela an' me decide we go to Honolulu like my bruddah say. I come fa tell you yestahday but you wasn't home. Same today."

"I was up north today. Painting." Neal tapped his bottle on the lava, thinking. "God, what a mess. You know what this is all about, don't you?"

"Yeah, da rocket ting. I tok to some people an' figgah it out. Dey start workin in da valley two days ago. Ey brah, dey wan' you place, too?"

"Looks like it. I got a couple of letters from Pacific Investment a while back about selling my land but I said no thanks. I got another letter today from CSS, the rocket company. They want to make an offer."

"What you gonna do?"

Neal shook his head. "I don't know. I don't want to go."

Kawika finished his beer. He put the bottle back in the carton and pulled out another, and they sat drinking in silence under the stars. The breeze floating in from the sea carried the clean tang of salt water.

"Why here?" Neal said. "I still can't believe it."

"Goddam right, brah," Kawika muttered. He blew into his bottle, making it hoot softly.

Neal found Susan asleep when he got home. He went back outside to the verandah and sat for another hour, gazing at the sea and stars, trying to imagine what the place was going to look like in the future.

When the moon finally rose from behind the bulk of Mauna Loa, dusting the hillside below with bluish light, it gave the sea an eerie metallic sheen that made the water look cold and hard.

Chapter Five

Neal picked a random spot on the Dr. Bronner's Pure-Castile-Soap bottle and read it. "*Absolute cleanliness is Godliness! So teach the Moral ABC that unites all mankind free in our Eternal Father's great All-One-God-Faith. Listen Children Eternal Father Eternal One! Exceptions eternally? Absolute None!*"

Standing in the bathroom, he paused to reflect upon precisely what in hell that meant. It was difficult to say. He had been studying Dr. Bronner's labels on and off for a couple of years and still didn't have a firm grasp on what the Essene rabbi soap makers were up to. But in a general way he felt they were on the right track.

He tried the bottle again. "*Mao wrote: 'Marxism, once in power, is utterly unworkable! Has less value than cowdung! Its power is the gun!'*"

This particular observation he understood. He left the bathroom and finished dressing.

In the kitchen, Kawika and Muriela were huddled over the stove. Kawika saw him and lifted a batter-covered spoon. "Monnin, brah. We cookin' pancakes."

"So I see. They smell great." He slid into the chair between Susan and Kealoha, ruffling the boy's hair, and got a milk-rimmed grin in return. "Susan's making you guys cook today, huh?"

"That's a laugh," Susan said, stirring her coffee. "They won't let me do anything."

"Das right," Muriela confirmed. "Our turn today.

Ey, Neal, how many pancakes? Six? Eight?"

"Actually, I think four would be more like it."

Muriela set a plate down in front of him. Aloud, he counted five pancakes, all enormous.

"You too *skinny*," she scolded.

"It's solid, rippling muscle," he said, dribbling syrup over his pancakes, and Muriela emitted a birdlike titter. It was good to hear her laugh. She had seemed in good spirits at Big Jim's Stationary New Year's Eve Cruise but for the last four days, since moving in to wait for their apartment in Honolulu to be readied, the Kahookes hadn't been their usual cheerful selves. Not that he blamed them. They had emptied the house the week before and most of what they owned was now waiting to be shipped from the warehouse in Kawaihae to Honolulu, where they didn't want to live. Muriela set a single pancake in front of Susan and deposited herself beside Kawika, who was digging into a mound of pancakes and bacon.

"How da cakes, brah?" Kawika asked.

"Great. You got a secret ingredient or something? "

"Shu. Poi."

Neal chuckled, somewhat uncertainly, and surreptitiously inspected the next couple of forkfuls until he caught Kawika elbowing his wife.

Susan was pouring her second cup of coffee when she suddenly lifted her head. "Hey. Did you hear that?"

"What?" Neal asked. "The boom?" A sound resembling a flat peal of thunder had buzzed the windowpanes a moment before. It was nothing new; blasting had been going on in the valley for the last few days.

"No, not that. Listen."

He heard it a moment later, a low growl.

"Bulldozers."

"Yeah, but it sounds close. Like it's right downhill."

"Hard to tell," Neal said, returning to his food. He avoided looking at Kawika and Muriela as he ate.

While the dishes were being stacked in the sink he slipped outside. Standing in the middle of the yard, away from the noise in the kitchen, he could hear the sound clearly: the throb of diesel engines, the squeal of lugs, and over that, the crackle of breaking trees. It was close. He glanced at the kitchen window and then crossed the yard, passing through the opening in the stone wall to the footpath that led down to the Kahookes' now-vacant house.

He reached their back yard in time to see two bulldozers emerge from the woods like blundering metal monsters. The machines rumbled across the back yard, their lugs digging up clods of earth, and halted beside the empty house.

One of the drivers spotted him and climbed down from his seat. He came over, brushing leaves from his shirt with a gloved hand, and nodded a greeting. "This your place?"

Neal shook his head. "No. Not mine.

"Dis my place."

Neal turned around. Kawika was standing behind him.

"Your place, hey?" The driver grinned. "Or *was* your place, I should say."

Kawika's head swiveled on his thick neck like a tank turret until his eyes lined up on the driver. The man's face sobered and he instinctively took a step back. "Well—you got everything out?"

"Yeah. What you gonna do?"

The driver wiped sweat from his forehead, leaving a

dirty streak like an extra eyebrow. "We're s'posed to clear out this area and level it for a building." He waved toward the house. "First thing we're s'posed to do is tear that down. So, if everything's out I guess we'll get to work."

The man went back to his bulldozer, looking over his shoulder before mounting the grumbling machine.

"I think you upset him, Kawika," Neal said. "Maybe he heard what you did to that guy's car."

"Probbly did," Kawika agreed glumly. "Frank Ninomiya toe me da company ask da police to come heah, so I don' make trouble. I toe Frank don' boddah, not gonna be no trouble." He turned to look at his former home. "No trouble."

The bulldozer operator pulled on a dust mask, and with a final look at Kawika he grabbed the control levers. The big machine vented a geyser of black exhaust and clanked forward, shoving its heavy blade into the side of the wooden house. Nails shrieked and boards popped as it moved relentlessly forward.

One pass was all it took to collapse the house. The bulldozer exited the far side of the building in a cloud of dust, a slab of ceiling riding on top of the driver's protective cage, electrical wires trailing behind. The house's corrugated metal roof slid almost intact onto Muriela's flower and vegetable garden below, flattening red and green *ti* plants.

Kawika stood watching as the bulldozer plowed through his home again, his sausage-like arms hanging at his sides. When it started across for a third time he turned to Neal and said thickly, "Goin' back."

Neal nodded. "See you at the house."

The bulldozer rolled back and forth over the remains of the house, grinding floorboards, clapboards, joists, and studs into a pile of kindling. The other machine, having trampled the dislodged roof flat, was shoving the remains uphill onto the rest of the debris. The garden was a ruin of churned-up dirt.

When the house was finished, both machines pointed their snouts toward the big palm trees and set to work knocking them over. Coconuts rained down as their blades bit into the smooth trunks.

Neal turned and headed up the footpath.

He was rounding a curve in the trail when he heard a noise from ahead. He stopped to listen and it came again, a whispering, wheezing sound. He crept forward quietly, peering through the trees until he saw a broken patch of bright color. Another step brought the pieces together; it was Kawika's shirt. He was facing away, squatting in the middle of the path, his head on his arms. His huge back shook as another sob forced itself out.

Neal removed his flip-flops and stepped off the path into the trees. He set off through the woods in a wide arc that would take him to the house, moving silently, his ears alert, his eyes unconsciously probing the underbrush for hidden trip-wires.

Chapter Six

The morning of the Kahookes' flight to Oahu, Neal and Kawika drove in separate vehicles to the forest above the small town of Captain Cook. After a short transaction Kawika left his pickup truck with the Japanese taro farmer who had made the best offer for it.

Neal drove home, Kawika slumping dejectedly in the passenger seat of Susan's Datsun station wagon. "Don't take it so hard, Kawika," Neal said. "Your truck was almost as big a piece of crap as mine."

"Yeah, but it ran good," Kawika said listlessly. "I had it fa long time. Like da boat."

Selling the boat had hit Kawika hard. It was just an old patched-up center console hull with a ratty-looking homemade Bimini top, but Kawika had spent thousands of hours in it, working the sea. Letting it go made the end of his former livelihood and the move from his home island cut that much more deeply.

By the time they got back to the house Muriela had finished the last-minute packing and Susan had made breakfast. They ate, then loaded everything in Neal's pickup and got underway, Muriela sitting up front with Susan, Kawika and Kealoha riding in back with the suitcases.

They pulled into Keahole Airport forty-five minutes before departure time. After paying for the tickets and checking the luggage, Kawika herded everyone to an open-air bar concession and paid for a round of overpriced Cokes. The morning humidity and the bar's stiff-backed plastic chairs did nothing to lessen the gloom.

Kawika finished his Coke first and said, "Scuse me," getting up from the table. "I bettah hit da men's room."

Neal also stood. "I'll go with you."

Inside the restroom Kawika nudged him. "I don' hafta take a leak or nuttin, brah. I came in heah to smoke dis." He held up a lumpy cigarette rolled in yellow paper. "A lil *pakalolo* make me fee mo bettah."

"I hope so," Neal said. "Sorry about everything, Kawika. Maybe it won't be so bad."

Kawika gave him a sheepish look. "Ey, iss areddy bad. I'm smokin' dis cause flyin' skeh da crap outta me." He lit the joint and inhaled, vaporizing a full third of the joint. "Ey brah," he said creakily, holding in the smoke, "you wanna toke?"

The resinous smell was inviting but Neal didn't feel like it. He faked a hit to keep Kawika company, holding the smoke in his mouth for a while and then slowly blowing it out. "You know," he said, "I'm really going to miss you and Muriela. You've done a lot for us. Taking us fishing, introducing your friends, showing us places and everything. It won't be the same."

Kawika blew out his own smoke. "Thanks, brah." He looked embarrassed. "I miss you too."

They were silent.

"Ey you know, Neal," Kawika said, pulling on his goatee, "lossa Hawaiians—I mean *kama'aina* like me— dey don' like *haoles*. Fac, dey don' like nobody but da Hawaiians. An' I don' blame em, really. *Haoles* come an' take da lan'. When you firs' move in I tink, Ol' Akoki an' his wife die, heah come a *haole*, grab a piece of da

50

islan'. Den I tok to ol' Kamuela one time. He toe me about da ting in Vie'nam. I been tellin' folks how come you got da Akoki place."

Neal felt his ears burn. "I wish you hadn't, Kawika. I'd like people to just take me for what I am now."

"Dey do, brah. But dis don' hurt none."

Kawika put out the joint and they went back to the table. Neal presented the Kahookes with the package he had brought along. "A going-away present from me and Susan," he said. "I hope you like it."

Muriela untied the strings on the flat cardboard box and lifted off the top. Inside was a small painting of their home. Beyond the palm trees and *ti* plants in the yard, the Pacific Ocean stretched gem-blue to the puffy-clouded horizon.

"Susan framed it herself at a shop here," Neal said.

Kawika and Muriela stared at it for some time. Finally Kawika said in a husky voice, not looking up, "Tank you."

The passenger boarding call came over the loudspeakers and they walked to the gate, Muriela dabbing her eyes with a handkerchief. Holding his mother's hand, Kealoha seemed to finally realize that they were moving away for good and began crying, too.

At the apron gate Susan kissed and hugged the three Kahookes. Kawika wrapped a heavy arm around Neal's shoulder and said, "See ya, brah."

Neal's eyes were stinging. He cleared his throat and said, "Keep in touch. Any time you guys need a place to stay here, you know where you can come."

The Kahookes waved one last time before disappearing behind the wall, and then they were gone.

On the way back to the truck Susan said, "You really look depressed, Neal."

"I am. And I'm mad. Here they are, not hurting anyone, minding their own business, and their life gets totally screwed up by people they'll never even see and they can't do a damn thing about it."

"They'll probably do okay in Honolulu," Susan said. "I mean, the rest of their family's there and everything."

"No. Kawika's not cut out for the city. Or being a garbage man."

They got in the truck. "What time did you tell Harry we'd come by?" Neal asked.

Susan looked at her watch. "About fifteen minutes from now."

"All right." Neal started the engine and gave it a couple of angry revs. "We can get something to eat."

"What? We just ate two hours ago."

"That explains it. Maybe we can talk Harry into taking a break from the shop."

*   *   *

Holding the screwdriver with his fingertips to get the correct feel, Harry Sturdivant tightened the grip screw on the Browning Hi-Power a fraction more.

Finito. He slipped the screwdriver into its rack slot, wiped off the pistol, and returned it to its box. Checking the wall clock, he saw there was time to do the plants before Neal and Susan arrived.

He grabbed his pipe and ambled down the hall to the front of the shop, pausing at the front gun display counter to light his pipe with a kitchen match from one of several strategically located jiggers full. When the stained cherrywood was going good he filled an atomizer bottle with distilled water and started misting the plants, starting in the back left corner and moving clockwise around the shop. It would be another slow day, he reflected, but then it always was after the holidays. No matter. It was good having time to goof around. Goofing around was what God made islands for.

Harry had lived in Hawaii since 1967. His wife suffered a fatal stroke that year, and after a lengthy period of grief and confusion, he sold his gun shop on South Broadway in Denver and moved to Honolulu, where he started up the business again. In time he developed a substantial clientele among Oahu's military personnel and established a solid trade with the Honolulu Police Department, which bought his .38 Special target reloads and used him exclusively for repair and tuning of its SWAT firearms. In addition to being a recognized authority on firearms Harry was a skilled craftsman who found genuine satisfaction in working on guns. He loved their clever, efficient, elegant mechanics, their polished beauty, the subtle joy of working up a perfect load.

At one corner of the shop Harry unfastened a cord from a wall-mounted cleat and paid it out, lowering a plant hanging from pulleys beneath the shop skylight, a *Cymbidium* Jungfrau with beautiful red and white blooms. He eased the pot down to waist level and belayed the cord to the cleat in a sailorly fashion.

When Honolulu became too much like any other big city Harry had moved to the less hectic environment of Hilo on the island of Hawaii. Hilo was only a modest-sized town but he had done a fair business. There was some hunting on the Big Island—goats, pigs, and sheep—and again he was able to supply the city and district police departments.

It was in Hilo that Harry's passion for orchids took root. He had always loved flowers because they reminded him of being a kid, of working in his mother's flower shop in Philly. He could close his eyes and bring back the smells of earth and perfume, the colors, the silent, moist air. That seemed a million years ago, but the feelings had come flooding back when he visited the town's Nani Mau Gardens. He fell in love with the orchids and bought his first one that day. He began collecting them. Before long he built a small hothouse around his back porch that quickly filled with the exotic plants and their offspring.

Harry checked the Jungfrau's water level. He sprayed the plant, and after consulting a chart taped to his filing cabinet he poured a quantity of pre-diluted 30-10-10 fertilizer solution into the pot. He inspected the leaves critically, judging their color, looking for any suspicious mottling, checking the leaf crevices for signs of black rot. The inspection was important. When he first started growing orchids he had overlooked the symptoms of a viral infection in one plant and the disease was transmitted to several other orchids via his own hands. He finally had to destroy a total of seven plants, one of them a favorite, an *Epidendrum ciliare* with delicate, fringed blooms, a descendant of the first orchid he ever bought.

Harry eventually grew restless in Hilo. His shop was too cramped and he was old enough to dread the days of no sun.

The more he thought about it the more he wanted to move to the other side of the island; the Kona coast saw the sun about 340 days a year. And he could afford the move. The shop had produced enough to cover all his bills and he still had his savings and the funds from Louise's life insurance policy. Though it wasn't a lot there was also his writing income. Since selling his first article in 1955 he had published over two hundred and eighty four articles in *Shooter's World, Gun Digest, Guns and Ammo*, and other magazines, and had authored two well-received books on firearms.

When he finally made up his mind he drove to Kailua-Kona on the west side of Hawaii, found a suitable space in the Kailua Industrial Area and a bungalow off Hualalai Road, and moved.

The three years since then had been a time of contentment. Sometimes, he thought, too much so.

Harry decided to leave the Jungfrau down for a while, to keep it out of the noonday sun streaming through the skylight. He moved to the stair step bench in the side window, which held several cattleyas and two out-of-bloom phalaenopsis species, and went through the spraying and inspection ritual. The phalaenopsis pots always had to be checked after new visitors left the shop; the pots of these orchids were tipped on their sides to avoid rot, and well-meaning people were always setting them back up.

Finished, Harry put up the atomizer and carefully washed the watering can. He saw that he was out of paper towels and ran his wet hands over his hair, which he had worn in an unvarying crew cut since 1938, and which had, within two years of Louise's death, turned from graying brown to snow white.

Harry was in the back mixing another batch of fertilizer solution when the door buzzer sounded.

"Anybody home?"

"Neal!" Harry called out. "Come on back!"

"Am I invited too?" Susan yelled.

There was a sound like a dry gargle, Harry's chuckle. "That goes double for you, kid."

Neal and Susan looked into the study, a small

cubicle furnished with a typewriter and hundreds of gun books, then pressed on to the workshop, a large, well-lit space equipped with two workbenches, various machine tools, reloading presses, and tiers of parts drawers.

"Hey, you guys!" Harry greeted them, drying off his hands. "How long's it been?"

Susan kissed him on the cheek. "Way too long."

"Almost seven weeks," Neal said, shaking his hand. "I figured it out driving over."

"Seven weeks!" Harry was genuinely surprised. "Boy, time flies when you're a codger."

"Come on," Susan chided. "You've got a few more years before you're a codger."

"Just a few?" Harry's gravelly voice sounding hurt. Susan bought it for a second and he laughed again. "Hey, you two have a good Christmas? I got your card from La-La Land."

"Yeah, we had a pretty good time," Neal said. "But I was ready to get back."

"I know what you mean. Being in Honolulu last week made me appreciate Kailua even more. And now that we're all here, by golly, I want to show you something." Harry swept a hand toward the door. "Step this way, please."

He led them down the hall, stopping in front of a heavy steel door. "I finally did it," he said, and pushed the door open.

The empty half of the building, formerly used for storage, had been turned into a small pistol range. "Maximum fifteen yard distance," Harry said, turning on the overhead lights. "You've got three shooting stations. You've got air conditioning, you've got a custom venting system to suck all the bad stuff out.

You've got individually adjustable target lighting and individual target retrieval controls. Is this modern or what?"

Neal nodded approvingly."Modern. Very nice."

"It's neat," Susan said. "But what about the noise? And what about a bullet going wild or something?"

"The walls and ceiling are covered with sound-absorbent tiles," Harry explained. "And there's sheet steel under that. Perfectly safe. You couldn't shoot through it with a .454 Casull." He held up a finger. "Speaking of which, no one's fired a shot in here yet. Don't move." He stepped out of the room and returned a moment later with the Hi-Power he had been working on earlier. He slid a loaded magazine into it and stepped into a booth, holding out the pistol. "Susan, care to do the honors?"

"Me? No guns for me, thanks. I'll watch."

"That hurts," Harry said. "but I'll try to get over it. Okay, it's you, Neal."

He hesitated. "How about you? It seems more fitting."

"Malarkey. I've been waiting for one of you guys to break this place in. Don't let me down, now."

"Well—all right." He stepped into the booth and took the pistol. "It's been a while," he said. "Years."

"Excuses already," Harry chuckled. "You're familiar with this weapon, right? Okay, then. Hold on a sec." He lifted two pairs of earmuff-type hearing protectors from wall pegs and handed them to Neal and Susan, then put a pair on himself. "Okay! Fire at will!"

Neal looked down at the automatic pistol in his hand. Over a decade and a half had passed since he last fired a pistol like this. He smiled grimly, working the safety with his thumb. Then gripped the slide with palm and fingers, tugged it all the way back, and let it fly forward, chambering a round. The target was a red bull's-eye in a black circle about ten yards distant. He stared at it a moment, then raised the gun with both hands and fired a single shot. The feel, the kick of the 9 millimeter were familiar. His heart thudded heavily for two or three beats.

"Not bad," Harry said, looking over his shoulder.

Neal studied the target. The hole was high two inches and right one. He set his feet, then smoothly raised the gun and fired two quick shots. He lowered the gun, raised it, and again fired twice, repeating the cycle until the slide locked back on an empty chamber. Brass cartridge casings littered the floor and the air reeked of burnt powder.

Harry squinted at the target. "Good grief, Neal," he said in a tone of awe. "I had no idea you could shoot like that."

"I guess it's like riding a bicycle." He checked the pistol's chamber and handed it back to Harry. "Well, the range is broken in. I appreciate the honor."

"It was worth the wait," Harry said, grinning. "And now that that's done I can show Susan something she might be a little more interested in. Got a few new orchids in bloom."

Harry wiped the pistol and put it away, then led them to the front of the shop, where he took Susan on a tour of the orchids.

"They're incredible," she said, moving from one to another. She stopped in front of an orchid sprouting from a mass of tree fern on the wall. "Ooh! What's this one called, Harry?"

Cylindrical leaves four feet long dangled like tentacles. At the base of each leaf, above a bulbous sheath, was a large bloom of pale yellow color, each marked with reddish-brown spots and stripes like some jungle beast.

"That's a *Scuticaria steeli.*" Harry pointed at the plant with his pipe. "Smell it."

Susan leaned close and sniffed. "Mmmm, that's wonderful," she said dreamily. "Even though its name sounds like a disease."

Harry barked out a laugh. "Kinda does," he agreed. He lifted a potted orchid from a shelf, a variety of lady's slipper with artistically mottled leaves, and held it in front of her. "This is one's a little nicer. See if you can get it the first time. *Paphilopedium bellatulum.*"

He laughed at the expression on her face, but she got it right on the second try. "Not bad," he said. "I'm glad it came so easy because it's yours. A belated Merry Christmas. I mean, *Mele Kalikimaka.*"

"Oh, Harry, are you kidding?"

"Usually, but not right now."

Susan took the pot from him carefully, staring at the orchid's speckled white bloom. "It's so beautiful. Harry, thank you."

"You're welcome. And now let's belatedly celebrate your return to the Big Island. I've got a bottle of champagne."

"Champagne!"

"I kid you not. If you two aren't busy we can go sailing and open it on the high seas. The *LuLu*'s all ready. What do you say?"

"Sounds great," Neal said.

"Susan? All right then! Let me close up the shop and we'll bug outta here."

Chapter Seven

The sound of heavy trucks traversing the ranch road woke Neal early in the morning, as they had every day since returning from California. He lay in bed, Susan breathing softly beside him, wondering about what was happening in the valley to the north. In one way he wanted to see the damage Concord Space Systems had done over the last few weeks and in another way he didn't. For the most part, when he caught himself thinking about the launch site, he tried to bend his thoughts away from it.

As he did now. He got up, careful not to wake Susan, and put on shoes and a pair of running shorts. On the verandah he stretched a few minutes and then went through a basic karate routine, performing the blocks and strikes with the smoothness of long practice, sweeping out the tight arcs, halting, and returning to position. By the time he finished he was perspiring.

He left a note for Susan on the kitchen table, donned a small rucksack, and bounded down the stairs, jogging across the yard to the entrance road. Just outside the stone wall surrounding the yard, the entrance road—two wheel ruts running through the trees—turned right and ran nearly straight uphill. He kept jogging as he followed it. Higher up the road curved left, passing through a gap in the ridge of exposed lava running across the upper part of his property, and then curved right and went in a more or less direct line all the way to Mokolea Road.

On Mokolea Neal picked up the pace. He descended a long downhill stretch with his eyes on the pitted asphalt. At the bottom the road swept left and followed a meandering course that climbed gradually upward through the trees. He struggled uphill in the growing heat and humidity, walking when he ran out of breath, and eventually spotted Yamata Store, his destination.

He arrived at the store sweating and panting. He stood under the big ohia tree outside while he caught his breath, then checked the mailbox. Inside was another certified letter slip. He put on the tee shirt he had brought along and went into the store.

Mrs. Yamata was already in her postal cubbyhole, sorting stamps.

"Morning, Mrs. Yamata."

"Ah! Goo monning, Nee! You up early."

"Yeah, getting a little exercise." He held up the slip. "Another letter, it looks like."

"Yes, yes." Mrs. Yamata located the letter and handed it over. "You know," she said, giving him a stub-toothed grin, I start thinking you big binissman!" She laughed wildly at this, as with all her own jokes.

"Not much chance of that," Neal said. He picked out a few items for breakfast and took them to the register, where Mrs. Yamata rang them up. As he was putting his purchases in the rucksack she pointed to the letter.

"Same people building place fo rocket?"

"Same people," he said. "I guess it'll be good for your business."

"Maybe goo fo biniss, Nee, but I don' keh. I don'

wan' rocket here. When I come to Hawaii fo marry Mr. Yamata, I living befo in Tokyo. Terrible place! So many people erry wheh! Dirt in sky! Maybe one day Hawaii be like Tokyo."

"I wouldn't be surprised, Mrs. Yamata. They've got a good start on it in Honolulu."

He said goodbye and started back to the house, jogging again after a short walk.

At the bottom of the final hill two trucks loaded with heavy equipment rumbled by, raising a cloud of dust. He stopped beside the road to let the breeze clear it away, and while he waited he thought of the letter. He took off the rucksack and pulled it out.

In a somewhat injured tone, Edward Treadway III reiterated his last message, closing with a request that he be contacted at the CSS office in Honolulu so that a meeting could be arranged.

Susan was making a pot of coffee when Neal returned. He put the letter in a drawer with the first one, saying nothing about it.

*   *   *

Eight days later, while Neal was reading on the verandah, a sky-blue Jeep Wagoneer emerged from the trees and pulled into the yard, filling it with the birdlike chirp of a loose compressor belt. He put down the book and watched as the car stopped near the breadfruit tree, close enough to make out the Concord Space Systems door decal.

The man who stepped from the vehicle wore a crisp-looking suit of light linen. He was trim and tanned, athletic in his movements, and had a full head of brown hair, groomed to the point of resembling a small tidy animal perched on his head. His age—middle forties, Neal guessed—was given away by a set of fluffy silver sideburns. These clashed with his overall youthfulness and seemed somehow bogus, as though pasted on for effect.

Unaware that he was being watched, the man gingerly removed his suit coat and leaned into the car to lay it on the seat, emerging with a leather briefcase. After bending to check his hair and nostrils in the outside mirror he started toward the house, and his eyes lifted to the verandah for the first time. He stopped in his tracks, surprised, but made a quick recovery. "Hello!" he called out, smiling and giving Neal a nod. "I didn't see you sitting there. You're Mr. Tate, I presume?"

"That's right."

"Ah, great!" The man gave his tie a pat. "Thought I'd gotten myself lost! Wouldn't be the first time."

"What can I do for you?" Neal asked.

The man put his tie-patting hand in his pocket. "Well, let me introduce myself. My name's Ed Treadway. I'm with Concord Space Systems. As you might recall, I wrote you a couple of letters."

"I recall."

"Well...I've been trying to get in touch with you for some time." Treadway's smile reappeared. "Since we never heard back, I came to Hawaii to, ah, combine a little business with pleasure. As I said in the letters, CSS may have an interest in buying your land."

Neal closed the book in his lap. "*May* have an interest?"

Treadway's eyes sharpened, reinforcing the somewhat vulpine look of his features. "Let me rephrase that. CSS *is* interested in buying your land—if the price is right. And, of course, if you're interested in selling. Is that a possibility?"

"Right now," Neal said, "—no."

"Oh. I see. Well, would you mind if we discussed this? I'm prepared to make you an offer right now, today."

Neal stared at the man. "If you have an offer you can leave it with me. I'll look it over."

"Well, I don't know if that's—"

"That's the way I want to do it. If your company's interested, make a proposal and I'll look it over."

Treadway returned his hand to his pocket and jingled some coins. "Mr. Tate," he said, his pained expression reflecting an unsuccessful struggle to remove the condescension in his voice, "land transactions are a little complicated. It's not like buying, oh, a..." He held up his briefcase. "A piece of luggage or something."

Neal said, "Sure it is."

Treadway smiled fleetingly. "Well, of course, there *are* similarities. But quite a difference in price and procedure. We've done a lot of research on property values in this area and we know what this land is good for, commercially speaking. As you know, the earning potential of real estate around here is severely limited."

Neal raised his eyebrows. "Is it? Then I guess your interest in my land is misplaced."

Treadway pursed his lips. He scratched his head with one manicured finger, a gold cufflink flashing in the sun, and the act exposed a small crescent of perspiration beneath his arm. "Look, Mr. Tate," he said, a hint of impatience creeping into his tone, "I don't want to waste your time or mine. I have with me a bona fide offer for your land, in contract form, and a check made out in your name to use as earnest money if we reach an agreement. Neither of these items has any figures filled in. I'd like to fill them in, today if possible.

"But," Treadway continued, holding up a hand, "I must tell you that while CSS *is* interested in your land for things that *might* come up in the future, it isn't absolutely necessary that we obtain this parcel. We want it so that if we *do* ever need it there's no hassle. You understand what I mean?"

"I understand what you're saying, anyway," Neal said.

Treadway smiled unenthusiastically. "Well—good enough. If you don't mind telling me, what would you consider a fair offer for your land?"

Neal shook his head. "I'm really not interested in selling."

Treadway couldn't conceal his disappointment. "I see. Well, perhaps you would be if we made the right offer. Is that a possibility?"

"I think not."

"Now look, Neal," Treadway said with an exasperated chuckle, "—if you don't mind my calling you that—I really think you should consider our proposal. Maybe you don't have a clear picture of this whole thing. I think I know how you feel about development and that sort of thing, but not everyone shares your views. And I think the important thing, the operative factor so to speak, is that the launch facility is being built *right now*. We've got crews working day and night out there."

"I'm well aware of that fact," Neal said. "The lights are pretty damn irritating when I'm outside trying to enjoy the stars. Not to mention the trucks going up and down the road at all hours."

"Well—I understand. But my point is, whether you're against the launch facility or not, it really doesn't matter. In a few months it'll be ready for the first launch. Now you have a chance to unload your land for a good price, a price you'll probably never get again. If you have an idea of what land goes for around here you know what I'm talking about."

Treadway took the continued silence to mean he was getting through. "My advice," he went on confidently, "is to think ahead, Neal. When the facility is fully functional there'll be a lot of traffic on Mokolea Road and our entrance road, right above you. And the rockets will make a little ruckus themselves. This won't harm anything of course, but it could be unpleasant if you're used to it being quiet around here. You really ought to think about that."

Treadway moved to the shade of the breadfruit tree and set his briefcase on the picnic table. He pulled a sheet of paper from inside and wrote on it. "I'll be staying in Kailua for the next few days," he said, clicking his pen closed. "What I'd like is for you to think this over and then we can get together and discuss it. Do lunch or something. I'm sure we can come up with some figures that'd be satisfactory to you." He held up the paper. "Here's a number where I can be reached in the meantime. I'll just bring it up to you."

"Don't bother," Neal said.

Treadway stopped. "Pardon?"

"I don't need your number. Everything you just said reminded me of why."

"What do you mean?"

"Your company ran my neighbors off their land. I don't like that. You're ruining the island and I don't like that either. So I won't help you do it."

Treadway chewed his lip. "I see. Well—I'm sorry to hear that, Neal. I think you're making a big mistake." He paused a moment and then returned to the table. "I tell you what. I'll just leave this phone number here anyway. Maybe you'll change your mind." Treadway snapped his briefcase shut and aimed a cold smile in Neal's direction. "I hope to hear from you. Have a good day."

On his way back to the car Treadway stopped and turned around. "I'd like to remind you of something, Mr. Tate. What we're trying to accomplish here will be good for the island and for the people on it. We care about Hawaii."

He strode back to the Wagoneer and climbed in. The car backed out of the yard and roared up the bumpy dirt drive, compressor belt squealing.

Susan stepped through the verandah doors in her underwear. "Boy, you weren't exactly Mr. Friendship, were you?"

Neal turned to look at her. "Not toward them. I haven't forgotten about Kawika and Muriela."

"Nor have I," Susan said. She leaned against the doorframe. "I just caught the end of it. What did he say?"

"Same thing. CSS wants to buy the place."

"I gather they didn't make an offer you couldn't refuse."

He shrugged shortly. "He didn't make an actual offer. He suggested we do lunch and work up an acceptable figure."

"But you're not going to?"

"Hell no."

Susan's eyebrows came together. "Why not just talk

to him? See what he says?"

"What do you mean?" Neal shoved himself out of his chair and paced back and forth along the verandah. "You think I should sell out? Just give up and let these jerks take over?"

"You don't have to raise your voice," Susan said. "You can blow off their offer, Neal, but whatever it is, it'll be a hell a lot more than Kawika and Muriela got."

"What's that got to do with it? Look, think about it. If we took their money a huge hunk would probably disappear in taxes. What are we going to do with what's left? Buy a mobile home on the edge of some cane field?"

"I'm sure we can do better than that."

He stared at her. "I don't think you understand. This is the land Dan's family left me. I don't *want* to sell it. Even if I did, and even if we found another place, we probably couldn't pay for the whole thing. We'd have mortgage payments to make." He held out his hands. "*I'm* not making any money right now, *you're* not making any money. In case you haven't noticed we're living off savings. For now we're stuck. And maybe that's for the best because I don't want CSS to have this place. I don't like them. I don't like people who think their big plans are more important than anything or anybody else. I don't like people who shove other people around like pawns in some frigging game. I got a gutful of that in Vietnam."

Susan eyed him coolly. "Fine. But I think you're not being realistic about this whole thing."

Neal suddenly felt drained. He slumped down into his chair and stared out over the ocean. A fishing boat, tiny in the distance, drew a thread-thin white wake on the blue water. "Let's just wait and see what happens," he said quietly.

That night, in the shower-steamed confines of the bathroom, he pulled a bottle of Dr. Bronner's off the shelf and read: "...*If I don't perfect 1st me who can? If I'm only for me, what am I then? If not now, when? Only hard work, trillion trees can save us...*"

He took this as a sign. It made him feel a little better about running Treadway off and about his decision not to sell.

Chapter Eight

Ed Treadway paused in his perusal of *Fortune* magazine to glance at his watch. He re-crossed his legs, took a casual look around the plush reception area of Komodo Incorporated's Honolulu offices, and then went back to the magazine. His left thumb worked busily as he pretended to read, rotating the diamond ring he wore.

Treadway's edginess had increased as his meeting with Hideo Kamada drew nearer. He had been face to face with Kamada only five times in his three years with Concord Space Systems, as most of his dealings were with Skip Schaefer or the other Japanese in California, but five times was enough. Kamada was not a barrel of laughs. Always cool and formal, all business. Interested in results, no time for excuses. He wouldn't be happy to hear that the Tate deal had hit a dead end.

Every now and then, when he suffered a rare lapse of introspection—even self-doubt, as now—Treadway feared for his future with CSS. The company was getting strung out, finance- and time-wise, but that wasn't the main thing. His primary concern was that he, Treadway, was the only Caucasian executive in his department. All the others were Japanese and they were all good at their jobs—compulsively good. He sometimes wondered if Kamada might not like to make a clean sweep of it, run off the last round-eye. What kept him from looking for another job was the certainty that CSS needed his American face and his facility with the language.

But even if he were delivering good news, even if he weren't worried at all about job security, he still wouldn't be looking forward to the meeting. In the way some people radiated personal warmth, Kamada exuded coolness. Actually he went beyond cool; he was cold. Cold as a...Treadway searched for the right word.

Lizard. Exactly. They didn't call him the Dragon for nothing.

The sound of a door opening and closing broke into Treadway's thoughts. A Japanese man in a dark blue suit emerged from the alcove outside Kamada's office, smiled and bowed quickly in Treadway's direction, and exited.

"Excuse me, Mr. Treadway," the Japanese receptionist said in her tinkling, wind-chime voice, "Mr. Kamada is ready to see you now."

Treadway stood and adjusted his tie, surreptitiously checking his shoulders for hairs and dandruff flakes. He hadn't done so well at convincing Tate to sell but at least he'd look good when he saw the goddamn Dragon.

*   *   *

"Since Tate was obviously in no mood for further discussion," Treadway said, concluding his account of the trip to the Big Island, "I left my telephone number and returned to Kailua."

Hideo Kamada, seated across the desk, said nothing.

Treadway searched Kamada's face for some sort of reaction, found none, and plunged ahead with what he considered to be a judicious display of open-mindedness. "Now it could be," he theorized, his voice betraying a belief that what was to follow was too absurd to be true, "that Tate just didn't like me personally. The impression I got, however, was that he's simply a hostile sort of person."

Treadway felt a drop of sweat trickle down his armpit. How the hell could he be sweating? The room was as cold as a goddamn refrigerator. In fact the room looked like a goddamn refrigerator. The carpet was white. The pebbled vinyl wallcovering was white. The curtains were white. Kamada's desk, a massive thing of marble and lacquered wood, was white, as was all the rest of the furniture except a few pieces made of chrome and glass. Even the flowers—roses on the coffee table and anthuriums on the desk—were white.

Hideo Kamada himself was the single anomaly, a thickset dangerous-looking Buddha in a perfectly tailored pearl-gray suit. He didn't move. He didn't rock his chair, he didn't tap his fingers, he didn't blink or, as far as Treadway could tell, even breathe. He just sat and stared, the heavy planes of his face a mask, waiting.

Treadway held his gaze on the slitted eyes across the white marble desktop, determined not to speak first. There was a feeling of being examined and found wanting and it made him angry.

Kamada's mouth opened slightly. "I am not surprised at the outcome of your visit. Tate has never answered any...correspondence. Not from us, and not from Pacific Investment Corporation. So...Edward. What do you recommend."

It bothered Treadway when Kamada spoke. He didn't talk like a human. It wasn't just the way his lips barely moved, though that was pretty damned disconcerting. Kamada spoke good English, but the noise seemed to be coming from an android. *How-are-*

you. We-are-having-great-difficulties. There was no emphasis, no inflection for questions, only pauses for unusual or hard-to-pronounce words.

"Well," Treadway said, "I'm not sure there's anything we can do, uh, Hideo."

"There is always something that can be done...Edward.

Edward. Treadway didn't care for that either. He liked Ed. "Of course you're right, Hideo," he said. "One thing we could do is offer him more for his property."

Kamada fell into his trance again. Treadway grew uncomfortable trying to detect signs of life in the two black slits and stared at Kamada's hair instead. Gray and heavily oiled, it swept back over a wide skull, pale lines of scalp showing in the furrows.

Kamada's mouth opened a fraction. "No. I do not think that is what we should do. If we raise our offer, he will detect that our...desire to purchase his land is very great. What is to prevent him from demanding still more. And there are other...considerations, also."

Treadway renewed his attentive look.

"If we pay a large price for the land belonging to this Mr. Tate," Hideo Kamada continued, not moving from the position he had settled into a quarter of an hour ago, "then we are, in effect, setting the market value for that area. Perhaps someday we will wish to buy more land. To expand. And there are the taxes. What is to prevent the state from...applying the price we paid for Tate's parcel to the land of the entire launch facility. The assessment difference would result in higher taxes. Over the years, perhaps hundreds of thousands of dollars more."

"Well, that's right," Treadway agreed cautiously.

"But what about the road?"

This got a reaction. Kamada turned his head a few degrees to one side and pulled back his lips until the tips of his teeth were bared. "Yesssss."

Treadway watched, fascinated. He could easily imagine a long blue tongue flicking from the man's mouth.

"Yessss," Kamada breathed again. "The road is a major concern."

The new road to the launch facility would peel off from the Mokolea road, which CSS would widen and repave, and lead straight toward the heart of the launch facility along a natural shelf of land. Unfortunately, the shelf crossed Tate's property. If they didn't get his land they would have to build a road further down, by the sea. Aside from being longer and less direct, an alternate entrance road would cost three or four times as much with all the blasting, carving, and shoring-up required.

"We need his property for the road," Kamada said. "If this Tate does not sell, we will have difficulties when the final...construction is begun. Already, his failure to cooperate has caused...delay."

Delay, Treadway thought. Construction at the Kona Launch Facility was two weeks ahead of schedule—really about three when the last shortcuts were figured in—and Kamada was unsatisfied. His decree of an initial test shot on May first had been pushing it, even for the stripped-down Phase One site requirements.

"If Mr. Tate cannot be soon convinced to sell his land...Edward. We will have to strengthen the existing road. And we will have to use extreme caution to deliver the rocket modules to the launch site. I think of the problems with the trucks of a few weeks past."

Kamada stared hard at Treadway. "It concerns me to think of a module lost in a similar manner."

Treadway nodded, remembering the incidents. One truck carrying a heavy load of re-bar up Mokolea Road had sheared a U-joint, and another truck that failed to properly negotiate a hairpin turn while driving down the winding valley road had ended up on its side. "Well," he said hopefully, "we still have the ability to offload from the barges."

Kamada lifted his short-fingered hand an inch off his desktop, then set it down again. "Using barges to deliver the modules will not be always safe. We will use it for now because we have no choice."

"What do you think we should do, then?"

Kamada's eyes bored into Treadway's as he said in his flat voice, "I believe that in this case...we will be doing something ...if we do nothing." The edges of Kamada's lips raised a millimeter. "We will speak to Mr. Tate later. I think he will change his mind...Edward"

Treadway wondered what was going to bring about this conversion but he didn't ask. It might be something he didn't want to hear. He could accept CSS paying for local political support—that was just business—but finding out about the hanky-panky with the Akoki will had bothered him.

A little, anyway.

Chapter Nine

"Hey!" Susan called out, "did you turn off the water?"

Neal stepped out from the storage area beneath the house where he was checking a termite-chewed floorboard and saw her leaning over the verandah rail. He said, "No. What's wrong?"

"What's wrong is the water's not running. I had the kitchen faucet on and it just quit. There's nothing from the bathroom faucets either."

"Great, another problem. Did it sputter, or what?"

"No, not really. It just slowed to a trickle and stopped. The water looked real dirty toward the end."

"Dirty?" Neal thought for a moment. "When was the last time you used that faucet?"

Susan shrugged. "I don't know. About three hours ago, I guess, after breakfast."

He went back beneath the house and checked for obvious leaks. There were none. He traced the water lines back to their source and came to a single PVC plastic pipe entering from uphill, at the rear of the excavated storage area. He walked around to the back of the house, worked his way delicately through a tangle of thorny bougainvillea and got down on his knees. Hidden in the weeds below the main shutoff valve was a faucet that tapped directly into the supply pipe. When he twisted it open murky water drooled out

He shut off the faucet and got to his feet, careful of

the bougainvillea thorns. From where he stood the supply pipe disappeared uphill into the brush. It suddenly occurred to him that the actual source of the water was a mystery; until now he'd just taken it for granted.

With nothing else left to do he pushed his way into the brush and followed the plastic pipe.

It ran through the trees beside a corroded steel pipe for about three hundred feet and then passed over the lava ridge that paralleled the level section of his entrance road. He climbed atop the outcropping, a feat made easy by eroded gas pockets in the igneous rock, and jumped the short distance to the ground on the other side. The pipe continued through a stand of trees that ended at the road, where it vanished beneath the ground.

The property a few yards beyond the far side of the road now belonged to Concord Space Systems. The trees and brush on that side had been cut back from the roadway, and down the center of the cleared strip was a line of survey markers, tiny red flags on wire staffs. Every few yards a new *KAPU—No Trespassing* sign was staked into the ground.

Crossing the road, Neal found where the pipe emerged from the ground. He had gone only a few steps when he located the problem. The supply pipe was broken. He looked up from the splintered end, which lay half-sunk in a puddle of muddy water, and saw more pipe. Long off-white sections of it stacked beside a pile of cleared brush like giant vermicelli waiting to be boiled. He stared at it, drops of sweat stinging his eyes. From somewhere downhill a jackhammer rattled over the moan of a diesel engine, the familiar sound of the work crew that had been digging fencepost holes all week. Above, on the ranch road, airbrakes wheezed as a truck from the launch site slowed before pulling onto Mokolea Road.

"They took out all the pipe?" Susan said in disbelief when he got back. She had given up on cleaning the kitchen and was eating a lunch of soup and crackers at the table.

"All the pipe on their land, it looks like."

"But they can't do that!"

Neal ripped a paper towel from the holder and wiped his face. "I wish you'd told them before they did it."

"Wait a second, now. Isn't a water line official property or something?"

"Hell, I don't know. I'm not even sure where the damn water comes from. It might come from one of those rainwater cisterns, which I doubt is official anything. I'm going to go check—oh, hell."

"What?"

"What if the water does come from a cistern? The whole thing might be draining out where they took out the pipe!" He grabbed the truck keys and hurried out.

*   *   *

Susan was on the verandah writing in a notebook when he returned an hour later. "That took long enough," she said as he climbed the stairs. "What'd you find out?"

"Well, we weren't losing any water, anyway. It was turned off at the source."

"And where is that?"

"Above Mokolea Road, where it turns left up there. Our pipe comes off a bigger pipe and runs straight down to here. Or did. The whole section crossing CSS property was taken out."

"Why would they do that?" Susan asked. "Even if they had the right to they should have notified us. That was incredibly shitty."

Neal lowered himself into one of the rattan chairs. "Maybe they forgot."

"Yeah, right." Susan closed her notebook and tossed it down. "Well, what now? We've got to have water."

"I don't know. I went to Yamata Store to call CSS; but the only number I could get was their Oahu office and I didn't have enough money for the call. I'm going back in a few minutes."

Susan fumed. "It still seems like there'd be some legal requirement that they notify us. What if we needed water for an emergency, like a fire or something?"

Neal snorted. "They'd probably be *glad*. Hell, I'd like..." The words faded and his expression went blank. "I just remembered something," he muttered. He got up and went inside, and returned a moment later studying a creased sheet of blue paper.

"What's that?" Susan asked.

"I remembered this when you said they should notify us." He read aloud from the paper: '*Dear Mr. Tate, it has come to our attention that a plastic above-ground pipe which supplies water to your residence lies partially on Concord Space Systems (CSS) property. A careful search by our legal department has failed to produce any record of an easement for this pipeline, nor is there any record on file with the Mokolea Town Council, which leases the water main which feeds your supply pipe. Please be advised that unless you are able to provide CSS with valid documentation of such an easement within the next thirty days all portions of the aforementioned pipeline lying on CSS property will be removed.*' He looked up. "It's got some guy's signature on it. Chief Engineer of the Kona Launch Facility."

Susan grabbed the paper from his hands and looked at it like a photo of a bad car wreck. "Where was this?"

"That came in the mail about a month ago. I thought it was another thing about selling the land and just stuck it in my back pocket. I put it with the rest of the CSS crap and never got around to reading it."

Susan handed the letter back. "This is really great."

"Yeah, it's great." He stuffed the letter into its envelope and sailed it through the verandah doors. "The most amazing thing it says is that Mokolea has a town council. If it actually does, the least amazing thing is that they can't find any records. Hell, maybe the Akokis had a verbal agreement about the pipe. With whoever owned the ranch before, I mean."

"And maybe they didn't," Susan said. "Maybe they just put it there."

Neal shook his head. "I don't think so. There's a rusted steel pipe running uphill next to the plastic one so it must have been there a long time. They must have had permission."

"That doesn't mean a damn thing if there's no record of it," Susan pointed out.

"No," Neal agreed. "Look, I'll drive to Mokolea and see what I can find out. Maybe Kamuela Napeahi knows something he's been here forever. While I'm doing that why don't you drive up to Captain Cook and get us some bottled water."

"Bottled water?" Susan said faintly. "You think we're going to cook and wash and bathe with just bottled water?"

"Unless you have any better ideas. You can get two or three five-gallon bottles. And we'll need a few feet of plastic tubing to use for a siphon."

Susan sat back carefully in her chair. "Just how long do you propose we do this, Neal?"

He shrugged. "I don't know. Let me see what I can find out in Mokolea first, and then we'll worry about it."

Mokolea was a small fishing village bordering the small bay north of the launch site. A short investigation made it clear that no one in the village knew anything about water records. Neal visited Ana Napeahi's stone bungalow and the old lady did recall that a town council was formed in the early sixties to negotiate with the developer of a proposed project in the area. The only remnant of the fizzled project was the four-inch water main that continued to supply Mokolea and into which the Akokis' line had tapped.

Back at the house Neal told Susan what he'd found out. "So it looks like we'll have to re-route the section of pipe that ran across CSS's frigging property." He shoved the last of five plastic water bottles into a corner of the kitchen and started to wash his hands in the sink. "Good grief," he said, "look at me." He shut off the dead faucet valves he'd just opened out of habit.

Susan was leaning back in a chair at the table, fanning herself from the effort of lugging the forty-pound water bottles up the stairs. She said, "How hard will it be to put in more pipe?"

"Not too hard, I think. You just glue it together. Tomorrow we can figure out where to run it and how much we'll need."

"Which brings up something I was thinking about, Neal. Who owns the rest of the land between the main water pipe and Mokolea Road? I don't want to do this again."

"I asked Kamuela's sister about that," he said. "The land belongs to a man she knows that lives in Hilo now. She said she'd call him to make sure everything's okay but she says there won't be a problem. The guy was a friend of the Akokis and he hates CSS."

Chapter Ten

Neal ordered the new water pipe through a friend of Big Jim's in Hilo. While they waited for it to come in he painted and Susan finished the first draft of a children's book she was writing, which cheered her up somewhat—just enough, Neal figured, to offset the irritation caused by the lack of running water.

Late in the week—the same morning they opened the last bottle of water—a stake-bed truck came inching down the entrance road and pulled into the yard with a load of PVC pipe. They helped the driver unload the bundles and then changed into shoes and long pants and went to work.

The missing section of water line was completely installed by the following afternoon. It now ran from below the rock outcropping across to Mokolea Road, under the road through a drainage culvert, and then zigged uphill to the supply main.

Since he was already in work mode Neal started on another repair job the next day. He'd been putting it off for months; the wood around the base of the toilet had rotted and water was leaking out around the base. He disconnected the toilet, spent most of the morning replacing the spongy flooring, and then made a list of items needed to put everything back in working order.

He found Susan in the front yard sunning on a blanket, covered in a suntan lotion that smelled like coconut custard. She rolled over and looked at him upside-down when he came outside.

"Finished?"

"Negative. I need some things from the hardware store. You want anything in Na'alehu?"

"Yeah, some earplugs. I'm tired of listening to that damn jackhammer."

The machine gun-like noise was coming from somewhere uphill, where the work crew was installing Concord Space Systems' new chain link fence. They had rapidly worked their way down Mokolea Road to a point just above the house.

"No kidding," Neal said. "But it looks like they'll be out of the vicinity pretty soon."

"Good." Susan stretched her arms and legs, yawning. "I could use some more suntan lotion, if you don't mind. But not this stuff. I feel like a big piece of candy."

Neal hung out his tongue and moaned. "That's exactly what you are, baby," he panted, "exactly what you are."

"You're very attractive when you do that," Susan said. "Especially with those brown streaks on your cheek."

Neal wiped his face with his shirt tail. "Don't think I don't know it," he said, and left.

He was bouncing along the ruts near the top of the entrance road, trailing a small cloud of blue smoke, when he saw the fence. He let up on the gas and stared in disbelief through the windshield. A section of new eight-foot chain link fabric crossed the road ahead, blocking his way. He slowly drove up to it and stopped the truck.

The fence, he saw when he walked up to it, ran in a straight line from the direction of Mokolea Road, gradually angling onto his entrance road until it cut off a section where the road took a hard right. He bent down and felt the concrete at the base of a pole. It had been poured earlier in the day. He put his eye next to the fence, looked along it, and saw something moving in the trees about a hundred yards to the left. He set off in that direction, following a swath of crushed vegetation.

Fifty yards along the fence fabric ended. From that point on there were only new holes with poles stuck loosely in them like large metal soda straws. He heard voices ahead and kept walking.

The drilling crew was a mixed bag of Portuguese, native, and oriental types. They gave him heat-dulled looks when he appeared from the trees and then went back to what they were doing, which was watching while one of the men measured the depth of a newly-bored hole. Neal looked around and spotted a pot-bellied Caucasian in a cowboy hat dozing in the shade, sitting in a folding chair leaned against the truck they were using to haul their diesel compressor. He walked over to the man.

"Excuse me."

The foreman jerked, letting his chair fall forward, and pushed back his hat, exposing froggy eyes that blinked at the light. "Howdy," he said in an odd gargling voice. "Can I help you?"

"I think you've made a mistake," Neal told him.

The man fought his way out of his chair to his feet, then turned his head and ejected a wiry stream of brown liquid from a gap in his teeth. "Uh *mustike?*"

"I believe so." Neal pointed in the direction of his truck. "Your fence crosses my road back there. How am I supposed to get out?"

"Get out?" Perplexed, the foreman pinched his lower lip, transforming himself from a frog into a monstrous fish. His eyes suddenly lit up and he patted his shirt pockets, coming up with a piece of paper that he laboriously unfolded. "Lessee," he said, running a finger across it, "are you Mr.—uh—Tate, by any chance?"

"That's right,"

The man's smile exposed a wad of brown mulch between his lower lip and teeth. "Well, Mr. Tate, the gennelman who is my boss said that we might be speakin' to you today. He said if we did I should give you this here."

Neal took the sweat-dampened paper from him and examined it. It was a photocopy of another letter from the Chief Engineer of the Concord Space Systems Kona Launch Facility. The gist of the text, fortified with directional and surveying references, was clear enough: a short segment of his entrance road lay on CSS property. Hand-written at the bottom of the page was the notation *Copy mailed to N. Tate on 3-08.*

Neal folded the letter copy and slid it into his shirt pocket. CSS had obviously known for some time that their fence would cut through his entrance drive but the notice had been mailed only two days before. It was probably sitting in his post office box now.

The foreman shot another stream of brown saliva from his mouth and cocked a thumb at the fence. "It's in the right place, ain't it?"

Neal smiled grimly. "Not for me." He thanked the foreman, walked back along the fence to the road and got into his pickup, where he sat contemplating the net of shiny chain link stretched in his path. The truck cab's dusty-smelling heat raised beads of perspiration on his face. Without the toilet parts there would be no toilet. He imagined Susan's reaction when he told her this.

He started the truck, stuck his head out the window, and backed up about fifty yards down the narrow road, where he stopped to buckle his seatbelt. He adjusted the shoulder strap and settled his sunglasses in place, then put the pickup in first gear and floored the accelerator.

He was in second gear when he hit the middle fence post. It folded out of sight in the blink of an eye, pulling the chain link fabric down with a metallic shriek. The fabric caught beneath the truck for an instant and then let go with a loud metallic chattering, after which the engine sounded different. As he blasted up the road, Neal glanced into his rear-view mirror and saw the pickup's muffler rocking in the dirt.

When he reached Mokolea Road he stopped and got out to inspect the truck. Other than losing the muffler and adding a few more dents and scrapes everything seemed fine. He got back in and pulled away. There were certain advantages, he reflected, to owning a junker.

*   *   *

The run-over section of fence had been propped back in place with two-by-fours by the time he got back from Na'alehu. He looked left and right, saw no one, and drove into the fence at low speed. The chain link fabric folded down again, accompanied by snapping boards and squealing nails, and popped up behind the tires with two scraping slaps. Neal parked the truck and got out to study the situation more carefully.

*   *   *

Susan was sitting up on the blanket watching him when Neal pulled into the yard and parked beneath the breadfruit tree. As he walked up to her she said, "What's wrong with the truck? It sounds funny."

"The muffler fell off," he said. "And that's the good news."

"Oh—no. What's the bad news?"

He set down the sack of toilet parts and sat on the blanket. "Right up there," he said, pointing, "CSS put up a fence that cuts across our entrance road."

"A fence?"

He pulled out the photocopied letter from the foreman and she read through it. "I still don't understand."

"Well, if you want to believe their surveyors, about forty feet of our road—right up there where it goes through the narrow place in that ridge of lava—is on CSS land. When they put in the road they used a natural gap in the ridge. The problem is, that little jag goes about five or six feet onto CSS property."

Susan brushed an ant off her thigh. "If that's all, then what's the problem? We just make it go onto our property."

"Unfortunately," he said, "it ain't that easy. The ridge is in the way. I got out and walked around. We'd have to change where the upper section of the road goes and take out a huge hunk of solid rock. I'm thinking the best thing might be to put in a whole new road."

Susan's face fell. "You're kidding. A new road?"

"Unless we buy a helicopter."

"But—where?"

88

"It'll have to come in from there," he said, pointing to the other side of the yard, "and go straight across to Mokolea Road."

"Oh, wonderful."

Neal stood. "I'm going to check it out on foot."

"Wait, I'll go with you. Let me get my shoes."

The distance from the house to Mokolea Road was roughly two hundred yards. The terrain in between was steeply sloped, cut by a deep ravine, and heavily wooded.

"Now we know why they put the road in up there," Neal said. "I'm starting to think a helicopter might actually be the best answer."

Susan pushed her hair back from her face, where it was sticking from sweat. "I don't think this is funny."

"What are you angry about?"

"I'll tell you what I'm angry about. We just put in a million feet of new water line, and now this happens. I'm sick of these damn problems."

"I am too, Susan, but there's not much we can do but fix 'em."

"How about moving?" Seeing his reaction she said, "Or at least look into this survey stuff. They might be lying."

Neal pondered a moment. "I doubt it. They wouldn't take the chance of getting sued. I'm sure they got all their facts straight."

Susan let out a hard sigh. "What about these trees?" she said, looking around. "This ravine? It'll take forever to make a new road. Think about it, Neal."

He looked at her.

"What?"

"That's the same thing Ed Treadway kept telling me."

"Well, my reasons for saying it are a hell of a lot different from his. But you *should* think about it."

"I have, Susan. Putting in a new road'll be hard but it can be done."

"Oh, come on, Neal," Susan said pleadingly. "Maybe it'd be better to just give in and sell."

"We've been through that. We can't afford it right now. And dammit, I don't want to knuckle under to these jerks."

"What about what *I* want? To tell you the truth I wouldn't mind living a little closer to civilization. And what about that thing," she said, waving a hand in the direction of the launch site. "That's going to screw up this whole area."

Neal's face softened. "Maybe so. But look, Susan, I still want to stay here for the time being. I don't feel right about selling out. Not yet, anyway."

"Okay, fine. Tell me this. What the hell are we going to do about getting in and out while—" She stopped and her face grew a puzzled frown. "Hey, how did you get back? You said they put a fence across the road."

"They did." He looked up and down the ravine. "I drove through it."

Susan stared at him. "I really think you've gone a little bonkers, Neal."

He look at her a moment and then lifted his eyebrows. "I never said I wasn't."

Chapter Eleven

The problem of getting to and from the house had a workable solution, which Neal found by scouting the area more thoroughly the next day.

"There's a clearing in the trees just off Mokolea road," he told Susan. "We can park the cars there and walk to the house."

He saw that she was less than thrilled with the proposal. "That's quite a hike if you're carrying something."

"It's not bad, only three or four minutes. There's an old trail that leads from there to here that I can fix up a little. Cut back some of the brush."

"What about putting in a new road?"

"Well, I think the clearing is actually a road somebody started and never finished. It's pretty level there and it's a good place to turn off from Mokolea Road."

"So what about it? Are we going to hike in to the house for the next year or what?"

"Just for a while, I guess."

Susan accepted this with a silent resignation that lasted exactly ten days, at which time she came hobbling into the yard after a shopping trip to Na'alehu while Neal was on the roof repairing a leak. "What happened?" he called down.

"I tripped," she said curtly. "The groceries are back there on the ground." She climbed up the stairs and went inside.

Neal helped wash her scraped ankle. He got her settled into a chair on the verandah and then took another sack back to where she had tripped. He picked up the cans and packages scattered along the ravine, thinking about the access problem.

Having no way to drive to the house was a major headache but he hadn't done anything about putting in a new road. He wasn't keen on hacking a corridor across the hillside. In general the idea of chopping down trees and gouging up the ground held no appeal for reasons that could be termed philosophical and esthetic, but the potential hypocrisy involved made it even worse. Although the damage would be minor in comparison with Concord Space System's depredations in the valley, it was just a matter of degree. A final consideration was lack of funds, which meant building the road by hand, and the only hands available were his and Susan's.

But the fact was, they needed a road. He pulled a can of Ranch Style Beans from under a vine and brushed it off, trying to picture himself and Susan laboring with pick and shovel. Not a pretty picture, but there was one mitigating factor, albeit a feeble one; not paying some stranger to bulldoze out the road made the idea seem more acceptable, more...natural. Or something.

The logic of this position, he knew, would crumble under close scrutiny so he avoided a potential philosophical dilemma by not scrutinizing closely. They needed a road.

He made a final visual sweep for missed grocery items and started back to the house.

*   *   *

Susan took off on a photography trip to the black sand beach at Punalu'u the next morning and Neal drove up the coast to Kailua. He got a new muffler installed on the Chevy and by eleven o'clock he was driving—much more quietly—to a hardware store in the industrial area, where he bought picks, shovels, a wheelbarrow, some rope and a block and tackle. He also bought a chainsaw, which actually soured his stomach. He didn't like the things and never had. They embodied, in one noisy, smoke-spewing, tree-eating unit, a lot of things going wrong on the planet. Owning one was another thing that didn't bear close scrutiny. He tossed the last of the equipment into the back of the pickup and drove to Harry's gun shop.

The shop's door buzzer sounded as he went in. "Be right with you," Harry growled from somewhere in the rear.

"No hurry," Neal called back. He wandered around the shop and looked over the orchids as muted pops of gunfire came from the indoor pistol range, then walked back to Harry's writing cubicle and stuck his head through the door.

"I see you're hard at work."

Harry swiveled around in his chair and pulled off his glasses. "Neal! I didn't even recognize your voice! Long time no see."

"That's why I came by." He nodded at the typewriter. "What are you working on?"

"Just plugging away at another article." Harry folded his glasses and set them down. "To answer your question a little more thoroughly, I'm writing about the old 1911 .45 ACP versus the 9 millimeter Beretta they picked for the new military sidearm."

"Huh." Neal leaned on the doorframe, getting comfortable. "What do you think about that?"

Harry stuck out his lips. "Well—the Beretta's a damn good gun, no question. A lot's been written about the change but I'm sort of tying it all together in one little mini-history. It's a good opportunity to give everybody the benefit of my profound experience and amazing wisdom."

"I'm sure they could use it."

"Hell yes. What I can't understand is why the Army didn't just ask *me* what gun to pick."

"They weren't thinking," Neal said. "What gun would you choose?"

Harry rubbed his palms together slowly. "It's a tough one. Sometimes I think that if you're going to give a guy a sidearm, make it something with some real punch. A .357 auto, maybe. Something like the Desert Eagle, the Israeli gun."

A string of rapid-fire shots came from the pistol range across the hall. Harry waited until they stopped. "Of course," he continued, "we've got the 10 millimeter auto-loaders now, like the Colt *Delta Elite* and the Springfield *Omega*. Which reminds me, Springfield's sending me an *Omega* to check out. They've been out for a while but I've never shot one."

"Yeah? Must be nice, people sending you guns to play with."

Harry's chuckle sounded like sand swirling in a bucket. "Yeah. You crank out enough articles and people think you know what you're talking about." He reached across the litter of books on his desk and lifted a well-used briar pipe from a cluttered rack. "Of course, writing the damn articles is a lot of work."

"I believe it."

"Well, don't," Harry said, laughing again. He picked up a pipe reamer and sat back. Neal watched as he began scraping the bowl of his briar with the care of a paleontologist cleaning a creodont skull. "Hell, I *love* writing about guns, as depraved as that is. It's usually pretty straightforward—this is this, that's that. I don't have to figure out a plot or make up characters or anything."

Another string of shots sounded across the hall and Neal gestured toward the range. "Doesn't that ever bother you?"

"Music to my ears." Harry knocked the pipe on his palm and eyed the bowl critically. Satisfied, he packed in a load of sweet-smelling tobacco and reached for a match, but his jigger was empty. He heaved himself out of his chair with a short grunt. "Let's mosey to the front. I need to get off my keister anyway."

"Been sailing lately?" Neal asked as he walked down the hall.

"Oh—no. But I am going this weekend. Me and, uh, a lady I met. Hey, Neal, you and Susan are welcome to come along. I'd like you to meet Vi."

"That sounds great, Harry, but I've got too much work to do. I'll take a rain check though."

"You got it." Harry snagged a match from another jigger and scratched it alight. He sucked in the flame, getting the pipe going with little popping puffs, working at it with the blissful concentration of a nursing baby. He shook the match out and exhaled a cloud of smoke. "So, what're you up to today?"

"Just buying some stuff for the house."

Harry nodded, puffing. "What about the art, now? Still painting away?"

"As much as I can. I've been doing a lot of house things lately."

"Yeah, well, I know how that goes." Harry's eyebrows suddenly lifted. "Hey, your place is pretty close to this rocket thing they're putting in, isn't it? The lady I'm going sailing with was telling me about that."

"Yeah," Neal said, "I'm near it all right."

"I see you're not too happy about that."

"No. I like things quiet. And I don't think it's good for the island. The hotels are bad enough, but we sure as hell don't need rockets blasting off all year long."

Harry's eyes shifted and Neal turned to see what he was looking at. A stocky, round-faced Hawaiian man stood in the hallway near the shooting range door, which closed itself with a soft hiss and clunk. The man had come in during the last part of their conversation. He held a suit coat in one hand and a large automatic pistol in the other, and a shoulder-holstered revolver was strapped to the side of his thick chest. His almond eyes moved lazily away from Neal.

Harry pulled the pipe from his mouth. "How's she work now, Sam?"

The man gave Harry a quick smile that exposed a row of white but slightly gapped teeth. "Perfec'." He came around to the customer side of the display cases and laid the automatic on the counter. "I used five different type cartridges, even some old corroded stuff." The man's clipped voice was flavored with the local accent. "No problems with anything."

Harry rapped the top of the display case with a knuckle. "I knew it! Just that little burr on the ramp snagging the cartridges." He nodded in Neal's direction and said, "Sam, this is Neal Tate. Neal, this is Sam Kane."

96

Kane's smile dried up. He shook hands perfunctorily and then turned back to Harry. "How much I owe?" he asked, pulling out his wallet.

Harry gave him the bill. Kane paid, said goodbye, and departed, giving Neal a short nod on the way out.

"Friendly guy."

Harry slid the register closed. "Sam's okay. I don't know what's eating him today."

"Does he live around here?" Neal asked.

"Nah. He's a police captain over in Hilo. I've known Sam since I opened my shop over there. He still brings me his business and he's sent me a lot of other customers." Harry shot a puff of smoke toward the ceiling. "You know, I think I'm ready for a break. Why don't we go get sloshed at Drysdale's?"

Neal laughed; it was a small joke between them. "I wouldn't mind a beer. Maybe something to eat."

"Sounds good." Harry squinted one eye. "You okay?"

"Me? Sure. I've just...got a lot on my mind lately."

Harry nodded. "Well, if there's anything I can help with, let me know."

Chapter Twelve

They had gotten sloshed at Drysdale's, literally, the first time they ever met. It happened a few weeks after Neal and Susan moved to the Big Island, while they were living in an apartment in Kailua-Kona and waiting for the probate problems with George Akoki's will to be resolved. Neal went for a walk around the bay by himself one evening and ended up wandering into Don Drysdale's Club 53, a bayside watering hole that served burgers and drinks with PG-rated names. He grabbed a stool at the bar and ordered a beer, and when it came he drank unhurriedly, enjoying the breeze.

The crowd in Drysdale's that night was mostly cruise ship tourists sporting new aloha shirts and new sunburns, but the table closest to him was occupied by locals. He'd seen them in Drysdale's a couple of times before—a bunch of old coots who sat around shooting the bull. He listened in on their conversation with half an ear, for a couple of reasons. First, he liked old coots, and second, it was hard not to listen since they were so close. And one of them had a voice that was hard to ignore. It sounded like he had strips of rawhide instead of vocal cords.

While Neal was working on his beer a waitress tripped over a chair leg and spilled her tray of drinks, dousing him and the rough-voiced man. They cracked a few jokes about it and Neal wound up sitting at the table for a round of drinks on the house. The first

98

round led to another, and another, and the longer Neal sat, the more he found himself liking Harry, the man with the voice. Harry did the least amount of talking, always a good sign, and when he did speak he showed a sharp wit.

Another thing Neal liked about Harry was the way he looked. Friendly was the most accurate description. When Harry smiled the lines on his face fit perfectly. A large nose and bristly white hair only added to the effect; the nose was comfortably battered-looking rather than aristocratic, the crew cut retro rather than pugnacious. But Harry's eyes were his most striking feature. They were brilliant blue, intelligent.

One thing that was impossible to miss was the scar on Harry's neck. The skin between his jaw line and collarbone was pale and gnarled, the disfigurement standing out plainly against his tan, and he had an unconscious habit of covering it with his hand.

One by one Harry's cronies departed until he and Neal were the only ones at the table. They ordered a last round of gin and tonics. When the waitress set them down and left Neal touched his own neck. "How did you hurt yourself there?"

Harry's hand automatically went to the scar. He gave it a familiar stroke, the way he might rub an old dog's muzzle. "Trying to shave while I was drunk," he said remorsefully.

"Hm. Must've been some razor."

Harry chuckled and drank some of his gin and tonic. He played with his plastic swizzle stick a moment, drawing a figure eight in the condensation on the table, and then he looked up. "It was in the war," he said.

Neal nodded. "Your arm too?"

The upper part of Harry's arm was also covered

with deep scars. "Same time, yeah. Not one of my better days."

"What happened?"

Harry took another drink. "It was...in the Pacific," he said slowly. The words seemed to be fighting their way out. He reached up to touch his scar again but stopped himself and placed his hands on the table, one gripped in the other. "In the Philippines."

"The Philippines." Neal murmured the words. He set his drink on the table and sat back.

Harry hesitated again. He wondered why he wanted to talk about it. He was a little drunk, but that wasn't it. Maybe...maybe he *had* to talk about it every so often. Maybe, from time to time, a person had to dredge up the things chewing on his soul and put them into words, to remind himself that they were, after all, simply things that had happened to a man, and weren't the dark, spreading forest they sometimes seemed.

He disconnected his hands long enough to take a drink and wipe the sweat from his forehead with a paper napkin. "It was in 1942," he told Neal.

The Japanese offensive that began on January ninth of that year, on the island of Luzon, had steadily pushed American troops under MacArthur south, forcing them to retreat down the Bataan Peninsula. The Japanese under General Homma were well-equipped, had extensive air and artillery support, and were numerically superior to the combined American-Filipino army, who by this time were in terrible shape, undersupplied, battered by the enemy, ravaged by heat, humidity, rain, fungus, and malaria. Harry—Pfc. Harold Sturdivant—was in and out of the fighting from the start of the offensive until MacArthur departed in early March, leaving General Wainwright in command on Corregidor.

On the twenty-fifth of March an incoming Japanese artillery round exploded and sent a chunk of tree into Harry's arm, slicing into his biceps and fracturing the humerus bone. Shrapnel from the same shell struck him in the throat, tore loose a patch of skin, and chopped a piece out of his larynx.

"The medic gave me a shot of morphine," Harry said, laying a hand on his old neck wound. "Then he cleaned me up and dumped on some sulfa powder and sewed the whole mess up. I watched him. Maybe that made a difference somehow, watching, I don't know, but I never got any serious infection. My neck and my arm swelled up but everything healed. I was lucky. "Harry pulled slowly at his nose, staring into his empty glass. "Even after we got to Camp O'Donnel," he added in a faded voice. His eyes lifted. "Ever heard of Camp O'Donnel?"

Neal studied the other man's face. It seemed weary, older than before. He said, "I don't think so." He wished he could have said yes because he knew it mattered.

Harry gave him a crooked smile. "Well, that's understandable." He drained his glass and wiped his mouth roughly. "People remember the victories, not the defeats. The Japs just kept coming until we couldn't go on. Then General King, the guy in charge on Luzon, surrendered everybody that was left on Bataan. Around twelve thousand Americans and sixty-five thousand Filipinos. There wasn't any choice, really. We'd had it."

Harry turned to stare across the dark water of Kailua Bay. A boat had come in late to the town pier. Under the lights a marlin was strung up on the weighing scales, the skin of the great fish shining like old silver.

"The Japs rounded us up at a place called Mariveles," he went on, watching the small figures on the pier. "They made us stand in the sun while they searched us and questioned us. It took hours. No water. No shade. No food. No medication for the guys that were sick or wounded. The Japs were...bad. They were bad. They beat us. One guy, an American officer, had some Japanese money on him. I guess they thought he took it off a dead soldier, who knows. They pushed him down in the dirt and cut his head off with a sword."

Harry pinched the bridge of his nose, closing his eyes. "I can still see it now, like it was yesterday. The guy's head just fell off and the blood gushed out. A big pool of blood in the sand." When he opened his eyes they were glistening. His voice hardened. "Then the Japs marched us—everybody, the sick ones, the wounded ones—from Mariveles to the railroad at San Fernando to ship us off. We walked...so *far*."

Harry put a hand over his eyes and rubbed them, hard. "You know," he said, "I never have looked to see exactly how far it was. It doesn't matter, really. It was too far for a lot of the guys. Five days it took us. The Japs didn't give us food or water or medicine. They beat us on the way for no reason. There was no shade. The men that fell behind or couldn't go on, they shot 'em or bayoneted 'em. Sometimes they'd beat the hell out of a guy, a sick man, a dying man. Just whip him until he was bloody and then kill him."

A drunken laugh erupted from the other side of Don Drysdale's Club 53. The television hanging over the bar droned.

"I do remember," Neal said quietly.

Harry seemed not to have heard at first. Slowly, though, his eyes focused. Between the two men time wandered off track

"I remember what you're talking about," Neal said again. "Bataan. The Death March."

Chapter Thirteen

The first few days of roadwork were exhausting. Neal cut down trees and sawed them into pieces and Susan dragged them off to one side. They went at the stumps with chainsaw and axe next, and then used the picks, shovels and a new sledgehammer for rough leveling of the roadbed. They kept at it for four days straight, working from just after sunrise to sunset.

On the morning of the fifth day Neal left Susan sleeping in bed. He ate a quick breakfast, loaded the wheelbarrow with tools, and rolled it through the woods to where they had left off work. Tugging on his gloves, he listened to the trucks whining uphill to the launch site entrance. The sound had become familiar; he could barely remember how quiet it used to be.

After dragging the last batch of brush and logs off the road he put in his earplugs and fired up the chainsaw. The plugs helped some, but every session with the saw made his bad ear sing for hours.

The chainsaw purred in his hands like a mechanical cat as he knelt in front of the day's first tree. He said, "Sorry, Mr. Tree," and squeezed the cat's balls. While it screamed and clawed he thought again about Harry. He hadn't told Harry about the launch site situation and he was trying to figure out why. He'd told Big Jim the details, and he'd kept Bernice Hollings up to date during visits to the Treasure Chest over the last three months.

The tree he was working on made splintering noises and he stepped back while it slowly toppled over. He cut off the limbs, then started on the trunk, chips spraying his bluejeans as the chain chewed into the wood.

On and off for the last few weeks he'd tried to convince himself that he'd cut Harry out of the loop because he didn't want to bother someone else with his problems. But that didn't explain Big Jim and Bernice.

The main reason behind the silence, he was beginning to see, was fear. Fear that Harry wouldn't understand his opposition to the launch site or his general opposition to developing the island. Fear that Harry wouldn't understand not selling his land. Or—worse—that Harry wouldn't really care one way or the other. He was afraid of what it would do to their friendship. They were from different generations, with different views of life.

Susan came down the footpath carrying her gloves and a Thermos bottle. She waved and said something and he pointed to his ears.

Coffee? she mouthed.

"Maybe in a few minutes," he shouted. He revved the saw, pumping the oiling button. Susan grimaced and walked down the road to get away from the noise.

Neal knelt down for the next cut, and as he did so another set of doubts boiled up, displacing Harry. It was the trees. By now he had slaughtered dozens of them, young and old alike, but he still hadn't gotten used to it. Or to the unavoidable comparison between building a road and building a launch site

Of course there was the difference of motivation—being forced to build a road to reach a house already in existence versus CSS screwing things up just to make

105

money. Then there was the difference of scale. One small road was certainly less damaging to the ecosystem than a sprawling, active launch site. Taking the long view, the road was fairly impermanent, whereas CSS was tearing things up on a grand scale, making changes that would take nature thousands of years to erase if it ever got the chance.

All of this, he knew, smacked of petty rationalization. Smacked of it like crazy. He revved up and put saw to wood. It would be good when the road was finished; he was sick of worrying about right and wrong and hypocrisy

*   *   *

Walking home after work that evening Susan said, "Looks like your estimate of how long it'd take to finish the road was a little off." Her tired laugh sounded borderline hysterical. "A week to get to the ravine, huh? And on the eighth day he rested."

Neal shrugged as he trundled the tool-filled wheelbarrow up the path. "Hey, I was wrong. It'll never happen again."

"Gosh, that's a relief." She mopped her forehead with her bandana. "Hey. How about taking a day off tomorrow?"

"Fine. I was hoping you'd say that a couple of days ago."

Susan stopped and stared at him. "What did you say?" She grabbed a shovel from the wheelbarrow. "That does it." She raised the shovel over her head and came at him. "You're gonna die right now."

Neal let out a high-pitched shriek and scuttled ahead with the wheelbarrow. A few yards up the path the wheelbarrow rammed a tree, sending him into a

106

somersault. He lay on his back laughing like an idiot as Susan walked up and sat on his chest.

"It's all over, pal" she said, menacing him with the shovel.

"I'm begging you to spare me," he wheezed.

She bounced up and down on his chest. "And go back to the damn rock pile? I don't think so."

"Do I get a last wish?"

"What?"

He pulled his arms from beneath her legs and slid both hands beneath her T-shirt. Her breasts were slippery with sweat. "Take a guess."

Susan lowered the shovel. "Okay," she said sternly.

*   *   *

They ate breakfast on the verandah the next morning.

Susan poured the last of the coffee into their cups and said, "What are you going to do today?"

"Nothing that feels like work," Neal said. He stretched and yawned. "I was thinking about taking Kawika's boat out."

"Boat? Oh, right," Kawika had left behind an Avon inflatable with an outboard motor on permanent loan. For the last two and a half months it had languished in the storage space under the house. "Is it safe?"

"Sure. It has a couple of patches but it's fine."

Susan blew on her coffee and took a sip. "Where are you going to take it?"

"Just down there," Neal said, waving to the north. "See what they're doing. Want to go?"

They ferried everything down the path to the pickup truck and then drove down Mokolea Road to the bottom of the hill. From there a rutted track led to the shore, where an old lava flow formed a natural boat ramp used by locals. The ramp was now a stone's toss from Concord Space Systems' security fence, which ran downhill to the high tide line and then turned and followed the shore.

Neal used a foot pump to inflate the boat. After a final inspection they stowed a few items on board, pulled it into the water and climbed in. Neal cranked up the motor and steered into the waves. Beyond the breakers he changed course and headed toward the small peninsula a mile and a half to the north.

He stopped the motor when they were directly offshore of the peninsula. From their vantage point on the undulating waves the entire valley could be seen. Three months of construction had transformed the narrow, weed-covered road leading from the top of the valley down to the peninsula into a wide gray scar. The road's curves had been altered, smoothed out here, strengthened with concrete buttresses there. Most of the valley was still untouched grass and trees but through binoculars Neal saw a low building of raw concrete perched on a blasted-out shelf midway up the valley floor. Where the old ranch house used to be there was a warehouse-like metal structure. Outside the valley proper a small white building was going up on the former site of the Kahookes' house.

"That's what most of the blasting was about," Neal said, pointing.

On the peninsula itself an area nearly the size of a football field had been leveled. A line of concrete pre-mix trucks, looking in the distance like horizontal tops, were in the process of filling the pouring forms surrounding the leveled area, while on the north shore a mobile crane offloaded shipping containers and steel trusses from a barge.

"It makes me sick to see this," Susan said. "I'm ready to go back when you are."

They motored back to shore, loaded up the boat, and drove home. Susan went inside to make sandwiches and tea while Neal walked down the footpath that once led to Kawika and Muriela's house.

The new fence stopped him where the Kahookes' back yard had started. He hooked his fingers in the mesh and watched workmen lift the last section of a small cylindrical building into place. He guessed it was the base of a small radar dome.

*   *   *

That afternoon when he turned on the kitchen faucet to fill the teapot the water came out in weak stream. He let it run until it died completely. Then he calmly set the pot in the sink, told Susan where he was going, and went to find the problem.

He took the path through the woods and came out on Mokolea Road. From there he walked uphill to where the new supply pipe crossed beneath the roadway.

The break was easy to locate; an artesian spring seemed to have erupted from the shallow ditch on the far side of the road. In the ground near the pipe he found, not to his great surprise, a set of deep tire tracks that angled purposefully off the road and passed over the rocks covering the pipe.

He plugged the pipe with a stick, drenching himself in the process, and walked back along the road to the clearing where he was parking his truck while they built the road. He rummaged around behind the seat and found a length of rubber hose and two clamps he kept there for an emergency. Back at the pipe break, he replaced the crushed section with the hose and clamps, covered it again with rocks—heavier ones that would resist a truck's weight—and started back to the house.

It seemed that CSS was trying to tell him something.

Chapter Fourteen

"I don't know if I can hack the road today."

Susan was slouched back in her chair at the kitchen table holding a coffee cup with both hands, her eyes puffy with fatigue. "I feel pretty wiped out from yesterday."

"Me too," Neal croaked. He set down his coffee and rubbed his eyes, blinking at the rectangle of blue sky showing through the kitchen window. Since their short trip in Kawika's inflatable boat they had put in two more days of work, pushing the road almost to the ravine. Getting past that obstacle was going to be difficult no matter how it was done. Just thinking about it made him tired.

He banged his fist on the table. "Let's do something fun for a change."

"Don't kid me."

"As Harry would say, I kid you not. I'm taking suggestions right now."

Susan *hmmd*, tapping her bottom lip with a finger. "I wouldn't mind driving somewhere. How about that place we keep passing? Pooka-hooka-now-now or whatever the hell it is."

"Excuse me," Neal said in a condescending tone, "are you referring to Pu'uhonua o Honaunau?"

"That's cheating," Susan said. "You actually studied the sign. You're supposed to *absorb* this stuff."

"Oh, I did." He breathed in deeply, nodding. "Oh

yes. That's it. Poo-oo! Honua! Oh-ho! Now now!"

*   *   *

The Visitors Center at Pu'uhonua o Honaunau National Historical Park was swarming with German and Japanese tourists whose buses had made an unfortunate simultaneous arrival. Neal and Susan bypassed the Center and walked down the paved path that wound its way through the park.

Susan read aloud from a guidebook she had purchased before they moved to the island. "'In the pre-white man era the site on Honaunau Bay had served a purpose similar to cathedrals and monasteries of medieval Europe. Hawaiians who violated a rule of kapu or committed a civil crime were safe from punishment if they could avoid capture long enough reach the Pu'uhonua, or Place of Refuge. There was good incentive to do so, as infractions of the law were commonly punished by death. Once inside the sanctuary, sinners or criminals, directed by priests, performed the rituals necessary to bring about purification and forgiveness of the gods, after which they were free to rejoin society.'"

"So, basically," Neal said, "things haven't changed all that much."

They strolled around the park grounds. Towering palms, their coconuts shorn for safety, shaded them with a rustling canopy of fronds. Tourists wandered aimlessly along the breezy intersecting paths, pointing and snapping pictures.

Susan stopped to sit on a bench. "What a great place," she said, looking around. "It's like an oasis."

Neal sat beside her. "Yeah. Those priests were no fools."

After resting a few minutes they took the path to a stone platform. According to the guidebook, rites of redemption had been performed atop it. They circled the platform and then walked down to the shore, following it to a small cove separated from the rest of Honaunau Bay by a partly submerged ridge of lava,

They walked around the cove. On the other side a road led them to a row of picnic tables shaded by trees. They sat, watching children splashing in pools of tidewater in the shelf of bare lava bordering the bay.

Neal was slumped on the table with his head on his arms when he felt someone staring at him. He turned around and saw Bernice Hollings standing in the road beside a tall man he didn't recognize.

"It is you!" Bernice said, laughing. "I can't believe it!" She came over to the table. The man, wearing a beard and a puzzled smile, ambled contentedly after her. "Tom and I were talking about you not twenty minutes ago."

"Tom Bailey," the man said, sticking out his hand. "Nice to meet you."

Susan gave him an odd smile as they shook hands. "Have we met before?"

"I don't think so," Bailey said affably. "Maybe you saw me around Kailua or something. I've done some serious loafing there."

Bailey's appearance lent credibility to this statement. He wore baggy shorts, scuffed huaraches, and a faded aloha shirt featuring green lizards cavorting on red leaves. He was bald on top, but his remaining gray-sprinkled brown hair was long enough to cover his collar.

Susan gestured toward the picnic table benches. "Have a seat."

113

They did, Bailey slouching sideways to stretch out his legs.

"Looks like summer's about here," Bernice said, flapping her blouse. "Amazing how a few more degrees makes such a difference. So what are you two up to?"

"Taking a break from working on the road," Neal told her.

"Oh, lord, that's right. How's that going?"

"Slowly."

"I'll bet. It sounds like very hard work. Listen, did you guys get the invitation I mailed you?"

Neal looked at Susan. "I guess not, but we haven't checked our mail in a while."

"Well then I'm doubly glad we ran into you. I'm having a party tomorrow to which you're cordially invited." Bernice pushed her sunglasses back and dug a pen and notepad from her shoulder bag. She wrote briefly, then tore out the page and handed it to Susan. "That's my address and home phone," she said, dropping her glasses back in place. "Tomorrow night, seven thirty—be there or be square."

Susan thanked her and tucked the address into her pocket. "If the slave driver here doesn't kill us," she said, aiming a glare at Neal, "we'll try to make it."

"Me?" Neal said, looking shocked. "Are you kidding? You may not be aware of this but in certain quarters I'm known as Mr. Relaxation. In fact I'm relaxing even as we speak."

"Maybe you can teach Tom how," Bernice said. "I had to practically tear him away from his writing and force him to come with me today."

Bailey laughed. "Yeah, sure."

"What are you writing?" Susan asked.

Bailey pursed his lips. "Well...basically, it's a book on

environmental law."

"Ahh," Neal broke in, "now I remember where I heard your name. You were doing legal work for GYRO, right?"

The lawyer's nod lacked enthusiasm. "Guilty as charged. We didn't exactly knock 'em dead, I'm afraid."

"Come on, now," Bernice chided, "this is a big, complex issue. And anyway it ain't over 'til it's over."

"Yes, but we should have—"

Shouts from the children on the shore cut short Bailey's response. They looked in the direction the children were pointing and saw dolphins surfacing in the middle of the small bay. The animals, maybe a dozen, churned up patches of white as they bobbed to the surface. As they moved in closer two of them suddenly exploded from the water, their sleek gray bodies twisting in the air and throwing off spirals of spray.

"Ooh, spinners!" Bernice exclaimed.

The dolphins stayed inside the bay for another two or three minutes and then headed out to sea, rolling to the surface like horses on a carrousel.

Bernice stared after them. "Aren't they beautiful? Maybe next lifetime we'll get promoted to dolphinhood." She turned to Bailey and set her palm on the table. "Well, Tom, if we're going down to Volcano we better get moving."

Bailey lifted his hands to indicate readiness, and they both stood.

"I hope you guys come tomorrow night," Bernice said. "And bring friends if you want. This is the first party I've had in a long time and I want to make it a killer."

Bernice and Tom Bailey said goodbye and walked

back to their car. They drove past on their way out, Bernice wiggling her fingers at them, Bailey, with a pipe protruding from the middle of his smile, raising a hand.

"I know I've seen him before," Susan said, watching the car drive off. "But he looked different somehow." She shrugged. "Oh, well. You want to go tomorrow?"

Neal gave her a look. "You realize we'll probably eat too much, drink too much, and stay up too late?"

"Yes.

"Okay then."

"Good. We can ask Big Jim to go."

Neal nodded vaguely in agreement, but his attention had been caught by a boat that had just motored into the bay, an open-hulled Boston Whaler pushed by a big black Mercury. The boat had throttled down to a sputtering idle as it headed toward the cove and boat ramp in the corner of the bay, but it was quickly nearing a broken line of lava rocks cutting across the mouth of the cove.

"What's he doing?" Susan said, watching the boat herself. "It looks like he's going to hit those rocks!"

A few feet from the jagged black humps the boat reversed its engine and held steady. While his two companions peered over the port and starboard gunwales, the man at the wheel looked astern. When the next large wave rolled in he shifted gears and pushed the throttle forward, riding the wave over the barrier.

"I'll be damned," Neal said. The trough of the wave had revealed a shallow gap in the rocks.

"Now I remember!" Susan suddenly said.

Neal turned to look at her.

"Tom Bailey!" she said, and burst out laughing. "He was the guy I saw picking up trash at the nude beach!"

116

Chapter Fifteen

Glowingly drunk, Tom Bailey leaned against the wall in Bernice Hollings' living room and heard, over the swirling strains of the Firebird Suite, the gritty snap of glass. He knew what it was instantly: he just leaned against a small framed photograph he had been admiring earlier but had forgotten about. With precise maneuvering of his feet Bailey altered his center of gravity and pulled away from the wall with what he hoped was a natural-looking movement.

The entire incident elicited no more than a slight ripple of disturbance in his brain, further proof of how far he had come since his six nerve-frying years with the firm.

Bailey took another sip of his double scotch and soda and reflected on the fact that, San Francisco or Hawaii, parties were about the same. Better here than San Francisco, though. Maybe California wouldn't be the next Atlantis, not for a while, but it had a damn good chance of being the home of the next Chernobyl.

In fact everything was better here, if only for the distance between himself and the law offices. His escape from the carpeted, wood-paneled hell of corporate litigation hadn't seemed real until he stepped off the 747 in Honolulu. No more alarm clocks, no more meetings, no more traffic. He had awakened from—as Henry Miller put it—the air-conditioned nightmare.

117

Or was it Arthur Miller?

The scotch was getting to him, Bailey decided. Either this one or the one he'd had before. Then again it could be the two beers he'd started off with. It didn't matter. After being cooped up with the book so long a little release of pressure was in order, Writing, he had discovered, wasn't easy. It was hard to sit in a chair and pat those plastic keys for hours on end.

The book he was working on, for which he was still trying to think of a clever title, would be an environmentalist's guide to winning legal battles, a handbook of strategy and tactics for laymen as well as lawyers. It would address a number of vital but arcane topics: which actions to take first in a legal confrontation and what to watch for in response; selecting the proper attorney for a particular job; redressing errors and corruptions of the legal process; countering falsehoods or statistical distortions favoring the "enemy"; understanding petition and referendum requirements. Other chapters would deal with subtler matters, such as effective interfacing with the news media, or ferreting out people and interest groups who might be willing to donate time, money, or name for reasons other than a love of nature.

Bailey considered himself qualified to write the book. He had plunged into the environmentalist fray before he graduated from law school, doing volunteer work for the Sierra Club, Friends of the Earth, and Greenpeace. From the very start he had studied the factors that determined success or failure of particular legal issues and over the years three filing cabinets had been filled with notes, analyses, and catalogued data sources relating to different environmental cases.

His last major battle was the fight to halt the Diablo

Canyon nuclear power plant, in which he served as legal coordinator for a coalition of environmental organizations. If ever a project deserved death, Bailey felt, Diablo Canyon was it, and when the plant was given the green light his enthusiasm suffered a meltdown of its own. He quit his position and went to work for his brother's law firm, where he devoted himself to making money.

Having money was a pleasant change. But after a time the fancy food, cool car and snappy clothes lost their thrill, and helping corporations make more money seemed pointless. In the end he unlocked his filing cabinets and started on the book. After finishing the outline and first two chapters the bug took hold firmly. He quit the law firm, bought a computer, and moved to Hawaii.

The Firebird Suite ended and, after a brief pause, Purple Rain started up.

Of course, Bailey thought as he downed a little more scotch, he'd gotten pretty slack at first, letting the book slide while he lay on the sand or went snorkeling. But hearing about Concord Space Systems had put him back on track. Rockets on Hawaii was some bad madness.

Since almost no one had a good word to say about the rockets except the business-boosters there seemed to be a fair chance of killing the plan. But GYRO had been outgunned, outflanked, out-politicked, and outspent by CSS. Bailey consoled himself with the reminder that he had entered late in the game and that working for GYRO had produced some positive spin-offs—like meeting a lot of good people and getting motivated to take the Hawaii bar exam.

Not to mention being motivated to work on the

book again. The usual schedule now was up at seven, write until eleven, take off a few hours for lunch and play, then back to the computer at six. Progress on the book was steady, but lately, sitting alone at night before the glowing monitor of his computer, he'd been thinking crazy things. The truth was that after years of protracted, carefully calculated legal skirmishing, the thought of grabbing an Uzi and running amok through the headquarters of a few environment-sliming mega-corporations had some appeal.

Bailey eyed his empty glass, wondering if he should go for another or hold off. Hold off a couple of minutes, he decided. Having made this decision, he turned his attention to the new arrivals at the front door. Two of them were the people he met yesterday at Pu'u-etcetera, the ones who lived near the launch site. He concentrated. The man: Tate, first name lost in the memory banks. The woman's name was easy, being the same as his sister's: Susan. The monster with the beard and Panama hat: unknown.

Rattling the ice cubes in his glass, Bailey tossed the last drops down the hatch and moseyed across the crowded room to greet them. He could tell Bernice about breaking the photo glass later.

"Aloha Susan, Mr. Tate," Bailey grinned, speaking loudly enough to be heard over the music. "Welcome to the madhouse."

Neal shook the offered hand. "Hi, Tom. Quite a horde here."

Bernice suddenly appeared with charms jangling. "You came.'" she said, squeezing their hands. "And you brought some wine, how nice!"

"We also brought along an actual party animal," Neal said. "Bernice and Tom, this is Jim Perkins. Most people just call him Large James."

"Only Neal," Big Jim said, shaking hands.

"Nice to meet you," Bernice said. "Now, first thing, you three go back outside and put your shoes on." She shooed them toward the door. "Too many feet in here for Hawaiian rules." They trooped outside, put their shoes on, and came back. Bernice crooked a finger. "Follow me to the pupus."

She led them through the crowded living room to the crowded kitchen, where a table laid with food was under siege.

"It's like vultures on a carcass," Susan shouted in Neal's ear.

"It certainly is," he agreed, and joined the pack.

He covered a paper plate with a pile of pupus and motioned for Susan and Big Jim to follow. The living room was packed with people drinking and trying to communicate over the blaring music, but they found an empty corner.

"How come nobody's dancing?" Susan yelled.

"Too busy eating and drinking," Neal yelled back.

Big Jim stuffed a squid sushi unit into his mouth and raised his beer. "I'm certainly doin'...my part."

One more pupu plate and two rounds of drinks later, the tape ended, leaving the hum of voices and scattered laughter.

"You know," Big Jim said, studying the crowd as he stroked his beard, "we've got some serious...boozin' goin' on." He suddenly looked worried. "Maybe they know something...we don't know."

"You didn't hear?" Susan said. "The volcano's about to blow up!"

Perkins polished off the remainder of his third beer and rumbled a belch into his fist. "Hey. Right now I could care less."

"You mean couldn't care less, Susan corrected. " 'Could care less' doesn't make sense."

"Hey," Big Jim said. "Right now I could care less."

Susan stepped on his toe. "As a writer I demand that you stop that. Grammar is important."

"It certainly is," a new voice said over Neal's shoulder. He twisted around. It was the pale man who had been staring at them from across the room.

"Although that particular misstatement is concerned more with logic than grammar," the man added. He gave them a pleasant smile. "My name is Jason York." He tilted his head toward Susan. "And you are...?"

"Susan McGregor."

She introduced Neal and Big Jim. Perkins shook York's hand and said, "Nice to meet you, Jason. And now I must...depart in search of more beer."

Big Jim lumbered off in the direction of the kitchen. Neal watched him go. He turned to find Jason York standing close to Susan, holding forth on the lamentable decline of the English language. He had trouble hearing York's low, sincere voice, and when the music started again he quit trying. He found the man simultaneously appealing and repellant. York's face— long and intelligent—was handsome in a smooth way, but his air of secret sorrow seemed affected. As did his clothes. He wore skin-tight jeans, white loafers without socks, and a shirt of black satiny material covered with tiny silver stars. The shirt was buttoned only halfway, exposing a twenty-dollar gold piece nestled in a patch of dark hair. As he spoke, gradually maneuvering himself closer to Susan until he was hovering over her, he emphasized his points by touching her gently on the forearm.

122

Neal slipped away when the discussion turned to California wines. Before he reached the kitchen Big Jim appeared and shoved a cold can of beer at him. "Where you goin', Neal?" he asked. "Leavin' the chick to the...mercy of Mr. Hollywood?"

"She's tough, she can take it," Neal said. He popped open his beer, took a swig. "Come with me."

He steered Big Jim into position near one of the speakers blasting out Creedence Clearwater Revival and slapped him on the back. "Now is this perfect or what?" he screamed.

"Close!" Perkins bellowed back. "Damn close!"

Somewhere toward the end of song Neal began to suspect that he was drunk, and moments later he had conclusive evidence. He watched in a kind of wild-ass detachment as his own hand reached down and cranked up the volume on the stereo. There was a loud hiss between songs and then the first sliding guitar notes of It Came Out of the Sky hit the room like a shockwave.

Big Jim let out a roar. "Yeah!" Beer in hand, he did a funky bent-over shuffle across the room through a sea of frozen faces and stopped in front of Susan. He bellowed at her, "Let's dance, baby!"

She put down her wine and danced. This broke the spell. In a matter of seconds the room was full of bodies jerking and bobbing to the music. Big Jim maneuvered backwards through the hips and elbows, passed Susan off to Neal, and picked up a woman on the sidelines. Neal danced with Susan into the next song, when Jason York came sliding through the crowd and put out a questioning hand.

Neal left Susan with York and worked his way into a corner near an open window. A moment later Bernice and Tom Bailey joined him.

Bernice was out of breath. "Boy I'm glad you did that!" she shouted. "I was afraid the party was gonna be a dud!"

Bailey grinned and said something that was swallowed by the blasting music and left. He returned with a precarious grip on three glasses of punch, which he handed out. He shouted, "Cheers," and downed most of his drink in one swallow.

Bernice drank some of her punch and then leaned close to Neal's ear. "I meant to ask you yesterday how your painting was coming along."

"Right now, with the road and house repairs, it's not."

"Sorry to hear that. But I want to remind you I was serious about my friend in Honolulu."

Bernice had offered to introduce him to a woman who owned an art gallery. Neal thanked her again. "I'll probably take you up on it when I have enough paintings done."

"Do that, hon. How's everything else? I mean with the launch site and all?"

He shrugged. "They're not blasting anymore but there's still a lot of noise and dust from the trucks driving by."

She gave him a sympathetic look.

"We went out in a boat and looked at the site," he told her. "They've done a lot. Fixed up the road, put up a couple of buildings. They were pouring the base of the launch pad, it looked like."

Bernice nodded. "It's going pretty fast, I heard. They pre-fabricated almost everything in Japan and then shipped it over. When the pad's ready they'll put up the temporary launch tower and they'll be ready to go."

"What do you mean, temporary?"

"Just for the test launches. When that's done they'll put in a permanent tower and finish the rest of the site." Bernice sighed heavily. "There still might be some way to stop this damn thing. We haven't given up the ship, have we, Tom?"

Bailey had listened silently but now he came to life. "We have not," he declared loudly. "It's too bad we weren't able to delay them a little longer, though. They were so desperate they might've gone somewhere else with their rockets."

"I'm not so sure," Bernice said. "The Japanese feel comfortable here."

Neal turned to Bernice. "That reminds me," he yelled. "You said CSS was basically a Japanese corporation but I read somewhere that it was Skip Schaefer's baby."

"Actually," she said, "Schaefer is co-director of CSS Incorporated, which is a 'Japanese-American consortium', as they call it. But that's stretching it. Komodo K.K.—the Japanese part—has all the money and power. The American part is Concord Technologies, which Skip Schaefer is CEO of. Concord Technologies is a registered U.S. corporation all right, but Komodo K.K. owns most of that, too. It's like a subsidiary."

"I didn't know that. All you read and hear about is Skip Schaefer."

"Because that's exactly what they want," Bernice told him. "Americans are sick of the Japanese taking over everything so that's the image CSS pushes. Komodo got Schaefer to head up Concord Technologies in California because, one, it's good PR to have an ex-astronaut's face to show the public, and two, Schaefer's name and contacts helped bring in U.S. aerospace engineers which CSS needed. I imagine his name hasn't hurt in other matters, like swinging the launch site deal here. The Japanese had it all figured out. I met Kamada once. He's no fool."

Neal looked at her. "Komodo is somebody?"

"No, Kamada. Hideo Kamada. He's the head of Komodo K.K. He's also in the hotel business. He owns one on Oahu and one on Maui."

"A hotel man," Neal said. "They're unstoppable."

"Maybe not. There may still be some monkey wrenches left to toss into the works. You remember Violet Gray, the woman I introduced you to in the kitchen?"

"Sure." She was an older woman, in her late fifties at least. Attractive in a mature way—straight-shouldered, dark eyebrows, silver hair done up in a chignon. "The marine biologist, right? She was nice."

"She is," Bernice agreed. "Violet's been working on a couple of angles but they're pretty iffy. One concerns the liquid fuel for the rocket's third stage. The stuff they're using is extremely toxic and they want to truck it in from Hilo or Kawaihae. The other thing is the Environmental Impact Study. The EIS says there'll only be minimal effect on the surrounding ecology, which of course is a crock. Violet's getting together data on what the adverse effects could be, especially on the bird life here, which is already on the way out. She also thinks the humpbacks used to come here to calve, like they do in Maalaea Bay on Maui. If the whale population increases then they may start coming here again and she thinks the southwest coast is a likely destination."

Bailey reactivated himself. "It'll be hard to make a case with that, though. How do you prove something is detrimental to something that might happen?" The lawyer took another hit of punch, and, lubricated, answered his own question. "Almost impossible, really, especially when the time spans are long. Anyway, if it ain't happening right this second people usually don't give a damn."

Bernice glumly agreed. "But we've still got other strategies, like showing the EIS was rammed through without enough study."

Neal was thoughtful. "What if it was proved that the rockets would disturb the whales or some other part of the ecology? Then what?"

"If we got to the right judge," Bailey said, "we could get a court injunction on launches or further construction. Anything that stalls their project hurts them financially."

Bernice put a hand on Neal's arm. "This reminds me. CSS announced their test launch schedule. The first one's supposed to be May first."

His face fell. "May first? That's—a month from now!"

"I know."

A moment later Bernice excused herself to go to the restroom. Bailey, holding up his empty glass, wandered off toward the kitchen.

Neal washed down Bernice's sour morsel of information with his last slug of punch and looked around the room. Big Jim was talking with a short woman in the opposite corner, looming over her like a shade tree. Susan had been cornered by Jason York, who was holding her hand and tracing a finger along a line in her palm.

He suddenly felt drained. The music was too loud, the room claustrophobic. He went outside and stood in the driveway a few minutes, cooling off, and then took a walk up the road.

The noise of the party faded behind him, becoming a mutter on the breeze. Below, through the trees, he could see the lights of Kailua-Kona. The town had grown like a weed in the last few years, Harry said. No doubt it would continue doing so. Things that made money grew like weeds, choking out things that didn't make money—forests, jungles. Empty valleys. That's how it worked, and people accepted it.

The problem was, he didn't accept it. He'd been beyond passively accepting things for a long time. It took a graveyard full of humans—including Dan, and almost himself—to bring him to that point, but when it happened the change was irreversible. The threat of a court-martial and prison had been meaningless. Thanks to a sympathetic officer, instead of spending time in the stockade his last weeks in Vietnam were spent in the rear doing essentially nothing.

Tilting his head back, Neal stared for a moment at the stars. He took in a few deep breaths, trying to clear his head. When he felt ready he walked back to Bernice's house.

It was after one o'clock when they finally left the party. Big Jim decided he needed air and rode in the back of the pickup. Neal rode inside, slumped against the passenger door with his eyes half closed. Susan, the most sober, drove. As they wound down the hillside toward town she said, "Jason is really an interesting guy."

"He must have been," Neal said drowsily. "You spent the whole night talking to him."

"Oh, I did not." She rolled down her window, letting in cool night air and the scent of ginger

128

blossoms. "He's doing research here, to finish up a screenplay he's working on."

"That's nice."

"Writing for the movies," Susan sighed. "How do people get into that?"

Neal craned his neck to peer through the rear window of the cab. In the back-glow of the taillights he could make out a sagging dark shape. Good, Big Jim hadn't rolled out onto the highway yet. He slouched into his corner again and said, "I think it has something to do with your clothes."

Susan laughed. "Aside from his clothes I thought Jason was nice. He invited us to go to Napo'opo'o with him next week, to the place where Captain Cook was killed. It sounds morbid but it might be interesting."

*　　*　　*

At breakfast the next morning the subject of the new road came up. Big Jim eased up his attack on the huge, greasy pancakes Fong's Chinese Kitchen was infamous for long enough to volunteer a hand.

"Got nothin' scheduled," he said, pawing at the crumbs in his beard. "And I wouldn't mind...splittin' town a while."

"We couldn't pay you much," Neal warned.

Perkins looked indignant. "Did I mention pay? Of course you could give me a...buddy price on a painting."

"Are you kidding?" Neal said, genuinely shocked. "You always make fun of my painting."

"Now, Neal," Big Jim said soothingly, "I just do that to...hurt your feelings."

"Hey," Susan broke in, tapping the Honolulu Advertiser lying in front of her, "speaking of hurt feelings, I can't believe we weren't invited to this yesterday." She read aloud from the newspaper. "'Completion of Launch Pad Pouring Toasted. Final concrete forms were removed from the Concord Space Services Kona Launch Facility launch pad Saturday. Company officials, including directors Hideo Kamada and former astronaut Laurance A. "Skip" Schaefer, marked the event with glasses of champagne and saki.'"

Neal pulled the paper across the table and looked over the article and accompanying photograph. He slid the paper back to Susan with no comment. Skip Schaefer's smiling features were familiar from the Apollo missions but this was his first look at Hideo Kamada: a humorless slab of a face mounted solidly atop a dark suit. The photo was a grainy mid-distance shot that reduced Kamada's features to almost a caricature, but not the kind apt to provoke a smile. It showed a hard man who would get what he wanted, whatever it took.

Chapter Sixteen

In the war-fevered early summer of 1945, air force inductee Hideo Kamada found himself involuntarily volunteered for patriotic duty in Admiral Onishi's Special Attack Corps. At first he was surprised at being selected, considering his lack of training, but after thinking about it he recognized the symmetry guiding his fate: his home and parents had burned to ashes during a night-time raid on Tokyo a few weeks before. This would complete the fiery annihilation of his family.

Although not eager to see his life end, he also recognized that the pilots in the Special Attack Corps were performing a holy mission. Like the great storm that had destroyed Kublai Khan's invading armada in 1281—the "Divine Wind" or Kamikaze after which they were named—the Corps would sweep the enemy's warships from the sea, this time with human-guided airplanes packed with high explosives.

At Gannosu Air Base in Fukuoka, Hideo was taught the fundamentals of flying, and not much more. There was no sense in wasting time and money on a pilot who would blow himself to pieces at the first opportunity. Much time was spent learning to identify various enemy ships from above and where their most vulnerable spots were. For example with an aircraft carrier—the most prized trophy—one dove one's plane into the central elevator near the base of the bridge.

As it so happened Hideo never utilized his skills. The final great assault on Japan did not come. Only the atomic bombs came, and their arrival saved his life and altered his philosophy.

When the bombs were dropped on Hiroshima and then Nagasaki, Hideo was horrified, amazed, and ultimately relieved. He was horrified by the death and destruction; he was amazed that the barbaric and uncultured Americans could develop such an awesome, almost mystical weapon; and once the initial shock had worn off Hideo was relieved because his initial resolve to become a part of the Divine Wind had been eroding for some time. Alone in his barracks bed at night he had tried to envision himself actually flying through a hail of anti-aircraft fire to dive at six hundred and fifty kilometers an hour into a giant gray ship. His imagination was good, and whenever it summoned up a realistic image of this hypothetical event something would come loose in his guts, as though his organs had all been untethered and were floating about freely.

What if he were shot from the air before ever reaching the ship? It would take a long time to reach an enemy vessel even in a near-vertical dive. What if, he thought, he made it through the flak and bullets but miscalculated the trajectory and missed the target? From high up a huge carrier was no bigger than a toy and he knew he wasn't an expert pilot to begin with.

The closer the time came for him to be sent off to do his duty for Emperor and country, the more Hideo wondered if there might not be some better way to serve. The simple truth was that, honor or not, he had been alive barely eighteen years and he wasn't ready to die. There were many things he wanted to see and do. He had never even slept with a girl.

Japan's surrender shortly after the atomic incineration of Nagasaki caused Hideo Kamada to view the world in a new way. He saw that, in spite of the barbarism, lack of culture, and the degraded form of life the Western world represented, and in spite of the cultural refinement and high form of life Japan represented—in spite of all this, the Americans had beaten the dung out of his country. They hadn't done it by coming ashore in wave after wave of hairy, snarling madmen bent on slaughter and pillage, either. They had done it through scientific finesse, if that word could be applied to something like an atomic bomb. And when the Americans didn't ravage his country after their victory but instead got busy repairing the social, economic, and physical damage of the war, he came to actually admire them. Not to like them, but to admire them. Obviously they were not the subhuman creatures he had been taught to believe they were.

In fact a lot of things were not the way he had been taught to believe they were. He saw now that the Emperor, whom his dead Shinto parents had so revered, was just a man, and not a very admirable one at that. He himself had been slated to die for the Emperor and the generals, but his death would have changed nothing. The thousands upon thousands of Japanese who had died in the war had done so for absolutely nothing. He himself had worked, prayed, and was ready to sacrifice his own life for Japan, and Japan had betrayed him.

All of this reduced his belief system to rubble. Other than that he was in good shape mentally. There was some sorrow that his parents were gone but he had never been very close to them. They had always favored his older brother and sister. Anyway, they were probably happier where they were now rather than living in a defeated Japan. As for himself, he was secretly glad. Glad to be alive when so many had died. Glad he hadn't committed suicide trying to sink a ship. Glad that he had been allowed to see things the way they really were. Glad to find a fellow soldier with a beginner's book on English, and glad it was no problem to steal this book just before his discharge from the military. When he discovered that he had a knack for English, he was glad about that, too.

And he was glad to have found a goal in life at a time when his friends were either dead, wounded, in mourning, or hopelessly confused. He reasoned that if the Emperor, a lucky but clearly ordinary man, could have all that power, why shouldn't he?

The easiest way to achieve power, he knew, was through money, and it was said that if Americans knew anything it was how to make money. It was said that in America any man with enough cunning and business sense could climb to the top, become a millionaire. Americans had no sense of hombun, one's proper station in life, but that was fine. He no longer did either. These gaijin, their country and their ways, represented the wave of the future.

It was through an American that Hideo got started in business. Always eager to practice his English, he had taken to offering his services as a guide to off-duty Occupation soldiers, and fate brought him into contact with Corporal Hank Tebbit of the Army Quartermaster Corps.

He had approached Tebbit in the streets of west Tokyo, as was his custom, and offered his usual opening line of "I be your guide show you city", but from that point on things became non-standard.

Corporal Tebbit was friendly but odd. He was more interested in the city's stores and shops—those that remained after the ravages of bombs and fire—than in the places foreigners usually wanted to see. Tebbit would pick out a shop, watch it from the outside for a time, and if pleased by some unknown qualities, he would enter and browse. Through Hideo he would speak with the store's proprietor, though he usually asked foolish questions about finding an item that was clearly unavailable in the store, sometimes unavailable anywhere in the city. Do you have this for sale? No? Where can I get it? How much of it could you sell if you had it? At what price?

It was clear that Corporal Tebbit was up to something but Hideo wasn't sure what. Sometimes the American played dumb with people they met and sometimes he took care not to appear dumb. When they left the store Tebbit would take a little brown notebook from his pocket and jot down something. Once, Hideo got a look at what he was writing. It was nothing but the name of the store and its address. In the margin next to the entries Tebbit would draw an X, a question mark, or a little five-pointed star.

Hideo never asked what Tebbit hoped to accomplish with his wandering and his questions. Americans, he was sure, were no different than Japanese when it came to nosy people, so he just translated and worked on improving his English, trying out different phrases, idioms, and the slang he picked up.

He also worked on assimilating an American demeanor. Americans didn't go for all the smiling and bowing customary to Japanese business dealings. When they talked business they were expressionless or serious or even morose. Being Japanese Hideo was already good at remaining expressionless so he practiced his serious and morose looks. He also learned to shake hands correctly, as Americans seemed to put a lot of stock in this unsanitary custom.

One day, after three weeks of cabs and walking, Corporal Tebbit showed up at the usual meeting place driving an Army jeep. Hideo accepted this unexpected improvement in transportation with a bland face and no questions and Tebbit was pleased with this apparent lack of interest. He saw it as further proof of Hideo's good sense. The kid was a sharp cookie all right—not goofy like other Japs, always smiling and nodding their heads like crazy, anxious to please the Americans—but that still wasn't the same as knowing when to keep your trap shut.

A little at a time over the next week—a word here, a look there—Tebbit sounded the kid out, and finally told him what the deal was.

It was basically simple. By doctoring receipts and manifests Tebbit and two other men working in an Army depot would become instant wholesalers. Working through six Japanese merchants Tebbit had carefully selected, they could supply anything from pens to penicillin, cheese to chocolate, scotch to cigarettes.

The operation went smoothly from the beginning. Once it started, Tebbit never let himself be seen by any Japanese except Hideo Kamada. He didn't trust them to have his best interest at heart. It was the Americans, after all, who had bombed the shit out of Tokyo. He made Hideo the sole link between the wholesale and retail ends of the scam, entrusting him with setting up the deals, handling the money, and delivering the goods picked up in secret rendezvous with Army trucks. When Hideo suggested that the Americans raise his expense account enough to cover the cost of hiring two Japanese friends for protection and speeding the unloading of trucks, Tebbit concurred.

As it turned out Hideo occasionally found it necessary to put his new underlings to other uses. The first time their job description expanded was when a merchant client, unhappy with the "delivery fee" Hideo had begun extorting from him, threatened to spill his guts to the nearest MP. Hideo had his hirelings break the man's leg, which ended the difficulty.

This mutually beneficial arrangement between Hideo and the Americans lasted nearly a year and a half, and then Corporal Tebbit was caught. The first Hideo knew of this unfortunate development was when his protection/delivery men, set up by a Japanese merchant threatened with prison, were picked up while walking through the back door of his store with a load of canned pears and beans.

At a secret meeting with the sergeant in the motor pool, who was in the clear, Hideo learned that Tebbit was keeping his mouth shut, refusing to implicate an officer suspected at the harbor end of the ring where the goods were initially diverted after offloading. The day after talking to the motor pool sergeant Hideo was picked up by the police and the tiny hut he rented from an old woman was searched. He had been fingered as the Japanese boss by his hired friends, who had crumbled at the threat of prison.

Hideo was detained for four days, during which he was questioned several times by Army Criminal Investigation Division personnel. He played dumb with them, acting embarrassed when the CID men told him their "sources" had named him as the Japanese boss of the ring. He had only said he was boss, he told the investigators, in order to impress people and give himself greater face. The truth was he was just a delivery boy, too.

The CID men were inclined to believe his story. Hideo seemed young and dull-witted and the clothes found in his hut, which was hardly the home of a crime boss, were nothing fancy. They didn't really care about nailing him anyway—it was the military people they were after. Still, dumb or not, an example had to be made, and in the end Hideo was sentenced to a year in prison.

The confinement of prison was intensely stifling to a young man of his drive and ambition but he endured it stoically. His constant battle against boredom took a turn for the better when he learned that the man in the next cell was proficient in the ancient art of origami, or paper-folding. To while away the long hours Hideo took up the art himself, practicing endlessly on pieces of newspaper obtained from a friendly guard. Origami turned out to be more than just a prison hobby. In origami he found a dual mental aid. With the paper under his fingertips he could either set his mind adrift, letting his fingers create on their own, or he could focus his thoughts on a subject with extreme precision. Many hours were spent plotting his future as carefully as he folded and creased the flimsy sheets of newsprint.

After serving six months Hideo was released early. He promptly set his plan in motion, getting a clerking job with one of the merchants he formerly supplied, who was properly grateful when Hideo recounted his unyielding refusal to inform on him even though the Army knew he dealt in pilfered goods.

He did not forget his ex-friends who had ratted on him. These loathsome dogs, whom he had taken off the streets and given high-paying jobs, had repaid him with betrayal. What really stuck in his craw was that Tebbit, a foreigner—and a crooked one at that—had kept his silence, refusing to implicate anyone else, and was now serving time back in the United States. Even in crime the Japanese had once again proved themselves inferior.

To maintain his honor and avenge himself for the months spent caged up like an animal, Hideo located the stool pigeons and laid in wait for them one at a time. He clubbed them senseless with a heavy stick, then propped up a leg and cracked the shin bone, just as they had done with the recalcitrant store owner.

At the end of ten months as a clerk, when he was certain the police and the Army were through with him, Hideo returned one night to the hut he rented before going to jail. He dug at a certain spot in the old woman's tiny rock garden and retrieved a wax-sealed jar. It contained all the money he had saved, buried the night before his arrest.

With this money he got back into business, this time dealing in bootleg liquor and drugs. Huge stores of war surplus amphetamines, manufactured by the Japanese government, were pouring onto the black market, and the demand for them was rising month after month.

He kept at this new enterprise for over two years. Having learned important lessons from Tebbit's operation, he ran the show from behind the scenes, using a trusted cousin as his front man. Hideo was always referred to by the name he gave himself, Ichisan, which was his own private joke. It meant Mr. One, but it also meant one-three, or thirteen, the number of the prison cell he had occupied for half a year.

As Ichi-san, Hideo Kamada paid his people well, whether they were policemen or city officials or deliverymen. He was completely honest in all his illegal transactions. He could not abide a thief or a liar and let it be known that anyone who cheated or stole from him would pay a terrible price. That was just good business.

At first, despite the warning, people frequently had to be cautioned or reprimanded in a physical way. Hideo was ruthless in seeing that the beatings and bone-breakings were well publicized within his "company". After a particularly heavy loss incurred by a driver making off with a shipment of opium, he decided the time had come for a more meaningful example. He had the thieving driver tracked down, and two days later did the rubout himself. There was no other choice, really. He trusted no one and didn't want to leave any loose ends. He constructed a crude silencer from a section of bamboo filled with heavy steel wool and taped it to the end of a Nambu 94 bought on the black market a few months before. After shooting the thieving driver in the head he took the gun apart, flattened the pieces with a sledgehammer, and threw them into the polluted waters of Tokyo Bay.

At the same time Hideo was running this business he began laying the foundation of the next step in his plans, pioneering a technique the Cosa Nostra would use heavily in the sixties and seventies. He went legitimate with his dirty money, investing it a little at a time in big corporations that were making a comeback and in smaller corporations just starting out. He invested safely and wisely, screening the possibilities with care before going ahead.

By 1951 he was completely out of all illegal activities. He was well off, but this was not obvious because he lived modestly. He still invested every cent he could spare in securities, and the cash he kept for possible emergencies was spread among several banks in Tokyo and the nearby cities of Yokohama and Yokosuka.

His next step, prompted by a desire to remove himself from the scene of his drug-dealing days, was to leave Tokyo and move to Kyoto. Though their names meant the same thing, the cities were unlike in appearance; Kyoto was visually more pleasant and had been left almost untouched by the war. Hideo devoted the next few months here to preparing for Kyoto University's notoriously difficult entrance examinations. Pragmatic as always, he accomplished this by hiring a teacher who was familiar with the tests to tutor him and easily passed the examinations. He stayed at the University for the next five years, taking degrees in business and civil engineering.

During this time he continued to invest his money in stocks, putting together an extensive portfolio of securities in various industries, including those that manufactured cameras, pharmaceuticals, heavy machinery, motorcycles, and automobiles. It gave him ironic pleasure to own shares in Mitsubishi Jukogyu K.K., the same corporation that had manufactured the excellent Zerosen series of fighters during the war, in whose product he came close to meeting his death as a kamikaze pilot.

The last two years at the university were nothing but constant work. As well as attending classes and studying, Hideo also ran a small trucking company he had purchased. He did have two diversions he utilized

141

to relax his mind. One was origami, a holdover from the prison days, and the other was women, a holdover from the drug dealing days. In Tokyo he had often visited the Yoshiwara "gay quarters" to satisfy his natural urges, and now, having little free time or desire for a girlfriend, even less for a wife, he continued to make use of prostitutes on a regular basis, a habit that stayed with him throughout his life.

In the spring of 1956, at the age of 29, Hideo moved to Hiroshima and started a construction company. Still in the process of rising, phoenix-like, from its own radioactive ashes, Hiroshima would be an unending source of lucrative contracts.

In Japan it was considered bad form to name a company after oneself but it was not unusual to give the company a name that was very similar to one's own. Hideo had read somewhere about the "komodo dragon", a large lizard of the monitor family that lived on an island in Indonesia. "Komodo" was nearly the same as own last name and he liked the idea of naming his company after a real dragon. Under his eagle eye and iron fist, Komodo Construction flourished.

All through these years Hideo had continued Americanizing himself. He dressed like an American, shunning traditional Japanese garb even at home. At great expense he had a small Western-style home built, one with heavy walls, wooden doors, carpets, adequate central heating, and a room with a toilet. He read books about Carnegie, Morgan, Rockefeller and other people he wished to emulate. Rather than pursue the old wakon-yosai principle, the blending of Western knowledge with the Japanese spirit, he preferred to embrace wholly the means and methods of the former enemy, though he was careful not to make the mistake of coming right out and saying this.

His ability to read and speak English came in handy since Komodo, Inc. often bought equipment and supplies from American companies. Because of this he required Komodo's corporate officers to take courses in English. When it was possible he hired American consultants and American firms to work for him, watching them closely to see how they operated.

Hideo Kamada ran his corporation like an American, for maximum profit, ruling it like a warlord, allowing no excuses for errors, firing incompetents or those who deviated from his own strict goals. Over the years the company diversified and expanded by buying up other companies, eventually becoming Komodo K.K., the Tokyo-based parent corporation of half a dozen subsidiaries. As the corporation moved into other fields it sent men to the United States to study and to learn the latest techniques in each.

Strangely, in spite of his devotion to things American, Hideo himself did not set foot on American soil until he was forty-four years old. In 1971 he decided it was time for a decent vacation, and having heard so much about Hawaii, he chose that as his destination. He fell in love with it. This was for him, the warmth, the sea, the restful climate, and the fact that he would not be regarded as a curiosity for his Western ways.

Although he had come to feel increasingly isolated in the country of his birth, Hideo had also come to feel a grudging admiration for it; Japan had come a long way since the war and was now a world economic power. The result of these conflicting emotions was that he felt torn between the culture he had renounced and the one he had adopted to further his compulsive ambition. Leaving Japan altogether, he decided on his third trip to Hawaii, would greatly alleviate this problem. He therefore formed an American branch of his Japanese empire—Komodo, Inc.—and based it in Honolulu, where he spent most of his time over the next years engrossed in the challenge of building up the fledgling corporation. He flew back to Japan only when business demanded.

Komodo, Inc. blossomed like the cherry trees in spring. Hawaii was a tropical gold mine waiting to be tapped. The corporation bought real estate at Waikiki and built a high-rise hotel, the Hale-o-Lono. Kamada loved the ironies of life, and like his old secret name Ichi-san, the name he chose for his hotel had a special ironic meaning for him. Literally translated from Japanese, kamikaze meant "spirit wind". Hale-o-Lono meant "house of Lono", Lono being the ancient Hawaiian deity who, among other things, was the god or spirit of the winds. The connection was subtle, but subtlety was something Hideo Kamada was Japanese enough to relish.

Hideo's worries that his career as a criminal would catch up with him had gradually tapered off. He had been extremely careful, always, and even the dreaded Yakuza had never learned who the mastermind of his small but efficient organization was. The only person who knew his secret was Kozo Hirasawa, the cousin who was his front man in the drug and liquor days and whose fortunes had risen along with Hideo's. Starting out as manager of the trucking company, Kozo had eventually become president of Island Inns, Inc., Komodo K.K.'s hotel subsidiary. When Kozo died in a JAL airliner crash in 1976, the last scrap of worry Kamada lived with vanished.

Time passed and the corporation grew by buying up profitable businesses and expanding those it already owned. By 1980 two more hotels were built, one in Japan and another on the Hawaiian island of Maui.

Hideo Kamada had now achieved all the goals of his youth. But the enormous personal power he had acquired seemed to grow stale year by year. He became increasingly restless, feeling the need of something new, something powerful, something that would challenge his abilities and, at the same time, reflect his own imagination and thrusting ambition.

Outer space filled the bill. One year after the idea to enter the satellite launching business first entered his head, and six months after he read a short magazine article on Colonel Laurence A. "Skip" Schaefer, who had recently left the U.S. space program, Concord Space Systems was born.

Chapter Seventeen

Big Jim Perkins drove down from Kailua the next Sunday afternoon. Over a dinner of Susan's lasagna and Neal's Greek salad they decided to start work on the road at daybreak the next morning.

"Workin' itself is...wrongheaded," Perkins stated somberly, "But workin' in the heat is crazy."

They went to bed after nightcaps of schnapps from the bottle Big Jim brought along, and before sunrise Neal was back in the kitchen brewing coffee and rattling pans.

That day was spent trimming and moving aside the trees felled the week before, and the next two were spent leveling the worst stumps and filling in low spots with rock and earth.

Thursday seemed to drag. Neal chainsawed the road corridor another thirty feet toward the house and then started cutting up the larger felled trees while Susan and Big Jim hauled away smaller trees and branches. At some point in the early afternoon, when they had cleared most of the new swath, Susan looked down the road and saw two men approaching.

"Somebody coming," she said, dumping an armload of trimmed limbs onto a growing stack. She stepped into the shade of the ohia sapling where Big Jim was sprawled on the ground taking a break. Neal set down his pick and took off his gloves to wipe sweat from his face, watching the men pick their way through the stumps.

The man on the left carried himself squarely erect, giving him a military air reinforced by his sharply-creased linen slacks, dress shirt with tie clipped in place, and a haircut short enough to show scalp when he looked down. His features were partly disguised by a pair of dark aviator sunglasses but Neal easily recognized him: Colonel Laurance A. "Skip" Schaefer, former Apollo astronaut, currently co-director of Concord Space Systems.

The man walking beside the ex-astronaut was taller, younger—probably in his late twenties—and heavily built, with a wide upper body that made his legs seem disproportionately thin. He also held himself rigidly but it seemed the result of inner tension rather than a military past. He wore a gray suit, tie, and sunglasses with pale yellow lenses of the kind favored by trap shooters.

Schaefer nodded a greeting and came to a halt a few steps away. He said, "Good afternoon, I'm looking for Neal Tate."

The friendliness in Schaefer's easy baritone sounded forced. Neal looked past him and inspected the larger man. He saw now that what he had mistaken for fat was actually muscle. The man's neck was about the same diameter as his head and a set of beefy biceps swelled his sleeves. He had a bland, puffy-looking face, dull pink in color. His reddish-blond hair, fine and tightly curled, had been trimmed with topiary precision until it resembled a fuzzy helmet. Stiffening under the scrutiny, the big man thrust out his massive chin and gave his close-cropped moustache a couple of pointless strokes with the joint of his index finger.

Neal turned back to Schaefer. "I'm Neal Tate."

The astronaut pried off his sunglasses, revealing a weathered face that turned boyish when he smiled. "Let me introduce myself. My name is—"

"I know who you are. What do you want?"

Schaefer's smile froze. Beside him, the bigger man shifted his weight and scowled.

Susan stepped from the shade and put a hand on Neal's arm. "Do you know these men?"

Schaefer broke eye contact first. He said, "Pardon me," and turned toward her, his smile loosening up. "My name is Laurance Schaefer. Most people call me Skip."

"Oh, of course! I thought I recognized you."

"Well, I'm flattered by that, Ms..."

"Susan McGregor." She shook his outstretched hand and then gestured toward Big Jim, who had gotten to his feet. "This is Jim Perkins."

They shook hands. Schaefer nodded toward his hulking companion. "This is Howard Tubbs, an, uh, associate."

Tubbs flashed a tight-lipped smile on and off like a nervous twitch but made no move to shake hands.

"Well," Schaefer said briskly, "I don't want to hold up your work here, so to get down to it Mr. Tate, the purpose of my visit is to ascertain exactly why it is that you're so..." He groped for the right word with a look of amused puzzlement. "—bound to this piece of property."

Neal looked at him. "Do I need a reason?"

The amused look became a neutral one. "No. You don't. And don't misunderstand me," Schaefer said, holding up a hand. "I'm not condemning you at all. But I understand you've only lived here a few months. It seems you've developed a strong attachment in very short order."

"That's right, I have."

"Well, that's understandable. It's a nice place."

"It'd be a hell of a lot nicer if your company wasn't tearing things up around here."

Schaefer managed to hold on to most of his smile. "I'm not sure I'd agree with your analysis of what's taking place here. To me it's something quite a bit different." He gestured downward to indicate the new road. "But speaking of tearing things up, what do you call this? Not beautification I imagine."

"I call it trying to get to my house," Neal said. "If you'd shifted a short section of your fence over about three yards I wouldn't be doing this."

Schaefer's mouth held firm but his eyebrows rose in little jerks. "I don't know anything about that."

"I'll bet."

"I don't know anything about it," Schaefer repeated, a trace of anger showing. "But I'll check into it. Look, I came here to make sure you understand what we're doing. If you decide to live here surrounded by our facilities then at least you'll be basing your decision on facts rather than emotions." Schaefer pointed toward the north. "That launch site is going to help people around here. The taxes we pay will benefit everyone, including yourself. Business is going to pick up on the island. People will be better off than before, have a stake in the future. They'll have jobs. In a few—"

"What jobs?" Neal interrupted. "A couple of locals in uniforms waving people through the gate? A couple more answering phones and waxing the floors at night? Is that how you'll help 'em out? What about the family you ran off that land right there, whose house you bulldozed. Maybe they wanted some say in their future.

149

Or do you decide what's best?"

"I don't know anything about that either."

"You don't know about that or about blocking my entrance road or breaking my water pipes. That's pretty convenient. You don't have to bother your conscience with facts. But here's a fact I can fill you in on right now. People around here don't want your rockets. That's what all those demonstrations and letters to politicians were about, remember? And if you think things've changed, go and ask around."

Schaefer's lips were a thin line. "I don't want to argue opinions with you, Mr. Tate. We're proceeding on the basis of our own findings in this matter. In any case my company is constructing a base to launch rockets here and it's going to function with or without your approval. And with or without your land as a part of the complex. You're only making things hard for yourself, though you apparently can't see it. You may laugh about it but I believe in the future. Having a clear concept of the future is good for this state. Good for the whole country, for that matter."

Neal nodded in the direction of the launch site. "So that's for America? Hell, I thought you were just trying to make a bunch of money."

Schaefer's upper lip had gradually sprouted droplets of sweat, and now a vein in temple seemed to wake up and stir. With his jaw clenched he said, "Listen son, I don't need some punk telling me how I think about my country. While you were crapping in your diapers I was shooting down MiGs over Korea."

"That's beside the point," Neal said. "We were talking about you ruining the island to make some dough." He motioned toward the hovering figure of Howard Tubbs. "Why don't you take your boy there and get the hell off my land."

Tubbs unfolded his arms and moved forward but a glance from Schaefer stopped him. The astronaut stood for a moment, working his jaw muscles. "Well," he said finally, "I did my best." He gave Susan and Big Jim a strained smile and then turned and started down the road, walking as briskly as the uneven ground allowed.

Howard Tubbs stood his ground until Schaefer was out of earshot and then he stepped up close to Neal. He pulled off his shooter's sunglasses and his eyes glittered from the pink expanse of his face, as hard and shallow as those of a stuffed animal. "If I catch you alone, my man," he said in a smooth, unaccented voice, "I might just kick your ass."

Neal returned Tubbs' stare for a moment, then jerked his head. "Beat it."

Tubbs' nostrils flared, developing small white creases in the corners, and he worked his fingers at his sides like a gunslinger. "I'll remember you." He jammed his sunglasses on and stomped away to catch up with Schaefer.

Big Jim was the first to speak. "For a second I thought he was gonna tell you to...get out of Hawaii by sundown."

Susan let out her breath. "Maybe it's a good time to take a lunch break." She started toward the spreading kiawe tree where she had left the food sack.

Big Jim looked at Neal and shrugged his hairy shoulders.

They joined Susan under the tree. She passed around pieces of chicken on paper towels and filled plastic cups with iced tea from a jug. They ate in silence, listening to the twitter of birds.

"Boy, that burned me up," Susan said.

"What?"

"When Schaefer gave you that business about Korea. I wanted to tell him you got a Silver Star."

"I'm glad you didn't." Neal picked at his chicken. "It's good that he came by. What Schaefer said was right."

"About what?"

"About the road. I think I want to stop right where we are." Susan's face fell. "Stop it? You're kidding."

"No. I mean—what is the difference between this and building a launch site? One's bigger, that's all. Maybe it sounds crazy but I'd like to just stop the road where we are. For now anyway."

Susan gave him a long, searching look. Saying nothing, she got up and wandered down the unfinished road, her arms crossed.

Big Jim slumped back against the tree trunk and wiped his fingers contemplatively on his pants. "A Silver Star, huh? That's somethin'."

"Maybe," Neal said. "I don't even know where it is."

"It's something, bro."

They sat quietly. Perkins licked his lips, smiling oddly. "It's funny," he said. "I almost forgot you were...in Nam. Susan mentioned it once. You never said anything yourself."

"It's not a favorite subject."

"I can relate. I don't like thinkin' about the...time I did on the Hancock." Perkins shook his head. "Those were the...bad old days."

Neal threw a chicken bone into the bushes. He said, "Yeah. They were."

Chapter Eighteen

Sometimes when he thinks back it seems like a movie.

A horror movie, with himself as one of the actors.

It happens in the jungle. It's hot, wet, the smells of both growth and decay heavy in the air. The morning light after a long, muddy night is a weak gray-green.

A North Vietnamese soldier appears from nowhere in the bad light and his involuntary cry of surprise breaks the humid silence. There is a sound like an enormous bumblebee and the NVA stumbles stiffly backwards, his tunic shredded by a burst from the silenced M-l0. As he drops out of sight in the foliage his finger triggers a single wild shot from his AK that hits Spaulding in the leg, shattering his fibula.

Captain Vollmer: "God dammit! Let's fuckin' didi mau!"

Neal Tate and Dan Akoki run toward Spaulding, who bites his lip in pain. "Go on! Leave me! Beat it!"

Captain Vollmer hesitates. "Leave him."

Sergeant Dan Akoki snarls. "Ey, fuck that!" Black-faced like the rest of the LRRPs on the team, his teeth show in a white grimace as he and Tate haul Spaulding to his feet. "Come on, man!"

DeLuca says in a low, fierce voice, "Shit, I can hear the fuckers coming!"

They can all hear it now, distant shouts from the jungle in quacking Vietnamese. Akoki and DeLuca take

153

up the rear, and with Tate's help Spaulding manages a limping run.

They blunder through the vines and bamboo, running toward the river, the smell of decomposing vegetation closing in like the walls of a huge, rotting coffin. From behind come the stuttering cracks of AK's. Bullets snap through the leaves, dropping debris from above, and the men twist around every few yards to loose short volleys toward the unseen enemy. Hindered by the wounded Spaulding, their progress is too slow.

A thumping explosion suddenly sounds from the upper end of the valley.

Tate, urgent but relieved: "That's our shit." Their satchel charges will pinpoint the underground arms cache for the air strike.

Vollmer jabs his chin at the sky. "We gotta get outta here before the flyboys blow our asses up." He looks around almost wildly and spies a break in the foliage. "There! Take the trail."

Tate and Akoki trade glances; they are in tune with one another. Taking the trail is stupid but Vollmer is a hardheaded asshole and there's no time to argue. DeLuca steadies the leg-shot Spaulding while Akoki trades places with Tate, who runs to the point. They need his eyes and sense of direction.

Fifty feet down the twisting path Tate leaps into the air, twists around and screams a warning but it is too late:

Captain Vollmer, following too close behind, snags the wire with his foot. Vollmer stops for and instant and then dives for the ground. Farther back on the path Dan Akoki shields Spaulding with his body and shoves him to the ground, and as he does so a hand grenade wired to a tree detonates and Akoki's camouflage fatigues are plucked by invisible fingers.

DeLuca gets up, untouched, and hurries forward. Tate is also unhurt and is already crouched over Vollmer. The Captain's head rocks one time, languidly, and becomes still, blood drooling from two black holes in his temple.

DeLuca stares at the shrapnel holes. "Oh, fuck," he snaps. He whips his head in one direction and then the other, looking angry. "Jesus H. Christ I'm turned around! How the fuck do we get out of this fuckhole?"

Tate drops beside Dan Akoki and feels the smooth brown skin of his neck. There is a pulse, a strong one. Glancing at Dan's wounds he makes a decision. He slings his weapon and Akoki's, then lifts his friend onto his shoulder. Dan is big but the adrenaline rush makes him seem light as a child. "Let's get off the fucking trail," he says to DeLuca. "Follow me."

Tate plunges into the bush. DeLuca hesitates only an instant before pulling Spaulding to his feet and following.

Tate heads for the river, less than a klick away. In his head he plays back their ingress route and moments later spots a familiar tree at the edge of a clearing. Smashing through the vines and leaves he thinks, Thank God it was Vollmer. He feels no shame for thinking this. He never liked Vollmer. Always mouthing off about recon. Starting to hate it, Vollmer says—it's so passive, no action.

Vollmer, drunk: "Gentlemen, a man needs to zap some fucking gooks now and then!"

What an asshole.

Halfway to the river they hear the scream of two F-4's overhead, seconds later the thunder of heavy bombs. Another flight of jets will follow this one to make sure the job is complete.

At the river Tate takes charge. He turns to DeLuca. "You take the radio across—and keep it dry!" To Spaulding: "Can you swim it yourself? With your gun?"

Spaulding nods, weak and queasy but game.

"Go across. Now."

As DeLuca strips the radio pack from Spaulding's back Tate examines Dan Akoki's head wound. It is ugly—a deep red furrow—but not fatal. The other four wounds are punctures into muscle tissue and their bleeding has already slowed to a clotted trickle.

The water splashes as DeLuca helps Spaulding into the water. Spaulding lets himself fall forward, his Ingram held above the surface, and then he begins side-stroking.

"When he's across, you go," Tate says to DeLuca. "We'll cover you."

"What about Akoki?" De Luca asks.

"I'll bring him over. You just keep the damn radio dry."

Moments later Spaulding drags himself like a crippled alligator across the mud and behind a log on the far side. DeLuca wades into the brown water, weapon and radio pack held to his chest. The stream has risen since yesterday and is now deep enough in the middle to require some swimming.

Crouching in the damp foliage on the bank, Tate regains his breath. A fuckup, getting boxed into the valley by patrols, but a worse fuckup to just sit there while the timer on the charges was ticking away. That was Vollmer's fuckup and it had cost him his life. Exactly the sort of fatal stupidity, Tate recalls, that he had hoped to escape when he volunteered for the Long

Range Reconnaissance and Patrol course. He had imagined lurps being more on their own, away from the everyday bullshit. He figured the intelligence they gathered would help keep the other poor bastards stuck in Nam from getting killed until they could all get out of this miserable fuckup of a war. The point of recon was supposed to be getting in and out without being spotted—no contact, no killing. And he had wanted desperately to escape the killing; he'd seen and done enough of it.

But here it was again, worse than ever. Last time out they had shredded five sleeping NVA regulars with silenced submachine guns after dispatching their sentry. Vollmer had loved it.

Tate presses his eyes to squeeze the sweat out. A phrase keeps coming back to him: Not my cup of tea. An inadequate, feeble expression, but he can't get it out of his head. Shooting? Garroting? Throat-cutting? Not my cup of tea.

DeLuca is two-thirds across now, side-stroking strongly, radio and Ingram up, when someone starts shooting at him from upriver. Tate lifts his M16 but decides not to return fire; the sniper's too well hidden to pinpoint and hosing down the general area will give away his own position.

As DeLuca approaches the far shore the sniper begins to get the range. His bullets slap the water closer and closer and the whine as they ricochet from the surface is unnerving.

Finally DeLuca wades onto the bank, radio against his belly, and scuttles into the brush near Spaulding. After an exchange of hand signals Tate slides into the slow-moving water, dragging Dan Akoki's slack body along. He gets an arm around his comrade—his friend—in a lifeguard's chest tow and strokes hard for the far shore. The sniper opens up again and Tate half expects a bullet to end it all.

Chapter Nineteen

Big Jim Perkins tossed his makeshift suitcase—a plastic garbage bag—into the cab of his pickup truck. "It's been arduous," he said, shaking Neal's hand. "Let me know if you...change your mind on the road."

"I will. Thanks again, Jim."

Susan raised herself on tiptoes to give Perkins a kiss. "See you soon," she said, patting his chest. "We'll do something fun instead of working."

"No more cards," he begged. "I can't afford playing with you."

She laughed and batted down the brim of his hat. "Practice up on your gin and you might win some back."

Perkins climbed into his truck and started it. "Adios, folks. And remember. The fishing offer's always open." He slammed the Ford in reverse and backed away, bouncing over stumps and rocks until he got to Mokolea Road.

Neal and Susan took the path back to the house. "What are you doing today?" he asked.

"Working on my story and finishing the book I'm reading. And I've got to make a phone call later. I told Jason York I'd let him know today about going to Napo'opo'o."

"Oh yeah. When is that?"

"He planned to go this weekend. Tomorrow."

"You going?"

"I think I'd like to. You're invited, remember."

Neal stopped to pick up a work glove someone had dropped. "I think I'll stay and do some painting," he said, slapping the glove against his palm. "I've been letting it slide lately."

They ate a leisurely breakfast of toast and eggs in the kitchen. After they cleaned up, Susan took her novel and manuscript onto the verandah and Neal retreated into the back room studio with a glass of iced tea.

He found the studio part of painting easy to put off since it meant staying inside. Once he got started, though, he seemed to fall into a trance. Hours evaporated. Today was no different; when he finally set aside the palette and capped the paint tubes it was already late afternoon. He swished the brushes in a can of paint thinner and took them into the kitchen for a final washing with dish detergent.

"Through, huh?" Susan said, coming inside.

"Yeah. I suddenly realized I was starving."

"Me too. I was thinking about going up to Yamata Store. You want anything?"

"Nah. You might check and see if we're out of milk, though."

Susan opened the refrigerator. "Hey. The light's burned out." She lifted the milk carton, then set it down and felt the metal rack. "Uh-oh."

"What?"

"The refrigerator's not working."

Neal rinsed his hands and came over. He checked the plug, then flipped the switch for the overhead light. It stayed off. "Might be a fuse. I'll check."

The screw-in fuses beneath the house were all intact. He walked to the side of the house and examined the wire leading from the roof's eave to a small transformer mounted on a pole.

Susan came to the window. "Everything's off inside. There's no electricity at all."

"Great," Neal said. "I can't find anything wrong here. I'm going to check the wire."

He walked uphill, following the single line that fed his house. At the boundary of his property the wire crossed over Concord Space Systems' chain link security fence. There was no top coil of barbed wire here; a few yards to his right was the section of fence he smashed through almost a month ago, which was still propped up with boards. Apparently they were waiting for repairs before installing the barbed wire. Neal climbed over the fence and continued his scrutiny, following the power line to the other side of the ranch road, now used by CSS as their main access to the launch site. Here, his power line connected with another power line that ran from Mokolea Road, on his right, across the mountainside to the old ranch house, on his left. Neal started toward Mokolea Road, where the CSS entry gate was.

The security guard at the gate was a baby-faced young man with short blond hair and a downy moustache. He was visibly flustered by the sight an unauthorized-looking person coming up the road on the wrong side. In a reedy voice he said, "Excuse me, are you with one of the construction crews?"

"No," Neal said. "I'm your neighbor."

The guard worked his lips and his hand dropped to the butt of his revolver. "Uh, you know that you're on—"

"Yeah, but don't shoot," Neal said, giving him a wink as he continued toward the open gate. "The power to my house went out and I'm following the lines to see if anything's wrong."

The guard trotted after him a few steps. "Excuse me. I think your problem might be up ahead, there. They had some kind of accident a little while ago."

Beyond the gate the old ranch road had been widened and leveled to form a broad, fenced-in corridor perhaps thirty yards long. Neal continued toward Mokolea Road. As he neared the intersection he saw a bulldozer parked in the trees to his left, on the other side of the fence. He walked past the hulking yellow machine onto the patchy, sun-baked asphalt of Mokolea Road.

From the road he could see the problem: a wooden power line pole had been knocked down. Two bulldozer tracks of plowed-up earth ran along either side of the felled pole, from the splintered stump at the bottom past the gray can transformer near the top. The transformer itself had been crushed beneath the machine's enormous lugs. The wire that supplied it, coming from a high-tension line that ran along Mokolea Road outside of the security fence, had been torn loose and now dangled a few feet above the ground giving off a fuzzy buzzing sound. The sharp smells of ozone and insulating oil wafted through the air.

Neal checked his watch. If he hurried he could get to Yamata Store and call the power company before they closed.

*   *   *

"What do you mean they don't know how long it'll be?"

Neal held up a hand. Susan was more than a little angry, which he understood perfectly since he felt the same way. He said, "All I can tell you is what the guy at the power company told me. The accident was reported by CSS right after it happened and Hapco is supposedly sending a truck to look at it."

"Well, that sucks!" Susan fumed. "I don't think this was an accident."

"Hell no it wasn't," Neal said. He gave an angry laugh. "The driver didn't even stop when he hit the pole. The bulldozer tracks went from the bottom of the pole to the top, right over the transformer."

"This is going too far, Neal. I can't believe CSS is doing this to us."

"Believe it," he said.

"But what about Skip Schaefer? I mean, he's a pompous ass but he seems so all-American. You think he'd go along with this stuff?"

Neal pulled out a chair from the kitchen table and sat. "I've been thinking about that," he said. "I don't think he was lying yesterday about not knowing what was going on."

"Then who does?" Susan demanded. "Somebody gave the order to rip up the water pipe. Somebody had them put the fence across our road without warning us. Somebody had the new water pipe broken and the pole knocked down." Susan exhaled sharply, trying not to scream. She walked to the kitchen window and looked out at the ocean. "It's going to get dark soon and we don't have any electricity. And—oh, dammit! I still haven't called Jason about tomorrow."

Neal got up. "Here're the keys if you want to drive to the store. I'm going to get the lantern from below and see if it works."

On the way down the verandah stairs the image of a face came unbidden to his mind. The man's features—

solid, closed—seemed foreboding even with a grudging smile. It came to him an instant later—it was the man with Skip Schaefer in the newspaper photo. Hideo Kamada.

Chapter Twenty

Neal lay on the futon listening to a gecko chirp into the sodden night air. He knew when he went to bed that he wouldn't get much sleep. The day had been lousy from the moment Susan left to meet Jason York and it hadn't gotten any better. None of the house repair projects he started had been completed, his fingernail throbbed where he had jammed a sliver of dried window putty under it, and his head throbbed from worrying about Susan.

He fumbled for his watch and pressed the illumination button. Almost two and she still wasn't back. Setting the watch down, he closed his eyes. The gecko resumed its trilling.

The lizard's calls were cut short by three rapid booms, like a backfiring truck. Neal raised his head from the pillow, instantly alert, and heard two more detonations coming from the direction of Mokolea Road. It wasn't a truck. He tossed off the sheet and hurried through the living room to the verandah.

Outside, a sluggish breeze ran over his naked body like a moist cloth. He listened, staring into the night. With no moon all he could see downhill was a formless black expanse sloping to a gray sea. To the right the blinking red beacon atop the rocket gantry, less than two miles away. The tower, completed almost a week ago, rose far enough above the intervening ridge to be an eyesore day and night.

A minute passed and then the sound of a car speeding away came from the direction of Mokolea Road.

He went back inside, his bare feet making delicate peeling noises on the painted wood floors, and felt his way through the darkness to the bedroom, where he switched on a flashlight and donned bluejeans and running shoes.

In the living room, just inside the walk-in closet, he pried away a loose section of wall paneling. The space between the wall studs held a long object wrapped in a plastic garbage bag. He took it to the sofa, switched on the battery-powered fluorescent camp light, and unwrapped the bag.

Inside was an M1 Garand rifle. The big wood-stocked U.S. military rifle had belonged to his father, a memento of time spent in France following D-Day. He ran his eye over both sides of the battered weapon, checking for fresh rust marks on the dark metal. The oil seemed to be doing its job. He pulled back the spring-loaded bolt halfway, looked at the top cartridges in the clip, and eased the bolt forward until it stopped. Then he pulled the bolt all the way back and let it fly forward, feeding a .30-06 cartridge into the rifle's chamber and locking into place. He turned off the light.

He used the flashlight to cross the yard to the footpath. The path took him through the trees to the aborted entrance road, where he stopped and sniffed the air. There was a burned smell. Stepping carefully around the stumps, he walked down the road to where his truck was parked.

From a distance the flashlight beam showed the pickup the same as always, a rusty, banged-up junker. As he got closer the burned smell grew strong and he could tell something was wrong. He walked around to the other side.

The truck's left rear tire was flat, its dust-grayed sidewalls mashed beneath the wheel rim like a fold of elephant skin. At the top of the tire was a ragged hole ringed with tufts of white nylon cord. Neal ran his flashlight over the side of the vehicle. The passenger door and the walls of the pickup bed were full of pea-sized holes and the entire outside rear of the cab, including the rack he used to transport paintings, was black and scorched, still smoking in places.

Most of the cab's rear window lay inside on the seat, broken into thousands of tiny diamond-like bits. The passenger window had also been hit but the glass was still in one piece, laced with a pattern of holes and shatter lines like the crystallized work of an insane spider. He tapped the window with the flashlight and half of it fell inward.

Moving to the front of the truck, he saw that the windshield was only slightly damaged. Three pellets had struck it from the inside, forming small shatter cones with radiating cracks.

Neal switched off his light and stood quietly in the dark. Having the truck shot and fire bombed wasn't particularly upsetting. A part of him was actually glad; the gut feeling that prompted him to bring the rifle wasn't paranoia after all. As for the truck, it would still run, and its ugliness factor had been increased only slightly. But if it hadn't rained earlier the painting rack and possibly the entire vehicle might have gone up in flames.

Neal turned on the flashlight and started back to the house, giving the pickup's hood a comforting pat on the way. There were definitely certain advantages to owning a junker.

*   *   *

Neal was slouched in a chair on the verandah with his second cup of coffee in hand when Susan returned home the next morning. She crossed the lawn with a firm stride, not seeing him behind the railing, and disappeared behind the plumeria tree. A moment later her running shoes made soft taps on the worn wood of the stairs. She was almost to the top when she suddenly stopped, looking at him with startled eyes. "Neal! You scared me!"

"Did I? Then we're even. I'm glad to see you're okay."

"Oh, I'm really sorry," she said, climbing the last steps. "I couldn't—wait a second, your truck! What happened to it?"

He blew on his coffee. "Someone shotgunned it and threw a Molotov cocktail at it. Not necessarily in that order."

"Shotgunned it? When?"

"About two in the morning."

"Who?"

"Beats the hell out of me. Who do you think?"

"How would I know? And why are you acting so snotty?"

He set his cup down. "I hope you don't mind if I ask where you were last night."

"I was in Kealakekua, at a friend of Jason's."

"Oh. I see."

Susan unslung her shoulder bag and stepped out of her shoes. "Neal, don't be angry. Look, we drove to this guy's house after we went to Napo'opo'o and had a few drinks. We ended up having dinner there and
168

staying late and I was just too tired to drive home. I slept on the couch and Jason slept on the floor." She closed her eyes and clasped her hands. "Air conditioning," she said blissfully. She looked at him. "I'm really sorry. I would have called you if we had a phone. Are you really mad?"

"I'll try not to be."

"I'd probably be at the bottom of a cliff if I'd tried to drive back."

"Then I'm glad you didn't drive."

Susan leaned against the railing. "You don't like Jason much, do you?"

He was about to answer when a wailing yelp came from the valley to the north. This sound was not something new; the warning siren at the Concord Space Systems launch site had been tested several times before. Neal glanced at the tower, a red steel box of girders and struts jutting over the trees on the ridge, and turned back to Susan. "I don't know Jason well enough to dislike him," he said, "but I admit I'm leery of guys who can't even button up their own shirts."

"You're in a bad mood."

"That's right. I got about thirty seconds of sleep last night worrying about you, I sweated off about five pounds because the fan doesn't work, somebody shotguns and torches my truck, and I spend all morning crawling around underneath the bastard getting the spare tire off and changing it." He jerked his head in the direction of launch site. "Now this." The siren blasts had been replaced by another unpleasantly familiar sound, a beeping horn, strident and nerve-grating even at this distance.

Susan picked up her shoulder bag and shoes. "Not very nice, is it? You know something, Neal? I wish you'd think about this. Things are going to be a lot worse when they start shooting off rockets." She stepped over to his chair and bent down to kiss the top of his head. "I'm sorry about your truck," she said. "Even though I've wanted to do the same thing to it."

"I hate to tell you this but it still runs fine."

"Who do you think did it?"

He stared ahead grimly. "I don't know."

"What about that guy that was with Skip Schaefer? Tubbs?"

"Maybe."

"Maybe it was just some testosterone-crazed teenagers."

He shook his head. "I don't think so."

Susan kissed him again. "I've got to go pee. Think about what I said, Neal. Things are just going to get worse here."

She went into the house, leaving him alone on the verandah.

Chapter Twenty-One

Susan was on her knees cleaning the inside of the now-empty refrigerator when Neal returned from Yamata Store Monday morning. "What's the scoop?" she asked him.

"Good question." He went to the sink and splashed water on his face.

"Oh, no. What did he say?" She dropped her sponge into the bucket of water and stood up, rubbing her knees. "How many more days will the electricity be off?"

Neal dried his face with a dishtowel and threw it back onto the counter. "Well, they aren't sure exactly when the electricity will be back on. But there is a bright spot-they're very sorry for the inconvenience."

"What's the problem? Why can't they fix it right away?"

"So many reasons. First they have to get a special crew to come and clean up the oil that spilled from the transformer. Apparently the oil's full of polychlorinated biphenyls, also known as PCB's, which are toxic or carcinogenic or both, I can't remember."

"Still," Susan said with a frown, "that couldn't take more than a couple of days."

"You'd think so. But that's just part of it. By an odd coincidence CSS just filed a request to have the power line to our house rerouted."

"What do you mean?"

171

Neal shoved his hands into his shorts pockets and leaned against the counter. "CSS wants all the poles and wires along the ranch road removed so they can widen and landscape it. They say they don't need them now anyway. They've got a new hook-up at the top of the valley. The problem is our line comes off the ranch road line.

"And?"

"The guy I talked to said Hapco's probably going to comply with CSS's request. I may be way off base but I bet this has something to do with the amount of electricity CSS uses compared to the amount we use."

Susan dropped into a chair. "What does this mean? What about our electricity?"

"It looks like it's going to be off for a while. The guy said Hapco's bogged down with a lot of other work."

"How long is a while," Susan asked in a low voice.

"Four to six weeks."

"What! A month and a half without electricity? Can't they just string a temporary line or something?"

"I asked," Neal told her. "They said that'd be as much work as doing it right. Some bullshit about satisfying their insurance company's safety requirements. He did say they'd reimburse us for renting a gasoline generator if we wanted to do that."

It rained that afternoon. Neal made an attempt to paint but found himself unable to concentrate. He gave up and opened one of the beers Kawika had left behind when the Kahookes moved to Honolulu. Agreeably mellowed after his second one, he made an enormous pot of spaghetti, baked a loaf of whole wheat bread, and set the table. Susan quit working when he called her. They ate in silence, listening to the rain drumming lightly on the roof.

When Susan was through eating she sat back with her glass of wine, curling her legs into her chair. "That was great," she said. "Thanks for fixing dinner, Neal."

His forehead wrinkled. "Was that dinner? I thought it was lunch. What time is it?"

"Probably about five. You're a little out of it, I think."

"I guess so." He nodded at the spaghetti pot on the table. "I fixed about ten times too much. If the..."

"What?"

"Nothing. I was going to say, if the Kahookes were still here we could've invited them over to eat."

Susan sipped her wine. "You really miss Kawika, don't you?"

"Yeah," he said quietly, staring at the table. "Kawika's a good guy. And Muriela. I liked 'em."

Susan gave him a crooked smile. "You know what? I really do love you."

He gazed into the orange-streaked wasteland of his plate. For some reason the way she said this made him sad.

For the next two days, while Susan edited and typed the final draft of her children's book—a process slowed by having to relearn the quirks of her manual machine—Neal submerged himself in painting. He stopped only to eat and sleep.

He was burned out by the end of the second day. The sun was settling into the ocean as he set the canvases against the wall and cleaned up, capping the paint tubes, pouring the turpentine into the settling can, washing the brushes. He found himself feeling almost good. Completing two canvases gave him a sense of satisfaction and left him feeling serene, or something like it. Susan also seemed to be in a better mood. She

173

had apparently adjusted to the idea of living without power for a while.

When she blew out the reading candles that night she rolled over in the bed and snuggled against him. "I really love you so much, Neal," she said quietly. She brushed her fingertips along his cheek, then kissed his eyes and nose. "Too much."

Neal turned toward her, but her face was a blur in the dark. He was about to ask what she meant when her leg slid over him and her lips found his. She kissed him softly on the mouth, then began a slow trail of kisses that started at neck and went down...down...down.

*   *   *

Footsteps sounded on the stairs outside. Neal put down the dish he was washing and rinsed his hands. Susan had driven to Captain Cook for groceries that morning while he stayed home to clean up, but it was too early for her to be back and they weren't her footsteps anyway. He dried his hands and was already headed for the front door when someone knocked on it.

The man standing outside wore a khaki uniform and a revolver He consulted the manila envelope in his hand and said, "I'm looking for, uh—Neal R. Tate."

"That's me."

"I'm with the constable's office, Mr. Tate." The man held out the envelope. "I'm here to deliver this."

"What is it?" Neal asked, taking it.

"I don't know. I'm just delivering it for the court."

The man left, his boots clumping on the stairs. Neal stepped onto the verandah and watched him march cross the yard toward the trees. When he was gone he

174

looked down at the envelope. Whatever was inside, it probably wasn't good tidings. He eased himself into the nearest chair, the rattan complaining in a dozen squeaky voices. When he felt relatively calm he tore the envelope open and read the documents inside.

Concord Space Systems was suing him.

*   *   *

Susan returned from shopping with sacks of canned goods and a huge red ice chest loaded with four blocks of ice. They wrestled the chest up the stairs and into a corner of the kitchen. Susan sat at the table with a soft drink while Neal began filling the chest with perishables.

He was squeezing a package of hot dogs next to the margarine when she said, "I talked to Jason while I was gone. He's going to Waipio valley Saturday and asked if we wanted go. I said I definitely did."

Neal looked up. "I thought *we* were going to go."

"We were, about five times. We still haven't in case you didn't notice."

"Yeah, well, in case you haven't noticed, we've had a few problems around here that seemed more important than driving to the other end of the island."

"Come on, Neal. I was trying to get you to go when we lived in Kailua."

"I've had a few other things to do. Like go to court and fix the house so we could live in it. I figured Waipio wouldn't disappear in the meantime." He started on the next sack of groceries.

"Do you want to go or not?" Susan asked.

"Not with York. You go ahead if you want."

"I really want to go. I've been wanting to see it for a long time."

175

"Great, fine, Susan. Have a good time."

"Thanks," She flexed the sides of her soft drink can, making it crackle. "I guess we'll be gone all day. We might camp out there if the weather's okay."

"Wonderful."

She got up and went to the bedroom, banging the door behind her.

Neal closed the ice chest and leaned on it. Being jealous over Jason York was not good. He made an effort to think positive.

A break from each other couldn't hurt. Susan would have a chance to get away from the house, have some fun.

In keeping with that last thought he decided to put off telling her about the lawsuit until after the weekend. She'd just worry about it the whole time she was gone.

That afternoon the water went out again. Neal gathered up the supplies purchased in anticipation of this event and set off through the woods.

He found the break on the far side of Mokolea Road, in the shallow ditch the water pipe crossed before entering the drainage culvert. Black marks from a set of truck tires ran off the road and over the rocks covering the pipe. It looked like some of the bigger rocks he'd laid over it the last time had been rolled off.

After a drenching struggle he repaired the break by splicing in a length of heavy rubber hose. Now 'accidentally' driving over the water line wouldn't break it. They would have to cut it deliberately. He covered the hose with rocks and walked back to the house.

Before going inside he tapped on the silver natural gas tank beside the house. From the sound it was at least half full. This was a small relief. With no road, the supply truck wouldn't be able to get in to refill the tank, but it was a problem he wouldn't have to deal with for a while.

He found Susan in the bedroom, sorting through her clothes.

"Just getting organized," she said in answer to his puzzled look.

"For what?"

"For nothing. Just organized. Getting rid of stuff I don't need." She added a few more items to the separate piles on the futon. "Neal. Have you given any more thought to selling the place?"

"Not a lot."

She looked at him. One corner of her mouth was pulled down with something that looked like worry. "You know, sometimes I think you're not dealing with reality."

"Oh?" He leaned against the doorframe. "What's reality? Selling the place? Letting someone shove you around whenever they feel like it?"

She looked away without answering.

Neal stood in the doorway. He wasn't in the mood for an argument, he decided. He turned and left, leaving her to her organizing.

Saturday, while Susan was off with Jason York, Neal took Big Jim up on his standing invitation to go along on a deep-sea fishing trip. His last sortie aboard the *Suzy Q* left him with mixed feelings. Landing a *mahimahi* and two large *ulua* had been fun, but getting sunburned and puking up his breakfast had not. To avoid a repeat performance he equipped himself with sunglasses, suntan lotion, aspirin, anti-nausea patches, and in an empty pill bottle the remainder of Kawika's joint. Aware of the *Suzy* Q's chronically empty larder, he also brought along a plastic bag of salted celery and carrot sticks, a Tupperware bowl crammed with tollhouse cookies, a small styrofoam ice chest packed with soft drinks, and a sack full of fried chicken, the latter being Big Jim's guaranteed seasickness remedy.

Once it was over and they had motored back to Kailua Harbor, Neal rated the expedition a success on two levels—good fishing and no puking. They pulled in a good-sized *mahimahi*, a six-foot thresher shark, and a two hundred-pound *ahi* tuna that nearly ripped the rod out of his hands and caused him to peel up the end of a fingernail when he grabbed for the reel crank. Balanced against a total absence of seasickness symptoms, the nail was nothing.

Big Jim took off to sell the fish, packed in ice in the back of his pickup, and Neal drove to a pay phone. He found Bernice's card in his wallet and dialed the number.

"Treasure Chest," she answered. "May I help you?"

"Probably so. This is Neal, Bernice."

"Well, I'll be damned. Tom and I were just talking about you. Were your ears burning?"

"A little, but I think it was the sun. I just got back from fishing with Big Jim, whom you may recall from your infamous party."

"Hey, I only look senile, Neal. Of course I remember Big Jim."

"He's pretty hard to miss. Listen, I know you're busy. I called for a couple of reasons. One, to say hello, and two, to see what the situation is with CSS."

"The situation is fine, for them. They just brought in their first set of rockets for testing. I guess you didn't see the trucks, huh?"

"No. I've been inside painting for a couple of days. When was this?"

"I think it was Wednesday. There was a thing in the paper. Hang on and I'll read it to you." She put down the phone and came back a moment later. "Okay," she said, clearing her throat, "it says here—this is a quote from Skip Schaefer—'*Everything's coming along perfectly on schedule, no real problems, I'm happy to say. My company is extremely glad to have found a home on the Big Island and we hope to be a real benefit to the community. We want to grow with Hawaii as it moves forward into the Space Age.*'" Bernice paused. "Gee. A Space Age Hawaii. Sort of grabs you, doesn't it?"

"Yeah. In the wrong place."

"Well, now that we're grabbed," she went on, "there's more." The newspaper rattled. "Let's see...blah, blah, blah. Ah—'*Launch readiness of the Keanapa Point complex, south of the village of Mokolea in the Big Island's Kona District, was confirmed after testing of the facility's electrical systems and its tracking and telemetry stations. Initial testing of the first "Independence" rocket, which will be the satellite launching service's workhorse payload carrier, is tentatively scheduled for May 1. Company spokesman Bernard Padgett said that there was "still a great deal of work to be done to assure that all of our testing objectives are met, but it looks good" (for the May 1 date).*'"

The paper rattled again. "May first," Bernice said. "That's just a couple of weeks away."

Chapter Twenty-Two

"Neal, I have to talk to you."

He looked up from his painting. Susan stood in the doorway of the studio with a strange expression on her face.

"Sure." He put down his brush.

She bit her lip. "First, I want to say this. I've thought about this for a long time and I'm not going to change my mind so please don't try to talk me out of it." She took a breath, and her voice turned husky as the words came out in a rush. "I'm going back to LA in three days. I'm going to stay there. For a while at least. I already made the ticket reservation."

Neal looked at her, stunned. "What? What do you mean? You're *leaving?*"

"Yes. For now, for a while."

"Just like that, without even talking about it?"

"I didn't want to talk about it. I didn't need to talk about it."

His mouth closed.

"I didn't want to talk about it because I knew we'd argue. I don't want to argue."

He nodded slowly, looking at her. "All right. Then—what, this is it? It's been nice knowing you, adios?"

Susan's eyes suddenly brimmed with tears. "It's not *like* that," she said angrily. "I knew you'd make this hard." Her eyes suddenly brimmed with tears. She spun around and walked away.

Neal followed her to the kitchen and stood, inert, while she washed her face at the sink. Through the window, where the Kahookes' house used to be, he could see the new CSS radar dome bulging over the treetops like a monstrous white mushroom.

"It's not what you think," Susan said, drying her face. "I don't want us to split up. It's just a—a vacation from each other, that's all."

"A vacation." Neal leaned against the refrigerator door. "I see. You just pick up and leave and it's a vacation."

"God dammit, Neal, I'm sick of everything here! All the problems! Can't you understand? We're living like cave people, no electricity, no lights, no refrigerator, no washing machine. Half the time no water, and we have to lug crap back and forth from here to the cars."

"That's temporary, and we do have electricity."

"The generator? Right, that thing's so loud we can't even turn on the fan at night. I'm sick of sweating in bed. And I *don't* want to finish the road, it's just a waste of time. *Think*, Neal," she said, imploring, "when the launch site's completed it'll be a mess here. There'll be more cars and trucks on Mokolea Road and the ranch road than there are now. You'll be right in the middle of this thing and you won't be happy with it. You're not happy with it *now* but you're just sitting here. Just face it, the peace and quiet's gone. I'm tired of waiting for you to get some damn sense into your head."

She wiped her cheek, wet with new tears. "It's not just that, though. It's me. You're painting, which is wonderful, and I know how much you've wanted this, but I'm not getting anywhere with *my* life. I feel like everything's been on hold since we moved here. It's been worse since this mess with CSS started, one problem after another. Now I have a chance to do something for myself and I'm going to do it."

"What are you talking about?"

Susan turned back to the window. "I got a job."

"What job? Where?"

"In LA. Doing research for the screenplay Jason's working on. When that's done he thinks he can help me get a job at one of the studios. He has friends at Universal and Lorimar. I might just be doing menial stuff but at least it's a start. Maybe I can finally do something with my English degree."

"York," Neal said. "What is it? Are you falling in love with this guy?"

"No. I *like* him, a lot. He's nice. And he's funny. You'd probably like him too if you gave him half a chance."

"I'm sure."

"Look," Susan said, turning around, "Jason's not the issue. I want to go for my own reasons. It doesn't have anything to do with him. Or you, really. It's what *I* need. Just try to understand that."

Neal looked at her. He started to say something but changed his mind and walked out of the kitchen.

His footsteps sounded on the verandah stairs, and Susan went to the window. Through a blur of tears she watched him stride across the yard and disappear into the trees.

Chapter Twenty-Three

"Okay." Susan blinked back her tears. "Call me soon."

Neal gave her a peck on the lips and stepped back. "Yeah, I will." He looked toward the gate separating the public area from the airport apron. "You better get going."

Susan shifted the shoulder strap of her carry-on bag, sniffing. "Don't forget to say goodbye to Big Jim and Harry. Tell them I'll write."

"I will."

"And thanks for taking care of my car. If you decide not to sell it that's fine."

"If I keep it I'll send you the money."

"It's not important." She gave him a hopeful look. "Can I have a smile? Just a small one?"

His smile was small. He gave her another peck on the cheek. "Bye, kid. Be careful."

"I will. You too. I love you. Bye."

She walked through the gate and disappeared from sight.

Numb, Neal walked back to the parking lot, unlocked the Datsun and got in. It was hot inside but he didn't touch the window crank. He sat still, the keys in his hand, thinking back over the last three days.

They'd been hellish. He had eaten little, slept badly. There were spells of clear thought in which he tried to sort things out in his head, to get an objective view of how things had happened and what had gone wrong.

His best analysis was that, basically, everything had turned to shit.

There were moments when he felt like a fool for not selling out to CSS, but when he went back and thought things over, when he looked at events singly and in the order they occurred, he always felt he'd done what he had to do. Not necessarily the absolute right thing but definitely nothing wrong.

What CSS was doing—what they had done to him, Kawika, the island—all that was definitely wrong.

But it all seemed superfluous when he thought about Susan. She'd said her feelings for him were the same but he wasn't so sure. Jason York was slinking around in there somewhere. York was picking her up at the airport in LA. That bothered the hell out of him, and the fact that it bothered the hell out of him bothered the hell out of him. More thought was required.

Nearly half an hour passed before he stirred. He was dripping sweat. He rolled down the windows, started the car and drove off. He wasn't sure where he was going at first, but as he neared town his hands steered the car into the industrial area.

Harry came from the back of the shop in response to the door buzzer. "Neal! How the heck are you?"

"I've been worse, I guess," Neal said, trying for an approximation of a smile. "How are things with you?"

"Well—good, really," Harry said, grinning. "Real good. How's Susan?"

"Oh, fine, fine. Actually, she just took off for California."

"Yeah?" Harry raised his eyebrows a bit. "She gonna stay there a while?"

"I don't know. She's got a job. Have to see if it works out, I guess."

Harry's forehead wrinkled. "Huh. Gee, I wish I'd seen her before she left."

"She didn't have time. She told me to say goodbye and that she'll write and that I'm in charge of her orchid."

Harry laughed. "Well, maybe I'll forgive her. So what brings you here?"

Neal pulled off his sunglasses and rubbed his eyes. "Nothing too important. Just thought I'd drop by and see what was new."

"Not much. Business is slow. Hey, I guess you know they're shooting off a rocket in a few days, huh?"

"Yeah."

"Yeah, well, I'm starting to feel like you do."

"What do you mean?"

Harry set his elbows on the counter, sniffing the Miltonia roezli under his nose before answering. "Well, I was pretty neutral about the rockets before," he said, staring at the orchid. "I guess I'm one of those people who sticks his head in the sand and lets the world run itself. But that's stupid. Like my wife used to say, everyone's part of the world so everyone has to take part in running it. Louise was right. I've been learning more about this rocket thing over the last few weeks. The more I know the less I like it." Harry turned his eyes toward Neal. "Did you know this? They're trying to ban boats from near the launch site when they shoot off the rockets."

"No, I hadn't heard," Neal said. "Where'd you hear this?"

"From Vi, the lady I've been seeing. But there was a thing in the paper this morning about it. Hang on a

185

sec." Harry went back to his writing room and returned with a newspaper clipping. "Here you go."

It was a short article from the Honolulu Advertiser. Concord Space Systems had requested a ban on vessels within a designated flight corridor extending from the launch facility out into the ocean. Neal handed the clipping back without comment.

"Can you believe that crap?" Harry asked gruffly. "I mean, if NASA does this at Cape Canaveral that's one thing, but that's the government. These people here, they're just some damn corporation. Why the hell should people stop sailing or fishing down there just because they're gonna blast off one of their rockets?"

Neal shrugged.

Harry flapped the paper. "It sort of chaps my ass. First the people come here and tear up the place, then they want to tell us when we can use the goddam ocean, which they're making unsafe! Even if the ban only lasts an hour or so it's the principle of the thing. Corporate control of the seas. To hell with that."

Neal pulled his head back. "What's gotten into you, Harry? I don't think I've ever seen you so bent out of shape."

Harry's angry look dissolved. He pulled thoughtfully at his sizeable nose. "Well, you know, I've been...I don't know, not caring about things for the last few years. I guess since Louise died. When I first came here, to Honolulu, I just wanted to leave Denver. Get away from the snow and the rat race. Honolulu was okay then, but it finally got as bad as any other city. Crowded, crime, all that. So I moved here and it's starting all over again. I guess I've sort of woken up. I feel like I should do something."

"Looks like it's too late with this particular thing,"

Neal said.

"Not totally," Harry said. He smacked the newspaper clipping. "Probably won't do any good, but I'm going to write the state congressmen—soon as I find out who the hell they are—and give 'em a piece of my mind on this thing."

"Sounds like a good idea. Couldn't hurt, anyway."

"Couldn't hurt," Harry agreed. "Well, let's change the subject. I want to show you something. Come on back here for a minute."

In the workroom, Harry pulled a large handgun from a foam-lined box. "We've got a serious weapon here, Neal," he said, working the slide open and handing it over. "That's the gun I told you about before, the Omega 10 millimeter auto."

"Right, I remember you saying they were going to send one." He hefted the pistol a couple of times. "It's heavy."

"Sure it's heavy, and the bastard ain't even loaded yet. But you've got a lot of gun there, a lot more than any nine millimeter or .357. With the right bullet it'd stop a friggin' truck."

"I guess it would."

"Well, sir," Harry said, pulling his nose vigorously, "why the heck don't we stop jabbering and go shoot that thing?"

"Now?"

"Sure! Hang on, I'll go lock the front door."

Harry came back with a box of 10 millimeter cartridges. "Anybody comes, they can buzz us from outside. I switched it to the pistol range." He held the range door open and followed Neal inside. "Wait 'til you see what's coming over from Honolulu. I won't tell you what it is, but when it comes we'll have some fun."

*   *   *

Leaving Harry's shop later, Neal considered tracking down Big Jim. He got the car and drove to the highway, but when he got to it he turned south, toward home. He needed to be alone.

He parked at the end of the new road and sat in the silence for fully half an hour. At last, needing to move, to do something, he got out and walked home.

Looking up at it from the yard, the old house had never seemed so empty. He didn't feel like going inside. Instead he walked the perimeter of his property, following the CSS fence on the downhill and north sides. At one point he sat down on the ground, thinking he ought to cry since supposedly it would make him feel better, but no tears came. He got up and trudged back to the house.

He rummaged around in the kitchen cabinets and located partly-full bottles of gin and scotch, leftovers from Big Jim's stay during the roadwork. Four shrunken limes turned up in a bowl atop the dead refrigerator.

With the help of the limes, gin, and ice chipped from the blocks in the chest, he got drunk.

He was careful not to get slamming around, tripping-over-the-feet drunk, which would end the party prematurely, and instead got glaze-eyed, numb-brained drunk. Whenever he felt himself going too far he slacked off. After a while the gin started to taste bad and he switched to scotch.

In the late afternoon, while he was in the bathroom taking perhaps his sixth leak of the day, he found himself staring at a bottle of Dr. Bronner's Pure-Castile-Soap on the shelf in front of his face. A line on the label popped out at him: *Love is like a willful bird, do you want it? It flies away!*

He snatched the bottle from the shelf, took it out on the verandah and hurled it. It bounced once on the far side of the yard and slapped into the low stone wall, shattering the plastic cap in a spray of liquid soap and bubbles. Sparkling with the sky's reflected light, the bubbles drifted unhurriedly across the lawn and into the trees.

He kept drinking into the evening, but still trying not to overdo it. The only thing he ate was part of a coconut Susan picked up on her last trip with Jason York. He set it on the counter and gave it one fierce whack with a hammer that blew juice and shell bits all over the counter. As he pried off hunks of the white meat with a knife he decided he was already adjusting pretty well to his new mental state, severe depression. He felt himself sliding into sync with his fate, too, whatever that might be. He could handle it. In fact if he just stayed drunk like this he could handle anything.

He could even handle looking into the mirror again. Seeing his reflection earlier had not been pleasant. His face was covered with beard stubble, his eyes were bloodshot, and his hair, which Susan had been on him to trim for the last month, looked like greased yak fur. But she wasn't there to see it, so who gave a shit.

Everything came back to her. The idea of losing Susan was more than he could really think about. It would be like losing a part of his mind, a hunk of his life. They'd known each other for so long. She knew more about him than anyone, and he knew more about her. She knew all about his nightmare in Vietnam, or at least more than he'd ever shared with anyone, or probably ever would. Once you'd gone far enough down the road with someone, opened up your soul with them, shared years of pain and joy and even boredom with them, they *did* become part of you. In a way that you could never re-create with another human. The thought of going through a fraction of their experiences with someone new made him feel weak and empty.

He drank and brooded until the sun drifted down to meet the clouds on the horizon, setting them afire and bathing the verandah in an orange glow. Neal stood at the railing with an empty glass in his hand, watching the endless shimmering sea, and whispered into the breeze, "Dan."

His voice sounded peculiar, like a stranger speaking inside his head.

"If you can hear me," he said softly, "I'm right here, in the house you told me about. Where you were born. It's really beautiful here, like you said. I'm trying to watch over it, man. I really am."

Something gave way inside him then. He sat down where he was standing and cried.

Around one in the morning fatigue set in solidly, sucking at him like the undertow of a wave, and he used the last of his strength to drag the futon from the airless bedroom onto the verandah, where he collapsed on it. He quickly fell into a leaden sleep, the scotch and gin bottles, nearly empty, standing guard.

Chapter Twenty-Four

Bernice Hollings' disembodied voice came from nowhere when Neal walked into the Treasure Chest.

"Hey, stranger! Just a sec."

He looked around the shop, which was empty of customers, and spotted her kneeling behind a glass case containing pearl jewelry. "There you are. Hi, Bernice."

Bernice closed the case and stood up. "How is everything, hon?" she asked, leaning across the counter to squeeze his hand.

"Not bad." He tried to lay a convincing smile over his hangover headache and queasiness. "How are you?"

"Just dandy. Business is pretty dead right now, as you can see. How's Susan?"

"She's—fine. She's in California right now."

"Oh, she is? Well, at least you're here. What brings you to my humble place of commerce?"

"Nothing in particular," Neal said. "I didn't feel like hanging around the house so I drove up here."

"I imagine it's pretty lonely down there with your gal gone. I sure like her. We talked quite a bit at the party."

"She told me."

"She said CSS made another try at buying your place."

Neal nodded. "That was some time ago, though. Back in January or February. They sent a guy out and I told him no thanks."

"And that was it?"

191

"For a while. Actually, Skip Schaefer came by about ten days ago."

Bernice's eyebrows went up. "Did he now! Did you get his autograph?"

Neal feigned smacking his forehead, carefully. "Damn, I forgot."

"What did he say?"

"The same sort of stuff you read me from the paper the other day. Space age. Good for mom, Hawaii, and America. Didn't mention his bank account for some reason."

Bernice laughed. "What did you tell him?"

"I said no thanks. Emphatically. We weren't fast friends when he left."

"Ah, well. I'm sure that won't make any difference if you change your mind and decide to sell."

"I'm really not inclined to do that. I don't think I like those people, Bernice."

She made a growling sound. "You ain't the only one, hon. They've pissed off a lot of people, pardon my language. They asked the Coast Guard to warn boats away from the rockets' flight path when they do their test shots."

"So I heard. There was a thing about it in the paper."

"Yes, but what the paper didn't say was that CSS is trying to get legislation pushed through to make it official, so boats have to stay out of the flight path. I imagine their insurance company had something to do with it."

Neal grunted. "I guess it could get expensive if a rocket landed on a cruise ship or something."

"Well, there's not much danger of that," Bernice said. "They have to have a range safety officer and self-destruct mechanisms on the rockets. It's required."

"That's comforting. What about this legislation? Can they do it?"

Bernice shrugged. "It's possible. CSS won't make any friends with it, though. The commercial fishermen and barge companies have got their collective danders up, and with any luck the recreational boaters will put their two cents in."

"I know one that's pretty disgruntled about it," Neal said. "You don't know Harry Sturdivant by any chance, do you? He owns a gun shop in the industrial area."

"As a matter of fact," Bernice said, "I just met him the other day. He and Violet Gray and I had dinner together."

"Violet Gray?" Neal cocked his head. "I didn't know...oh, right! I'll be damned! He mentioned he was seeing someone named Vi, but I didn't make the connection. I guess it is a small world."

"Real small, hon. We're on an island."

Neal laughed. "Good point. Anyway, Harry's the one who showed me the newspaper article about keeping boats out of the flight path. He was pretty peeved about it."

"Good," Bernice said. She glanced toward the door, then leaned toward him, her charm bracelet tinkling on the glass counter top as she set her palms on it. "You know hon," she said quietly, "I found out something you might be interested to hear. Let me ask you something—the name of the people who left you their land was Akoki, right?"

"That's right."

Bernice nodded. "Okay now, this shouldn't go beyond you and Susan, because it might get someone in trouble. I have a friend who works in the probate court in Honolulu. I was talking to her a few days ago and our conversation got around to your situation, being surrounded by CSS and so forth. I mentioned the name Akoki, and to make a long story short she told me that about a year and a half ago she pulled some files for a fellow named Jack Milliken—whom I would imagine you remember."

Neal nodded. "Good old Jack Milliken."

"My friend told me about the hassle you had with the state over the land. Anyway, the files she pulled for Milliken were on George Akoki. Now here's the thing, and you can just take it for what it's worth. My friend was eating lunch with a friend of hers a few days ago and they ran into this Milliken. He didn't recognize her but she remembered him because your case was unusual. Anyway, they talk a while and it turns out Milliken doesn't work for the state anymore." Bernice straightened up and crossed her arms. "Okay, here's the question, Neal. Who does he work for now?"

He chewed his lip a moment. "Pacific Investment."

"You win the prize.

"You know," Neal said slowly, "I'm really naive. I should have known things were even more rotten than they were. He turned toward the shop windows, narrowing his eyes at the glare outside. "Now the whole trial makes sense. The way things went."

"What trial?"

He turned back to Bernice. "When the state contested the will in court," he said. "They called it a trial. And believe me it was. I thought it was just a routine thing, the state automatically trying to grab something for nothing."

"But maybe not."

"Probably not, if this thing about Milliken is true."

194

His brow furrowed. "But—now I'm wondering if Milliken went after me because of a job offer from Pacific Investment or...

"If the push came from the state itself?"

"Yeah. Or from some state official with something to gain from it."

"Hell, Neal, it could be all three," Bernice said. "If the state had screwed you out of the land and sold it to CSS for a nice hunk of cash, I'm sure a lot of people would've been happy."

"Yeah. This whole thing stinks."

"Tell me about it," Bernice said drily. "So, what happened in this trial thing, Neal? I just got a quick rundown from my friend."

He took a deep breath. His head was pounding worse than before. "What happened is, George Akoki wrote out his will a few months after his wife died from a stroke. He did it himself, by hand. The state—Milliken—claimed that George was mentally incompetent when he wrote it, which would make it invalid."

"Well," Bernice said, "was he?"

"I couldn't say since I never met him. Milliken pointed out his shaky handwriting and his grammar and spelling, which weren't great. But I don't think he was incompetent. He had enough sense to have two people witness his will."

"He did? Who?"

"One was an old friend of his, a man named Kamuela Napeahi, and the other was Frank Ninomiya, a policeman here on the island. Frank's older brother went to high school with Dan Akoki."

"Dan Akoki was George Akoki's son, right? The one who's life you saved."

"It...yeah."

"What happened at the trial?"

"Milliken brought up all this garbage about George. Like he was depressed from his wife's death, and he drank a lot, and he was trying to give his land away to a haole he never even met. That sort of crap. When Frank and Kamuela finally testified, Milliken started hammering away at them, trying to make them look bad, too. He twisted everything around. The judge finally chewed him out. Kamuela and Frank testified that George was fine when he wrote the will, and Frank said he told George to have it done right by a lawyer. George said he would, but he died before it happened."

"When did he die?" Bernice asked.

"A few days after Frank witnessed the will. Some kids found his body washed up on the shore. Apparently he slipped while he was fishing and hit his head on the rocks."

"Ohh. That's sad."

"Yeah. Anyway, his will named me the main beneficiary. Frank and Kamuela got some personal possessions and some money, which Milliken harped on. They would have gotten everything if I'd been dead."

"And what was the problem with finding you?"

"The main problem was that George didn't know where I lived. He only knew my name and a few other things from the letters Dan sent from Nam—from Vietnam. Like my rank and our division and company, that sort of thing. He wrote it down in the will. It took them four months to track me down."

"At least they did it," Bernice said. "Though I'm sure a lot of people wish you had been dead. Well, there's not much that can be done about this Milliken creep, but I thought you'd be interested."

"Yeah. Thanks. It just reminds me what I'm dealing with. Which reminds me of something else. Does Tom Bailey practice regular law here?"

"He's sure thinking about it. In fact he just passed the bar here about a month ago. Why?"

"Just a small legal problem. Do you think he'd mind if I gave him a call?"

"No, not at all," Bernice said. "Here." She turned to a flip-up directory on the counter. "Let me give you his number."

Neal left the Treasure chest a few minutes later and walked down to the pay phone, where he dialed Tom Bailey's number. The lawyer answered the telephone himself.

"There's something of a legal nature I'd like to ask you about," Neal said after they exchanged greetings.

"Sure. Shoot."

"Okay. Concord Space Systems is suing me. They want me to pay for some damage to a section of their fence."

"I see. Did you damage the fence?"

"I drove my truck through the bastard."

"I see. Well, as you can probably imagine, I'm wondering how this came about."

"It came about because they put the fence right across the road that leads to my house, which kept me from going anywhere. I decided to clear the path."

"I see. Hm. Was the fence put up legally?"

"I assume it was. But that road's been there for probably twenty years."

"I see. Did anyone witness the, ah, destruction?"

"Not to my knowledge."

"I see, I see. Now, did the court contact you?"

"Yeah, they sent me a notice that I was being sued and telling me how and when and where I should respond. Dates and times."

"Right," Bailey said. He cleared his throat. "Well, if you're asking me what to do I'd say if you don't feel you should pay for the damage then just deny the allegations on the form and send it in. That may end the matter if they don't have a witness."

Neal pondered. "I hate to lie about it. What happens if I don't respond?"

"Well, if you can't show a good reason for not responding then CSS will probably go through the motions to have the judgment made against you in default. And they'll probably get it. If you do respond, they can still go ahead with the suit and have the court require you to come and give a deposition on the matter."

"And if I don't do that?"

"Then you're in the same fix as before. They can file a request to have your previous response set aside and move to have the judge grant a default judgment."

"Good lord," Neal said. "What a hassle."

Bailey chuckled, somewhat mischievously. "That's what law is all about."

When he hung up after talking to Bailey he was still uncertain about what to do. That being the case, he decided, the best thing would be to postpone a response. He walked down to Billy Boy's and bought an iced tea, then walked back to the Datsun. He drove north out of town, heading for Honokohau harbor.

A gap in the line of masts where the Suzy Q's tuna tower should have been told him Big Jim was out. He continued to the mouth of the harbor and parked near the entrance light. Rummaging in the glove box, he found some aspirin. He swallowed two with the last of his tea, then changed into his swimsuit inside the car and walked down to the water.

Broken blocks of gray lava lined the shore in this protected corner of the bay. Neal found one that was flat on top and sat down. With the sun beating on his shoulders, he stared into the crystalline shallows at his feet. Black urchins, ignorant of his presence, waved needle-like spines. The thick orange spines of pencil urchins moved almost imperceptibly. From a few feet out, where the water turned blue, there were quick flashes of yellow from trumpet fish.

He kicked off his flip-flops, waded out to knee-depth, and dove in. The water was cold since the upper three-foot layer was fed by a freshwater spring. He swam in a large circle, his teeth together, head pounding, and then hauled himself onto the rocks again, covered with goosebumps.

When the sun dried and warmed him again he went back to the car and got a dive mask, a rolled-up reed mat, and a towel from behind the seat and set off for the nude beach.

He spent the next three hours lying on the sand. He went into the water twice, the first time to cool off and the second time, with the mask and snorkel, to explore the lava reef lying just offshore. Swimming slowly above the sunken, seaweed-covered ridge, he caught a glimpse of an octopus. A small puffer crossed his path and he nabbed it, holding the spiny fish in a gentle grip as it bloated itself with water, its eyes goggling seriously.

Back on shore he lay down and dozed off. A pack of naked, squealing children woke him up some time later. He watched them for a minute with one lidded eye and then dragged his mat into the shade and fell asleep again.

When he awoke late in the afternoon his headache had faded to a mild band of pain encircling his skull. He pulled on his shorts and headed north along the curved beach with his flip-flops in hand. The beach looked like the site of a failed amphibious invasion of nudists; bodies were everywhere, sprawled motionless in the sand, and more bobbed just offshore on floats, moving limply as the waves passed under them.

At the far end of the beach the sand turned into lava pebbles, which farther on became a stretch of solid rock. Neal kept walking, following half-remembered directions Big Jim had given him months ago. He finally spotted a path leading into the scrub brush. The path led through a stand of trees and ended at the edge of a wide, open plain covered with bare, crumbled a'a lava. Except for a few stunted trees and patches of yellowed grass there was nothing to see but the lava. He shaded his eyes, searching the heat-wriggling landscape. In the distance were two or three heaps of rock.

That had to be it.

He headed away from the sea, staying on a broken trail that skirted the edge of the ancient flow. The path took him abreast of the dark humps he had seen from the trees and then, cutting left, out to them.

They turned out to be pillars, just over head high, made from thousands of lava chunks stacked together without mortar. He walked past the primitive constructions until he came to the place Big Jim had described: a pit in the barren lava field about thirty feet across and forty long, at the bottom of which was a pool of clear, fresh water surrounded by green plants and brush. Neal climbed down into the depression and waded into the pool, cooling his feet. When he squatted down to wash his face he saw tiny shrimp swimming around his legs.

He watched them, mesmerized, until images from nearly a year ago suddenly flooded his thoughts.

He saw the creased clasp envelope with the remnants of a price sticker clinging to the back that George Akoki had bought to hold his last testament. On the front, printed carefully in pencil, Will of George N. Akoki. Inside, along with the will and the notes about himself, were two curled Polaroid photographs. The first was taken in front of the training office of the MACV Recondo School compound at Nha Trang. It showed himself and Dan in fatigues squinting into the sun with their arms hung across one another's shoulders. Each pointed to the other's right breast, where new Recondo patches were sewn on.

The second photograph was taken in Okinawa and showed Dan mugging the camera from a hospital bed, a cigarette in one hand and a beer in the other. His head, right leg, and a portion of his right arm were covered with gauze bandages. On one side of the bed a hand reached into the picture holding a piece of cardboard on which was drawn, in felt-tip marker, a magnet. Zigzag lines of force radiated from the magnet tips toward Dan. On the other side of the bed, with the TATE on his name patch legible, was himself holding up a piece of cardboard saying MR. MAGNETIC PERSONALITY, a joke about the shrapnel removed from Dan's body.

The images were suddenly replaced by the pointed, too-clever features of State's Attorney Jack Milliken. Milliken's peculiar eagerness to prove his case made more sense now, as did his antagonism toward the defense witnesses. In the end, though, it had gotten him nowhere. Neal remembered the judge leaning forward in his chair and tugging off his glasses. "Precisely what is going on here, Mr. Milliken? I see no purpose being served by going into this further. All the testimony so far indicates that Mr. Akoki was a reasonably intelligent and stable man, if a bit lax in handling personal matters of legal consequence. However this does not automatically indicate mental incompetence."

The judge, holding up a sheet of paper: "I have here a copy of Mr. Akoki's will. I have to say that despite— or rather because of—its lack of lawyeristic verbiage, Mr. Akoki's intent couldn't be clearer. In fact I consider this will to be an excellent example of brevity and lucidity. Now, this document has been witnessed by Mr. Ninomiya and Mr. Napeahi, who appear to be gentlemen of good character. So why don't we end this matter before I become any angrier than already am?"

The trial had turned out in his favor, but Neal remembered the way it made him feel. As if dirty hands had gone through his personal belongings. He also felt, despite having never met them, a sense of defilement for George and Api Akoki.

He climbed out of the water and sat on a ledge. Milliken pushing to void the will because of a job offer. The Kahookes, run out of their home. Himself, squeezed and harassed. If all this, then what else had they done to get the launch site built? How much that he didn't know about, or couldn't even guess?

Another image came to him then, something he had only imagined but which always made him feel sick at heart: George Akoki's lifeless body floating in the sea, moving with the waves, alone.

*   *   *

Big Jim Perkins was hosing suds off the Suzy Q's foredeck and listening to slack-key guitar buzzing from the ruptured speaker of his radio when he saw Neal on the harbor walkway. "Eyyy brah!" he yelled out. "Ain't seen your ass in a while."

"Over two weeks," Neal said. "How'd we survive?"

Perkins hung the hose over the bow rail. "Turn off the water for me and...come aboard."

Neal cranked the faucet closed. A long step took him from the walkway to the stern of the Suzy Q. "So, howzit yourself, Large James?"

Perkins wiped his hands on his tattered cut-offs and turned down the radio. "It is okay." He scratched at the mat of hair on his chest. "Where's the chick? My main woman?"

"The chick has split."

Perkins stopped scratching. "Split?" His furry shoulders sagged. "When? To where?"

"Yesterday, to sunny Californ-eye-a. She went to LA. Got a job offer and decided to check it out."

"I'll be damned. Didn't even say goodbye."

"It happened pretty fast. She told me to say goodbye, sorry she didn't have a chance to. She said she'd write."

Perkins' eyebrows did a dance. "You guys aren't, uh, ...breaking up, are you?"

"No. It's...she's taking a vacation. Sort of."

"Oh. Good. I thought all that crap with the...rocket deal was causing a problem." Perkins picked up the hose, coiling it roughly as he moved sternward. "Hell," he snorted, "you got the better deal stayin' here." He heaved the hose onto the walkway and leaned against the gunwale.

Neal looked him over. Perkins was red-faced and perspiring, his beard and hair sticking out in various directions. "Poor old Large James," he said, shaking his head. "You look like you just got out of electroshock therapy."

"Well. How do you know I didn't?" Perkins leered. He slapped his belly. "I'm through workin'. Time to celebrate."

He lumbered in the cabin. Neal fell into one of the cushioned chairs on the aft deck, dazed from a day in the sun. He felt his headache returning. Closing his eyes, he concentrated on the harbor sounds. The lapping of wavelets against pilings. Halyards clapping against masts like giant wind chimes. A gull's cry. Inside the cabin, the rattle of glasses and the slam of a cabinet door.

"Heard anything from my old...fishin' colleague?" Big Jim called from inside.

"Kawika? I got a postcard a few days ago. He's apparently finding his job as a garbage man less than satisfying."

"Not too thrilled, huh?" Another cabinet door slapped shut.

"What the hell are you doing in there, Large James?"

"Fixin' celebration drinks, of course."

"Oh man, no," Neal groaned. "I got sort of drunk last night. My head's still hurting."

"Hair of the dog!" Perkins cried lustily. He came outside with two tall glasses filled to slopping over with chunks of ice and a pinkish liquid. Holding one out, he said, "My own secret recipe for...planter's punch."

Neal looked dubious, but he took the dripping tumbler.

Perkins lifted his drink over his head. "How about this—to Concord Space Systems. May all their rockets...blow to bits!"

Neal looked up. Blocking the afternoon sun, Big Jim's head was a dark oval surrounded by a glowing halo of wild hair, and above that his glass of punch hovered like a pink UFO.

The glass descended. As Neal raised his own to meet it an idea skittered across the top of his thoughts, vague but somehow calming, like a bat flitting across the back yard on a summer evening.

Chapter Twenty-Five

A frantic clanging filled the Suzy Q's cabin the next morning. Neal lurched from his bunk and stumbled across the deck searching for the source of the hellish noise. He found the fat brass windup alarm clock in the head, its clapper batting between two clam-sized bells, and subdued it with frantic slaps. He groped his way back to the bunk and sat rubbing his whisker stubble a moment, thinking, and then he went back to the head to check the time.

Charter clients were due to arrive in forty-five minutes.

Big Jim was laid out like a corpse on the opposite bunk, one arm hanging off the bunk and one eye pulled open enough to show a little white.

"Rise and shine, Large James."

The words produced no detectable reaction.

From all outward signs Perkins could have been brain-dead. Neal raised his voice. "Hey! Rise and shine!"

Still getting no response, Neal shuffled across the cabin and shook his friend a few times but got only a soft moan for his efforts. He scooped a glass of ice water from the beer cooler and poured it over Perkins' head. Big Jim mumbled something and his eyes blinked open. With much effort he sat up, wiping his face and flicking water from his beard as though it were part of the normal morning routine. "What time is it?" he croaked.

"Late," Neal informed him. "Seven twenty."

"Holy shit! I gotta get. Organized." Perkins staggered upright, swaying as he got his balance. "First things first. Breakfast." He fumbled a beer from the cooler and popped the tab, grabbed a half-empty bag of Doritos and pawed it open. He ate standing up, cramming chips into his mouth and chasing them with swigs of beer.

"I'll say it again," Neal said. "You're an animal."

Big Jim poured the last Dorito crumbs from the sack into his mouth. "Now I'm hurt," he said around the particles. He wadded up the bag, drained the beer can, belched, and fell back onto his bunk.

Neal shook his head. "This is a damn horror show." He found his pants and pulled them on. "Hey. What do you have to do to get ready?"

Perkins issued orders from his bunk and Neal carried them out as fast as he could. The single glitch was locating a sack that contained five teaser lures bought the day before. As the deadline approached, Perkins struggled from his bunk to join the search. He found the sack behind a six-pack of beer in the refrigerator just as his clients pulled up in a rented Subaru.

Neal turned down an invitation to go along as mate and jumped ship. He drove into town, parked, and headed for Wing's Chinese Kitchen.

Four cups of coffee later he felt alive enough to pick up the Kona Gazette he had bought outside. A headline on the front page jumped out at him: CSS Readies Rocket for Launch. Below that, in smaller type, Space Company's Hopes and Future Ride on Success Of Test Series.

He took it as a sign.

When he finished breakfast he drove to a hardware store in the industrial area. He sat in the truck half an hour making a list and then went inside. He bought eight spray cans of enamel paint—five flat black, two dark green, one gray—a can of light oil, a roll of black plastic sheeting, three large corks, and a box of heavy-duty black plastic garbage bags. He sat outside in his pickup after paying and thought for a while, then went back in and bought a roll of duct tape.

Driving south toward home on the highway, he avoided thinking about what he was going to do and focused instead on the passing scenery. A scarlet poinsettia bush against a rock wall. A jacaranda tree thrusting a lavender-blossomed limb over the road. The long arc of a palm tree against the blue backdrop of the ocean.

It worked pretty well for the most part. He'd have to keep doing it for a while because when he started thinking, the doubts rushed in and there was no room for doubt any more.

Chapter Twenty-Six

The launch of Concord Space Systems' first complete Independence rocket was a spectacular failure. The entire sequence of events was visible from several places along the highway where scores of cars had pulled over to watch, but the best vantage point was from a small hill on the coastline about a mile and a half north of the launch pad. Detective Sam Kane of the Hilo Police department had climbed to the top of that hill with his wife Sunny about an hour before the scheduled launch. They were sitting on a picnic blanket, Kane with his binoculars pressed to his eyes, when the first bleats of the warning siren floated across the intervening water.

As they watched, the rocket belched out a massive cloud of flame and smoke and climbed—slowly at first, then faster and faster—straight into the sky, thundering now, a thin tapering white stick pulling a fat trail of flame and smoke until, out over the ocean, it became almost too small to see, at which point it exploded with a brilliant but silent flash of light. The muted sound of the explosion wafted down several seconds later, and by that time the spider-like cloud punctuating the end of the rocket's exhaust trail was already being slowly bent and twisted by the wind.

Sam Kane took his eyes off the cloud and chuckled without smiling. "Dis happen again," he said, "I can fahget da job."

Sunny Kane took a last look up at the complex skywriting left behind by the rocket, made a clucking sound, and retreated into the shade of a stunted tree. She settled her wide bottom on the blanket they had spread out earlier and took a sip from her open can of beer. Covering a soft burp with her hand, she said, "Not a good way to stot off, fa shu,".

Sunny was a hapa-haole, half-Hawaiian and half white, and growing up with her native mother in Hilo had left her with an island way of speaking. But like her full-blooded Hawaiian husband, she could speak haole when she wanted to and often switched back and forth during a conversation.

Two fishermen from Mokolea had also climbed the low hill to watch the launch. One of them said something, the other laughed, and then both started down to their car, parked near the natural boat-launching site at the bottom of the hill. Sunny drank her beer and patted her wind-ruffled bouffant hair. Only half-joking she said, "Maybe dis a sign or sometin, Sam. Maybe mo bettah you tink 'bout dis again."

"Tink about?" Kane cried. "Damn, Sunny, you don' lissen." He jerked a thumb toward the CSS launch site. "Broke da head tinkin 'bout dis."

Kane made an effort to calm down. He tended to revert to pidgin when he was excited and he was trying to rid himself of the habit.

Sunny smoothed a strand of black hair back in place and gave Kane a sharp look. "Don't get mad at me. I listen. But I don't want you to cut your own throat."

Kane turned away. Hands on his hips, he watched the smoke drift away from the launch pad and float uphill to blot out a huge patch of the mountainside. "The only way I'm gonna cut my throat," he said, "is if

I stay a cop."

He pronounced each word carefully, wondering again if he sounded okay during the interview at the Concord Space Services offices in Honolulu.

"It's no good with the force any more, Sunny. I make detective, then sergeant, and now captain for four years. I used to think, okay, I'm doing a good job, moving up the ladder, I'll be police chief one of these days. So what happens? Li retires and, bam, Cayetano gets chief. Hell, I'm twice as qualified as him. And Cayetano's gonna be chief a long time, everybody loves his ass. He's gonna stay chief even if we get a new mayor. He's good at the politics and I'm not."

A fly landed on Kane's arm. He glanced down at the insect without moving his head. The fly walked in a circle, stopping every so often to briskly rub its fly-palms together. Kane slowly lifted the arm with the insect on it and moved his opposite hand into position. "Cayetano's got a little more education than me," he admitted, "but I've got more experience. I've been a detective three years longer than him."

With a lightning snatch he caught the fly. Cocking his arm back, he said, "I guess that don't count for shit," and hurled the fly at a nearby pile of rocks. It bounced off and tumbled to the ground, lifeless.

Kane moved nearer to his wife, who had stretched out on the blanket, and sat on a slab of lava. He blew out a long breath. "Ever since I became a cop all I wanted was to be chief of police. Now I see what's gonna happen. I gotta face the facts, which is I got no connections. I got no political buddies. Oh, maybe if I stick around until I'm a hundred they'll feel sorry for me and let me be chief. Hell with it. Anyway I think I'm tired of bein' a cop."

He reached into the styrofoam cooler beside the tree and pulled a beer can from the ice water. Popping the tab with a thick forefinger, he took a hefty slug from the can.

"You worry too much, Sam," Sunny said.

"Maybe."

"You worry enough, you gonna get a heart attack. Den you not gonna be police chief or security chief at da rocket place or nuttin. You gonna be dead."

"Dead mo bettah I wait twenny years fa police chief."

Sunny set her beer down and rolled onto her side to face her husband, propping her head on one hand. She smoothed out folds in the blanket with the other, lost in thought for a moment. "How long til you fine out 'bout da job?"

"Mmmmm. The guy said it'd be at least two or three months. That was a couple of months ago."

"I don' believe all dis time go and you jus' tell me today."

"Look. I didn't want anyone to know since I wasn't sure. Maybe you'd accidentally say somethin' to somebody if I told you."

"Huh! Well...what happen to da security guy dey got now?"

Kane smiled. He leaned forward to tell the story, his stolid face becoming animated and his speech gradually lapsing into the old patterns. "I foun' out from Hap. While he workin' there he hear da security chief say he go back to Oahu in a few mont'. So I call 'bout a innaview an' say I hear maybe a position come open fa security chief. Da man say mattah fac' yeah, but dey probbly don' decide fa leas' two mont'."

"Why you shu dey wan' you?"

The thought of being Chief of Security for the Concord Space Systems Kona Launch Facility made Kane sit up straight and clean up his speech. "Well, I asked. I told the guy at the interview that, you know, I was thinkin' about moving into the private sector. But I said I didn't know whether I should resign now and maybe move to another island or the mainland or what, so I need to know if I'm wastin' my time with them. The guy says he read my resume and it looks very, very good. The way he says it, I don't think he's bullshittin' me. Hell, I'm a police captain, I been on the island all my life, I'd be perfect. Anyway, the guy called me two weeks ago and said he'd advise not goin' anywhere yet."

Sunny looked dubious. "Dat all he say? Don' go nowhere yet?"

Kane gave her an exasperated look. "What else could he say? He ain't the guy, isn't the guy, who does the final hiring, he just screens everyone and gives a recommendation. I think what he said sounds pretty solid."

Sunny furrowed her brow.

"What?" Kane said. "You don't like this?"

"Why you say?"

"Because everything you say about that company's been bad."

"Not everything," Sunny said defensively, switching to the speech she used at work. She snorted. "Anyway, I've been telling you what I've heard other people say about the rockets, not what I think."

Kane looked sideways at her. "The way you say it I think you feel the same."

Sunny didn't contradict him. She knew after fifteen years of marriage that she couldn't fool her husband even if she wanted to. "Maybe I have my reasons," she said.

"What? What reasons?"

"I don't know. I'm sick of seeing people come here and buy up the island. First the whites and now the Japanese. Anyway, I like the island nice and quiet, like it was before." She flicked a hand toward the launch site. "Not with all that."

Kane turned away from his wife and looked out over the ocean. "It's already done," he said. "The rockets are here. The company's here. It's gonna be big, a big place when it's finished. Important. I'd be crazy not to get in now, while they just startin' up." He crinkled his beer can, shaking his head. "I don't want to...I don't want to be number two in the police force, Sunny. I got a chance to be number one over there an' make a lot more money at the same time. Anyway, we'll be gettin' my retirement pay from the force so even if nothin' happens we'll be okay. I thought about it a long time. It's what I want."

Sunny pushed herself into a sitting position. She drank some of her beer, studying her husband's blunt profile. She knew he had been unhappy for the last year or two, and that once he set his mind to do something it was hard to sway him away from his goal. He had probably sized up the police force situation correctly. If he did get the job with CSS and it did pay more, well...

"Sammy." She reached out and patted his arm. "If that's what you want, then that's what I want."

Kane bowed his head and rubbed a hand over his thick salt-and-pepper hair. Short on the sides, it stuck up on top like a patch of uncut grass. He squeezed his beer can a few more times and then said, "Thanks."

"Ey. Shu."

He grinned. "You okay, Sunny. Maybe I marry you."

214

"Chry fahget it, bad idea."

Kane tried to pinch his wife's cheek with his knuckles but she slapped his hand away before it got near her coiffed hair, just as he knew she would. "Ey," he laughed. " I fee' bettah. Now we do sometin' make you happy. What you wan'?"

Sunny leaned back on her elbows and closed her eyes, feeling the steady breeze from the sea flowing over her body. "I wan' is do nuttin. Stay ri' heah an' drink beah. Den take a nap undah dis tree, den have mo beah, and den we tink what we do."

The Kanes were still alone on top of the hill when the stars came out, finishing off the last two beers in the cooler. They sipped lazily, watching the hundreds of sparkling points of lights growing brighter in the sky.

Sam Kane heard the motor first. He squinted, searching the rippling surface of the ocean below, and finally spied a dim white wake. The boat was headed straight for them. With nothing better to do, Kane pulled his big military binoculars from their case again and focused them on the approaching boat. Sunny Kane sat up straighter, trying to see what had caught her husband's attention.

"What is it?"

"Nothin', just a boat. Hear the motor?"

Through the binoculars, Kane could make out a man in shorts and light-colored T-shirt, riding in what looked like a black inflatable boat. He rested the binoculars in his lap and took another pull at his beer. Seeing where the boat was headed, he assumed the person in it owned the pickup parked at the base of the hill. It was a piece of junk, dented and rusted and missing the rear window. Someone had blasted one side of it with a shotgun, it looked like.

215

Kane finished his beer and lifted the binoculars again. He liked watching people who didn't know they were being watched. As the black inflatable buzzed up to the tiny cove below, the man cut his motor to a purr and rode the waves in, goosing the throttle to avoid the larger humps of lava. A few feet from the lava ramp he killed the outboard and tilted it up, then jumped out and towed the boat ashore with the bowline.

Kane watched him unhitch the motor from the transom and carry it to his truck, setting it in the rear with a thud that carried to the top of the hill. The man leaned against his pickup, catching his breath and eyeing Kane's Chevy Blazer, parked nearby. He looked around and Kane instinctively ducked when he turned to look up the hill. When Kane raised his head again the man was back at the boat, unloading it. There wasn't enough light to see well but everything he carried from the boat to the truck seemed to be black in color. Kane figured it was diving gear. When he glimpsed something that looked like a speargun he was sure he was right.

"Now what you watchin'?" Sunny asked.

"Oh. Same thing, the guy with the boat."

Sunny craned her neck to see over the rocks and grass blocking her view. "Not messin' wit da cah? I lef' my purse."

"No. Loadin' his stuff. I'm just watchin' for fun."

The thin rim of lavender on the western horizon had become black and the moon had risen over the mountain by the time the man finished tying down his boat. He gave it a final shove to check the ropes and then opened the door of the pickup. Instead of getting in, however, he stepped up on the doorsill and took a last look around.

Observing through his binoculars, the police captain hunched down again, but not before getting a last look at the guy's face in the moonlight. He had a feeling he'd seen him somewhere before.

Chapter Twenty-Seven

Sitting in the frigid whiteness of Hideo Kamada's office, Laurance A. "Skip" Schaefer rubbed his temples, trying to massage the numbness from his brain. "They've gone over every detail ten times, Hideo," he said. His voice was rough with fatigue. "It all checks out."

The flight from California had exhausted him but he acquiesced to Kamada's demand for an immediate conference and came straight from the airport to the offices of Komodo, Inc. In his view the meeting could have waited, blown up rocket or not. He needed sleep. That was something he hadn't been getting enough of in the last few months. All the talking, plotting, meeting, and shuttling back and forth between Oahu and the mainland, not to mention dealing with his own personal problems, was wearing him down.

Seated behind his desk, Kamada moved his arid gaze from Schaefer to the windows where, looking over a wall of beachfront hotels, he could see the ocean. It was calm today. Unlike his insides, where an invisible dagger seemed to twist in his stomach. The ulcer was coming back.

Kamada spoke. "It is obvious," he said in a menacing staccato, "that something has been overlooked. The rocket engines have all performed...satisfactorily...in the static tests. The electronic systems also have performed well. But the rocket has malfunctioned." He turned his head to glare at Schaefer. "There is a reason."

Schaefer wasn't sure how to take Kamada when he came on like this, sulky and growling. It often seemed like a personal attack, and more than once Schaefer had been tempted to let loose and blast the man. But if he did, things would never be the same between them. Kamada was that kind of guy. He'd lose face or something and they had to keep working together.

"There's a reason all right," Schaefer agreed, nodding wearily, "but apparently finding it's a bear."

A bear, Kamada thought. He was trying not to hate Schaefer and his crude idioms today—a real bugger, piss-poor, kicking ass, bugs—but it was difficult.

"Whatever the case," Schaefer went on, "I hope you see my point. Replacing the reassembly personnel will just mean more delay for the next launch. Hell, those guys are doing the best they can."

Kamada sat still, as though waiting for Schaefer to continue. The astronaut obliged.

"Let's just keep cool and wait until the team gets here from California. They'll go over the next one with a fine-tooth comb." Schaefer rubbed his jaw, slightly sandpapery with the beginning of a shadow, and stared through the windows himself. "It's a damn shame we had to blow the bastard up. Would've been nice to get it back in one or two pieces and look it over."

Kamada made a guttural noise. "We shall do as you suggest, Skip, and wait." He tapped his forefinger on the desk. "There is another matter about which I would like to remind you. This person Tate. He has still shown no intentions of selling his land."

Schaefer absorbed the news in silence. This was not a subject he cared to hear about, though Kamada never seemed to tire of it. "Yeah, well. Tate seemed pretty clear on that point. It's a bad kink in our plans but we can't force him to sell."

"Can we not," Kamada asked in his monotone. "Aside from offering him a great quantity of money, which would not be in our long-term interest, is there no way."

"You're asking me? No, I don't think so. I don't think he'd take the money anyway."

Kamada scrutinized the airspace just to Schaefer's left for several seconds. "I see," he said at last. "However, in my opinion Mr. Tate is becoming a burden. A large burden."

Schaefer examined his partner through puffy red eyes. "He's causing us problems, Hideo," he conceded, "but we'll have to work around him for now."

Both men were quiet.

"Well," Schaefer said, pushing himself out of his chair, "about the rockets, we can't do much right now. I'll get back with you tomorrow morning on the latest from California." He straightened his coat and tie. "I think I'm gonna go get myself a drink and a bite to eat. You want to join me?"

Kamada rose from his chair and held up a palm. "That is good of you...Skip. But I am not hungry. I hope you enjoy your meal."

Kamada saw Schaefer to the door and bade him goodbye.

When the astronaut was gone Kamada crossed his office and stood at the windows. He looked out over the ocean, brooding.

Time was running out. How many years could a corporation operate at a loss? Not only was the budget getting tight, but as a new company they had to provide continual, consistent results to keep the money flowing, to keep corporate morale up, to keep from stalling and perhaps going into a nose-dive. It was no good when the company's final product, its only product, malfunctioned and had to be destroyed in flight. There was no way to undo the credibility damage caused by the faulty rocket. Schaefer didn't seem to appreciate the trouble they were in. He wasn't a bad man, just naive at times. Naive enough that he wouldn't still be a partner if he weren't so good with the investors. They trusted him. He was...how did they say it? All-American. A good boy. No, a good old boy.

Kamada was not a good old boy and he knew it. He had no desire to be a good old boy.

I am the Dragon, he thought.

The Dragon had to breathe fire, to scorch people in order to bring out the best in them. Why did Schaefer try to keep him from breathing a little fire, from making it hot for these fools who couldn't make their own rocket work?

Kamada dipped a hand into his pocket and removed a card covered with Gelusil tablets in little plastic blisters. Half of the tablets were already gone. He pried another one out and ate it.

Concord Space Systems had become a severe test of his business acumen. Of his personal strength, even. He had never been involved with a business failure up to this point and he had no intention of marring his record now. As was to be expected with any new enterprise, CSS had had problems getting on its feet from the very start. Arranging finances, locating qualified personnel, getting the Research Center into operation, acquiring permits for a million and one things. But for a time—almost a year ago, now—

221

everything seemed to fall into place. All was moving along smoothly.

Then the problems. First the old man who wouldn't sell, not even for an amount of money that went beyond reasonable. The idea of persuading him to sell by simply burning his miserable house down had been a stroke of genius. Had the old fool not come home late that night, had he not tried to stop the arsonist, he would now be living out his worthless life in comfort. Instead of ending it with a broken skull, tossed into the ocean. His death had seemed the perfect solution at first, but with the dog Tate now in ownership of the property the problem was even worse. Two "accidents" would certainly raise suspicions.

And now this. The rockets didn't function as designed and no one could say why. It was probably something simple both times, Kamada felt, something overlooked or done incorrectly. Caused, no doubt, by a decline in discipline during manufacture or—his theory—during reassembly. Now that the first rush of excitement was gone everyone was relaxing. He imagined the rockets being thrown together in California, taken apart and shipped to Hawaii, then thrown together again to be launched. There was an ugly-sounding American word for doing things with such a lack of care...sloppy. Sloppy manufacturing, sloppy control, sloppy handling, sloppy assembly.

And the other irritations, an array of nettling problems that seemed to grow every day. He wished for a magical sword to hack a clear path through them. Like the problem with this Tate fool, who wouldn't sell them his land so they could build a proper access road. A thorn in his side, a stinging thorn. He wasn't used to suffering such irritation, and he didn't intend to endure it long. Things would change. Things would change.

When the glowing knot in his stomach had loosened Kamada went back to his desk and eased himself into his white leather chair. From a drawer he pulled a square of polished wood, like a flat, smooth cutting board, and a sheaf of rice paper. For the next hour, moving nothing but his hands, Kamada folded the stiff paper into birds. Birds with long tails, birds whose wings flapped, fat birds, thin birds. Birds that would have glided gracefully through the air if he had tossed them, which he did not.

After turning out a score of the translucent creatures, lining them up in front of himself on the white marble desktop, he stopped. For another quarter of an hour he sat still, gazing alternately at the avian origami and at the telephone set on his desk, his black eyes nearly shut. Then, slowly, he reached out and crumpled the paper birds one at a time, the crackle of rice paper resembling the sound of tiny bones breaking. When the last bird was crushed Kamada lifted the receiver and put through a call on his private line.

*   *   *

Skip Schaefer settled back in his chair in the dining room of the Hale Lono and waited for his order of lobster. His second martini rested on the linen tablecloth in front of him, its olive slowly revolving in the icy liquid like a lone biological specimen. He shivered slightly as the last chill of Hideo Kamada's office finally left his bones.

The chill came partly from the arctic air of that bloodless room and—he allowed himself to admit—partly from Kamada himself.

He'd spent a lot of time thinking about his partner

223

lately. Hideo was a strange one. Like upstairs just now. The problem with the rocket was eating at him, bad. He'd lost some sleep over it, too, but he felt that everything would work out okay. The next rocket would work fine.

The thing about Hideo was that he wanted it all now and any holdups he took personally. Businesswise that wasn't necessarily a fault, and he did know how to get people moving and how to run a company. No doubt about that.

It was possible, Schaefer reflected, that Kamada's current foul mood might be the result of something more than the glitches in the Independence. But if so it would remain a secret since Kamada never opened up and said how he felt about things. Not in any personal way. In all this time, Schaefer thought, he still didn't feel any closer to Kamada than when they first talked, which was years ago. It was hard to accept the idea that he probably never would.

Schaefer downed half his martini, working the freezing mixture around his tongue to warm it before swallowing. Aside from this the main complaint he had with Kamada was his pushiness. It was dressed up in polite talk, but pushy was pushy. He admitted that it was partly his own fault. He'd fallen into the habit of letting Kamada call most of the shots, especially when it had to do with organization or personnel. Kamada had years in business and seemed the natural expert on that sort of stuff. But it was time, Schaefer thought, to take a more active part in the day-to-day operations and policy decisions. The fact was, even though he was the chief liaison between CSS and the investors, he was relatively ignorant of CSS's total financial picture. And—what with keeping the investors informed and pumped up, doing all the PR gigs, ironing out problems at the California headquarters—he'd lost touch with what was going on with the Launch Facility on Hawaii. The easy thing had been to let Hideo handle all that since his background in finance and engineering and construction made him the best man for the job.

The irritating thing, Schaefer thought as he took another drink, was now that he wanted to find out what was going on it was like pulling teeth. When he asked questions of Kamada it was always, I will take care of that detail. Don't worry about this. That will be arranged. He'd been happy to let Kamada handle the details before, but now he wished he hadn't.

The deal with the Launch Facility was a case in point. The legal and environmental snafus had put them way behind schedule and he let Hideo talk him into stepping up the pace of construction. It had cost the company big bucks in overtime and rush fees. Enormous bucks. Kamada's rationale had been that even a small lead in this business at this time was worth the expense.

By the time he was nearing the bottom of his second martini Schaefer's outlook had undergone a metamorphosis. It began with the realization, a sudden ethanol-released insight, that he'd been avoiding the real issue. The things he was going over in his mind weren't just an accumulation of business problems that would solve themselves or smooth out in time. Simply put, he was feeling and acting like a poor relation in the company. More like an employee than a boss, a founder. He'd been suppressing that admission until now because it meant he wasn't in charge, that Kamada had been able to manipulate him successfully, either by force of personality or by being a better leader.

But it wasn't just his subordination that bothered him. As a means to an end he could handle subordination—he'd gone through that in the Air Force. It was other things about Kamada. The man made him feel...uncomfortable. Disturbed him in a fundamental way.

Like when he told Kamada about the trip to Tate's place. Kamada had squinched up his eyes and started doing some heavy nose-breathing, asking questions in that hard-ass tone. And the things he'd said—calling Tate a 'dog', for crying out loud. He didn't like Tate either, but 'dog'? What the hell kind of Jap weirdness was that? And what did he mean by saying Tate was 'becoming a large burden'? That they ought to have the guy assassinated or what? He couldn't decide whether, when Kamada said things like that, he seemed truly alien or whether he seemed...too American. In a Mafia sort of way.

There was other weirdness, too, Schaefer thought. He had the feeling that things were going on just out of his sight that he didn't know about, thing that he should know about. What, for instance, had happened to the political noises against building the Launch Facility in Hawaii? Most of it had just vanished a few months ago.

Schaefer drained the last of his martini. Probably some kind of backroom stuff. Schaefer prided himself on being above-board, a straight shooter, but he had a feeling Hideo was a little different. A bit twisted.

Which brought up the really hard question: why had he let a guy like Kamada manipulate him so easily? For example why the fuck had he, the great moon-stomping astronaut, been the one to fly to the Big Island and talk to this Tate asshole? Why not Kamada?

Ostensibly it was for the same reasons that he ended up doing all the back-slapping PR work with the investors and politicos—because Tate would relate to an American better. Because he, Schaefer, was a famous name, an astronaut, and his mere presence would carry weight. Because he was so good at dealing with people, selling them. All sound reasons, but would a guy like Hideo Kamada have gone to see Tate if good ol' Skip hadn't been there to send along?

Hell no. That wasn't Kamada's style. His style was to sit in his god damn meat locker all day, keeping cool, barely twitching a muscle except to pick up the phone, directing from above while he, the great astronaut, went stumbling over stumps in the hot sun to get insulted by some shaggy-headed turd.

Jesus. He felt like the guy with the handkerchief, what's his face—Rodney Dangerfield. No respect.

No respect, not even from his own wife. She sure as hell didn't hold him in awe. She wanted a divorce. "For all I've gotten out of this marriage in the last ten years you might as well have stayed on the god damned moon!" Worse, no respect from the kids. They were on her side, he could see that. They didn't come right out and say it but from the things they didn't say, holding back when he talked to them on the phone, he could tell. Now that they were grown up and had their own families they'd gotten judgmental on him. True, wrapped up in the space program he hadn't been the best family man but he had provided for them, every damn thing they could ever want.

And what had it gotten him?

Well. A trip to the moon. To the moon. How could you ever measure the worth of that? And fame, yes. But it was slipping away year by year, a diminishing resource. A resource never huge to begin with since his mission flew at the end of the Apollo series and the public was bored with it by then.

Fuck it all, Schaefer thought, and flagged down the waitress for another martini.

*   *   *

At the same time Skip Schaefer fell into bed in his suite at the Hale Lono, drunk and exhausted, Hideo Kamada opened the door to his penthouse suite to admit the person who had just arrived on his private elevator.

The visitor, a young woman of Japanese ancestry, said nothing as she stepped into Kamada's suite, but she did twist her lips into a semblance of a smile as she passed him. Once inside she avoided looking directly at her host.

The woman had a secretarial air. Her thick black hair was pulled back tightly from her face, braided and coiled into a bun, and she wore large gold-rimmed spectacles that gave her a studious look. She had on a high-collared blouse with long sleeves and a simple black calf-length skirt with a short slit up either side. Over one shoulder was a black shoulder bag, and she carried a leather attaché' case.

Closing the door behind the woman, Kamada gave her a cool, knowing smile. He gave her the slightest bow said, "Good evening, Odemae." He gestured toward the hallway leading from his open living room. Like his office on the floor below, the living room suffered no shortage of geometrically shaped glass, Lucite, and chrome. The woman took her cue and strode off down the hallway, disappearing through the door at the end.

Still dressed in his business suit, Hideo Kamada settled into his couch. He gazed with heavy-lidded eyes at the black half-mirror of his balcony windows, watching the lights of Honolulu.

Half an hour later three gentle buzzes sounded on the intercom. Kamada roused himself, straightened his coat and tie, and made his way to the closed room at the end of the hall.

Just inside the door was a small entryway where he paused to take off his shoes and socks. From here he climbed up three small steps into the room proper, the floor of which was raised two feet above the level of the rest of the suite.

Entering the room was like stepping across the ocean. With a few minor departures it was a reproduction of the guest quarters of a traditional Japanese home. The ceiling was a wide latticework of dark wood with squares of heavy cloth stretched between the narrow beams. The floor was covered with tatami, square mats of woven straw. Two of the walls were overlaid with non-functional fusuma, sliding doors made of wood and heavy paper. The other two walls were made of highly polished cypress wood, though one of these walls—the one to the far left of the small genkan, or entry—was not visible because of a wood-and-paper partition and shoji that formed a separate cubicle. The wooden wall held several sumi paintings of landscapes, though they were difficult to see because of the light shed by four ornamental paper lamps and the haze of incense in the air. Below the paintings, pushed against the wall, was a large futon covered with a silk comforter.

The woman Kamada had called "Odemae" waited on a tatami in the middle of the room, holding out the first cup of heated sake. She had transformed herself from a secretary into a geisha. Above her intricately embroidered silk kimono tied with the wide obi, her neck and face were heavily powdered to a snowy white. Her eyes were lined and her eyebrows were carefully penciled over. Her hair was pulled back and sprayed stiffly, artfully pierced with a wooden comb and ivory pins that glinted as she moved, catching light from the two scented candles resting at either end of the low wooden table she sat behind. Atop the table were lacquered wooden bowls holding various delicacies: fern tips, sashimi, smoked octopus, tangerines, sake-marinated loach, lichee fruit.

Kamada seated himself and took the cup of sake and drank deeply, staring impassively at the woman. She stared back with the same expressionless look, a porcelain figurine brought to life. Her outward composure, in contrast to the more alert demeanor she presented when first arriving at Kamada's door, was not due solely to the role she now played. Much of it came from two downers she popped while riding the elevator to the penthouse.

Kamada finished his second cup of sake. The woman, moving with a dreamy languor, helped him out of his coat and loosened his tie. She brought out a pan of hot water from behind the partition and, while he ate with chopsticks from the bowls, washed his feet and massaged them with oil.

Kamada's hunger was soon satiated. By this time he was also reeling drunk. He finished off the last drops of warm sake in his cup and stood. "Show me," he hissed.

He said this in English. Despite her authentic look the woman spoke only a little Japanese.

She looked down and said softly, "No. I can't."

"Come," Kamada insisted roughly, taking a step back to keep his balance, "Take off your clothes. Show me."

She shook her head, still not looking.

He leaned over, leering, his face covered with a sheen of perspiration. "You will take off your kimono now."

Again the woman made a meek refusal.

Kamada was now directly over her. He reached down and slapped her on the face, hard enough to make a fleshy pop. The sound died instantly, absorbed by the layer of acoustic tile hidden behind the room's false interior. The woman had rolled her head when Kamada struck but the slap still stung. Kamada grabbed her hair and pulled back her head, slapping her again, then again. She winced with each blow but kept silent.

With a slack-jawed but still intent look on his face, Kamada released the woman and straightened up. He stepped directly in front of her and unzipped the fly of his trousers and pulled out his penis. The uncircumcised member hung like a large brownish grub directly over the woman's head. Her careful coiffure was in disarray, loose strands waving in the air. Kamada seized the woman's hair again and pulled her up, dragging her face toward his penis. With apparent reluctance she opened her mouth and engulfed it. Kamada used his hands to move the woman's head back and forth until he was stiff and then pushed her away.

"Take off your clothes!" he commanded. His erect penis bobbed in the air as he took a step toward her, lifting his hand. The woman whimpered and lifted her hands to protect herself as he slapped her wherever he

231

could find an opening. Breathing hard, Kamada stopped long enough to strip off the rest of his suit, which he tossed into one corner of the room. A fine sheen of perspiration glistened on the layer of hard flab covering his body. Naked, he went over to a lacquered cabinet and took out a small whip. The handle was a short dowel attached to dozens of thin black thongs.

Kamada shook the whip to straighten the thongs and moved toward the woman, who still cowered on the tatami-covered floor. She held a hand to her mouth and cried, "No! No! Please!", but Kamada brought the whip down on her backside, which she had obligingly turned to him. The thongs whistled through the air and landed with a leathery slap, and the woman let out a surprised-sounding yelp.

"Take them off!" Kamada ordered, and hit her with the whip again.

The woman was breathing heavily herself. She reached back and pulled at the hem of her kimono, lifting it a few inches. Kamada struck at the exposed flesh, catching her hand with some of the thongs. She drew the hand back, but she seemed to be moving in slow motion. She reached back again and pulled the hem up even further, to her calves. Kamada gave the creamy skin a whack with the whip and new cluster of pink stripes appeared above the first ones. The hem-raising process continued until, after numerous lashes of the whip and pained cries, the rounded lobes of the woman's buttocks peeked from behind the silken folds of the kimono. Kamada's penis stiffened even more, waving like a conductor's baton as he staggered to get the best angle from which to strike. The woman continued her ineffectual moans and protestations but kept raising her kimono until the whole of her heart-shaped buttocks was exposed. Kamada flailed at the soft flesh, covering it with a hatchwork of pink. He stepped around until he was directly behind her. In the dark-haired cleft between the cheeks he could see her hidden treasure engorged, parted. He threw down the whip, knelt, and thrust himself into the waiting orifice. The woman moaned, closing her eyes, arching her back, pressing herself against the rhythmic thrusts jolting her from behind. She reached between her legs with her left hand and cupped the bouncing testicles, while her right hand felt on the floor until she found the whip. Still moaning and gasping, she drew back her arm and, like a jockey whipping a horse, cracked the thongs across Hideo Kamada's legs and plunging buttocks.

Over and over.

Chapter Twenty-Eight

Detective Captain Sam Kane stood on the hill where he had watched the first Concord Space Systems rocket explode in flames just over three weeks before. Sunny hadn't been able to get off work today but he had come anyway, primarily so that he could tell the people at CSS he'd personally seen all their launches, but also because, truth to tell, the first launch had been pretty exciting. The explosion was a bonus, better than fireworks on the Fourth.

Kane looked at his watch. Ten more minutes.

Two men and a woman—all from Mokolea, he found out during a brief chat—were on the hill with him. Kane looked down at the clearing at the foot of the hill and saw their ratty-looking little Suzuki jeep parked beside his own Blazer, but what interested him more were the other two vehicles. One was a lavender-colored Toyota pickup, the other the old green Chevy pickup with holes in it. The same one that was parked there last time. The black-boat man who drove the Chevy was nowhere to be seen. But he did see the Toyota's owner. A woman.

Kane moved into the shade of the scrub tree he and Sunny had picnicked under and put his binoculars on her again, the woman who'd driven up in the Toyota. Nothing had changed. She was still just sitting there in her boat, which hadn't moved.

He had watched her on and off for about an hour,

from the time she arrived, and got a pretty good look at her when she got out. Fifty-five, maybe older. Tall, silver hair, not bad-looking from what he could see. She wore a khaki safari shirt, navy culottes, purple deck shoes and a wide-brimmed straw hat. He had watched as she dragged a small inflatable boat from her truck to the water and hooked a tiny outboard motor to it. After loading the boat with camera bags and a metal case of some kind she'd started up the motor and headed out to sea, maneuvering the inflatable over the waves like a pro.

Kane had followed the woman through his binoculars as she buzzed off in the direction of the CSS peninsula. She stopped her boat at about the halfway point, unpacked a camera, and took a few pictures, her big hat flashing in the sun. He had watched with interest when a small Coast Guard patrol boat swung by to check her out. It looked like she talked to the Coast Guard guys a few minutes and then bigger boat moved off, leaving the woman where she was. He had put the binoculars on her a few more times but she seemed to be just sitting there.

Kane checked his watch again. Four minutes to go. He loosened his tie, reconsidered, and pulled it off, unbuttoning his collar. Even off duty he liked to dress neatly but it was too hot to worry about that. He took another sip of water from his jug, waiting for the launch with the patience of a stone.

Moments later the warning siren hooted across the water. Kane took a quick look at the rocket through his binoculars: no change. He lowered the glasses a few degrees and saw that the woman had started up the motor of her little boat and was moving, bounding over the waves toward the launch site. She finally stopped about a hundred yards from the low cliffs of the peninsula. Kane let the binoculars hang on the neck strap, frowning. She was on the safe side of the rocket, behind the rear wall of the pad and away from the blast deflector, but no more than a quarter of a mile from it. People, Kane thought, just didn't have good sense.

The launch siren died and the blatting beep of the one-minute warning began, the sound shrunken by the distance. He lifted the binoculars.

A puff of smoke signaled the ignition of the rocket's first stage. A thick, yellowish cloud suddenly blossomed outward from the base of the rocket, the gantry arm dropped loose, and the rocket moved upward. Seconds later the sound reached the hill, a fat rumble.

By shifting his binoculars down a fraction Kane was able to get the woman in the boat into his field of view. She was taking photographs. He was about to switch back to the rocket when the woman abruptly lowered her camera and stared toward the peninsula. Kane swung the binoculars toward the rocket to see what had caught her attention.

The rocket was rising past the top of the gantry, moving up steadily.

He moved back to the woman and found her sitting the same stiff way, camera lowered, not looking at the rocket but at something on the peninsula. Kane scanned the peninsula shoreline, saw nothing, and went back to her. She was taking pictures again, not of the rocket but of something straight across from her, and for the next few seconds Kane ignored the rocket and watched.

He broke off when one of the men on the hill started jabbering excitedly and pointing upward. Kane stepped from under his tree to get an unobstructed view. Through the binoculars he could see the rocket climbing smoothly, a white dot atop a glowing yellow dot. The exhaust trail looked odd, however; it had split in two and was getting thicker and thinner in spurts. As he watched, the rocket flame brightened and grew into an irregular blob of light.

Kane lowered his binoculars and stared at the smoky trail. It was now a long thin line that dead-ended in a fat white spider, just like last time. A few moments later a sound like distant thunder reached the ground.

Kane put the binoculars away, cursing under his breath. Another fuckup. He grabbed his water jug and headed down the hill to the car. His plans for the future seemed less certain all the time.

* * *

Kane pulled onto the shoulder of the Mamalahoa Highway and stopped to watch in his rear-view mirror as Frank Ninomiya handed a citation to the driver of a red Fiero. A moment later the Fiero started up, swung back onto the road, and accelerated past his car, leaving the young officer standing next to his cruiser trying to figure out why the Blazer had pulled off the road ahead. Kane smiled to himself as Ninomiya tossed his ticket book into the police car and strode up the highway.

"Ey, ey, Captain!" Ninomiya said when he saw who it was. He reached through the window to shake Kane's hand. "Good to see you! I didn't recognize the car."

"Course not," Kane growled, mock-severe. "You never seen it. And you never seen it 'cause you never visit, bum!"

Ninomiya looked down, flustered but still smiling. "I don't get over to Hilo all that much. Anyway, I figure you're busy."

"Never too busy to see you, Frank," Kane said. He grinned. "Ey, you still seein', ah, Louisa?"

"Oh, sure, yeah."

"And how's your worthless old man? I haven't talked to him for a while."

Ninomiya's thin features broke into a smile. "He's fine, Captain."

Kane wagged a finger. "Just you and me, Frank, you call me Sam like always. Captain only if somebody else's around."

"Okay. Sam."

Kane patted his own trunk-like thigh. "So how're things with you? Not tired of bein' a cop yet?"

"No, not yet. I like it. I knew I would. It's pretty slow, though."

"Not like on TV, ey?"

Ninomiya laughed. "No. Not like TV, but that's okay with me." The young officer took off his cap and scratched his head, his little finger making small neat strokes. "Ey, Captain, you see the rocket go off?"

"Yeah," Kane said. "It blew up."

"Again? Shee, wish I'd been watchin', I might've seen it from here."

Kane grunted. "Well, I better get my butt back to Hilo. I told Sunny I'd do some chores today. Stop in to see us if you're in town, Frank."

Kane stopped in Naalehu for gas and a leak, bought a Coke from a machine and headed out again, thinking about what he had to do back home. Fix the fence. Mow the lawn. Weed the flower beds. Buy a new hose if the old one couldn't be taped. Fix the leak in the bathroom. The kind of crap he hated doing, but that was the price of having a house.

In the middle of a repugnant vision—himself, floundering around on the bathroom linoleum as he pulled slimy pipes apart beneath the sink—Kane suddenly remembered where he'd seen the guy with the black boat. He was the guy in Harry's shop, the guy bad-mouthing the rockets. What the hell was his name?

He got on his radio and called the Naalehu station and Frank Ninomiya's voice came through the radio a few moments later. *"Captain Kane? This is Frank here."*

"Yeah, Frank. I wanted to ask you, you know anybody drives an old green Chevy pickup? All messed up, you know, burned, with holes in it."

"Holes?"

"Yeah, like it's been shot up or somethin'. I think maybe he lives down south somewhere."

"Oh yeah, sure, Sam—Captain. That's probably Neal Tate."

"Yeah? You know him?"

"Yeah, yessir, Neal's a friend. He's a good guy."

Rolling along the highway toward Pahala, microphone in hand, Kane frowned.

"Ey, Captain. How come? He hasn't done anything, has he?"

Kane pressed the mike button. "No, no. I saw his truck and I remembered I met him once. I just forgot his name."

There was another pause and then Ninomiya's voice came through, scratchy. *"I see. Well, Neal Tate. Anything else?"*

"No. Well—yeah. You ever hear him say anything about CSS?"

"Who?"

"CSS. The rocket people."

"Oh, right. Well—sure, we've talked some."

239

Kane thumbed his button again. "What about?"

"Well, they own all the property around him, you know. They've been tryin' to buy it but Neal, he doesn't want to sell."

There was a pause and then a sound came through the speaker, jumbled and overlaid with a burst of static.

"Frank," Kane said, "I couldn't hear you. Say that again."

Frank's laugh came over the radio. *"I said he doesn't like 'em too much, I can tell you that."*

Chapter Twenty-Nine

"A rifle?" Harry pulled the pipe from his mouth and tucked in his chin. "What kind of rifle?"

"Well," Neal said, casually looking around at the orchids in the gun shop, "I thought you might help me with that, Harry."

"Sure. Be glad to help. But what the heck are you gonna use it for?"

"Hunting."

"Yeah? Hunting what?"

"Oh...I keep hearing about wild goats and pigs you can hunt here."

Harry ran the pipe back into his mouth and puffed out a couple of smoke signals. He laid his palms on the display case in front of him and drummed his fingers on the glass. "Well, I might be able to help you out. I didn't think you were much of a hunter, Neal, for some reason."

"To tell the truth I haven't done any hunting in a long time. I thought I might try it again." Cornered like this, he promised himself he would actually go hunt for a damn goat so he wouldn't technically be lying. He didn't have to actually shoot one.

"Pigs and goats, huh?" Harry considered the problem professionally, softening the look on his weatherworn face. He spoke to the ceiling. "Well, let's see. You'll want something with some range. I'd say nothing less than a .270 if you really plan on pigs.

241

Other than that, you could go as light as a .243."

Neal ran a hand thoughtfully through his hair, which reminded him he needed to get a haircut pretty soon. "Hmm. I was thinking something a little heavier. As long as I'm spending the bucks on a rifle I want something I could use for other things. Who knows, I might go to Alaska someday."

Harry's eyebrows shot up. "Alaska! You're not leaving us, are you?"

"No, no. But I'd like to see it sometime. Maybe go hunting, I don't know."

"North to Alasky!" Harry grinned. "Boy, I'd love to go back there."

"You've been?"

"Oh yes! Hey—it'd be fun to go together, wouldn't it?"

Neal smiled and nodded, feeling even guiltier. "If I go, you're invited. But right now it's just a thought."

"Just let me know when you get the urge." Harry rubbed his hands together. "So you want a gun big enough for Alaska. Well you know, Neal, a rifle big enough for Alaskan game is sort of oversized for here."

"I know that. But better too big than too small, right?"

"Uh huh. But a couple of things. Ammo costs a lot for one of the big boys. We're talking anywhere from twenty-five to fifty bucks for a box of twenty, depending on the caliber."

"Wow." This was actually surprising but he didn't really give a damn about the cost. "Hell, Harry, how many boxes are you going to shoot up? Anyway, that'd still be a small percentage of any hunting trip's cost."

"True," Harry agreed, "but the main problem is, people who buy a gun like that tend to not practice with it. And not just because of ammo cost. The big bores kick the crap out of you. I'm just giving you fair warning."

"I'll consider myself warned."

"All right," Harry said dubiously. "I just want you to be sure before you blow a bunch of dough."

"I appreciate that."

"Okay. Let's check out a few items. Follow me." As they walked down the hall Harry said, "I used to get some trade from people going to the Big A, but that was almost entirely in Honolulu. I still have a few rifles tucked away that might suit you."

They went into a small storage room toward the back of the store. Harry unlocked a tall gray gun safe that, by Neal's guess, had to weigh a quarter of a ton. A simple theft deterrent. Harry ran an eye over the row of rifles, pulled one out, and cranked open the bolt. "This is a dandy," he said, tapping the barrel with the stem of his pipe. "I've shot it myself. Like new. It's a Sako seven millimeter Remington Magnum. What they call the 'Classic Sporter.' A pretty decent scope, too, an old Redfield."

Neal took the gun in both hands and looked it over. It was a beautifully finished firearm, the wooden stock shining like agate under a protective layer of urethane varnish. "Seven millimeter magnum, huh?"

"Right."

"Hm. Correct me if I'm wrong but that seems about the minimum gun I could use for—well, like to take to Alaska."

Harry pursed his lips. "That's true," he conceded, "if you're talking moose or bear."

Neal handed the rifle back. "I'd like option. Something heavier, I think."

"Heavier. Okay, let's see." Harry replaced the pipe in his mouth and put the rifle back in the rack. "I have four or five rifles that are larger caliber." He glanced over his shoulder. "Are you sure about this?"

Neal gave him a look.

"Okay, okay. I guess you can always sell the thing if you decide you made a mistake." He pointed into the safe. "That one is a Remington 700, which is a great gun tried and true in any caliber. This one's a .308. Now this one here," he said, indicating another rifle "is a Harrington and Richards in .30-06, which ain't a hell of a lot different from the .308. That's their model 340. No scope, as you can see." He looked up. "You gonna want a scope? I just assumed you would."

"Definitely want a scope."

"Right. Well, you can always stick one on. I've got some used ones in good shape. Now, this rifle here," he said, "is another .30-06. It's a Colt Sauer with a..." He slipped his glasses from his pocket and held them in front of his eyes as he leaned closer. "...Weaver 6X." He put away the glasses and touched the next gun. "Okay, getting into the really heavy-duty weapons, we've got these three. A DuBiel in .458 Win-mag. No scope, though I think you won't be wanting this cannon anyway. Some guy was going to Africa but he never made it. He offered me this gun so cheap I had to take it, though I'll never be able to sell it." He chuckled, a rusty wheeze. "And I sure as hell don't want to shoot the thing. It'd bust my arm."

He pointed to the next rifle in the safe. "That's a classic gun, a Weatherby Mark V. The caliber on that is .378 Weatherby Mag, which would take care of anything in Alaska and most everything in Africa. Not going there are you?"

Neal made a wry face. "Not any time soon."

Harry nodded. "Well, that's about it in the high-caliber department."

Neal pointed at the last rifle in the gun safe. "What's that?"

Harry looked. "That? Oh, you don't want that. It's all screwed up."

"Screwed up how?"

Harry pulled the gun from the rack, slid back the bolt, and handed it over. "Look at the thing."

Neal turned the rifle over in his hands, examining it. "Weatherby."

"Yeah. Weatherby Vanguard. They make it in Japan."

He read the barrel stamp. ".300 Winchester Magnum."

"Yeah. But Neal, you don't want that gun. The bluing's all messed up, it's got scratches, it's covered with little rust pits. The stock's been beaten to hell. The scope is dinged up too."

"Anything wrong with either? Gun or scope?"

"Oh, no. Both work fine. The scope's a good Leupold. I've shot it myself. Inside of the barrel is near perfect. They just look like hell. A widow sold me her husband's guns. Said he used that one in Alaska a few times. Used it pretty hard, I'd say."

Neal eyed the barrel again. It had a very small taper. A desirable feature for his needs.

Neal worked the bolt a few times. "I'm not real familiar with the .300 magnum caliber. What can you tell me about it?"

Harry rubbed his hands again, perking up. He loved technical gun talk. "The .300 magnum," he intoned sonorously, setting the stage. "Well first of all you've got no less than three different .300 magnums. There's the .300 Weatherby Magnum, the .300 Winchester Magnum and the .300 H&H Magnum. Of the three, the Weatherby cartridge is bit hotter, but not much. Now the interesting thing about the .300 magnums is the power they have at long range. At 300 yards, even a little 150-grain bullet out of that .300 has more energy, in foot-pounds, than a lot of your super-heavy calibers like the .458. At eight hundred yards—now that's nearly half a mile—a 150-grain bullet from a .300 magnum, any of 'em, is cooking along at about the same rate as a hot factory .357 magnum at the muzzle. The comparable .357 bullet would be 158 grains, of course, pretty much the same weight."

Neal worked the bolt again. "I think I want it."

"What, that? Neal, do yourself a favor and get a decent-looking gun."

"Nah, this is perfect. I don't want a great gun, just one that shoots straight. And I'd rather have one that's messed up so I don't have to worry about scratching the damn thing."

Harry looked troubled. "Well...I sort of agree with you, but—"

"This is the one, Harry. If it's for sale."

The crow's feet around Harry's eyes snugged as his disconcerted look turned mischievous. "Well, as a matter of fact it's not." He waited a beat. "I'll give it to you, though."

Neal protested and argued but Harry wouldn't back down. "Not only am I giving you the rifle," he said, lifting four small but heavy boxes off another shelf, "but I'm also giving you these." He held out the boxes of .300 Winchester Magnum cartridges, compelling Neal to take them. "They came with the rifle. Supposed to be the rifle's favorite load according to a tag the guy had attached to the rifle."

"Hell, Harry, let me give you something."

"No way," he growled. "By the way, if you want to shoot that thing any time soon I have an idea. Remember when I said something was coming from Honolulu that you might want to see?"

"Sure, I remember."

"Well," Harry said, waggling his eyebrows exaggeratedly, "it's here. Came in yesterday. Follow me."

Lying on Harry's workbench were several large machined and welded pieces of blackish phospate-treated steel. Harry started grabbing pieces and fitting them together. In a few minutes he had assembled a massive, bizarre-looking rifle that looked to Neal like something built in a high-school metal shop.

"What the hell is that?"

Harry chortled. "It's a test rifle. Hold on." He grabbed another dark metal contraption from a nearby shelf and clamped it to the round steel tube protruding below the barrel of the rifle. It was a set of bipod legs. Spreading the legs apart, Harry propped the rifle upright on the bench.

"Where'd you get it?" Neal asked.

"From a guy I know." With a mild grunt Harry lifted the rifle a couple of inches and set it back down. "Thing's heavy. Twenty-five pounds."

"That's heavy all right," Neal agreed.

"Yeah, but for good reasons. First, the barrel and chamber and bolt are way overbuilt so you can experiment with really hot loads. Don't want it to blow up. And second, the weight minimizes recoil, which makes it less painful if you're doing a lot of shooting in one session. And third, the weight helps minimizes shooter-induced error if you're testing for accuracy.

Neal studied the rifle. "What caliber is it?"

"Well now, that's the thing!" Harry said. He tugged open a drawer and lifted out a box from which he extracted a finger-sized rifle cartridge that resembled a somewhat larger version of .30-06 ammunition. "This is a new cartridge idea the U.S. military is working on. Or was working on, we'll see what happens. They're looking for an anti-materiel sniper round. You know, to disable vehicles or puncture storage tanks or what have you. Of course they're looking at the .50 BMG round but they also wanted something they could shoot out of a lighter rifle."

"Twenty-five pounds is light?"

"Well, remember, this is a test rifle. Anyway, this guy I know owns a company called RAP and he's working on the project. What this is," Harry said, holding up the cartridge, "Is a .416 Rigby case that's been necked down to .338 caliber. It's got a 250-grain bullet stuck in it."

Neal eyed the cartridge. "The Rigby, that's an African hunting cartridge, right?"

"Right. As of now they can't get this big ol' bullet travelling fast enough for the proposed military specs, which is 3,000 feet per second. The case isn't strong enough to hold the pressure. I asked Jerry why not use a lighter bullet made out of steel or pure copper or brass? It would reach the right speed and ought to penetrate armor better than jacketed lead. Anyway, we talked some more and I said I was interested in fooling with the idea and he sent me the rifle and a bunch of brass and bullets."

"It's not, uh...classified or something?" Neal asked.

"Oh, no, not at this point." Harry returned the cartridge to its box. "In fact I know another guy who's writing a magazine article about it."

Neal frowned. "Could you shoot it here in the shop?"

Harry chuckled. "I guess so, theoretically. But the Honolulu PD got me permission to use a target range up in the Saddle."

Neal was familiar with the Saddle. He and Susan had driven through it once, crossing from one side of the island to the other on a sightseeing jaunt. It was a high, flat expanse of land lying between Mauna Loa and Mauna Kea, the two main volcanic peaks on the island. Most of the Saddle was semi-arid, covered with scrub and scattered hardwood trees, but several square miles of the central area was mantled by crumbly black a'a lava that appeared devoid of life. Near the western edge of the Saddle, between the peaks of Mauna Loa and Hualalai, were the ruins of Ahu a Umi, a fifteenth-century monument and would-be capitol city constructed by Umi, first recorded ruler of Hawaii. A few miles from Ahu a Umi was Pohakuba, where the United States Army and the Army Reserve held maneuvers. They had heard the booming reports of artillery pieces as they drove through.

They both stared at the gun. A big, blackish insect perched on the bench. "I'm gonna try it out day after tomorrow," Harry said. "I told 'em I might need an assistant. You want to go with me? As added attractions we can try the suppressor they sent along with this thing. And you can bring your new .300 Win Mag to try out."

Neal didn't have to think about it. "Sure. You got yourself an assistant."

They both walked outside to the car. Harry aimed his pipe at Susan's Datsun. "Your truck still working?"

"Yeah," Neal said, unlocking the car. "But this thing's more comfortable." That was the truth, but it was also true that Harry hadn't seen the burned and shot-up pickup. The less he knew, the better.

Neal said goodbye and drove off. He went three blocks, turned onto the next street, and stopped at the hardware store. Inside, he picked up two more cans of flat black paint and a carton of coarse steel wool, and then went up and down the aisles, searching for the other items on his list.

He found what he was looking for in the electrical section; four-inch pancake junction boxes, shallow dishes of stamped metal with large holes for passing wires through and smaller holes for mounting. He got eight of them. Next he picked out a sack of machine screws, a drill bit, hose clamps, a section of galvanized pipe, three tubes of black silicone sealer, and several threaded rods with nuts and washers to fit them.

He paid for everything, drove to a metal fabricating shop a few blocks away and picked up a length of steel pipe with a four-inch inside diameter, and drove back through Kailua, heading home.

Chapter Thirty

Standing a few feet to the rear of Harry's prone form, Neal watched him squeeze off another round from the big black test rifle. With each shot the blast from the muzzle brake raised a cloud of dust from the ground. Even through his ear protection the report was fearsome.

Neal put his eye to the spotting scope and scrutinized a target two hundred yards away over the baked, barren terrain. "Looks like, oh, a quarter of an inch to the left of the last one."

Harry wrote something in the notebook resting on the tarpaulin on which he was lying and pushed himself to his knees, letting out a bear-like groan. "Well, that's about as good as it gets," he said, pulling off his ear protectors. Beside him on the tarpaulin lay a heap of empty .338 caliber brass. "You want to shoot it again? We could put the suppressor back on if you want."

Neal pulled his own ear protectors down around his neck. "I guess I've had enough if you have." The big booms were getting to him and the odor of burnt powder—enough to send him into a near-swoon of excitement when he was a kid, when it conjured up reed-covered duck blinds or flushing doves from an afternoon pasture—now smelled like death and blood and madness.

Harry got off his knees and stood, grunting some more in the process. "I guess that wraps it up, then."

251

Neal hesitated. "If you wouldn't mind, since we're all through with the .338 I'd like to sight in the Weatherby. I don't know when I'll have another chance like this"

Harry tapped his forehead with his knuckles. "I'm sorry, I flat forgot about that. Sure! Heck yes!" He gestured at the test rifle. "Let's pack this baby away first. And the chronograph unless you want to use it."

"Nope. Just want to zero the scope."

They loaded the big test rifle and its accessory equipment into Harry's Volvo station wagon.

"Okay," Harry said, "what range are you looking at? Two hundred?"

Neal squinted toward the distant targets. "I was thinking about sighting it in at three hundred and fifty yards."

Harry pushed out his lips. "Might not be a bad idea. That rifle shoots pretty flat so anything less than that'll only be a little high. You could memorize the ballistics for shorter shots."

"Exactly what I had in mind. You know—if you have the time I'd like to do a few shots farther than three-fifty. Like five or six hundred yards, maybe more. Just to check the bullet drop."

"What are you gonna do, man?" Harry asked, "Pick off cattle on the Parker ranch from home?"

Neal smiled. "No. But I've heard of people bagging bighorn sheep at a thousand yards. I'd like to see what I can do a ways out."

Harry nodded. "All right. Let's see."

They zeroed in Neal's new rifle and returned to town late in the afternoon. After buying Harry a drink at the Club 53, Neal drove home.

Cruising along the highway, he consciously noted that he was feeling uncommonly good. It wasn't just the beer. The afternoon was beautiful, the temperature perfect. Brassy sunlight on the skyscraping palms, ocean air and the scents of growing things all around. Feeling good like this made him want to ignore the nagging matter at the back of his mind, but not getting sent to prison was a powerful motivation to give it serious attention. Another launch was coming up and he had to weigh new risks.

He settled into the truck's cracked seat as he drove, mentally reviewing the first 'rocket op', as he mentally termed it.

* * *

He had woken up from a nightmare but instantly realized that the mortar round explosions in his dream were actually the slap of waves on rock a few feet from his head.

The bad dream faded as he rubbed his face awake and checked his watch. Half past nine, which meant he'd been hiding in the crack for six hours, since three thirty in the morning. He felt for the small stone that had been digging into his thigh, pried it loose, and tossed it toward the back of the crack.

The crack itself ran through the middle of a truck-sized mass of lava that had split off the cliffs a few yards away. Three days ago he had used the inflatable boat and a pair of binoculars to reconnoiter the peninsula and had selected three possible hiding places, the big split rock being one. His first close look at the crack was in moonlight in the early dawn hours, and it was better than he expected. Wide enough for him to easily fit inside and taller than his head toward the far end, it provided good concealment except from the direction of the short cliffs that rose from the shore up to the fairly level top of the peninsula.

He worked himself to a squatting position and duck-walked to the open end of the crack, where he cautiously poked his head out.

The inflatable, which he had painted flat black, was pretty well hidden. He had pushed it into a crack in the cliff face and the part of the boat that protruded was covered with a piece of black plastic sheeting spray-painted with splotches of gray to match the lava. The outboard motor and gas tank, also painted flat black, lay among a jumble of lava boulders on the shore.

He had camouflaged himself also. Burnt cork on his face and hands. Black socks and a black knit cap. Bluejeans, shoes, and long-sleeved shirt sprayed black.

He retreated to the rear of the crack and stood up to stretch his legs. He took a few deep breaths and lifted his knees one at a time, flexing the muscles to restore circulation. With a glance toward the top of the cliff, he stepped on a hunk of lava wedged into the floor of the crack and pushed up until he could look out and see the ocean.

It was a calm day, the ocean a restless, rippling plane of blue. No boats in the immediate vicinity, but a few could be seen in the distance, maybe three or four miles off. He guessed there would be more spectator boats before liftoff; the upcoming launch had been in the news.

He dropped back into the crack and sat on a boat cushion. He checked the rifle one more time. Safety on. When he tugged back on the bolt lever he saw the gleam of cartridges in the eight-round clip.

Satisfied, he pulled from a plastic garbage sack a device fashioned from heavy steel wire and an amputated section of bluejean leg. It was a brass catcher, a bag to trap spent cartridge cases ejected after firing. Using duct tape, he attached it to the M1's receiver.

When the brass catcher was secured he set the rifle out of the way. He opened another plastic sack and took out an apple, some Saran-Wrapped oatmeal cookies, and a small carton of milk.

When he was through eating he stretched out on his stomach and dipped a handful of seawater from the rear of the crack to rinse his mouth. It felt so good to lie down that he decided to stay where he was. He arranged the food sack to block the wave spray getting in through the crevices, tucked the boat cushion under his head as a pillow, and took a final, uneasy look upward. He could see nothing but a narrow vertical slice of the lava cliff face and a section of the barbed wire coil topping the CSS security fence. He felt relatively secure; a person standing at the edge of the cliff could see him, but they would be outside the security fence.

Resetting his watch alarm for 1:45, he settled down and closed his eyes...

The launch warning siren shattered the afternoon calm like a hammer on glass. He was already alert, but the howling noise triggered a jolt of adrenaline that made him shiver. He checked the time: three-sixteen. The launch had been delayed over an hour. During the morning a series of announcements had come over the launch site public address system but the words had been unintelligible.

He picked up the M1 and duck-walked to the mouth of the crack, the sweat-damp jeans clinging uncomfortably, his breath coming faster. Putting his head out, he looked both directions along the curved shoreline below the cliffs. To the right he could see part of the inlet formed by the projecting peninsula. To the left, toward the tip of the peninsula, his view was blocked by large rocks. He was tempted to move back and stand up for another look around, but the only boats he had seen had been a good three miles away, well out of the flight path.

He stayed crouched where he was. Heat poured off the gray-black mass of the cliff in front of him. He breathed deeply, pressing his shirt sleeve against his forehead; the rough painted cloth blotted sweat poorly.

The siren stopped, replaced by the harsh bleats of the warning horn. He cleared away extraneous thoughts, focusing on the patch of sky above the cliff face. It was a view he had seen in his mind's eye so many times over the last few days that it seemed both familiar and unreal.

When the rocket engine finally ignited he felt it before he heard it, the rock humming under his knees and hands a second or two before the sound hit, sending another adrenaline shock ran through his body and making his heart thud hard. He edged farther toward the mouth of the crack and steadied himself, pushing the rifle's safety off with his trigger finger.

The rumble grew louder. A bile-colored cloud suddenly surged into the sky behind the silvery coil of barbed wire, boiling upwards like a gigantic cauliflower, and an instant later the rocket rose into sight, seeming enormous at this close range. As the exhaust nozzle came into view the noise became a crushing roar. He felt his body trembling under the impact of the sound waves. Screaming into the blast, Neal lifted the M1, aimed, and squeezed the trigger.

A stone seemed to drop into his stomach: the rifle

hadn't fired. He pushed his finger forward against the safety lever again—it was off, as it should be. He tore off the brass-catcher, sighted on the rising rocket, and pulled the trigger again. The rifle bucked and an empty case spun out, bouncing off the lava rock near the top of the crack and dropping down to hit his leg. In an instant he realized that the first shot had actually fired but the rifle's report had been swallowed by the roar of the rocket and the recoil overwhelmed by adrenaline.

Again he put the sights on the accelerating rocket, led it heavily, and squeezed off the remaining rounds. His target was the third stage, the top section where the relatively delicate wiring and piping of the liquid fuel motor and the vehicle's guidance system were covered by a relatively thin metal hull.

The noise level seemed to take another jump and Neal rolled back into the crack, dropping the rifle, covering his ears with his hands. As the exhaust cloud filled the sky and rolled toward him like an angry monster he scrambled to the rear of the crack and lay flat, pressing himself against the wet lava rock. A wave rolled in and sluiced seawater into the fissure, splashing his face.

The roar faded. He rolled over in the crack and saw a patch of blue above.

He stood on the rock inside and peered out. The rocket's smoke had stopped before reaching the edge of the peninsula and was now being swept landward by the breeze. His eyes climbed the exhaust trail until he spotted the Independence, now foreshortened to a spike riding a spot of brilliant flame. The rocket seemed to be functioning perfectly as it angled out over the ocean.

He stepped down and snatched up the binoculars.

257

Through them, he saw the first sign of trouble: a thin line of white vapor streaming down one side of the launch vehicle. In the next instant the rocket became a rushing mass of flame and smoke as it exploded, throwing off chunks of solid fuel that glowed like hundreds of signal flares as they fell.

The solid fuel debris burned out on the long plunge to the sea and pieces of booster casing, visible from the smoke they trailed, hit the water miles from the nearest boats. He stared at the sky a moment longer and then stepped down into the crack and began picking up spent cartridge cases, counting them as he did.

*   *   *

Neal bore down on the gas pedal as the highway climbed, still thinking about the two rocket ops. The morning after the first operation he had bought a *Star-Bulletin* in Kailua and read it as he ate breakfast. The headline at the bottom of page one read *First Hawaii Launch Ends In Failure*. Below, it said *Rocket Destroyed Over Ocean*. The article said that the first launch of an Independence, Concord Space Systems' workhorse payload carrier, had not been a success. The rocket's first stage had burned and separated perfectly, the second stage had ignited without problems, but shortly afterward data transmissions were sent back indicating serious trouble with the third stage fuel system. When the rocket was two miles downrange, 12 miles in altitude, the company's range safety officer had issued the destruct signal. CSS spokesman Bernard Padgett was certain that the source of the rocket's problems would be quickly uncovered and dealt with before the next launch.

Bernard had been wrong about that, Neal reflected

as he drove homeward through the balmy night. The second rocket had also mysteriously malfunctioned and had also been destroyed by the CSS range safety officer.

In most ways the second rocket op had gone more smoothly than the first—ear plugs this time—but then there had been The Woman In The Boat. A few minutes after the second rocket blew up far out over the ocean he had heard an outboard motor start up. And it sounded pretty close. He had belly-crawled out of the crack and peered out. The woman was perhaps four hundred feet away, sitting in an inflatable boat, wearing a big straw hat. She looked in his direction two or three times in a way that told him she had seen something, and that something must have been him. Probably a part of his arm and the business end of the rifle.

Neal had crawled back into the crack and thought hard, and by nightfall had reached a few conclusions.

One, he should have stayed totally inside the crack to shoot, despite the restricted field of fire.

Two, wearing earplugs had its drawbacks—the combination of wave noise and earplugs had prevented him from hearing the boat approaching the peninsula.

Three, he would do a more extensive search for the two cartridge cases missing from the first rocket op. He had searched the crack thoroughly so they must have flown out onto the lava rock shoreline. He hadn't been able to search the shore area because on both operations he had arrived at night and stayed inside the crack until dark and he sure as hell hadn't ever dared to use a flashlight. He would come back in a day or two, when it was light, just a guy just combing the peninsula rocks for *opihi*, and doing it legally since Hawaiian law said that every inch of shoreline below the high water mark was public property.

The fourth conclusion was that, if he shot another rocket it would have to be from somewhere else, not here in this crack. That meant somewhere much farther away, which meant he would need a rifle using a cartridge more powerful than the M1 Garand's .30-06.

The fifth and final conclusion he had reached while waiting in the crack concerned the woman herself. He got only split-second look before ducking down when she turned his way, not enough to identify her behind her sunglasses but enough to see that her hair was gray or silver. So he had an older woman taking pictures from a possibly dangerous location during a rocket launch, and significantly this woman had *not* gone back and told the authorities that she'd seen someone shooting at the rocket. If she had he would now be in custody, since he hadn't moved from the shore of the peninsula for that last few hours as he awaited nightfall. Therefore The Woman In The Boat was no friend of CSS. All of these facts pointed to one person. She had to be Bernice's friend, and Harry's friend, the woman he met at Bernice's party—Violet Gray.

As Neal navigated a long curve on the dark highway he reconsidered his decision to continue punching holes in rockets. Having someone know what he was doing scared him badly, even if she was on his side. He was pretty sure prison would be a bad experience.

He took his foot off the accelerator as a mongoose darted across the highway, its legs a blur.

The bottom line: he probably wouldn't get caught if he shot from the new location. The general plan was already mapped out. The more powerful and accurate rifle required was now in his possession, thanks to

Harry. And after tomorrow the sound suppressor to muffle its report—the parts for which he had bought in the hardware store the other day—would be finished.

Chapter Thirty-One

Sam Kane read the metal numbers affixed to the house, matching them with the ones on the slip of paper in his hand. It was the right place. He stuffed the paper back into his shirt pocket, pulled into the driveway, and parked the Blazer.

It was nice up here in Kona Palisades. The houses sat on big plots of carefully landscaped mountainside. This one was surrounded by hedges and a thick lava-rock wall covered with purple bougainvillea. Kane looked around, smelling the freshly-mowed lawn, taking in the artfully planted flowers, the grove of papaya and mango trees. Nice. Money. So what the hell was this lady doing bouncing around in that little boat?

He would soon find out. He ran a comb through his hair, tightened his tie, and got out.

The woman who answered the doorbell was definitely the same one from Saturday—tall, straight-backed, silver-haired—but up close, through a set of ornate burglar bars, she looked different than he had imagined.

"Yes?" she said, pulling off a pair of gold reading glasses. "Can I help you?"

Kane already had his ID wallet out. He unfolded it and held it up to display the badge. "I'm Captain Kane with the Hilo Police Department. If you don't mind I'd like to—"

"I'm sorry, Captain—Carney?"

262

"Kah-nay." He pronounced the two syllables of the Hawaiian word distinctly.

"Yes. I'm sorry, but if you don't mind I'd like to see your identification again."

He had just put away the wallet. He pulled it out and opened it again, holding it close so she could see. The woman reached through the bars and whisked it out of his hand. "Just a minute, please" she said, and closed the door in his face. He heard the deadbolt being thrown.

Kane stepped back from the door. This sure as hell hadn't happened before. The woman's appearance had flustered him somewhat. He knew Violet Gray was sixty one years old, but her face had retained a youthful look, and the young woman she had been was easily visible. Full lips, smooth jaw line, with only a trace of fullness below the chin. Her eyes especially had escaped the usual depredations of time. They were green, clear, and alert, boring into him from beneath dark eyebrows. Kane was unsettled at feeling an immediate attraction for a woman old enough to be his mother.

In any case his ID was gone. He started to shout something through the door but changed his mind and reached for the doorbell button. The door swung open before his finger made contact and the woman, an impish smile on her face, poked his wallet through the bars. "I'm sorry, Mr. Kane. I live alone and I have to be a little cautious with strange visitors."

Kane took his wallet back, wondering about her choice of words. "That's fine," he said. "Ah, you are Violet Gray, right?"

"Yes, I am."

"Well, Miz Gray, I'd like to ask you some questions if you don't mind."

She smiled patiently. "I won't know if I mind until I know what the questions are, of course. Could you tell me what this is about?"

"Well, sure. Were you out in a boat near the Concord rocket launch site last Saturday?"

Violet Gray studied Kane's face for a moment, not quite frowning. "I'm sorry but you still haven't told me the purpose of your visit, Mr. Kane. I think I'll have to know why you're here before I answer any questions."

He put an understanding smile on his face. "All right."

I'm investigating a report of, uh, possible legal violations during the launch."

The woman gave him a reproachful look. "Oh, now. If you're here about my observing the launch in spite of the Coast Guard warning I'm afraid our talk is over. That was perfectly legal. No laws have been passed prohibiting it so far as I know. Isn't that correct?"

"Yeah, yes, that's correct, Miz Gray. But I'm not here to ask you anything about that." Kane pulled at his fingers, his single nervous habit. "Would you mind if I came in to talk?"

The woman hesitated, then unlocked the wrought iron burglar bars and stepped away from the door. "Please come in."

She directed the police captain to an armchair in the living room. He sat down heavily, straightening his coattail and lapels.

"Would you like something to drink, Mr. Kane? Water? Iced tea?"

"Oh, sure, that'd be great. Tea, I tink. Think."

While she was in the kitchen he looked around the living room. Pictures of sea creatures on the wall, a lot of them weird-looking things, black and blue, with shiny eyes and giant mouths full of needle-like teeth. One picture, off in a corner, was of a man in a brown sweater holding a cigar and laughing. A huge bookcase full of books. He squinted. *The World's Whales. Underwater Photography, Catalogue of Marine Zooplankton*, and next to it, *Catalogue of Marine Phytoplankton*. A tall one called *Octopuses, Squids, and Cuttlefish.*

Strange lady. As for the room, everything was tidy, ordered, feminine, with no current trace of the man on the wall. He guessed he was her husband and that he was dead.

Violet Gray came back and handed the police captain a tall, narrow glass of pale tea. "It's already sweetened a little," she told him. "I hope you don't mind."

He gave her a short smile of thanks. "I like it that way," he said, and thirstily drank half of it down. "Hot out there."

"Yes." The woman sat across from him.

Kane set his glass on a small round table at his elbow and pulled out a notebook and pen. That always made it look like you were serious. "Well, Miz Gray, I'd like to ask you a few questions. Nothing about what *you* were doing, which isn't my business. I, uh, I wonder if you saw anything odd that day."

"Odd?"

"Yeah. Like...did you see anyone when you were out in the boat?"

"Just one moment, Mr. Kane. How did you know I was out in the boat? And how did you find out who I was?"

"Oh, well, I was there watching the launch and I saw you put your boat in the water." He chuckled. "I notice stuff. It's my job, y'know. So when I saw you go out there I wrote down the license plate of your truck."

"I see," Violet Gray said disapprovingly. "Did you watch me when I was in the boat as part of your job?"

Kane wiped his hand on his knee. He was starting to feel like a snoop. "Well, no, not really. I was mainly there to watch the rocket. I had some binoculars and I did see you out there. But getting back to this, did you see anyone?"

"See anyone where?"

Kane paused, watching her face carefully. "Anywhere on CSS property," he said. "Anywhere where they shouldn't be."

Violet Gray held Kane's stare for a long moment, then looked upward, as if thinking back. "No," she said at last. "I didn't see anyone."

Kane studied the floor in disappointment. He sighed heavily, then dropped the notebook and pen into his coat pocket. He drank the remainder of his tea in one gulp and set it back on the table. Why'd they made these damn scrawny tube glasses? Put a couple of ice cubes in 'em and there wasn't enough room left for an ant to piss in. "Well," he said, slapping his knees, "I guess that's it." He shoved himself out of the chair. "Thanks for your help, Miz Gray. And thanks for the tea."

She got up with him, looking perplexed. "That's it?"

"Yep." Kane gave her a pleasant smile. "Sorry to take up your time."

"Oh, no bother at all."

Violet Gray followed the police captain to her front and saw him out. She said, "If I can be of help again just let me know."

"I sure will, Miz Gray. Have a good day." Kane started up his Blazer, which, parked in the summer sun, was living up to its name. He moved the air conditioning lever from NORM to MAX, put the fan on high, and adjusted the vents to blow cold air directly on his face.

It looked like his hunch might pay off. The big question was, why was the lady lying?

He put the car into reverse and backed out of the driveway. If it ever got down to proving things he could have a search warrant sworn out and come back for the pictures she had taken. But right now he was going to drop in on cousin Danny in town and borrow a few things.

*　　*　　*

Kane stepped from the aluminum runabout into thigh-deep water. Keeping one hand on the gunwale, he waded through the seaweed-covered shallows to the bow, grabbed the line, and towed the boat until it bumped against the bottom. When the next wave came he pushed the lightweight craft onto the narrow pebbly beach and secured the bowline to a rock.

The waves were rough today. He was soaked up to his thick waist.

Taking a plastic canteen from the beached boat, Kane walked over to a flat rock, his tennis shoes squishing, and sat. He took long pull from the canteen, surveying the shoreline in both directions. He was approximately halfway from the outermost tip of the rounded peninsula on which the Concord Space Systems launch pad was built. As near as he remembered, this was where Violet Gray had been looking during the launch.

When he felt rested Kane tossed the canteen back into the boat and started off down the wave-lapped stretch of lava, scanning the ground.

It took a little over twenty minutes. As he neared the massive lava boulder that marked his starting point, he saw something gleaming in a crack at his feet. He got on knees and worked his hand into the fissure. The lava dug his skin. When he pulled his hand out he held, pinched between his fingers like a cigarette, a dripping and slightly dented rifle cartridge case. It looked fairly new. He brought it up to his eyes and read the characters stamped around the circumference of the base: *FC 30-06 SPRG.*

Kane pulled a handkerchief from his back pocket and wrapped the brass case in it. He plodded the few feet to the cliff that rose above him and sat down on a chunk of lava. Pulling a pack of Winstons from his shirt pocket, he lit up, taking a long puff into his mouth. The idea of smoke in his lungs was disgusting but he liked the taste.

The woman, Violet Gray. Say she really had taken some pictures that day. Say they actually showed something, like a man with a rifle. With a search warrant he might—if she hadn't destroyed them or hidden them somewhere—get his hands on the photos.

He exhaled and took another puff, squinting up at the sky. There were problems with that approach.

To get the warrant he would have to tell some judge what he thought was going on. The judge just might tell him he was out of his mind, no way could he issue a warrant on evidence that flimsy. And if he did believe him, then what? Something like this was way out of the Hilo Police Department's jurisdiction. The judge would go to the state police, maybe the FBI, who the hell knew. Quicker than a cat craps, everybody would know about it. Just through regular procedures it was bound to get around. Nobody could keep a secret around here. If the guy, Tate, had any brains at all, the first hint of anyone nosing around and he'd forget about doing it again. And that would be that. Case closed. One empty cartridge case meant nothing and the only other evidence, the rockets, were blown all to hell, the pieces sunk under thousands of feet of water.

In any event, Kane thought, once the other authorities found out it would be out of his hands. He would no longer be directly involved. If they somehow made a case against the guy, then sure, good old Sam Kane might get a little snot-dab of credit somewhere way down the line, but only after all the real work was done. Whatever else was true about cops—any kind— they weren't fond of sharing the glory.

But all that was just bullshit. To make it stick they would have to catch the guy in action. Question: had the woman told anybody about what she saw? If she hadn't told anybody yet, a bunch of detectives showing up at her door with a warrant might stir up the neighbors' interest, and if they poked their noses in she might spill the beans to the first sympathetic ear she could find. Maybe someone in...whatsit, GYRO. If that happened word could get back to the shooter somehow.

This was one of those dilemma things, Kane thought. Kind of an all-or-nothing deal. He had to tell somebody but it had to be someone who would keep the secret or else the shooter would be tipped off and quit and they would never catch him or even *see* his ass, which would make the theory of the shooter seem like crap based purely on circumstantial evidence and a hunch. Whoever he told would have to give him proper credit and let him stay involved. If he could actually make the collar, or at least be in on it, that would absolutely clinch the job with CSS.

Kane flicked the end of his cigarette with his thumb to dislodge the growing ash, trying to figure out how to get the maximum mileage out of the situation.

Chapter Thirty-Two

A chime like a single xylophone note sounded in the lobby, announcing the elevator's arrival. As the door slid open Calvin Wilmotte, director of the Concord Space Systems Kona Launch Facility, gestured with his hand. "After you, Captain."

Detective Captain Sam Kane stepped inside and Wilmotte followed, punching in the floor number. The door closed and the elevator rose smoothly, administering a dose of soft Muzak to its occupants.

Wilmotte glanced at his watch. Seeing Kane's eyes on him he said, "Mr. Kamada's a bit of a stickler for punctuality." A half-hearted smile lifted one corner of his mouth. "I like to humor him whenever possible."

Kane nodded noncommittally. Wilmotte wasn't what he had expected from talking to him on the telephone. The director's deep voice gave the impression of size and power, but in person he cut a generally unimpressive figure. Although his suit was expensive, tailored to fit his narrow build, he had a tendency to slump his shoulders and jam his hands into his back pants pockets. Increasing the debits, Wilmotte's nose was red from recent exposure to the sun and stood out like a chili pepper against his sallow complexion. His eyes, dark-lashed and intense behind his glasses, were heavily pouched. He looked like he'd been losing sleep. As if to confirm this Wilmotte volunteered in a confidential tone, "Mr. Kamada's been pretty upset with all this...trouble we've been having. Of course, we've all been concerned."

Kane nodded again. He brushed his fingertips across his midriff to make sure his suit coat was buttoned, clasped his hands behind his back, and stared up at the plastic panels covering the elevator's overhead lights. They looked, he thought, like tray dividers for making little bitty ice cubes.

The elevator halted and let the two men out. They walked down a short hallway to a glass partition whose door read, in gold block letters, Komodo, Inc. Below was a stylized dragon logo, also in gold. On the far side of the glass, an attractive young woman of Japanese parentage raised her head and smiled at Calvin Wilmotte. Her complexion and makeup seemed so unreally perfect to Captain Kane that he had the sudden impression of a store mannequin come to life. The woman pressed a button on her desk and the glass door slid open silently.

"Good morning, Mr. Wilmotte!" the receptionist said perkily. She tilted her head and her straight black bangs swayed like tiny draperies. "How are you today?"

"Fine, thanks. Ah—Tina, this is Mr. Kane."

The receptionist held out a slim white hand. "Very good to meet you, Mr. Kane."

Kane took her hand in a soft grip, smiling as though in pain. He always felt awkward shaking hands with women.

"Tina," Wilmotte said, glancing at his watch again, "Mr. Kane and I have a meeting with Mr. Kamada at ten."

"Yes, of course. Let me buzz him." She lifted her phone and stabbed the intercom button with a red-nailed finger. "Mr. Kamada, Mr. Wilmotte and Mr.

Kane are here...All right, very well." She set down the receiver and smiled up at the men. "You can go right in." As they started away she said, "Nice to meet you, Mr. Kane," and gave him a brief display of teeth like cultured pearls. Kane replayed his handshake smile and followed Wilmotte toward a set of heavy wooden doors.

Kane's first sight of Hideo Kamada was from across a large and astonishingly white office. Kamada rose from a white leather chair as though lifted by helium balloons and waited, a stocky, blank-faced, gray-suited statue, as his visitors waded across the snowy pile carpet.

"It is good to see you...Calvin," Kamada said in a deep monotone. He shook the director's hand, released it, and swiveled his arm sideways like a robot Santa. "Captain Kane. I am pleased to meet you."

Kane gave Kamada his best eyeball-to-eyeball look. "Nice to meet you, too." Crisp, precise enunciation. He wondered if Kamada, a Jap, would be able to appreciate this.

Kamada pointed to the chairs in front of his desk. "Please sit."

Kane sat. He watched Kamada descend into his own white leather chair, noticing that the man didn't adjust his pants or fool with his coat or move around to get comfortable once he touched down. He just sat.

Kamada began the meeting with no further formalities. "Captain Kane. Calvin has told me you have a theory about what is causing our rockets to fail. Please, tell me."

Kane shifted in his chair, sitting up a fraction straighter. "Well, I have to tell you up front that I don't know anything," he cautioned. "It's what I think."

"Please tell me what you think."

The police captain experienced a sudden flash of fear. The possibility that he had committed a monumental blunder in coming here paralyzed his tongue momentarily, but just as quickly the anxiety passed. His shoulders, which had somehow gotten all bunched up, relaxed. It was too late now.

"All right. I'll tell you what I think."

Watching his diction, Kane repeated the speech he had rehearsed over the last week. He laid out the facts in chronological order, breaking into the sequence only to emphasize a step of logic. To maintain an appearance of professionalism he used no names, referring to "the suspect" and "the female witness." He didn't mention the cartridge case because he didn't want to hand it over to anyone at this point, but instead claimed he had found "signs" that someone had been hiding in the rock crack. As he talked he was aware of becoming more and more sure of himself even as his story sounded less and less plausible, merely a collection of interesting circumstantial evidence. Curiously, he was not bothered by this.

"I have to say again," Kane concluded, "this is all just a theory, a possibility." The police captain laced his fingers together and laid them in his lap, watching the man across from him. He thought he was pretty good at reading other people's thoughts but he was running into a brick wall here. Kamada had sat as motionless as a corpse during the entire recitation, his expression an unyielding neutral. The only slight change was in his eyes. They had gradually narrowed from thin black slits to extremely thin black slits. Kane was reminded of a cat feigning sleep while the birds hopped a little closer.

Calvin Wilmotte, unlike his superior, seemed to

have taken on a supply of excess energy. From the corner of his eye Kane saw the man tap a finger on his palm, cross his legs, scratch his temple with a forefinger. The launch site director cleared his throat, Adam's apple pumping, but did not speak.

Kamada's eyes widened a degree and his nearly lipless mouth moved just enough to release the weirdly flat sound of his voice. "Captain Kane. Have you reported any of these things to the police department."

"No, I haven't."

"Have you reported them to any other authorities."

"No."

"Why have you not."

Kane hesitated, wondering again if Kamada was aware that he had applied for the Chief of Security position at the Kona Launch Facility. He should have asked Wilmotte before. "Well," he said, "I didn't tell anybody for a couple of reasons. In the first place it's all circumstantial, like I said. There's no real proof of anything. I don't want to start saying these things, accusing someone, you know, and be wrong. In any case all the investigating I've done has been on my own time. I couldn't use police time on something that was so uncertain."

Kamada nodded his head with hypnotic slowness.

"And there's other reasons," Kane continued. "Hilo, you know, it's a pretty small place. In the police department everybody knows everybody pretty good. People talk. If this got out you'd never catch this guy. He'd hear about it from somebody and stop." He leaned forward in his chair, holding the pause for effect. "But maybe he just stops for a while, you know. Maybe he decides to shoot your rockets again sometime. The thing is, you won't ever know when.

You'll always be wonderin' if it's going to happen again." He sat back. "That's why I think we need to catch the guy in the act."

He had decided it would be good to say we.

Kamada kept his eyes on the police captain for several seconds. "Captain Kane," he said. "I am quite grateful to you for telling us your...thoughts. It is even more...gratifying, since you do not believe your theory strong enough to involve the police. But in a sense, it appears that you are holding the...safety of Concord Space Systems above, perhaps, your own job."

Kane played Kamada's game, saying nothing.

"Mr. Wilmotte says that you insisted upon telling these things to me, personally."

"That's right, I did. As long as I was sticking my neck out—you know, taking a risk—I wanted to be sure you got everything straight. And to cut down on the chances of this being mentioned where it shouldn't be."

Kamada nodded once. His eyes shrank to slits again, and there was another wait. At length he said, "Perhaps you have certain ideas about stopping this person."

"Yes," Kane replied. "I do."

"Which will involve the police."

"Not at first, no. Not unless this guy shows himself. From what I know, I think we could handle it with your own security people."

"You wish to be a part of the...work, then."

"I'd like to very much. But unofficially. Like an observer or something. I know a lot about the island and I have some ideas about how to set this thing up. A plan."

Kamada turned to Wilmotte. "Do you have an opinion on this matter...Calvin."

276

Wilmotte cleared his throat and uncrossed his legs. "Well, Hideo, I think—with no slur on Ben Hurley's abilities intended—we have an expert here who's willing to help, who's gone out on a limb for us, so perhaps we should take advantage of the opportunity. We sure can't afford to lose another rocket. About going through regular channels, I would defer to Captain Kane's judgment. A leak would probably kill our chances of catching this person, whoever he is. And as Captain Kane pointed out, he could cause us much worse trouble down the line. Anyway there's nothing illegal with us doing our own security work and we can call in the police at any time we feel it's appropriate."

Kane watched Kamada for a sign. The man's mouth worked slowly, as though he were chewing something about the size of BB with his front teeth. His eyes, glinting like wet stones, slid toward the launch director and clung.

"Calvin. Does Laurance Schaefer know of this."

"No," Wilmotte said. "As far as I know, the only people who know are myself, Captain Kane, and yourself."

"Good. I will inform Mr. Schaefer myself. Captain Kane. If you would soon draw up an outline of your plans for capturing this person, I would like to see them. Please include any equipment requirements. You can deliver the plans to Mr. Wilmotte and they will be brought over here by...courier."

This last word, Kane noticed, caused Kamada unusual difficulty. He worked his jaws oddly in saying it, then wiped the tip of his tongue over his lips, like a lizard sweeping in the antennae of a freshly-caught roach. Kane was so distracted by the performance that he almost forgot to respond. "Sure, fine," he said hastily.

"Captain Kane. What days are your weekly...holidays."

"Ah—Sunday and Monday, usually."

Kamada consulted a small calendar on his desk. "Our next launch will be in...eighteen days. Monday, June twenty-four."

"Excuse me, Hideo," Wilmotte broke in, "but our next launch is scheduled for July 10. We're still going over data from the last shot, and if we have to make any major changes it could slip further."

Kamada turned and fixed Wilmotte with a stare. "The next launch will be Monday, June twenty-four. I believe we have discovered the source of our problems. The facts fit together, ours and Mr. Kane's. There is no point in delay. Captain Kane. Please draw up your...requirements, and give them to Mr. Wilmotte."

Kane started to ask a question but the meeting was apparently at an end, as Kamada levitated from his chair and held out a hand. "I thank you for coming to us. Captain Kane. If we may assist you in the future, please come to me."

Kamada walked the men to the door of the office. Calvin Wilmotte departed first, and as Kane was about to pass through the door he felt a touch on his forearm.

"Please pardon me. Captain. I wish to know the name of the man you suspect. Be certain that I will tell no one."

Kane had expected Kamada to ask earlier and he had intended to profess ignorance, but it no longer seemed to matter. Keeping his voice low enough stay within the office, he said, "It's just my theory, like I said. You probably know this guy, because of where he lives. His name is Neal Tate."

Chapter Thirty-Three

The watch alarm beeped at two o'clock in the morning. Neal fumbled at his wrist and pinched the button, then rolled over on his back. The room was in total darkness except for a slice of silver moonlight slanting across the wall. He stared at it, letting his mind wake up, and then threw off the single sheet and got out of bed. He dressed quickly, putting on an old pair of army fatigues and a dark green shirt with long sleeves.

In the kitchen he lit a candle and ate a quick breakfast of oatmeal stirred into yogurt. Then he went to work.

The moon was nearly down by the time the Datsun was loaded. Standing beside the car's open door, he pulled a list from his pocket and ran a finger down it, mentally checking off entries. Satisfied, he lit the slip of paper with a butane lighter and set it on the ground, watching until the orange flames died and became winking spots of light that gradually faded out.

A cloud overhead reflected enough moonlight to see by. Keeping the car lights off, he backed down the bumpy half-finished road, the pale disks of tree stumps disappearing beneath the rear window.

A quarter mile past the end of Concord Space Systems' fence on Mokolea Road he slowed the car to a crawl and aimed a flashlight into the trees. When he saw a red gleam he stopped and got out, leaving the

Datsun's motor running, and checked out the area again. It looked good. On the way back to the car he pulled off the bicycle reflector he'd nailed to the tree three days ago. He drove off the road into the dense brush, killed the engine and lights, and went back with the flashlight to straighten up the bushes he had run over, fluffing their branches out.

After laying his gear on the Datsun's roof he sat in the front seat and blackened his face with burnt cork. When this was done he popped the car hood, wiggled the ignition coil cable until it was loose, and re-closed the hood. He locked the vehicle's doors and hid an extra set of keys at the base of a nearby tree.

Neal strapped on the rucksack, slung his new Weatherby rifle over his shoulder, fitted a pair of clear safety goggles over his eyes, and set off down the mountainside, holding his hands up to fend off branches. When he was well away from the road he switched on the flashlight again.

It took almost forty minutes to make the long curve down the mountainside and intercept the CSS perimeter fence. He followed it farther downward, the going made easier by the narrow corridor CSS had cleared along the fence line, and in a few minutes came to the first navigational checkpoint, a decisive outward curve of the fence. This was part of a large zigzag in the property line that showed on a map of the launch site in a CSS brochure he'd gotten from Bernice. He continued downhill, passing the blurred shapes of *KAPU* signs every few yards, until he came to the second leg of the zigzag.

Neal unslung the rifle and rucksack and scouted the fence line until he found a natural dip in the ground that passed beneath the fence. Using a dead tree branch, he levered up the fence fabric and propped the gap open with a rock. He pushed the rucksack and rifle through, then wormed his way beneath the barrier on his back. On the other side he pulled the prop rock out and leaned a dead branch against the fence to mark the spot.

Switching to a smaller flashlight, he moved through the woods on a line roughly perpendicular to the fence. The land began to fall away on a steady incline. After twenty minutes of pushing through the trees and bushes he saw lights blinking through the leaves. He put away the flashlight and changed course, heading directly for them. The land began to drop off even more steeply and within minutes he came to an opening in the trees at the edge of the valley.

Neal crouched down and moved forward until he had a complete view of the Concord Space Systems Kona Launch Facility. To his left a string of lights snaked downhill along the main road at the bottom of the valley. The road wound past a mobile home used for the launch site construction office. Farther down were two small tilt-wall buildings, each with a tiny illuminated dirt parking area. Farther below them, in a huge step blasted into the rock, was the large metal building used for rocket reassembly. Sodium vapor lamps mounted on poles around the building made its sky-blue color a dirty gray. From the door of the reassembly building a separate road—wide, smooth, and well lit—traced an *S* down to the small peninsula at the foot of the valley where the actual launch pad was located. The rocket stood beside the gantry in middle of a cleared area the size of a football field.

Three hundred yards uphill from the rocket was the launch-control center, a low, bunker-like structure.

Neal made out two tiny figures standing in the asphalt-covered parking area at the rear. He pulled out his binoculars and focused on them. The man to his left, thin looking, was dressed in a pale short-sleeve shirt with tie. The other, from his clothing and the dark shape of a holster on his hip, was obviously a security guard. Sitting beside the guard was the unmistakable black form of a Doberman Pinscher.

Neal turned the binoculars toward the floodlit launch pad. At the base of the gantry, two men in light blue coveralls moved a large black cable while another wheeled something on a dolly to the far side of the rocket. He spotted another security guard, this one standing near the edge of the concrete pad. As he watched, the man raised a walkie-talkie to his mouth.

Neal tucked the binoculars away. Keeping trees and bushes between himself and the valley floor, he moved down the side of the ridge. When he estimated his distance from the rocket to be about five hundred yards he began to look for a place to hide. A short search produced a promising spot—a mound of weathered lava protruding from the ground in the middle of a grove of small trees. The downhill side of the mound was bordered by thick brush but the uphill side was relatively open.

He hunkered down and peered over the rocky mound and through the trees until he had a fix on the blinking red gantry light. The angle looked good. He unslung the rifle and rucksack, pulled the knife from his belt sheath, and crawled atop the lava mound to hack at the branches until he had cleared a vertical swath in the leaves. Dropping behind the rock again he checked and saw that he had a clear view of the floodlit rocket from its midpoint up.

Neal set the timer on his watch. He moved a few rocks out of the way and stretched out along the base of the mound.

The watch beeper woke him hourly. Each time, he turned it off, listened for a moment, and reset it.

*   *   *

The watch beeper woke him again just before sunrise. Neal pinched it off and rolled into a sitting position. His stomach was sour, his neck hurt, his muscles were stiff, his hip bone throbbed from pressing into the ground, and his eyes felt full of grit.

He massaged his face until it felt like his own, then dragged the rucksack over to him. A long drink from the water bottle soothed his stomach. He pulled a can of kippered herring from the sack, changed his mind, and traded it for two Beef Stix. It was too early for dead fish.

After masticating the last bite of Beef Stix into submission and washing it down with water he stowed the wrappers and opened the rucksack's main compartment. Inside was a blanket-wrapped bundle, which he unrolled to reveal a black metal cylinder almost two feet in length. The cylinder, perforated with dozens of holes and studded with machine screw heads, was capped at both ends with pancake junction boxes that showed the tips of four threaded rods. He had tested this home-made sound suppressor on the big Weatherby only once, out in the yard. The rifle's normal ear-splitting boom had been reduced to a powerful thudding hiss surrounding the bullet's sharper sonic crack. Still loud, but no match for the rocket's overwhelming roar.

Neal dug into the rucksack and pulled out a length

of galvanized pipe and a section of rubber hose. He slid the hose over the rifle's sightless barrel and fastened it with a hose clamp near the stock's fore-end, then screwed one end of the galvanized pipe into the suppressor and tightened it with a pair of Vise-Grips. He worked the other end of the pipe, which was split with a hacksaw, onto the hose-covered barrel and used more clamps to hold it firmly in place. Last, he put three cartridges into the rifle's magazine and snapped the hinged floor-plate shut.

He drank some more water, stowed the bottle, set the watch timer, and lay down again, pillowing his head on one arm. The launch was scheduled for one p.m., over six hours away.

* * *

"Further in that direction."

Neal's eyes snapped open to see blue sky. He held still and listened, his heart beating hard. The shout had come from downhill. Rolling onto his belly he elbow-crawled to the bushes at the end of the rock and worked his way into the leaves, where he raised himself to his knees and carefully moved the branches aside.

Fifty yards downhill a man wearing the blue shirt and khaki pants of a CSS security guard was speaking into a walkie-talkie and making pushing motions in the air. Neal craned his neck and spotted the object of his signals—another guard, standing about two hundred yards down the valley.

Neal eased the branches back in place and watched the men through gaps in the leaves. The first guard holstered his walkie-talkie and started uphill, and as he did Neal spotted something that gave him a prick of fear: the guard was followed by a leashed Doberman. It was a different dog from last night. That one had been black with brown underneath and this one was a deep rust all over.

The prick of fear became a general adrenaline tingle as the guard kept climbing, heading toward his hiding place as though drawn by a homing signal. The glossy, pointed head of the Doberman appeared behind his legs every few steps, tongue dangling like a strip of pink liver. Neal estimated that if they kept coming they would be on him in about a minute, and the prognosis from that point on was poor. When the guard saw him it was easily conceivable that he would let go of the Doberman's leash and reach for his gun, and it was easily conceivable that the dog would go bat-shit and attack. Neal dropped down and silently backed out of the brush, spurred on by the image of the seal-sleek creature sinking its fangs into his own personal ass as he scrambled uphill.

He unzipped the back pocket of the rucksack and pulled out a pistol, a battered Ruger .22 auto, and held it against his stomach to muffle the sound as he worked the action and chambered a round. Whatever else happened, the dog wasn't going to bite his ass. He shouldered the pack and slung on the rifle, cumbersome with the heavy suppressor, and crouched down behind the lava to wait, pistol in hand. His watch timer suddenly beeped and he frantically clawed at his wrist to shut it off.

The security guard's voice came from below a few moments later. "You don't smell nothin', do you girl? No ma'am. No ma'am."

The dog answered with a plaintive whine.

"Hang on, girl. Hold it there. Now sit. Good girl." There was a pause, followed by the hiss of radio static.

"Hey, Jimbo, you hear me?"

The hiss jumped up a notch in volume and a garbled voice responded. From the sound, Neal guessed the security guard was about thirty feet away. He looked up at the top of the trees; the breeze was blowing from the sea. The dog might miss his scent if it didn't come closer. Good thing he hadn't opened the herring.

The guard spoke into his radio again. "Jimbo, you see where I am? Come on up here." There was a pause and then the guard said to the dog in baby talk, "Yeah, you's gettin' hot, huh? Gettin' *tirsty*, huh, girl?"

Neal waited, crouched down in the brush, sweat running into his eyes. Minutes passed. The bushes rustled and there was another impatient dog whine. A new voice said, "Any boogymen, Larry?"

"Nope. Whoo, it's a hot one. I'm sweatin' my ass off."

"Huh. That'll take some time."

"Hey, fuck you, Jim. Want me to sic this dog on your pecker?"

The new man laughed again, less heartily. "Sure, Larry. Give 'im the word. I'd shoot that fuckin' dog so fulla holes he'll whistle in the breeze."

"It's a *she*, bird-brain." The first guard rolled out a long sigh. "Well, hell, Jimbo. I guess we oughta get on with it. Let's head up the valley. We can spread out some. How 'bout you take the high road?"

Neal heard the whisk and slap of branches against their pants as they set off. One set of footsteps came closer and he backed to the far end of the rock. The dogless guard came into view no more than five steps distant. He was moving away, walking at a slight angle up the side of the valley. Pressed against the rock, Neal watched the guard's sweat-stained back disappear behind a tree. He waited another five minutes and then moved to the rear of the rock. He shucked the rifle and pack, got out the binoculars and crept into the bushes again.

Through the glasses he saw the security men moving up the valley at a quick pace. He watched as they finished a wide sweep that took them back to the road.

Neal crawled out of the bushes and sat down with his back to the big rock, shaken. The guards' conversation gave the impression that their search wasn't standard procedure. He checked his watch: twelve twenty-six.

The minutes crept past as he sat thinking. Having come this far, he was reluctant to back out now. When his watch showed twelve forty he decided to go ahead with the mission.

*   *   *

A CSS security man in a light blue Suzuki Samurai drove Captain Sam Kane to the launch control center. Kane saw Calvin Wilmotte waiting outside in the rear parking area, squinting up at the sky. Kane was sweating heavily, even with his coat off and his tie loosened, but Wilmotte looked fresh in his suit and tie. He had been in the air-conditioned control center all morning.

"Nothing, I presume?" Wilmotte said as the police captain climbed from the cramped vehicle.

Kane reached a hand around and tugged his damp shirt away from his back. "No. Nothin' so far."

Wilmotte considered. "Well, what do you think then? How much of the site has been searched?"

"Everywhere I think he might be. And some places

288

he probably wouldn't be."

Wilmotte stepped closer to the low-roofed control center, putting himself in a wedge of shade that shielded his body but left his head in the sun. "Well, hmm, Captain. How about—" He cleared his throat and glanced furtively around, lowering his voice. "How about the men waiting on Mokolea Road?"

"I talked to 'em again about fifteen minutes ago," Kane said. "Neither man saw anything that looked like the suspect's pickup. But maybe he already left or maybe he went on foot this time."

"I guess that's possible." Wilmotte patted his palm with the back of his other hand. Kane saw tiny droplets of sweat, fine as dew, forming on his bald head. "You know," Wilmotte said, "maybe this...could your theory be wrong?"

"Yeah. Could be."

"But you really don't think so."

"No," Kane said flatly.

Wilmotte looked up at the sky. "Well, I don't know what to think." When Kane offered no response, he gestured toward the control center door. "You know, Captain, I've been discussing this with Mr. Kamada. We appreciate all your efforts, but of course we can't live in fear of a hypothetical saboteur forever. We can't slip the schedule much more. If nothing turns up in the next..." He looked at his watch. "...hour and a half, we're going ahead with the launch." He said this as though breaking bad news. "The media people are here. We've got to let them know if it's on or not. Do you have any suggestions at this point?"

Kane shrugged. "No. Everything *looks* okay. But I got a bad feeling."

Wilmotte gave the police captain a look of

apprehension tinged with disapproval. "I certainly hope you're wrong. Well—I've got to get back inside. Would you like to speak with Mr. Kamada?"

Kane shook his head. Kamada wasn't the kind of guy you wanted to chat with when you weren't producing results. "I think I'm gonna go down and get on the boat," he said. "I'll just stick with the plan."

Wilmotte smiled, somewhat sourly. "You'll be keeping in touch with us on the radio, correct?"

"Yeah. I'll call back in an hour or so."

"All right. Pending your next report, then, the launch is on for four o'clock."

* * *

Kane waited for lift-off at sea in a sixteen-foot Starcraft with a fifty-horse outboard that CSS had provided at his request. Two other men were with him in the boat, which floated a few hundred yards to the south of the launch site peninsula. The security guard with the pockmarked face and luxuriant waxed mustache had been introduced as "Duffy" McDuff. McDuff wore his full guard's uniform, including gun, cap, and shiny black leather brogans, but in contrast to his un-nautical appearance, Kane observed that the man handled the boat's controls with practiced ease. Now that they were stopped, McDuff stood near the driver's seat with one hand on the windshield, scanning the shoreline.

Only moments after meeting the second man in the boat—Howard something, a big, fuzzy-haired, red-faced haole with a congenital surly look—Kane had him categorized as a Born Asshole. Howard wore a military-cut green denim shirt, sleeves rolled up to expose his thick forearms, and brand-new camouflage fatigues tucked into G.I. jungle boots. His gear included a small knapsack and a black web belt holding a stainless-steel .45 auto and extra magazines in pouches. Howard's exact position in the company had not been made clear, which didn't sit well with Kane. He had both an instinctive and a professional aversion to mysteries. Howard, who had kept to himself on the boat and during the foot search of the shore, now sat in the stern with his swollen arms folded over his chest, glaring at the valley. A couple of times Kane had been tempted to tell him to use the other pair of binoculars but he'd resisted the urge. Although the guy had followed his orders so far, it was clear how he felt about it.

Kane continued his own binocular search. There was a good view of the entire valley from the boat, which was the only vessel near the peninsula. A red and white Coast Guard cutter patrolled the waters about two miles to the north, and half a mile beyond the cutter several boats sat on the ocean's rolling surface. The cautionary request to maintain a safe distance from the launch site had been taken to heart, with some further incentive provided, no doubt, by the last two failed launches.

Kane checked his watch. The rocket was scheduled to go in twenty minutes. He started to raise the binoculars again when his walkie-talkie crackled.

"Recon 2 to Seaview. Over."

Kane grabbed the radio unit. "Yeah, Seaview here." The voice hissing through the little speaker sounded anxious. "Yes, ah, Seaview. I'm at the aforementioned surveillance location and the target vehicle is here. I repeat, target vehicle is here. Over."

This meant the pickup with the holes in it was

parked at the end of the new road on Tate's property. As a final precaution he had sent a man in to check on it. "Okay," Kane replied. "Now listen. I want you to go to the residence of the owner at your surveillance site. You know what I'm talking about?"

The voice hissed back uncertainly, "Well, affirmative, I believe, but perhaps you could, ah...clarify. Over."

They'd been talking this secret-agent crap all morning and Kane was tired of it. He could clarify all right. "Go to the guy's fucking house, okay? I want you to walk—no, run—to the guy's house. He don't have any 'no trespass' signs. Go to the door and knock on it and say you're there to remind him of the launch. Like it's a—a courtesy or somethin'. If he ain't there, call me immediately. If he's there and gets pissed off, just apologize. Be nice and then leave. Don't say anything else. When you're out of sight, call me. Hey, Recon 1, you there?"

A different voice came over the walkie-talkie, crisp and sing-songy. "Ahhh, roger, Recon 1 here, Seaview. Ahhh, Over."

These guys, Kane thought. Too much TV. "You hear all that, what I told Recon 2?" he asked.

"Roger. That's affirmative, Seaview. Over."

"Good. Get in your car and go pick up Recon 2 when he comes out to the road. Go now."

Without waiting for confirmation, Kane dropped the walkie-talkie on the seat and picked up his binoculars. He started scanning again. He was going to look damn dumb if Tate was home.

*   *   *

The dull metallic voice from the launch site PA

system seemed to have been droning on for hours when it finally broke through the layers of heavy sleep. Neal opened his eyes and struggled into a sitting position, brushing an ant off his cheek. He was pouring sweat. His upper body was in the shade but his legs, exposed to the sun, felt microwaved. He checked his watch. Three fifty-four. Time was not flying by. Moving sluggishly, he pulled his legs into the shade and pushed the rucksack between himself and the rock to make a backrest, then shuffled his rear end around to get the right spot on the rocks. Just as he got comfortable the PA came to life again, but this time the words had a hard-edged insistence.

"All personnel clear the launch area. We have T-minus six minutes. Clear the launch area."

Neal grabbed the binoculars from the rucksack and crawled to the end of the rock. Through the glasses he saw that there was no one near the rocket, the third stage of which was now releasing a small plume of white vapor. Nor was there anyone anywhere on the peninsula. He hopped to the other end of the rock, pushed through the bushes, and glassed the upper valley and launch control center. It was the same. No vehicles moving, no one in sight.

The launch warning siren suddenly blared, filling the valley with its long, rising whoops.

"Holy shit."

He scuttled back behind the rock. Moving as fast as possible, he fished the foam protectors from his pocket and fitted them into his ears. He snatched up the rifle, worked the bolt, and shoved the rucksack onto the flat top of the rock. With the forestock lying across the makeshift rest, he settled into a kneeling position and found the rocket's third stage through the rifle scope.

His homemade sound suppressor made the rifle end-heavy and filled the bottom of the scope's sight picture with a fuzzy black hump, but the crosshairs were clear. He picked the top letter in the rocket's *CSS* logo as his mark and waited, his heartbeat rhythmically jogging the view through the scope.

*　　*　　*

Kane's walkie-talkie came to life a moment before the final countdown horn began its harsh bleat. *"Recon 2 to Seaview. Recon 2 to Seaview."*

Kane snatched up the unit. "Yeah. What you find?"

"Nobody home. We knocked for a while and no one answered, so we went around the whole place tapping on the windows and looking in, just to be sure. I hope that was okay."

"You did good," Kane said. "Now get the hell outta there and join up with Group 2."

"Right. Over and out."

Kane felt a little better. He checked his watch again. Forty seconds to go.

*　　*　　*

When the rocket engine ignited Neal felt the tension drain from his muscles. His view through the scope steadied as the exhaust blast, diminished by the earplugs, built to a rumbling peak. The big rocket seemed to shudder slightly and then it lifted off. Neal followed his aiming point smoothly, letting the crosshairs glide upward past the rocket, and then squeezed the trigger. There was a deep thudding sound and the rifle stock sledgehammered his shoulder, causing the rocket to disappear from view for an instant. He kept his eye to the scope, worked the bolt,

294

found the rocket again, and fired another round. He fired the last round hastily from an awkward crouched position and the recoil booted him onto his rear end.

It was over. Neal dragged the rucksack off the rock and used the tools from the back pocket to detach the suppressor. He shoved it in the sack, followed by the binoculars, and got to his knees to locate the three ejected cartridge cases. Only when they were safely in his back pocket did he look upward.

The Independence rocket was already small, going strong. He watched until the exhaust cloud from the launch pad blocked his view.

The cloud itself drifted uphill and was on him in moments, a thick yellow miasma that made his eyes and nose burn. He grabbed up the rucksack, slung the gun over his shoulder, and ran. The plan to stay in place until dark no longer seemed smart, and the noxious cloud provided a handy smokescreen for an early exit. He didn't know how long he could have breathed it anyway.

Darting from tree to tree, Neal worked his way uphill, halting every few yards to make sure he didn't outrun the smoke, but before he reached the trees it had dissipated into a light veil. He stopped and lay flat on the ground, lungs laboring and throat closing.

Just before the smoke thinned out completely he pushed himself up and made a final dash into the woods.

*   *   *

Sam Kane ran his binoculars over the body of the Independence twice, watching for anything unusual during the liftoff. Nothing. He shifted to the sides of the valley, covering it with overlapping sweeps. It would be a long shot from there but a sniper would have good cover.

Kane heard the sound of the rocket intensify. He put the binoculars back on the Independence as it rose from the swelling exhaust cloud on a fat pillar of fire and climbed into the sky. He still saw nothing amiss so he switched back to the valley and began another sweep. The drifting exhaust smoke thwarted his surveillance of the valley's north side. He shifted to the south, scoured it from top to bottom, and returned to the north side. High up, the cloud of smoke thinned momentarily, enough for him to spot a small figure disappearing into the trees.

Chapter Thirty-Four

Neal slowed down in the trees to suck air into his lungs. He tried to catch a glimpse of the rocket through the branches but the leaves were too thick.

He slumped to the ground where he was, suddenly feeling weak and nauseated. Sliding the rifle and pack off, he laid his head on his knees, forcing himself to take slow, deep breaths

The queasiness abated. A drink from the water bottle washed away the Beef Stix-flavored belches

He used a piece of soap and more water to remove the burnt cork from his face. Cleaning his face sharpened his desire to get out of the woods and back home. He wanted to soak in the tub. Nice, hot water, dosed with Dr. Bronner's Almond Scented All-One-God Essene Rabbi Pure Castile Soap. Not only would this feel excellent, it would—if he remembered correctly—*clean body-mind-soul-spirit instantly*. Exactly what he needed. He rested a few more minutes and then shouldered the rucksack and started toward the exit point.

*   *   *

Neal spotted two CSS security guards through a break in the trees and ducked behind a vine-swathed stump. The two men stood by the fence a few feet from his marker stick, one holding the leash of a

297

straining Doberman, the other speaking into a walkie-talkie.

He retreated quietly, moving farther into the woods, and headed toward the sea. After a few hundred yards he changed directions and veered right to intersect the fence again. When he felt he was close to it he slowed his pace and made a cautious approach.

Another security guard was stationed by the fence, this one with a German shepherd for company. The guard was picking his nose but seemed otherwise alert, looking up and down the fence line. Neal backtracked a safe distance and continued toward the sea.

His third try was also a strikeout. Another guard, this one without a dog.

The next attempt produced two more guards and another Doberman. Neal retreated into the woods again. It looked like the entire north boundary had been staked out, which indicated that he had been seen or had given himself away somehow. If that were true they might be planning an active search. He altered his course, moving as quickly and silently as possible straight toward the launch site valley.

At the rim of the valley, where the trees thinned out, he crawled through a thick patch of grass and raised his head until he could see below. It wasn't good. Blue-shirted guards with riot batons dangling from their belts were making their way up the slope in a broken line. He counted five more dogs moving up with them, three Dobermans and two German shepherds.

Fighting off a rising panic, Neal thought out his options. The main priority was to get off CSS property and the north fence still seemed the quickest route out. He could worry about being arrested or charged later. They might not know who he was and they might not be certain of what he was doing.

He crawled back into the trees.

The next fence approach was promising. Two guards were in sight, one posted within shouting distance uphill and the other a stone's throw downhill, but there were no dogs. Between them a shallow, weed-choked ravine appeared to intersect the fence line. Neal slipped through the trees to the ravine, dropped to his stomach, and crawled.

He tried to move silently. Grass and branches snagged his clothes, raked his face and hands. He had made it almost to the fence before he saw it was a bust. The ravine he was crawling in had been filled with stone and cement where it passed under the security fence, and the fence fabric itself was anchored to metal rods. He had a pair of wire cutters in the rucksack, but cutting through without being seen would be impossible. He crawled backwards, an alligator in reverse, until he was in the trees again.

The half-exposed roots of a big *ohia* seemed like welcoming arms, and he sank into their embrace, his back against the trunk, catching his breath. Sweat ran down his face and arms, making scores of tiny scratches sting. Time was running out. The launch site was big but a systematic search by the men and dogs would probably flush him out.

He rested a few moments longer and pulled himself up. There was nothing he could do at this point but keep trying the fence.

He had gone only a few steps when a faint sound reached his ears. He sank into a crouch, listening, and the noise came back again, clear enough to recognize. A helicopter. The patting of the rotor grew louder and he caught a glimpse of the distant machine through the branches. It was small bubble-canopied Hughes.

Things were not looking up. He kept moving.

He checked for exit points half a dozen more times, always travelling farther downhill, but there was no place that wasn't being watched over by the security men. The cleared corridor and the relative straightness of the fence line enabled each guard to surveille a lengthy section. He couldn't just climb the fence and make a run for it because of the razor wire coil on top.

Twice during his search for an exit the helicopter had passed close enough to force him to hide. At this point Neal estimated his position to be a few hundred yards from the sea, where the fence dead-ended at a high cliff. Simply stepping around the end was not an option. Through binoculars he had seen a barrier made of pipe and barbed wire at the fence terminus. Given a few moments, he could probably use the wire cutters to cut his way through it, but if a guard was posted there he was screwed.

*   *   *

Hideo Kamada sat in the driver's seat of a sky-blue CSS security sedan parked with its doors open in front of the reassembly building. Calvin Wilmotte and Skip Schaefer stood outside the car, coats off, armpits dark with perspiration as the voice of Ben Hurley, Concord Space Systems Chief of Security, came from the vehicle's radio. *"He seems to be gone from this area but we're still watchin' the fence. He has to be on company property still."*

Hideo Kamada held the radio microphone in one hand. The tips of his other thumb and forefinger were pressed together, as though holding a needle. Into the microphone he said, "I see." Kamada released the invisible needle and looked out through the car window at Schaefer and Wilmotte. "Gentlemen. Please enter the automobile."

Kamada pulled his legs in, closed the door, and started the car's engine. Schaefer and Wilmotte traded a quick glance and got in, Wilmotte taking the back seat. It was a moment before Schaefer realized they weren't going to drive anywhere; Kamada had commandeered the vehicle in order to use its air conditioner, which he put on the maximum setting.

Kamada turned to the astronaut. "Do you have any suggestions...Skip."

Schaefer shook his head. "All we can do now is check the area. If we see him, we circle and close in."

Kamada's eyes blinked sluggishly. He lifted the microphone. "I am calling...the Seaview. Captain Kane, are you able to hear me."

The reply was a few seconds in coming. It sounded distant and washed-out. *"This is Kane. I can hear you fine."*

"Mr. Kane. What do you suggest we do at this time."

"Just what we're doing," Kane replied. *"Tryin' to make sure he don't—doesn't—get through the fence. I think I should stay in the boat for right now. We got a pretty good view of the place. If the guy's spotted again we'll come ashore."*

"Fine." Kamada set the microphone in his lap. "This man cannot be allowed to escape," he said quietly to Schaefer. He raised the microphone again. "Mr. Hurley. Can you hear me."

"Yessir, I can."

"How long has it been since the...person was seen."

"Ahh. It's gettin' close to seven now. So almost three hours ago. Mr. Kamada, we'll catch this guy. We've got men with dogs combin' the ridge now."

"Yes," Kamada said. "But with such a great area it is

301

possible that he will exclude you, Mr. Hurley."

Schaefer's eyebrows flickered. He had never heard Kamada use a word so wrongly.

"This person must *not* escape," Kamada said into the microphone. "I believe we must release the dogs."

"Release the dogs?" Hurley's crackling voice inquired. *"Did I hear you right?"*

"Wait a second, Hideo," Schaefer protested. "That might be a big mistake."

Kamada said, "One moment," and set the microphone in his lap. He turned to Schaefer.

"What if the dogs chew this guy up?" Schaefer said. "What if they put him in a hospital? What if he's not doing what we think he is? Maybe he's just snooping, or maybe he's some guy that sneaked in to take photos. We don't want a million-dollar lawsuit on our hands."

The blast of the air conditioner ruffled strands of Kamada's steel-colored hair. "Skip," he said calmly, "Captain Kane reported that the man was carrying a rifle."

"Appeared to be."

"The helicopter men believe they saw him perhaps an hour past, and he was still on our property. I am convinced now that Captain Kane was correct. This man has been shooting bullets at our rockets. If it is so, he has costed us perhaps millions of dollars in money and time, and he has costed us a large amount of loss in credibility."

"We *think* he has. We *think* this is the guy. But if—"

"We have been forced to destroy another rocket today!" Kamada snapped. His eyes became razor-slits. "It is becoming late. If we do not act while we have the opportunity, we may lose this person. At the least, he is an illegal *trespasser.*"

"Yes, but that doesn't—"

"He is *attacking* me!" Kamada hissed violently, his eyes bulging open briefly. "He is *attacking* my plans! He is *attacking* my goals!"

Kamada's skin seemed to have tightened over his skull, stretching his mouth into a grimace that reminded Schaefer of a *kabuki* mask. The astronaut was so stunned by the fury of the outburst that it took a few seconds for the self-centeredness of it to register. Recovering, he said, "I think it would be a mistake to take a chance on the dogs ripping this guy up without being sure who the hell he is."

"I am sure," Kamada said, breathing hard. "It will be dark soon and this man will *escape*. If you wish, you may step from the car and I will take responsibility for the action. You will *not* change my mind."

Schaefer thought briefly about grabbing the microphone and ordering Ben Hurley not to let the dogs go, but the idea of wrestling Kamada for it seemed absurd. And a part of him wanted to let the dogs loose. It was entirely possible that several years of his life had been flushed down the toilet by some maniac with a gun. But Kamada's venomous reaction to reason had crystallized the doubts that had been plaguing him, and in an instant his decision was made. The relief was like a heavy black burden shucked from his shoulders. Whatever the outcome of this particular day, his association with Hideo Kamada—with CSS, if need be—would be of limited duration.

Schaefer pushed open the car door. "Do what you want, Hideo," he said, getting out. "Maybe the idiot will have the sense to climb a tree."

Calvin Wilmotte opened his own door and set one foot on the ground, not wanting to take sides.

*   *   *

When he first heard the noise it sounded like someone trying to sneak through the woods behind him and doing a bad job of it. Then it sounded like a man running, but that wasn't right either. Neal bent lower, peering through the welter of branches and leaves, and his heart jumped. Uphill, a black shape darted through the deepening shadows.

A Doberman.

Neal lowered himself to his knees and backed into the cover of a bush. If the dog didn't blunder right into him he might just pass him by since the animal's heading wouldn't cross his scent trail. But he had to be ready for the worst. He worked open the top of the rucksack and slid his hand inside.

The rapid patter of the dog's feet grew closer. He could hear the Doberman padding one way and then the other, making light sniffing and snorting noises. The sounds abruptly stopped. Risking a look, Neal slowly pushed aside a branch. The dog had stopped a few yards away and was staring directly at him, its eyes glistening darkly.

The jig was up. Neal shoved himself to his feet, ripping through small branches and dragging along vines. The dog stiffened and backed up from this sudden apparition, neck hairs bristling. Then it started forward at a stiff trot, growling, its muzzle working into a mass of wrinkles.

Neal pulled his hand from the rucksack and the dog hesitated at the sight of the black object, but not for long. It made a deep, sucking snarl and lunged.

The first shot hit the dog in the chest. The startled animal dodged to one side and kept coming. Neal mashed the button again, sending the stream of liquid straight into the Dobermans's face. This time it yelped and dove headfirst to the ground, somersaulting blindly into Neal's legs and sending him sprawling.

Rolling to his feet, Neal backed away. The Doberman floundered on the ground like a wounded shark, snorting and sneezing, wiping its tear-gassed snout in the leaves. He hosed it down for good measure and then ran.

The sun was low enough that it was getting harder to see. Neal hurried through the woods as quietly as possible, moving seaward toward the cliffs, his face lashed by branches, his feet tripped up by rocks and roots. Somewhere far uphill a voice shouted over a bullhorn. He ducked under a limb and the rifle caught it and slammed him to the ground, the sling biting into his neck. He got up and hurried on, barely feeling the burn.

The sun was suspended less than a hand's width above the horizon when he reached the cliffs. He slowed his pace and moved cautiously toward the murmur of the sea, keeping a look out for security guards.

A few yards from the cliffs he saw a man silhouetted against the orange glow of low-lying clouds. The man was facing away; dual bulges of pistol and walkie-talkie showed at his hip and he held a stick of some sort, but he wasn't wearing a guard's cap.

Neal kept his eyes on him as he edged toward the cover of a scrubby tree. When his foot settled on a dry leaf the man lifted his head. Neal dropped down, pressing himself into the brush.

The man's long shadow played over the leaves as he approached. Neal took advantage of a wave pounding the rocks below to unsling the rifle, and when a boot came nosing through the grass almost within reach he stood and swung the weapon.

The man was looking away but he was alert and almost blocked the blow with an upward snap of his arm. Not quickly enough, however; the rifle butt thumped against his temple and he dropped to the ground.

Neal knelt to check the man's pulse and got a look at his face. It was Skip Schaefer's bad-ass driver, Howard. Howard's pulse was excellent. He was lying atop the stick he had been carrying. Neal tugged on the end poking out and discovered that it was in fact two sticks, connected at their ends by a short length of nylon cord. A *nunchaku*. The weapon went sailing into the trees, followed by Howard's .45 auto. Neal started to toss the walkie-talkie too, but changed his mind. Instead he slipped off his rucksack and shoved the radio unit inside.

Neal left Howard slumbering in the dusk and made his way toward the end of the fence, dropping to his hands and knees as the undergrowth became sparse. He was within a few yards of the barrier when a soft clank alerted him. He crept through the grass until he could see along the fence.

Uphill a lone security guard stood beside a tree, his back to the sea. Neal sank to his belly and snaked across the rough lava toward the razor-wire barricade at the end of the fence. Reaching it, he peered over the edge of the cliff. The drop was a good sixty feet. There was a narrow, uneven ledge a few feet below that ran beneath the barricade, but the thought of standing on it was terrifying. He set his forehead on the rock. It was either over the edge or back into the woods.

A stream of obscenities that suddenly erupted from the trees saved him the trouble of deciding. Howard was back among the conscious.

"God damn son of a *bitch!* You *hear* me? He's *here!*"

The guard shouted a reply and came running.

Neal lowered himself over the edge of the cliff. His rifle sling caught on a rock and held him half-suspended, toes barely touched the ledge. Without thinking, he let go with his right hand, slid it between his chest and the cliff, and dislodged the sling. It let go with a soft thud and he dropped the rest of the way to the broken shelf of rock.

He extended his left foot, set it, found new handholds, and then moved his right foot. He did it again, sidestepping across the face of the cliff until he was past the barbed wire barricade and then started climbing.

As he came over the lip of the cliff Howard saw him from other side of the fence and let out a roar. Neal clawed the rest of the way up and ran for the trees.

He plunged uphill through the darkened woods, cut left, and ran until the burning in his lungs forced him to stop. He sagged to the ground, his chest heaving. While he rested the helicopter came batting overhead, probing the trees with a spotlight. Neal suddenly remembered the walkie-talkie in his pack. He pulled it out and switched it on in time to hear the tail end of a transmission.

"...car we spotted in the trees up by the road."

The radio hissed and another voice came on.

"It's covered. We got a team with some dogs fannin' out downhill from there and another one coming from the valley toward you."

"Roger on that."

307

A new voice, louder and more distinct, followed the first two.

"All security personnel. The subject may have his hands on a radio unit, so for now keep your units on for instructions but don't respond unless I ask you to. If anybody breaks silence give them the message. That's all, over."

Neal switched off the walkie-talkie. It was strange and depressing to hear himself spoken of as "the subject". Even more depressing to hear they had found the subject's car, because circling back to it was now out of the question. He rested a minute longer and then headed back toward the sea. There was one more card to play.

The possibility of being cut off from the overland return route had occurred to him during planning, so two days ago he had cached the inflatable boat on the shore just outside the launch site, at the point where the cliffs tapered down to the sea again.

By the time he reached the slope leading down to the shore the sun was long gone, but a mass of clouds over the horizon were still giving off a dull red glow. Enough for him to make out two men climbing up toward his position from below. He hid in the scrub brush and waited.

The men moved up the grassy slope at a brisk pace, not talking. The one in slacks and short-sleeved shirt carried binoculars and the other, wearing a CSS Security uniform, carried a walkie-talkie. Neal kept his head down as they approached. He heard them pass by, both breathing heavily, and when they had disappeared into the trees above he scrambled downhill toward the shore.

The men had pulled their fiberglass-hulled runabout onto a patch of gravelly lava beach at the bottom of the slope. Neal pulled out his knife, waded into the water, and cut the fuel line to the outboard. As he waded back he heard shouts from above and saw the two men coming down the slope toward him, moving at a stumbling run in the twilight.

Neal jogged farther down the shore to a stand of scrub trees and pushed his way in. He yanked the painted plastic sheet off the inflatable, stuffed it into the stern, and dragged the boat to the water, climbing in just as the helicopter came roaring over the cliffs and swinging around in his direction, its running lights on.

With the boat tossing on the waves, Neal squeezed the fuel pump bulb a few times and cranked the motor. It started on the first try. He twisted the throttle gently, easing the revs higher until the engine smoothed out, then put the motor in gear and whipped the little boat around.

He headed north, away from the peninsula, the inflatable bucking over the waves, spray flying over the bow.

Less than a minute later the helicopter's powerful spotlight suddenly hit him from above. He kept his head down and twisted the throttle further open. The helicopter swooped low, blasting him with rotor wash, and a voice made huge by a megaphone poured over him with almost palpable weight.

"Halt. Halt. You're under arrest."

Neal kept the boat's speed steady as he bounced over the water. Points of light from the fishing village of Mokolea were in sight when helicopter unexpectedly cut its spotlight and zoomed off, rotors beating the air.

*　　*　　*

Kane watched from the driver's seat as Duffy

McDuff struggled to reconnect the fuel line in the heaving stern of the boat. When the cut end was re-clamped to the inlet nipple Kane started the motor, keeping the boat in position while McDuff sloshed ashore in the surging water to untie the ropes.

Away from the shore McDuff took over the wheel. Kane slid into the passenger seat and picked up the walkie-talkie. He spoke into it tersely, switched it off, and tucked it between his legs. Glaring at McDuff, he said, "This as fast as it goes?"

*   *   *

The little Avon banged across the water, following the coastline. Neal wiped the bow spray from his eyes and glanced up. The first stars were showing. That was good—the darker the better. He could find a place to land, hide the boat, and hike up to the highway.

When he looked back a few minutes later he saw two tiny, bobbing lights in the distance, one red and one green, which he recognized as a boat's running lights. He sped up slightly. The bow spray increased, dousing him with each bounce, stinging his eyes and soaking his shirt.

The boat lights behind him stayed in sight as he covered the next two miles of curving coastline. Their increasing brightness meant it was slowly closing in. He steered toward shore, riding just outside the first breakers, and searched the dark shoreline for a place to land. What he saw was not encouraging. The rocks along the shore formed a continuous, jagged barrier, and the terrain immediately above was steep and sparsely vegetated. He leaned forward and twisted the throttle tighter.

Even with increased speed the boat lights grew

310

perceptibly brighter. Neal felt a touch of panic again. There was still no place to put in and it was getting harder to see; the land was a featureless gray and the water was a black void marked near the shore with the dim white of breakers running onto the rocks. He reached into the wide canvas pocket screwed to the transom and dug through the greasy tools and spare parts until he felt the thing he was looking for: an eighteen-inch long piece of plastic pipe, one end wrapped with tape to make a non-slip handle. Slowing down, he jammed the throttle extension over the handgrip and moved to mid-boat, pushing a lifejacket under his knees. The outboard was ten horses heavier than the inflatable's maximum rating, and when he twisted the throttle all the way the boat dug into the water and bolted ahead.

With his weight forward now the bow of the little Avon didn't fly up so much when it caught the air after a bounce. It shot over the water, climbing each swell and sailing over the crest, slamming down again and skittering over the surface until it climbed the next swell.

Neal kept up the punishing pace, half expecting the boat's plywood transom to rip loose. His back and knees began to hurt. When it registered on him that he could actually see the front of the inflatable he took a quick look back. Another spotlight had been trained on him from the following boat, too far away to give his pursuers a good look but close enough to send a chill down his back. The possibility of being caught suddenly seemed much more real.

He swerved the boat seaward a hundred feet, losing the spotlight long enough to grab the rifle and toss it overboard. The empty brass casings from his back pocket went into the water next, followed by three live cartridges from his shirt pockets. He snagged the rucksack and dragged it close, pulling out the pistol. He hesitated; the gun was a graduation present from his father and it held a lot of memories.

Over the side it went, along with the spare magazine. He couldn't use the gun if he was in prison.

The dark coastline took on a more familiar look and Neal felt his hopes rise. His plan wasn't a good one, but it was the only one he had. He concentrated on handling the bucking boat.

The pursuing spotlight grew gradually brighter, making the sides and floorboards of the inflatable stand out against the black shadows and water. His own hand looked corpse-colored when he glanced at his watch. He had been on the water over half an hour.

A voice, small and tinny, cut through the raucous thrumming of the outboard.

"Halt!"

The command over the distant loudhailer struck Neal as an absurd cliché. He burst out laughing.

"Halt your boat!" the miniature voice ordered. *"Stop you damn boat up there!"*

Straining his eyes, Neal saw the long stretch of palm trees to his right and the winking dots of light back in the trees. He was approaching Pu'uhonua 'O' Honaunau, the City of Refuge. The park would be closed at this hour, and being Monday, the bayside picnic area would be fairly empty.

He careened around the point of land at the end of the palms, the boat dancing sideways over the swells. The spotlight would be off his back for the next few moments. He steered toward the little beach in the corner of the bay, straining to pick out the lava barrier in the dark. The rocks were nearly submerged by high tide but spots of white foam marked their location. Making his best guess, he slowed the motor to catch the next swell, then gunned it all the way. The boat shot through the gap in the rocks without a scrape.

Safely inside the cove, he put the motor in neutral and twisted furiously at the clamps holding it to the transom. When they were loose he put the boat in gear again and ran it closer to the shore, then yanked out the fuel line and heaved the sputtering outboard up and back, dumping it into the water.

He turned to look for the other boat. It was approaching the point, motor roaring, its spotlight blinking on and off as it raced along the grove of palm trees. Neal jumped out of the inflatable, which had coasted close to the shore, and pulled it onto the beach. He heard faint music coming from the picnic area, where a lantern hung from a tree. Closer, a car's interior light glowed yellow, but he was too far away to be seen.

The Avon made a hollow, scraping sound as he dragged it onto the lane leading from the shore to the parking lot above. He was fifty yards up the lane when he looked up and saw the pursuing boat pass the point. It slowed and the spotlight raked across the bay. Finding nothing, the light swept along the shoreline, starting at the far end and whipping closer. It settled on the beach of the little cove and the boat swung around and roared toward the beach.

As the boat neared the cove the beam of light crawled up the darkened lane. Neal crouched reflexively but the light never reached him. It suddenly jerked skyward and then snapped down, accompanied by a booming crunch from the water. The crunch became a squeal as the boat's momentum rammed it onto the lava ridge across the inlet. A following swell sent it bow down, the outboard motor racing wildly until the boat slewed sideways and the propeller blades struck rock with a chattering, cracking noise. The next wave rolled the boat onto its starboard beam. The downward-cocked spotlight illuminated a rush of water cascading over the gunwales and two figures paddling in the churning foam.

Seeing both men unhurt, Neal dragged the inflatable farther up the lane. He stopped beside the low rock wall bordering one side, lifted out the fuel tank, then shoved the boat over the wall. He hopped over and dragged the boat across a small field and into a stand of trees.

Neal slashed the sides of the boat open with his knife and it deflated with a rush of stale, rubbery air. With the collapsed boat on its side, the floorboards holding it up, he dragged it into a denser patch of saplings. He broke down three of the saplings to make room and laid the boat flat, covering it with the broken-off trees.

A sealed plastic bag was stuffed in the point of the bow. He pulled it out. Inside was a pair of underwear, a pair of shorts, and a tee shirt.

Neal jogged back across the field, vaulted over the low stone wall, grabbed the fuel can, and ran up the road toward the pay phone at Park headquarters. Before setting out last night he had wisely taped four quarters together and dropped them in his pants pocket.

Chapter Thirty-Five

"You know," Big Jim said when the waitress at Wing's departed with their breakfast orders, "I figured you were in some...bad *trouble* when you called last night."

"Why?" Neal asked. "Did I sound funny or something?" He had congratulated himself on sounding normal considering the circumstances.

"Not any funnier than usual," Perkins said, doling his words out at snail speed. "Which is not at all." He blew on his coffee and took a sip, wiping his moustache with a wrist. "Gettin' it on the radio was sorta...*odd*."

"There wasn't any other way," Neal said. Perkins hadn't answered at his apartment so he'd called Kona Fish and Dive Charters and had the girl at the desk radio the *Suzy Q*. She held the mike up to the telephone receiver to complete the call. An hour later Big Jim arrived in his truck at Napo'opo'o, four miles north of the City of Refuge.

"Still don't wanta. Tell me what you were *doin'* there?"

"I told you," Neal said. "I got stranded there after a boat ride."

Perkins sighed.

"Look, Jim, I'm gonna pay you back for this."

"You will," Perkins said. "One way or another. Anyway, you'd do the same for me, right?"

315

"Absolutely not."

Perkins lifted his hands. "See? You're payin' me back right now. I *love* that kind of abuse."

The waitress brought their food. Perkins jammed half a slice of buttered toast into his mouth and said around it, "Heard anything from Susan?"

"Yeah." Neal poked his eggs and watched the yolk ooze out. "I got a letter from her the other day."

"How's she doin'?"

"Okay, I guess. Everything seems fine.

"That's good." Perkins focused on his hash browns, forking them into his mouth like a farmer pitching hay. He chewed complacently for a moment. "How about you?" he asked. "How's the painting goin'?"

"Not bad," Neal said, glad to change the subject. "I've gotten a few things finished since you were there."

"Not pushin' yourself too hard?"

Neal looked up from his plate. "No. Why do you ask?"

"I don't know. You seem a little...*ragged* lookin'."

"Do I?"

"Yeah. Maybe you should take it easy. Go fishing or somethin'."

"Fishing?"

"You know. Catch fish," Perkins said. "In fact, we could go this mornin'."

Neal mulled over the offer. "You know what," he said, nodding, "that sounds good."

*　　*　　*

It turned out to be a good trip. They caught two big *mahimahi* and blue a marlin that weighed in at 437 pounds on the Kailua pier scales. From the dock Big Jim sold the marlin and one of the *mahimahi* to a hotel restaurant. They motored back to Honokohau Harbor, moored the *Suzy Q*, and hiked out to the nude beach.

They stayed on the beach until nearly sunset. By the time they got back to the harbor they were dragging a bit, but Neal mustered the energy to cook *mahimahi* steaks on the *Suzy Q*'s gallery, seasoning the fish with butter, pepper, and oregano the way Susan did. A third round of beers finished them off. Too tired to drive to Perkins' apartment in town, they spent the night on the *Suzy Q*, falling asleep to the soothing drone of an electric fan.

Kona Fish and Dive Charters radioed the *Suzy Q* early the following morning. "Two clients for this afternoon," Big Jim said, hanging up the mike. "You're invited as first mate."

"Can't do it," Neal told him. "But I'll take a rain check. Slaughtering fish is starting to grow on me."

"It does. So. You need to use my truck?"

Neal shook his head. "Nah, thanks. I can hitchhike back."

He helped Perkins get the *Suzy Q* ready for the charter and then thumbed a ride into Kailua. He ate breakfast at Wing's and started hitching again, catching a ride to Kainaliu and another all the way to Mokolea Road. From there he walked the three miles home.

Once he stepped off Mokolea Road into the trees he started feeling edgy. He walked slowly to the end of the unfinished road and saw that his pickup truck was sitting there just the way he left it. He continued along the footpath and stopped at the edge of the yard to watch the house for a minute. Everything seemed normal. Across the lawn, up the stairs, and still no evidence of visitors. Good.

He gathered up a few items inside, returned to the

truck, and drove back to the highway, heading north to Pu'uhonua 0 Honaunau National Historical Park.

Neal parked near a picnic table on the shore of Honaunau Bay and for the next half hour wandered up and down the lava shelf beside the water, pretending to study the fish trapped in the tide pools. When he was sure no one was watching he drove the truck down to the cove in the corner of the bay, and under the scrutiny of four brown grade-schoolers playing in the shallows he took off his shirt and shoes, donned a mask, and waded into the water.

The outboard motor was still there, lying in five feet of water, its contours partially obscured by a layer of sand. From the surface it looked like a patch of lava on the seabed. He swam back to shore, planning to return for the motor at night.

Neal dried off and drove his truck up the lane leading from the small beach where he'd come ashore the night before. Stopping beside the stone wall bordering the lane, he put on his tee shirt and shoes and hopped the wall, striding directly for the stand of trees where he had hidden the inflatable boat.

He pulled away the branches and manhandled the flabby black carcass out of the trees, feeling conspicuous as he dragged it across the empty lot and into the truck bed, but no one seemed to be watching. He covered it with a piece of plastic sheeting and climbed back into the cab, relieved. That was it. With any luck the only other piece of evidence of yesterday night, the inflatable's fuel tank, was already long gone; he'd buried it beneath the trash in the park dumpster.

Neal started the truck and drove up the lane toward the park entrance, stopping to let a man in a blue aloha shirt and Bermuda shorts cross the road. But the man didn't cross. He walked to the middle of the road and faced the truck, his mirrored sunglasses flashing blankly, and pulled a snub-nosed revolver from beneath his shirt with his right hand and a badge holder from his pocket with his left. Holding both up, he stepped to the windowless passenger side of the truck and said, "You under arrest, my friend."

Neal recognized him as the cop from Harry's shop, Kane. He said, "For what?"

Kane shoved the badge holder back into his pants. "Trespassin', for starters." He opened the door and got in. "Drive up to the parkin' lot."

Neal complied. At the parking lot Kane pointed to a brown Taurus in one corner, and he wheeled the pickup over to it.

Kane said, "Okay, my friend, get out."

The policeman unlocked the plainclothes car and made a call on a hand-held radio unit. They both waited in the shade of a coconut palm, Kane standing with arms folded, his gun back in his waistband and the mirrored sunglasses back on his face, watching the park entrance gate.

Moments later a state police cruiser drove through the gate and rolled to a stop beside the truck. A mournful-looking Frank Ninomiya got out, taking off his own mirrored glasses. Ninomiya walked reluctantly around the cruiser to join the two men.

"H'lo Captain. Ey, Neal."

Neal nodded. "Ey, Frank. What's this all about?"

The younger officer stepped to the back of the pickup truck and pulled up the plastic sheet, exposing the deflated Avon.

"It's about this, Neal."

"What about it?"

"Frank," Kane broke in impatiently, "you gonna do it or what?"

Ninomiya took off his hat and wiped his forehead with a hand. "I got a warrant for your arrest, Neal. Somebody came on CSS property Monday. They maced a dog, did some damage to a boat, and then left the scene." Ninomiya pointed at the limp Avon in the back of the truck. "In a boat just like that."

Neal shrugged. "Lots of boats like that."

"Painted black?"

"Beats me. Anyway, I just found it there. Somebody must've dumped it."

Ninomiya looked at Kane. The police captain's face was a rock. "Look, Neal, I'm sorry," Ninomiya said, "but you're under arrest for trespassing and vandalism." He took a small card from his shirt pocket. "You have the right to remain silent," he read.

*   *   *

At the police station in Captain Cook he was booked, fingerprinted, photographed, and locked in a small cell. He waited on the bench bolted to the wall, the smell of lemon-scented disinfectant and his own acrid sweat filling his nostrils. Fifteen minutes later an officer with squeaking shoes unlocked the cell and escorted him to a room down the hall.

The walls of the room were blank, painted with a pale green enamel that reflected the glare of a bare fluorescent light fixture that hung, humming, from the ceiling. The room was furnished with only a Formica-topped desk, a swivel chair behind it and a straight-backed wooden chair in front. The squeaky-shoed officer pointed to the wooden chair and left, the door clunking closed behind him.

320

Another officer entered a moment later, a sheaf of papers in hand, and sat behind the desk in the swivel chair. Neal read the officer's name tag: *Capt. J.D. Gilbert.* Gilbert, a smooth-faced man with the look of a misplaced high-school teacher, pulled a pencil from his breast pocket and tapped the eraser end on the desk as he pored over his papers. When he finally spoke he didn't look up.

He said, "Let's see, Mr. Tate," and ran his pencil down a form, reading from it in a cheerful, informative tone, as though reciting facts to a civics class. "You're charged with two separate counts of trespassing, theft of private property, three counts of malicious vandalism, unlawfully carrying a firearm, reckless endangerment of lives and property, fleeing an officer attempting arrest, and finally, abandoning a vehicle on a public right-of-way."

Neal shifted his position in the wooden chair. The sheer volume of the charges was impressive, but one fact left him with an unexpected spark of hope—there was no mention of rockets.

Gilbert bit his bottom lip thoughtfully. "Mr. Tate, you've been given your rights, haven't you? To an attorney and so forth?"

"Yes. But what I really want is to find out what this business is all about."

"This business," Gilbert said shortly, "is about the charges I just read, which could result in substantial fines or jail time. Now, I'd like to ask you a few questions. First, Mr. Tate, do you want to contact an attorney at this time?"

"Yeah," he said. "I do."

*   *   *

Two hours later he was led from the holding cell to a counter in the processing room, where another officer handed him an envelope containing his wallet and the keys to the Datsun.

"Where are my truck keys?"

The officer behind the counter, a heavyset man wearing horn-rimmed glasses, looked up from his writing. "Your truck's been impounded. We got the keys."

"Impounded? For how long?"

"I have no idea. Check with Captain Gilbert. Right now I need you to sign for this stuff."

Neal signed and pocketed the wallet and keys. "Which way to the front?"

"Through that door and straight ahead."

Tom Bailey was waiting for him in the lobby of the police station, puffing on a pipe and looking competent in slacks and tie. Neal shook his hand. "Thanks, Tom," he said. "I really appreciate this."

"I should thank you," the lawyer said affably. "I've been writing all morning. I was glad to have an excuse to get away."

"This is a poor excuse."

"Not at all." Bailey swept an arm toward the door. "Shall we depart?"

Outside Neal said, "I hate to bother you any further but I need a ride. They impounded my truck."

"I know." Bailey pointed with his pipe. "I'm parked right over there. We can talk while we drive."

Bailey re-lit his pipe inside the car, a Honda Civic that had seen better days. "I understand your other vehicle died on you somewhere," he said, shaking out his match and dropping it in the ashtray. "The one they said you abandoned."

322

"That's where I'd like to go," Neal said. "I think I can get it started."

"All righty. Let's go."

Following directions, Bailey pulled onto the main thoroughfare of the little town headed south. His pipe clattered against his teeth as he shifted it in his mouth. "Okay," he said. "First the good news, Neal. There was no bail to get you out and they dropped all the charges having to do with Concord Space Systems for lack of evidence. The bad news is they didn't dismiss the trespassing charge for the place near the City of Refuge or the theft charge for this boat you say you found. Also, of course, they have your truck, which they got a warrant to search, I know not why." Bailey passed a slow-moving vehicle in front of them. "What I can't figure out," he said, pulling back into his lane, "is one, why all this unsubstantiated stuff about CSS, and two, as far as the other charge goes, why they're making such a big deal out of nothing. It's like harassment."

When this indirect query produced no response Bailey tried a more straightforward approach. "What's the thing with CSS, Neal? You growing marijuana on their land or something?"

Neal laughed and said, "No, but it's an interesting idea." He gave the lawyer a look. "They didn't tell you anything at the police station?"

Bailey's forehead grew a crop of wrinkles. "Well— not exactly. But something odd happened. While I was waiting for you a cop came up to me, an oriental guy. Frank something, starts with an N."

"Ninomiya?"

"That's it. He asked if I was your attorney and I said yes. He said to meet him in the men's room in five minutes. I thought what the hell, so I did. He said to tell you Connie asked him to arrest you." Bailey glanced away from the road. "Who's Connie? The woman who owns the land where you dumped the boat?"

"It's kah-nay," Neal said, and spelled it. "He's another cop, a captain from Hilo. That's strange about Frank, since Kane was the one who stopped me."

"Maybe he was out of his jurisdiction or something," Bailey suggested. "Or he wanted to keep at arm's length for some reason. Paperwork, maybe."

"Maybe. Did Frank say anything else?"

Bailey scratched his beard, which had undergone a recent trimming. "Yes, he did. He said to tell you Kane and Kamada know what you've been doing."

Neal felt a weight pressing him into the seat. The news wasn't entirely unexpected, but hearing it was different. He stared out his window in silence, watching the trees crawl by. The trees gave way to weathered buildings as they entered the little town of Honaunau.

Neal said, "Let me ask you something, Tom. If I end up needing a lawyer, will you be it?"

"Sure," Bailey said promptly. "I've only done a little defense work but I did okay." He puffed his pipe as he drove. "So. Any idea what it is Kane and Kamada—I assume that's Kamada of CSS—think you've been doing?"

Neal made a sound through his nose. "Yeah. They think I've been shooting the rockets."

"Shooting the rockets?" Bailey said incredulously. "Like—with a gun?"

"Right."

Bailey burst out laughing. He had to grab at his pipe to keep from losing it. "That's absurd!" he said. "I mean, that's..." The lawyer's grin slowly faded and he glanced away from the road again. "I mean—it *is* ridiculous, isn't it?"

*   *   *

A police cruiser was parked on Mokolea Road close to where the Datsun was hidden in the trees. Under the impassive gaze of two officers, Neal went through the charade of trying to find the problem with the car. He tinkered under the hood while Tom Bailey sat helpfully in the front seat, turning over the engine when asked. When he got around to reconnecting the coil wire the engine immediately started. Bailey surrendered the driver's seat and Neal backed the Datsun out of the trees onto the road.

"Looks like you're in business again," Bailey said, watching the police cruiser drive off.

"Such as it is," Neal said. He suddenly felt very tired. How about a drink at my place, Tom? I think I've still got ice in the chest. We can talk."

"Sounds good," Bailey said. He sounded almost chipper.

Chapter Thirty-Six

Tom Bailey spent the night on the sofa in the living room. After seeing him off the next morning Neal went back to bed. He woke up two hours later feeling rested, if not calm.

He brewed a cup of tea in the kitchen. While it was steeping he paced around the house trying to work off excess tension. He hoisted the barbells a few times, thinking it would help, but it made him queasy. He returned to the kitchen, sugared his tea, and took it out on the verandah along with the spy novel he'd been plugging away at.

He lasted about five minutes with the paperback before he set it down and stared out at the ocean. His gaze wandered, eventually settling on the ridge to the north where the top of the CSS launch tower was a stroke of dull red protruding over the green of the trees. With a little effort he could recall, more or less, the way his mind was working when he decided to shoot the rockets.

From the present perspective it was like looking back at a different person. Not someone who was wrong or crazy, just different. More determined, more certain. He saw himself in his mind's eye making lists, buying things at the hardware store, making the suppressor, reconnoitering the peninsula. And then going to shoot the rockets. Launching the boat in the middle of the night, crossing the black, rolling water, hiding on the shore, seeing the rocket rise over the cliffs—all that seemed strangely dreamlike now. Unreal in its lack of connection to the normal flow of life. Surreal. His memories of Vietnam, condensed by time into shorthand images, had the same quality.

Neal thought of Susan. She'd been on his mind every day since she left, the first thing he thought of when he woke and the last thing before he fell asleep. The idea that her face, her voice, all the things they'd done together might also be just a sifted-down handful of shifting memories someday—that was too painful to think about.

He picked up the cup and book and stood up. He didn't feel like being alone.

He packed some things into a paper bag, locked up the house and headed down the path to the car.

* * *

The *Suzy Q*'s slip was empty. Neal continued down the harbor road until it dead-ended and parked the Datsun with the other cars. He tucked a towel and a beach mat under his arm and walked across the tide-exposed stretch of lava to the nude beach.

He floated in the breakers, lay in the sun, and dozed in the shade of the trees, trying not to think about anything. In the early afternoon a mass of drifting clouds blocked the sun, but he was ready to leave anyway.

Driving out, he spotted the *Suzy Q*'s tuna tower jutting above the lip of the sunken harbor and pulled over.

Big Jim sat cross-legged on the afterdeck of his big sportfisher, bathed in sharp sunlight as he worked on something in his hands.

"Exactly what the hell are you doing?" Neal asked from the walkway.

Perkins raised his head. "Ey, brah! Come aboard."

Neal crossed the gangplank and flopped into one of the chairs on deck. "I repeat, exactly what the hell are you doing?"

Perkins held up a foot-long plastic cylinder from which dangled multiple strips of aluminized plastic. "It's an el cheapo teaser lure," he said with a trace of pride. "Made from junk. PVC pipe. Wire. Piece of space blanket. Only thing I bought was the...duct tape." He jiggled it. "Whaddaya think?"

Neal took the fishing lure from him and examined it. "Crude, yet primitive. Not unlike yourself, Large James."

Perkins shook his head. "I'm tellin' you. I'm immune to flattery." He took a slug of beer from the bottle beside him and belched raucously. "Hey. Ready to go fishin' again?"

"Hell yes," Neal said. "When?"

"Tomorrow morning."

"Okay. You taking clients?"

"Negatory," Perkins drawled. "Just you and me, sweetheart. Why, you wanta invite somebody?"

Neal gave the question some thought. "Yeah," he said, "Remember Harry, from Drysdale's?"

"Sure, owns the *LuLu* over there. We've talked a couple of times." Perkins stifled another belch with a fist. "Ask him along."

Neal stood up and dug in his pocket for change. "By God, I'll call him right now."

Harry said hell yes he wanted to go.

*　　*　　*

328

From his perch in the *Suzy Q*'s tuna tower, where he'd stationed himself with a cup of coffee to watch the sun come up, Neal spotted Harry trudging solidly along with two grocery sacks in his arms. He was wearing baggy white shorts, white deck shoes, and a white aloha shirt printed with red boomerangs. As Harry descended to the walkway Neal called out, "You're looking mighty gay this morning."

Harry looked up. "Hey, Neal! I didn't see you there. Gay, huh?" He stopped and looked down at himself. "Thanks, I think."

"Come aboard," Neal said, climbing down from the tower. "Jim's still comatose."

Harry walked the plank sure-footedly and set his sacks on the deck. "You're looking pretty good, too," he said, shaking hands, "for so early. How's everything going?"

"Not bad. How about you?"

"Pretty darn good, if I do say so. Oh yeah, Vi says hello."

Big Jim suddenly appeared in the cabin door, blinking and groaning. He tottered out clutching an oversized mug of coffee and croaked, "Welcome aboard," pumping Harry's hand. "We're gonna...*murder* 'em today."

"I'm ready," Harry said. He pointed to his sacks. "Even if we don't we're gonna eat good. We've got fried chicken, rolls, potato salad, and assorted other crap."

Swaying unsteadily, Big Jim focused on Neal. "This is a man I could grow to love."

*　　*　　*

They pulled in an ulua and two ahi and lost a

poorly-hooked marlin before noon, at which time a lunch break was called. They ate on the rear deck in the rolling silence of the open ocean.

"Excellent victuals, Harold," Big Jim said, washing a last bite of roll down with beer. He patted his bare, hairy stomach. "And now," he said, "I shall retire to the foredeck and...fall on my face." He got to his feet laboriously and started forward. "If you hear a splash," he said, "be sure and wake me up."

Harry and Neal sprawled on the rear deck, shirts off and beers in hand. The sky was clear. A cooling breeze blew over them as the Suzy Q rose and fell on the long swells. Harry stared up at the sky and scratched his chest contentedly. "Jeez, what did I do to deserve this?"

"You know the right people," Neal told him.

"That I do. Jim seems like a really nice guy."

"I hate to admit it but he is.

Harry raised his beer. "Anyone who takes me fishing is all right in my book." He took a drink and sat up with a groan. "Gravity's pretty strong today. Hey, Neal. You remember that police captain you met in my shop?"

Neal experienced a sinking sensation. "Yeah," he said. "Sam Kane."

"Yeah, Sam. He came by the shop yesterday. He asked me a bunch of questions, mostly about you."

"Yeah? Like what?"

Harry adjusted his monster sunglasses and ran a hand over his crewcut. "He asked if you'd been by lately and I told him the last time you were in. Then he asked if you owned a gun. I almost answered him, but I asked what was going on and he said you were arrested for trespassing and vandalism." Harry grimaced questioningly. "Is that right?"

Neal squeezed out an unhappy smile from behind his own sunglasses. "That's correct. What else did he want to know?"

"Well, he asked if you'd bought any ammunition lately. I told him my transactions were confidential and that he'd have to go through the proper channels for that. Of course I was nice about it and all. Sam's a friend. But anyway, what's this all about?"

Neal worked himself into a sitting position with his back against the gunwale. "I'm not sure if I should talk about it."

Harry scowled. "Is this—big trouble you're in?"

"I don't know. Maybe."

"Oh. Well—can I help you in any way?"

"I don't think so.

Harry tugged on his nose. "Look, Neal. We're friends, aren't we?"

"I hope so.

"Me too. I mean, since you moved down south we don't see each other as much, and maybe we don't keep each other posted on everything. But, you know...I like you. A lot."

"I feel the same."

"And I feel—it seems silly to say it out loud—we've got a mutual respect."

"That's true from my end."

"Okay, then," Harry said, "now that all the mushy stuff's aside I'll say this. Whatever happened, we're still friends. Whatever you say is between you and me. Doctors and lawyers aren't the only folks entitled to— what you call it. Confidentiality. I won't be spilling my guts just because someone asks me a question."

Neal felt his chest tighten. Then the fear ebbed. He rubbed a hand over his scalp, trying to drive out a trace of dizziness. His hair felt hot from the sun.

"All right, Harry. I'll tell you what this is about. I shot the rockets that Concord Space Systems launched."

Harry's forehead knotted. "You did what?"

"I shot the rockets with a rifle. I hid near the launch site and shot 'em when they took off. That's why they keep having to blow the things up."

Harry removed his sunglasses and squinted at him, more in disbelief than from the glare. "But...why?"

"Why?" Neal sat back. "Hell, I don't know where to start."

"But, Neal, for cryin' out loud! They could put you in jail for that."

"Yeah. But there 're worse things than prison."

The lines on Harry's face drew together. "I don't understand."

"A lot of things've happened that you don't know about," Neal said. "Things I didn't tell you because..." He shrugged. "I don't know. Everybody has enough problems of their own."

"Well, hell, Neal. A person always has room for a friend's problems. I want to know what happened."

Neal tilted his head back and rested it against the gunwale. Far above, a lone seagull floated in the cloudless void, a spot of white on blue. The bird flapped its wings twice, tilted, and slowly soared from view. He looked down again and said, "All right, I'll tell you."

He gave Harry a bare account of his escalating troubles with Concord Space Systems, starting with the probate problems and the eviction of the Kahooke family. Harry listened with hunched shoulders.

When Neal finished he said, "I realize CSS had the

right to cut off my access road and to take out my old water line, but they didn't have the right to slander George Akoki and try to wipe out his will. They didn't have the right to shotgun and burn my truck or to keep breaking the water line or to knock out my electricity. I have to tell you, Harry, that stuff pissed me off."

Harry nodded, stroking his jaw. "I can see how it would. Is that why you decided to shoot the rockets?"

"Not really. Those things were just a symptom of the problem, which is the fact that if you've got a bunch of money you can do whatever the hell you want. Other people don't matter. To CSS, Kawika and Muriela were nothing. Not people, just a problem. Which they solved pretty easily. Then I was the problem, another thing they had to kick out of the way. And the awful thing is we're all so brainwashed by the idea of business that once in a while I'd start to think like that myself."

Harry's brow wrinkled. "What do you mean?"

"I mean every now and then I saw myself as this stubborn little nothing guy in his little house who was standing in the way of big people doing big things. That's what I meant about worse things than prison. The last time I felt that way was in Vietnam. I wondered what they hell we were doing there but I figured there had to be a reason. But the ugly secret is there doesn't have to be. Or if there is one, it could be based on nothing more than greed or stupidity or whim. By the time I finally figured that out I'd done some terrible things and I'd lost a lot of my self-respect. That's something that when you lose it, it's hard to get it back, and maybe pieces of it are lost forever. So you have to hold on like hell to what you have."

Harry massaged the scar on his neck, thinking. "I

think what you say helps me understand. Why you did it, I mean. But what about someone getting hurt, Neal? Did you think about that?"

"Of course I did. But no one lives within two miles of the launch pad. They're keeping boats out of the flight path. During the launch all the CSS people are inside the control center, and it's designed to take an explosion. The thing that decided me was the simple fact that the authorities—whoever the hell they are— gave CSS the OK to launch from the peninsula. Obviously they figured from the start that a rocket might go haywire and would have to be blown up. And that's what happened, and nobody's come close to getting hurt."

"I guess that makes sense," Harry said. He switched from his scar to his nose, pulling on it slowly. "But now I'm wondering why you shot the rockets when they took off. Why didn't you just shoot 'em when they were sitting on the launch pad?"

"Because CSS would've caught on the first time and stopped launching. This way the evidence was erased when they blew up the rockets over the ocean."

Harry was silent. "I don't know Neal," he said at last. "I'm still just not sure it was the right thing."

"I'm not either," Neal said. "But I don't feel like I did something bad. Just the opposite. Maybe that means I've gone a little crazy. Maybe a part of it, somewhere, is I blame them for Susan leaving. I don't know. But I knew I couldn't live with letting them run me off. I owed more than that to George Akoki. And to Dan. He loved the island. He used to talk about it all the time."

Neal pulled himself to his feet and crossed to the other side of the boat. He leaned on the gunwale, looking across the swells. In the distance the green slopes of the Big Island hung over the ocean like a mirage. He was suddenly aware of how quiet it was; the only sound was of water lapping and swirling around the hull of the Suzy Q.

"You know, Harry," he said, "there's more to it than the things I've said. Something bigger, the reason why people were fighting to stop the launch site a long time ago."

Harry looked up, a hand shading his face, the blue of his eyes intensified by the sea and sky. "What's that, Neal?"

"It's the islands." He spoke slowly and intently. "Hawaii's a special place. It's not just some real estate waiting to be developed. It's not just some place for hotels and golf courses and launch sites. Hawaii's too beautiful for that. Too valuable. Too valuable as a...a sanctuary. A refuge from all the craziness, from the ugly side of civilization. But one a piece at a time it's turning into a copy of the same old shit. And the people who lose out aren't just us, either. Everyone who comes after us loses." His shoulders drooped. "I'm not saying that all development on the island is bad, but rockets? Where does it end?"

Harry looked away, thoughtful.

Neal put his hands out. "Here, you've got some corporation. Here, the island and the people on it. Who determines what happens to this place? Who gets to say?" He dropped his hands. "The answer is the corporation. Why is that? GYRO and everyone else tried to fight CSS. They fought fair, they played the game by the rules. And they lost because the game is rigged like a son of a bitch. I just quit playing. The way I see it the only thing missing is a few rockets, and a rocket is just a machine. The island is something else."

Neal slumped down into a sitting position again. "You know, Harry, what I regret most about this whole thing is bullshitting you about the rifle. What I said about hunting was true, in its own way, but I was still lying. I just didn't know any way around it. I hope you can forgive me for that."

Harry made a small dismissing movement with his hand. He got to his feet and lumbered heavily to the ice chest. "You want another beer?" he asked, flipping the lid open.

Neal thunked a fist on the deck listlessly. "Sure."

A voice bellowed at them from above. "You guys want beer? I'll give you beer!"

A loose shower of cold beer rained down on them. Harry howled as it hit his sun-reddened skin and Neal scrambled to the stern of the boat. "God dammit!" he shouted, "what the hell are you doing?"

"Being obnoxious!" Big Jim roared from the tuna tower. Cackling, he picked up another can. Harry ducked into the cabin as another shower struck.

Neal held up his hands in a futile attempt to block the spray and then gave up. He stepped onto the gunwale and jumped overboard.

Harry barked out a laugh from the cabin. "Hold on," he cried, dancing gingerly out onto the beer-slicked deck. "I'm a-comin'!" He snatched a life ring from the cabin wall and a beer from the cooler and launched himself feet-first into the water.

*   *   *

With the *Suzy Q* made fast in its slip at Honokohau Harbor, Big Jim said, "I've gotta take the fish into town. We'll get something to eat after that. I'm buyin'."

Harry had to decline. "I was up pretty late last night. You get as old as me and you gotta have your beauty sleep." He departed with a chunk of *ulua* on ice.

Neal helped Big Jim load the *ahi* in the back of his truck for delivery. "How about Drysdale's?" he suggested. "Something like piña coladas and burgers."

Perkins nodded. "Excellent."

"But you're not buying. I'm not a complete freeloader."

"Not complete," Perkins agreed. "But I'm buyin'. As a token of my awe and respect."

"For what?"

"For you, sweetheart," Perkins said. He reached over and patted Neal's hand. "You crazy rocket-shootin' bastard."

Neal blanched. "You heard us talking."

Perkins nodded solemnly. "Big Jim sees all, hears all."

Chapter Thirty-Seven

The evening was unusually hot and humid. Honolulu's five-thirty traffic droned heavily in the streets, tourists returning from a hard day of play, islanders going home or heading for evening jobs. Limousines, rental cars, navy cars, business vehicles, taxis, a multicolored herd clogging the city's arteries.

High above the automotive turmoil the offices of Komodo, Incorporated were isolated from the noise and heat.

"I am outraged even still," Hideo Kamada said in a guttural growl, looking down at the traffic. "They simply released the...the fool. This is not justice."

Skip Schaefer pinched the bridge of his nose; his sinuses were reacting poorly to the arctic environment of Kamada's office. "They have to have evidence, Hideo," he said didactically. "That's the way it works in this country."

Schaefer was feeling poorly in general. The long flight from LA to Honolulu had left him stiff and rumpled. He felt like he'd made the trip in his own suitcase.

The truth was, he hadn't felt too hot when he boarded the 747. Things had not gone well the last two weeks. After flying back to California following the last launch disaster he'd been assailed by letters and phone calls from angry investors and besieged by a horde of reporters and blood-sniffing environmentalists. Even the man from Aviation Week had seemed, beneath the polite veneer, almost wary. Which he understood perfectly. With so much money and power and prestige at stake, anything that might sully the image of the aerospace industry—like a string of launch screw-ups—was as welcome as a fart in a spacesuit. The round of personal appearances on the Fourth of July had only made things worse. Maybe it was paranoia but everyone seemed to be looking at him funny—more like a man whose company was sliding down the tubes than an ex-astronaut.

Kamada turned away from the window and gave Schaefer a narrow look. "I am aware of how the legal process operates...Laurance." He let a breath hiss out. "Let us discuss something else for the moment. Our primary concern for now is to repair the damage done to the company. I have given much thought to this matter. I believe that the solution I have...devised, will prove to be the most productive."

"And what is that solution?" Schaefer's interest was real, if not keen. Deep soul-searching over the last few days—accompanied by an unusually high intake of alcoholic beverages—had culminated in a decision to stay with Concord Space Systems until the current crisis had safely passed. The decision did not leave him feeling renewed, determined, or satisfied. It just seemed required.

"It is this," Kamada said. "We will tell our shareholders the truth. In private communications, we will inform them that our rockets have failed because of...sabotage."

Schaefer looked skeptical.

"We will not tell them how the rockets were sabotaged," Kamada added.

"You think we can just say it was sabotage and they'll accept that, Hideo? These are people who invested tens of thousands of dollars over the last few years. Every day I get phone calls asking what gives and I'm running out of answers. We say sabotage, they're going to want to know who, what, when, where, how."

Schaefer watched as Kamada took two calculated steps across the dense white carpet and stopped. This was as close as he ever came to pacing. "I think not," Kamada said. "If we say that we know what the problem was, and that it will not occur again, and our...subsequent test launches prove that the rockets are reliable, they will be satisfied. We will say that we cannot provide further information at this time for legal reasons. Which is true, in a manner. In time, if it appears to be wise, perhaps the full story may be presented. But our current concern is to see that the next test launch is...flawless."

Schaefer tapped his fingers on the arm of his chair. "What's our schedule looking like?"

"The launch will be on Saturday. July twenty."

"The twentieth? Jesus, that's just two weeks from now!"

"The rocket will be thoroughly examined," Kamada said emphatically. "I have commanded the testing procedure to be done three times completely. Calvin Wilmotte informs me that everything is in perfect order at the launch facility. There are excellent reasons to go ahead soon. One is to assure our investors that everything is indeed under control. Another is to make room in the assembly building for the two new rockets, which will arrive next week. And another is to move ahead before other troubles hold us back."

"What other troubles? You mean money? Our

backers?"

"Not only them," Kamada said. "I have been in touch with our...political friends. It is not good. Their support is becoming less reliable. They wish to have our company here, but they are under an increase of pressure to move the launch operations elsewhere. Great pressure, they are saying."

Kamada turned his head to look out the office window. It was still dazzlingly bright outside, even at this hour. "There is more," he said. "Yesterday some of the fools who are against us filed a lawsuit. The people in the town of Mokolea have asked for an...injunction, against further launches. They are saying that their fishing is interrupted."

"Well," Schaefer said, "maybe they've got a point."

Kamada stared at him coolly. "There is another lawsuit filed against us today. It claims that the smoke and the sound produced by the rockets will affect the...quality, of the Natural Area Reserve to the south of the facility."

"I see," Schaefer said. "With the EPA thing from last month, I guess that makes it about an even dozen lawsuits pending against us for one reason or another."

"Yes. Perhaps a dozen. And there will be more irritations to come, large and small. On the Saturday of next week, for example, there is to be a...demonstration. Against us."

"Oh?"

"Yes." The corner of Kamada's mouth twitched downward. "As you know, that is the day scheduled for the arrival of the two new rockets. Someone, Laurance, is a traitor."

"A—what?'

"I cannot believe this is merely a coincidence. Some

person has revealed the schedule, in spite of my command not to."

"Hell, Hideo," Schaefer said, "even if it's not a coincidence it's hard to keep that sort of thing quiet. Someone in the trucking company probably let it slip."

"Yesss. We will never use them again. But to return to the subject. One demonstration will be held in front of the governor's home here, on Oahu. At the same time, one will be held at the entrance to the Kona Launch Facility. Advertisements are located in several of the newspapers. I will show you one if you wish."

"No thanks," Schaefer said. He changed the subject. "So, what about the investigation? How's that going?"

Kamada's next set of steps put him beside his desk, where he had begun his abbreviated perambulation. "I have been in contact with the police and with Captain Kane. It is not yet known if Tate owns a rifle. As for the last rocket, only very small pieces of it have been picked up, but they show no unusual damage."

"Where are these pieces?"

"In the assembly building." Kamada's eyelids dropped until they were almost closed. "You know, Laurance. I think you should look at them."

"I will," Schaefer said. "But I don't imagine I'll find anything our people haven't spotted."

"I do not mean for that reason. I thought perhaps it would remind you of..." Kamada paused and his teeth came together tightly. "Of what has been done to us."

Schaefer flushed. "I don't need anything to remind me of what's been done."

"No? You seem to accept all of this with much...calmness."

"What do you want me to do? Flip out?"

"I think not."

"I think not, either."

The men locked eyes.

Kamada turned away first. He looked out the window, fixing his gaze on the thin white lines of breakers crawling in from the sea. He was right about Schaefer, he reflected. If not for the astronaut's valuable contacts and the image he imparted to the company, he would prefer to buy the man out. Schaefer no longer had the will to fight. He had lost his ...what was the word? His drive.

"Is there anything else we need to discuss?" Schaefer asked.

Kamada carefully sat in his white chair behind his white desk. "Yes," he said heavily. "It is a serious matter. I would like to have your suggestions for protecting the next rocket from this dog Tate."

Schaefer lifted a hand. "I don't think he'll try anything. He knows we're on to him. He's not crazy. I doubt he wants to go to jail."

"Laurance," Kamada said, unable to mask the impatience in his voice, "I doubt that he wanted to go to jail before. As for his condition of sanity, that is a matter of opinion."

"I suppose it is. But he probably feels lucky that he got away with just some trespassing charges. I don't think he'll press his luck again, especially when he knows we'll be watching him."

Below the desk, out of sight of the astronaut's eyes, Kamada crushed his hands together. The man simply had no forethought. Schaefer would have to be led, like a child, to the correct decision.

"Laurance," he said, releasing his hands, "what if our investigation of Tate is, in the end...inconclusive. What if we have no evidence which will put him in jail."

"You think that's going to be the case, Hideo?"

"I do not know. I am only...supposing. But if this happened, Tate would escape all punishment."

Schaefer started to respond but Kamada held up a hand. "However, let us say that enough evidence is gathered to prove what he has done. Then, I think, it would not be wise to involve the federal government, nor any authorities. It would not be wise to bring this matter to the courts."

Schaefer screwed up his forehead. "What? For Christ's sake, what's the point of gathering evidence, then?"

Kamada cleared his throat, a low cough. "The point would be to use it to persuade Tate to...cooperate."

"Cooperate? You mean...sell us his land?"

"Yes. Of course. That is what we needed from him all along. That is the...source, of our problems."

"Just that? What about everyone else who wants us out? What about all the lawsuits? Did you forget about them?"

"I have not forgotten," Kamada said frostily. "But once Tate is out of the way, and we have a record of successful launches, then we can complete the launch facilities properly. When we are in place totally there will be no reason to stop us."

"So we tell Tate to sell out or we prosecute. But what about the cops? Kane's already involved. Other people could find out, or guess. If the Feds hear about it they'll raise hell."

Kamada spread his hands. "That is exactly my point. Some persons may now suspect what Tate was doing, because he was seen with a rifle. But they do not know, because we have said nothing of that matter."

"What about Kane?"

"Captain Kane has assured me that he will say nothing until we decide to, for the good of everyone. Think of this, Laurance. Once the police or Federal agencies are involved, it will be out of our control. We will have no...leverage, to remove Tate. Perhaps he would be placed in prison, but his land will still be his—not ours."

Kamada stood and moved to the window again. "What also concerns me is that openly accusing Tate of shooting the rockets —this will result in much publicity on the matter. As you know, we seem to have enemies on the island. What if there are others as...demented as he. What if another fool is...inspired, by Tate's acts, and decides to shoot at our rockets also. What if this is a problem we were forced to deal with for years."

The first gentle throbs of an oncoming headache floated to the top of Schaefer's head, soft bubbles of diffused pain. He pressed his eyeballs with a thumb and forefinger, wondering if he should take an aspirin or a Tylenol. "I guess it's possible," he said irritably. "You know, it's too bad we didn't assess the local sentiment a little more closely on that damned island."

Kamada's eyes slowly blinked. "The local...sentiment," he said harshly. "It is fortunate, Laurance, that the pioneer settlers in America did not assess the local sentiment very carefully, or the United States would not exist."

Schaefer opened his mouth, then closed it. He had no ready response. But even if Kamada was right he didn't need some foreign bastard preaching to him about his own country.

"Skip," Kamada said, his face softening minutely, "the fools who oppose us—what they think is unimportant. In any case, the sentiment will change.

345

The people will more and more grow...accustomed to us. We will give them jobs. In time they will not care."

Schaefer listened to this with half an ear. Kamada's use of his nickname, a rare event, bothered him inordinately.

"I think this," Kamada said. "I think we should collect all the evidence we can against Tate. We should retain the services of a private investigator to aid us. I believe Mr. Kane might be able to advise us in that matter. When we have enough evidence to..." Kamada snatched at the air and squeezed his hands together. "...to strangle Tate, then we will show it to him. He will understand what will happen if he does not cooperate."

Schaefer considered this. Kamada, as he had seen before on many occasions, was unstoppable at getting what he wanted. If only he weren't so obsessive, if only his personality were more bearable, he would be the ultimate business partner. But that wasn't the case. Increasingly he'd become an egocentric, power-hungry manipulator. Schaefer's jaw tightened; the decision he had made in the car would not change.

"You know, Laurance," Kamada said, "we have still not solved another important problem. That is, how to make certain that our next launches come to no harm from Tate. I would still appreciate your advice."

Schaefer shifted in his chair. "I have no advice. Like I said, I really don't think he'll try anything. Maybe we should just go to him now and tell him we're on to what he's doing. We can tell him that the cops suspect him. We can throw in the FBI and the FAA and the goddam CIA for that matter, and scare his ass so bad he won't want to leave his house."

"I am not so sure," Kamada said. "If we tell him these things, perhaps he will think that he has nothing to lose by shooting another rocket."

Schaefer was in no mood to explore the psychological intricacies of the problem. He had just decided that a scotch on the rocks would be better than aspirin or Tylenol. He said, "We'll just have to keep a close watch on him."

Kamada's face clouded. "As you know, to perform the last search operation, we brought in from California many more security personnel. And still Tate evaded us. Still he damaged our rocket, which we were forced to destroy. Unless we tell the police what is truly occurring, they will not concern themselves to help us. But we do not wish to tell the police. You say we must watch Tate, Skip. Tell me how. Will we watch him every day. Will we watch him just before the launches. Will a man follow him at every moment." Kamada leaned forward from the waist, and a strand of his gray hair came loose and dangled in the air. "Will we have a man live in his house."

His point made, Kamada straightened up and smoothed his hair back in place. Schaefer was glad for this; somehow the loose strand made the man look a little too insane for comfort. He said, "Look, Hideo, I don't know what you want me to say, or what you're getting at. But if we just tell Tate we're on to him I don't think we'll have to worry about him anymore. Anyway, without going to the authorities, I can't think of a damn thing we can do but watch him as best we can."

Kamada's eyes seemed to shrivel. He pivoted his chair around to face the windows and emitted another adder-like exhalation. "It may be so, Laurance. I, also, intend to stop worrying about him."

Kamada remained in his office after the astronaut

left. Sitting at his desk, he ate a Gelusil tablet and picked up the telephone. He punched in a number, waited, and made arrangements for a girl to be sent up to his suite after dinner. It would be a new one this time; he had offered more money, but the last bitch refused to come back again.

Chapter Thirty-Eight

Neal waited outside on a patch of grass shaded by a mimosa tree while Big Jim went into the Kailua post office to check his mailbox. They had just come from a quick blitz of the grocery store across the street, a mission rendered essential after nine days of eating fast food and everything edible in Perkin's apartment and aboard the *Suzy Q*.

Neal had been in town since the fishing trip with Harry. He crewed for Big Jim on fishing charters, helped with boat maintenance while not incidentally maintaining a distance between himself and the Concord Space Systems Kona Launch Facility.

Sitting on the grass patch, Neal picked up a fallen mimosa blossom and twirled the fuzzy pink puff between thumb and forefinger, watching people go in and out of the building. Except for Big Jim the only person he'd spent any time talking to was Tom Bailey.

Bailey had discovered that a church owned the property involved in the trespassing charge. "It seems the police keep an eye on it to discourage dumping and vandalism," the lawyer explained at their meeting, "but you're the first person they've ever actually arrested. The cops are supposedly checking to see if the boat you took off the property was stolen. In any event, if the church doesn't pursue the matter that'll be the end of it." In Bailey's opinion the fence-damage suit was also a dead issue. "The main things," he said, "are,

349

one—no eyewitnesses, and two—we responded to the suit within the proper time frame. Since you denied all the allegations, what I imagine CSS's attorneys will do is introduce a motion to set aside our response and grant a summary judgment against you. But that's just *pro forma*. It won't happen."

The meeting with Bailey took a load off his mind. Now—aside from Susan's absence—only one other thing was hanging over his head—the situation with Harry. Their parting after the fishing trip had been awkward and restrained. Given the situation, that was understandable but still troubling. They hadn't spoken since then. Three times he started to go by the gun shop but hadn't gone through with it. The truth was, Neal admitted to himself, he needed Harry to make the first move.

His thoughts were interrupted when Big Jim came striding across the grass with a fistful of mail. "Got somethin' from Kawika," Perkins said. He squatted in the shade next to Neal and picked out the envelope, ripping off one end with his teeth.

Watching him dig out the letter Neal said, "Don't take this wrong, but you bear a striking resemblance to a Neanderthal going after bone marrow."

"Sometimes I wish I was," Perkins admitted with a wistful look. He pulled out a single sheet of ruled loose-leaf paper that he unfolded and read with a look of pained concentration. The frown gradually gave way to a broad smile. "All right!" Perkins chortled, slapping his knee. "He's comin' back!"

Neal flicked away the mimosa blossom. "Yeah? What's the deal?"

Perkins handed over the letter and Neal skimmed through Kawika's block printing. "This is great. It'll be

good to see him."

"Sure will." Perkins took the letter back and dropped it onto the rest of his mail. He sat back heavily on the grass. "Man, shoppin' wore me out."

"Yeah," Neal said dryly, "we must've been in there a solid twenty minutes. Half of which was you figuring out which cookies you were going to buy." He stretched out his legs. "What're you going to tell Kawika?"

"You mean about fishin' with me?" Perkins shrugged. "Hell, I can put his...fat ass to *work* for a while."

"You're a good friend, Large James."

"Not really. Kawika's a killer fisherman." Perkins grinned slyly and bobbed his eyebrows. "I can steal the bastard's *tricks.*"

*   *   *

Neal drove home the next morning while Big Jim was having breakfast with a new set of clients. His only stop was at Yamata Store. He bought ice and some food items and checked his post office box, where he found three pieces of junk mail, a letter from Susan, and a postcard from Kawika. The picture side of the postcard showed a bare-breasted, mai-tai-toting *wahine* wading in the surf, and the other side was filled with a shrunken version of the printing and contents of the letter to Big Jim.

Neal tossed the junk mail into a garbage can and drove home. He put away the food and sat at the kitchen table to read Susan's letter. She wrote, in a depressingly cheerful tone, that she was doing fine and missed him.

He changed into shorts, made a big glass of iced

351

water, and took a book and a blanket out to the yard, where he read until he fell asleep.

He woke up groggy and hungry. He gathered up everything and went back to the house. As he was pushing open the verandah door he suddenly stopped, then squatted down and examined the door latch. The edges of the double doors were marked with two shallow, squared-off indentations, as though someone had tried to pry them apart with a screwdriver to get at the bolt. He'd painted the door just over a month ago so the marks were definitely new.

Neal went straight to the loose panel in the closet and checked to see if the rifle was still there. It was. He replaced the panel and made an inspection tour of the house. As far as he could tell, everything was where he left it ten days ago. Everything except the door of the empty refrigerator, which he kept open an inch for air circulation. Someone had closed it.

He went down to the storage area beneath the house and dug into the ground near a piling. The boxes of rifle and pistol cartridges were still there, double-sealed inside a plastic bag and a Tupperware container.

He reburied the cartridges and went back upstairs, bothered. The question of going for another rocket had been in the back of his mind. It seemed a shame not to keep up the pressure on CSS, but making the attempt when they knew about it—and when someone had broken into the house for no obvious reason—seemed stupid. He was disinclined to push his luck any further.

What he really wanted to do was paint. Just paint for a few days, and forget everything else.

Chapter Thirty-Nine

Neal clapped the cabinet door shut and slumped to the counter, rubbing his eyes. Out of coffee. After four days of painting—a solid four days of stroking oil on canvas, working on a series of big, sunny views of the coastline that helped lift him out of his general depression—he'd started cleaning up the studio and hadn't stopped until almost two in the morning. He couldn't sleep after the sun came up, so he needed some coffee, bad.

He laced on his running shoes, slipped on a small daypack and set out jogging for Yamata Store.

After he'd gotten some air into his lungs and the initial stiffness melted away the run became almost pleasurable. The first mile of Mokolea road disappeared under his feet, then another half mile.

As he neared the final uphill stretch a string of cars heading in the opposite direction passed him. He slowed to a walk, puzzled. Five more cars, all loaded with passengers, rolled by in quick succession, and by the time he reached the store parking lot vehicles of every kind were coming in a steady flow. A placard that said NO ROCKETS!! taped to the side of a school bus solved the mystery. Tom Bailey had mentioned the anti-CSS demonstration the last time they spoke but he'd forgotten about it.

Mr. Yamata was minding the store. "Mrs. Yamata's sick, I hope," Neal asked, setting a can of coffee and a box of donuts on the counter.

"No," the old man said testily. He jabbed at the register keys with a gnarled forefinger. "She out wessin dam' time."

He started to ask how she was wasting her time but thought better of it. Apparently the loss of fishing hours had put Mr. Yamata in a foul mood. Neal said goodbye and retreated.

From the pay phone outside Neal dialed the police station in Kealakekua. Cars were still streaming down Mokolea Road. A woman identifying herself as Sergeant Moy answered and Neal asked to speak with Captain Gilbert.

"Captain Gilbert is gone for the weekend," she said. "Can I help you?"

"Possibly. This is Neal Tate. My pickup truck was impounded and I need to know when I can come get it."

The officer put him on hold. A moment later she came back on. "Mr. Tate? They're through with your vehicle but there's no one here who can release it. Captain Gilbert will be back Monday, if you want to try then."

He thanked her and hung up. After transferring the coffee and donuts to the daypack he started home at a jog.

The traffic on Mokolea Road had not let up, and the closer he got to the house the more congested the road became. Two more buses passed him, raising a nose-itching haze of dust.

When he rounded the curve below his own property he saw cars parked on both shoulders all the way to the top of the rise. He stashed the daypack a few yards into his entrance road, backtracked, and made his way uphill.

The demonstrators, many of them carrying protest signs mounted on sticks, appeared to be converging across the road from the launch site gate. The road widened at that point into an area of bare ground that CSS had used during construction to transfer trailered-in earth-moving vehicles. As he got closer he saw that the clearing was filled with cars and a large flatbed truck carrying what looked like a podium and band equipment. He darted across the road between a police car and a news van and joined the line of people filing uphill between the traffic and the parked cars.

A moment later the line slowed and then stopped. Craning his head, Neal saw a woman in khaki culottes and a straw sunhat tugging a bundle of new NO ROCKETS!! signs from the back of a station wagon. The line started forward again as she began handing them out, and he moved along with them. When he reached the station wagon the woman turned toward him and he felt a small jolt of recognition.

"Violet!" He held out his hand. "Hello! Neal Tate, Harry's friend."

"Hello, Neal!" Violet Gray took his hand in hers. "We were wondering if you'd show up today." She laughed. "I wasn't sure I'd recognize you, though, since I haven't seen you since..." She let the sentence trail off.

"Since Bernice's party, I guess," he said.

"Yes, that must be it."

Neal felt his ears burning, wondering if she was playing with him. He looked around. "A lot of people showed up."

"It's a pretty good turnout, all right," Violet said, giving away her last sign. She closed the station wagon tailgate. "We're getting people from all over the island.

Just about the whole village of Mokolea, from what Bernice says.

That's great. Where is Bernice, by the way?"

Violet pointed. "She should be by the truck up there, the loudspeakers and things on it. And Harry's around somewhere."

Neal thanked her and excused himself. He worked his way through the crowd in the clearing, heading for the makeshift stage. Bernice was on the far side, talking to a plump haole holding a walkie-talkie who trotted away as he came up.

"There he is," Bernice crowed. She started to embrace him and stopped herself. "Hey, wait a darn second, I'm mad at you! You haven't come to see me in weeks and weeks!"

"I know, I'm a jerk. Sorry."

"You sure are. Oh, well." She gave him a quick hug. "I hear you've been getting into trouble, hon. Trespassing or some other vicious crime."

"Afraid so. Who told you? Tom?"

"No, Harry Sturdivant mentioned it. Speaking of Tom, he should be here pretty soon with a banner and some more signs. And did you happen to see Harry or Violet?"

"I saw Violet. I was telling her you got a nice turnout."

"Not bad," Bernice said. "News-wise, it's excellent. They're delivering two more rockets this morning."

"Did you plan it like that?"

"Absolutely. I just got news that the trucks should be here pretty soon." Bernice lifted her head. "Ah, there's Tom. I'd better scoot. If you're looking for Harry, hon, he said he'd be down the road by that jacaranda tree."

There was no more vehicular traffic on Mokolea Road; the flow of cars from downhill had been cut off, leaving a stream of pedestrians only. Making his way downhill through the throng, Neal nearly walked over a small figure in horn-rimmed sunglasses and a woven palm-leaf hat.

"Hey, Mrs. Yamata. I wondered why you weren't in the store."

"Goo' reason," she said. "No rocket! Also, I make ol' foo' wuk today. Ha ha! He need pratice."

Neal said goodbye and kept moving, leaving her giggling. A little farther downhill he spied Harry coming in the opposite direction with a sign laced through one arm.

Harry grinned and hailed him as he trudged up. "Hey, stranger! I've been keeping an eye out for you. I was trying to find the road to your place but I can't figure out where it is. We're close, right?"

"It's down a little farther. Pretty hard to see. I'll give you a tour of the place later if you want."

"Hell yes."

"It ain't much," Neal warned. "However, I do have some gin and a chest full of ice."

Harry clapped him on the arm, chuckling hoarsely. "You got my number!"

Violet Gray appeared beside them with a sign on her shoulder. "I've been looking all over for you two."

"You found us, kid," Harry said. "Obviously you and Neal already re-met each other, right?"

"We did indeed. I came to tell you gentlemen that Bernice is about to get things going, if you want to move closer."

They started up the road but a shriek of amplified feedback stopped them. The crowd turned toward the platform as Bernice stepped up to the microphone on the makeshift rostrum, now hung with a banner reading The Islands Belong to Everyone—NO ROCKETS!. She greeted the protesters with a few words and segued into a prepared speech.

Bernice had been talking for only a few moments when she suddenly stopped and pointed downhill. "Hey, speak of the devils!"

Neal turned around along with the rest of the crowd. Through a forest of protest signs he saw a light blue sedan with flashing yellow roof lights rounding the curve at the bottom of the hill, followed closely by a tractor-trailer rig carrying a single huge cylinder strapped in place with nylon webbing and covered with blue tarpaulins. As more of the big trucks came into sight the crowd spontaneously booed.

The eighteen-wheelers, a total of six, climbed slowly up the hill, their air brakes hissing as they eased between the parked cars and ranks of protesters. One by one the big rigs crawled through the crowd and negotiated the turn onto the CSS entrance road, leaving in their wake a cloud of diesel exhaust. The protesters chanted No rockets as they closed in behind.

Neal was a few steps ahead of Harry and Violet Gray when a car started honking furiously. He stood on his toes and saw a black limousine barreling uphill, sending protestors scurrying out of the way. As the limo came closer he recognized Howard Tubbs in the driver's seat, glaring from behind the windshield like some angry life form trapped in ice.

Neal had moved to the shoulder of the road when he heard people shouting and saw a knot of demonstrators jumping from the path of the horn-honking limousine. The vehicle swerved to miss two people and struck Violet Gray, sending her spinning to the ground, her sign slapping into the vehicle's rear window.

The big black car slithered to a stop, its tires squealing, and Neal was forced back by the crowd. Through the press of bodies he caught a glimpse of Harry kneeling in the road beside Violet, and he pushed his way toward them. As he did the limousine's tinted rear window whirred down and Hideo Kamada, easily recognizable from the newspaper photo, thrust his head from the darkened interior like a malignant jack-in-the-box.

"Who has done this?" Kamada hissed furiously, his features contorted with rage. He slammed a hand on the door. "Who has struck this car?"

A few of the demonstrators near the limousine shouted heatedly and pointed back along the road. Grudgingly, Kamada started to turn and look, but he changed his mind and pulled his head in. The tinted window hummed shut. With a steady blast of the horn the big automobile jerked forward menacingly, clearing away the protesters, and drove off.

Violet Gray had been carried into the shade of a tree. Neal found her sitting against the trunk, surrounded by a small crowd, clutching her thigh as Harry knelt beside her and wiped her face with a wet bandana.

"I guess I'm slowing down, Neal," Violet said with a breathless laugh.

"He was going too fast," Neal said. "Maybe you should lie down, Violet. You look sort of pale."

"I think he's right, kiddo," Harry said. "Let's just scoot you down a bit."

They helped her lie down with her head elevated on

a folded blanket somebody brought over.

"How's the leg look?" Neal asked.

Harry grunted angrily. "At the minimum she's gonna have a nasty bruise on her leg and a sore foot," he said. "The car ran over her toes. I don't think anything's broken."

"I'm fine," Violet said. "Just let me lie here a bit."

She rested a few minutes, and then Neal and Harry made a chair with their arms and carried her to the station wagon. Harry fussed around getting her comfortable in the back seat until she shooed him away. He slid behind the wheel with his mouth set tight and Neal got in on the other side. Raising a finger, Violet said in a tired but credible English accent, "Hospital, James."

Chapter Forty

At the outer edges of his thoughts Neal noticed that the bedroom walls had turned from gray to a glowing pinkish hue. He had been awake for nearly an hour, lying in bed as morning sunlight gradually crept across the curtains Susan had sewn, with images from last Saturday's demonstration floating through his mind. Bernice. Harry. Violet at the hospital. The crowds of protestors. Tubbs' face behind the windshield. The blue-shrouded rocket sections on the trucks, the limo knocking Violet down, Kamada.

From a distance of five days the jumbled scenes coalesced into a single complex event, and the overall tone of that event reinforced his belief that his war on Concord Space Systems was basically right-minded.

From the start he realized that his hatred of CSS carried in it a load of personal baggage, and he knew that his sabotage of the launches, while subjectively satisfying, could be objectively labeled radical and/or stupid. These things, plus having to make almost all his decisions concerning CSS without anyone else's input, had made his reasoning processes regarding CSS suspect, more abstract than concrete.

On the other hand none of the people who now knew what he was doing—Tom Bailey, Harry, Big Jim—had seemed stunned or horrified. But there was no way to extract their true, bottom-line feelings. He suspected they didn't really know how they felt themselves, not entirely.

But Saturday had changed things, at least in his own mind. If he wasn't totally right about CSS he was definitely on the right track, on the right side. He didn't feel so alone any more.

Neal sat up and stretched, wondering what Susan was doing in Los Angeles right then. The question was a standard part of his waking routine, almost a reflex. Thinking it and then shoving it to the back of his mind seemed to clear some kind of mental path, letting him get on with his day.

He wolfed down a bowl of cereal and went straight to the studio, where he flipped through the stacked canvases and picked out two that were almost finished. Taking them out to the verandah along with the easel, paints, and brushes, he set everything up and started work on a view of Kealakekua Bay, where in 1779 Captain James Cook had gotten his head bashed in by a mob of disgruntled Hawaiians.

In six hours of work, including a sandwich break, he completed the two paintings and quit for the day.

After cleaning up he drove Susan's car to Yamata Store and telephoned the police station in Captain Cook. His truck had been released.

Inside the store Mrs. Yamata looked up from her Japanese newspaper and gave him a peg-toothed smile. "Hallo, Nee! How you do?"

"Pretty good, Mrs. Yamata, thanks. I was wondering—would you mind if I left my car parked outside for a while? I'll be gone for about an hour."

"Shu, of coss. But maybe I sell why you gone!"

He left her staggering in a little circle behind the counter, her sides shaking. As he parked the Datsun it crossed his mind that she might be at least half bonkers. But who wasn't.

Neal walked up Mokolea Road to the highway and thumbed down the first car that passed. It was a rental driven by a middle-aged tourist couple, a paunchy salesman type with thinning hair and a booze-ravaged nose, and his wife, a tanned redhead who didn't look up from emery-boarding her fingernails when he got in.

The man peered in the rear-view mirror as they accelerated up the highway. "You live here?"

Neal said, "Sure do."

The man shook his head. "Jesus, must be nice. This place is goddam paradise." He looked at his wife, then slapped her thigh. "Ain't it, honey? A goddam paradise?"

The steady, insectile rasping didn't stop as she said, "It's lovely."

"Told ya it would be." The man belched into his hand and the smell of alcohol drifted into the back seat. "We're on a sort of golf vacation," he said, grinning into the mirror. "But today we're takin' a vacation from our vacation."

Chuckling, he swerved into the other lane.

"Went up to the Volcano House this mornin'," he went on, ignoring the dark look from his wife. "Now we're just cruisin' around. Already did the courses on Maui. When we're through here we'll do Oahu. I tell you one thing, those Japs may be buying up the place but they really know how to make a golf course." His forehead bunched up earnestly in the mirror. "You play golf?"

"Never took it up," Neal said.

"No? Great game, great game." The man twisted his head around and winked. "You get to be old farts like us, it's the only reason for gettin' up in the mornin'."

He laughed, slapped his wife's thigh again, and drove onto the shoulder of the road.

"Watch where you're going," the woman warned. "And speak for yourself."

Jack steered back into his lane, momentarily chastened. "Say," he said, glancing into the mirror again, "we anywhere near that rocket place?"

"Pretty near," Neal told him. "It's off to your left about four miles."

"No kiddin'? Boy, I'd love to see a rocket go off! Know when they're gonna shoot up the next one?"

"I really don't know for sure." In fact it was one of the things he wanted to find out.

Jack and his wife let Neal off at the police station in Kealakekua. He picked up his keys at the desk and drove the truck from the fenced-in compound to the nearest pay phone, where he called the offices of the *Kona Gazette.* The next test launch was scheduled for the coming Saturday.

After driving the pickup truck home Neal walked the two miles back to Yamata Store for the Datsun. He thanked Mrs. Yamata for not selling it, which disabled her for a full minute, drove home again, took a shower, and fell exhausted on the futon.

When he woke up he brewed a cup of tea and took it out on the verandah to watch the sunset. It was a pretty good one, cloud-wise. He stayed outside, thinking, until the first stars came out. Dinner was spaghetti seasoned with garlic butter, which he ate by candlelight at the kitchen table.

After dinner he settled on the sofa with a gin and tonic to read' but the harsh light of the battery-powered fluorescent camp lantern seemed to have a soporific effect. He closed the book and went to bed.

*   *   *

The whine of a mosquito woke him. Neal dragged a hand from under the sheet and waved it sluggishly over his face, driving the insect away. He was slipping comfortably back into his dream when a creaking sound came from the next room. He lifted his head, instantly awake. The noise came again, slightly different this time, and his skin suddenly seemed to be covered with a film of cold oil. Someone was in the living room.

In one motion he pulled the sheet aside and stood on the futon, keeping his eyes on the open bedroom door, a blurry black rectangle against dark gray walls. One long step put him close to the chest of drawers. He lifted a pair of cut-offs from atop it, slipped them on, and moved silently to the front window of the bedroom. He was about to unfasten the screen hook when he heard whispering on the other side of the window, outside.

He knelt down and listened. Over the whine in his bad ear came the faint sound of the verandah doors being unlatched, followed by a soft squeak as they opened and then a series of drawn-out floor creaks. Another person had been let inside.

Neal stepped back to the futon. Moving quickly but quietly he laid the two pillows end to end and pulled the sheet over them. He lifted the electric fan from atop the chest of drawers by the bed, ran his hand down the cord to the plug and pried it from the socket, then squatted into the patch of gloom on the side away from the door.

He waited, sweat running down his ribs. Whoever was in the house knew he was here since both cars were at the end of the road.

Another creak came from just outside the door, along with the soft scuffing sound of a foot. Neal tightened his grip on the fan, putting his other hand on the wall behind him. The shape of a man, black from head to foot, appeared over the top of the dresser and moved toward the futon. There was a faint rustle of cloth as the intruder bent over the pillow dummy.

Neal pushed off from the wall and slammed the fan into the man's head, following it with a kick to his chest that produced an explosive grunt. The man staggered sideways and crumpled to the floor, sucking air into his lungs with mewing gasps.

The dark shape of the bedroom door seemed to wobble as another black-clad figure rushed into the room. Swinging the fan from his hip, Neal caught him on the arm and sent him stumbling into the chest of drawers. The man snarled something in a language that wasn't English and Neal straight-armed the fan at the source of noise, drawing a howl of pain.

The first man staggered upright with an angry groan. Neal drove a sidekick into his stomach, slamming him against the window, and the man's head snapped back and shattered the glass behind the curtain. He went down again.

Plunging through the bedroom door, Neal barreled into another black-clad intruder. Their heads struck with a wooden clunk and the man let out a squawk of pain and surprise. Neal pressed a hand to his forehead where he had hit and lunged blindly toward the front doors, but something swept his feet from under him and sent him flying. He rolled as he hit the floor and scrambled to get up. A foot smashed into his right arm and chest, flipping him onto his back and knocking out his breath. He kept rolling and crashed into one of the spindly end tables by the sofa, which fell across his back. Fighting the urge to suck in air uncontrollably, Neal got a grip on one leg of the table and dragged it with him behind the sofa. He drew a steady breath into his lungs, forced it out, and drew in another, pulling himself to his feet as the man who had kicked him came around the other end of the sofa.

All he could see was a moving shadow, but that was enough. He swung the end table with both hands. It connected solidly, cracking off the legs. He used one of them to club the man to the floor. As he went down the man screamed out a stream obscenities, definitely in English.

Neal backed away, his lungs heaving. A fist hammered him from behind but the blow was badly aimed and glanced off his ribs. He whirled around and beat at the new attacker with the table leg.

The fluorescent lantern suddenly snapped on. Neal crouched down, holding up a hand to shield his eyes. Before they adjusted to the light he was tackled from the right. The attacker's momentum propelled them both into the closet door, splitting the center panel, and the impact forced his left arm partway through the crack.

The man who had tackled him shifted his grip and Neal snapped an elbow into his chin, sending him walking backwards on his heels, arms windmilling. With a violent heave he freed his trapped arm from the door and turned to face his attackers, getting his first good look at them.

He saw three. Two were edging toward him in fighting stances, hands up, while the third was getting to his feet beside the sofa. All wore black nylon windbreakers, black leather gloves, black chinos, and dark running shoes. Their heads were covered by dark blue ski masks with red-rimmed openings for the eyes and mouth.

The two closer men attacked at the same time. He swiped the table leg at one, nicking him on the head, and snapped a kick at the other, scoring a direct hit. The man shrieked and clutched at his crotch, hobbling away.

The other man stepped in, parrying a second blow from the table leg, and threw a front kick. Neal twisted away as it landed but he was still knocked into the wall. He recovered as his attacker charged and delivered a spinning back kick that lifted the man into the air. When his feet touched down the man did a frantic backward tap-dance into the sofa and somersaulting over it with a startled cry.

Two of the intruders were on their feet again, breathing hard and shooting glances at each other, when an incoherent bellow came from the bedroom and the man he'd hit with the fan lumbered into the living room. He was taller and heavier than the other three but dressed similarly in dark shoes and pants. Instead of a black windbreaker he wore a black turtleneck pullover and a *ninja*-style hood, split in the middle for the eyes, hid his features.

The man who had been kicked in the groin staggered to his feet. "Son of a bitch!" he screamed, heading for the verandah doors, "you *lied* about this!"

The big man pointed a finger at him, his eyes glittering behind the slit in his hood. In a distorted growl he said, "Don't move, you chickenshit! You leave and I'll come after you and kick your fuckin' guts out."

"Fuck you!" the man screamed, and bolted through the doors.

Neal sprinted toward the back of the room.

"*Stop him!*" the big man bellowed, lunging around the sofa.

Neal changed his mind about jumping through the window. Instead he pushed off the wall to turn himself around and leaped into the air, lashing a foot at the head of the closest man. The man ducked and fended off the blow with a forearm, and Neal came down awkwardly. He was regaining his footing when a foot slammed into his head and knocked him down.

He managed to get to his knees just as the three men crowded in, kicking savagely. The blows didn't hurt but he could tell from the sickening thuds that they would later. He grabbed a foot and struggled upright as he twisted the foot in his hands, toppling its owner. Jumping over the fallen man, he headed for the front of the room.

One of the assailants vaulted over the sofa and made a grab as he passed, snagging his wrist and stopping his forward motion with a jerk. Neal swung with his free fist. The blow skimmed along the man's ski-masked cheek into his nose, breaking it with an audible pop, and the man let out a short scream and clutched at his face.

Neal lunged toward the doors again but an arm wrapped around his neck, his knee was kicked from behind, and he was dragged backwards and down. As he fell he clawed at the gloved fingers on his throat, prying two of them loose. He bent them back and the big man let out an inarticulate scream and went down on his knees to ease the pressure.

Keeping a grip on the fingers, Neal tried to stand. A foot caught him in the gut and he fell over again. Another foot slammed into his temple and the room went black.

*   *   *

A loud smacking noise brought him back to consciousness. He felt his head move with the next smack and realized he was being slapped. He tried to lift his hands but they wouldn't move. He could make out, through barely opened eyes, one of the ski-masked men pinning his right arm, and he knew from pressure that his left arm was also pinned. Moving his eyes, he saw the big man silhouetted against the lantern-lit ceiling, poised for another slap.

Neal cocked his leg and kicked upward, and the big man made a huffing sound and disappeared from view. Twisting to one side, he kept kicking, concentrating on the man holding his right arm. The man rose from his crouch enough to boot him in the ribs. The pain of the blow was paralyzing; all he could do was lie stiffly on the floor, gasping for air. Through the blur of pain he saw the big man appear over him like a black cloud. The man pulled a *nunchaku* from behind his back, whirled one stick in the air, and swung. Neal felt the stick crack into his shin. He screamed, as much in anger as in pain, and fought to get up. The big man stepped around to his head and kicked and he faded into a state of semi-consciousness.

He was aware of what happened next but it seemed to be taking place in a distorted mirror, one that moved every time his eyes did. He felt himself dragged across the floor and pulled onto the sofa. A ski-masked man jerked him into a sitting position, his head hanging forward loosely, and stretched his arms out along the sofa's backrest, one man holding each wrist. The big man shoved the *nunchaku* sticks under his chin and

370

forced his head up. "I got somethin' for you, shithead. Special delivery. You won't be doin' any shootin' for a while."

Straightening up, the big man adjusted his *ninja* mask and pointed with his *nunchaku*, making a brushing motion. "Move back some."

The man holding his right wrist moved to one side while keeping his grip. The big man let a *nunchaku* stick fall free and then whipped it down. There was a thudding snap as an arm bone broke. Neal screamed again and fought feebly to free himself.

"Hold him," the big man ordered. Repositioning himself, he drew the *nunchaku* back for a blow to the other arm.

It never came.

There was a thumping noise outside and the verandah doors burst inward in a shower of glass and wood as Big Jim Perkins charged into the room. Without stopping he lowered his shoulder and slammed into the *nunchaku* man, knocking him off his feet.

The two ski-masked men released their grip and backed away from the sofa, digging into their pockets and pulling out stainless steel *balisong* knives that they opened with smooth wrist-flicks. They rounded the sofa to help their boss, whose head was being slammed into the floor by Perkins.

Dimly aware of a new sound, Neal moved his eyes enough to see Kawika Kahooke lumber through the shattered front doors, snorting and heaving like a rogue elephant. Kawika spotted the men with the knives, bellowed, grabbed up a chair and swung it. A knife-wielder slammed into his companion, who inadvertently stabbed the first man in the buttocks as they floundered to the floor. Both men jumped up immediately, the one with the punctured buttocks cursing shrilly, but they went down again as Kawika plowed into them, stomping and kicking with his sandaled feet. The men rolled clear and scrambled up again, backing away with knives waving.

Kawika advanced relentlessly toward the near one. The other let go of his injured buttocks long enough to dart in and stab. Kawika howled as the knife jabbed him but he twisted around and caught the man's hand as he withdrew the blade. There was a frenzied struggle and the knife vanished just before Kawika snapped his opponent's arm over his knee. The man screamed and fell back, staring in disbelief at the odd new angle his limb had acquired. Kawika turned on the second man and closed in.

Across the room the big *ninja*-masked man freed one of his arms and struck Big Jim in the eye with a fist. Perkins made an open-handed swipe at the man's face that caught his mask and pulled down the bottom half, and then he rolled off, releasing his foe. The man with the broken arm picked up a loose table leg and clubbed Perkins, left-handed, across the shoulders. Big Jim was turning to fend off the blows when the man in the *ninja* mask slugged him in the solar plexus. Grunting with pain, Perkins hunched over and felt the *nunchaku* whip down on his back again. As he gasped for air he saw the big man slip past and run through the broken doors into the night.

The attacker with the broken arm and bleeding buttocks eyed Big Jim, who was blocking his way to the door, and then hobbled forward and swung his table leg. Perkins dodged the clumsy blow and knocked him cold with a backhand across the temple.

Backed against the wall by Kawika, the remaining uninjured intruder suddenly let out a cry and attacked, his knife slashing. Kawika fended off the blade and caught the man in his arms. With a grunt of effort he lifted him over his head like a writhing black octopus and tossed him toward the verandah doors, which had swung almost closed. The doors splintered outward as the man sailed through and hit the verandah deck, bouncing once and striking the railing head-first. He went slack.

Kawika hurried over to Big Jim. "You okay, brah?"

Perkins nodded, breathing in gasps, and waved him toward the sofa.

Neal had slumped down and fallen sideways on the pillows, a red smear tracing the path of his head. Kawika gently placed a finger on his neck. Relieved to feel a strong pulse, he surveyed his friend's injuries. Neal's face was cut and swollen, one eye puffed shut, his lips split. Blood ran from his nose and red welts bloomed beneath the scrapes on his ribs. His left arm was covered with deep scratches and his right bore a purplish lump.

"He don' look so good," Kawika said anxiously. "Bettah get him to da doctah."

Neal dragged one eye open. In a cracked whisper he said, "Hey, Kawika, welcome back."

Kawika covered Neal's hand with his own. "Tanks, brah. Ey, you gonna be okay."

Big Jim came over clutching his chest. Between pants he said, "Guess we...crashed the...party."

Neal laughed, a hissing sound that ended in a spray of blood. "That's okay," he said weakly. "It was getting kinda dull."

Big Jim lowered himself onto the arm of the sofa

with a groan. He lifted his arm feebly and pointed. "Hey, Kawika," he said, "you savin' that?"

Kawika looked down, then lifted his shirt. Protruding from the left side of his enormous belly was the handle of a *balisong*.

"Eeeeee! I *tought* I feel sumtin'!"

Grimacing, he pulled the knife out with a quick jerk. He inspected it briefly, then folded the bloody handles around the blade and put it in his pocket.

Big Jim let out a weary sigh. He pushed himself off the sofa and reached out, yanking another knife from Kawika's back. "Here," he said, holding it out. "May as well have this one, too."

Chapter Forty-One

Bernice Hollings rose from her chair as Harry Sturdivant and Violet Gray entered the waiting room at the small hospital in Kealakekua. She embraced Violet. "How's your foot, hon?"

"A lot better." Violet indicated her crutches. "Only a couple more days on these things."

"That's good news, at least. How are you, Harry?"

"I'm fine, Bernice. Have you seen Neal yet?"

"No, I just got here. The doctor's with him right now."

Harry looked at Violet, who was balancing uncomfortably on her crutches. "May as well have a seat, then."

Harry and Violet settled into the blandly upholstered sofa in the windowed waiting room and Bernice returned to her armchair, where she sat tentatively on the edge. "Violet," she said in a low voice, "thanks for calling me about Neal."

"Oh, sure. I just wish we'd known yesterday. Jim Perkins called both of us a few times but we were gone, and Harry just checked his answering machine at the shop this morning."

Bernice sighed. "It's probably just as well since the nurse said Neal was out all yesterday. I don't know if they meant sleeping or unconscious or from drugs."

"Did you get in touch with Tom Bailey?"

"I did. He should be here soon." Bernice let out a

quavery breath and sat back in her chair. "I can't understand why someone would do a thing like this."

Tom Bailey arrived a few minutes later. He bent to give Bernice a peck on the cheek and clasped hands with Violet Gray, who said, "You and Harry met, didn't you?" she asked.

"Briefly, at the demonstration," the lawyer said. The men shook hands. "How's Neal?"

"We're still waiting to see him," Harry answered.

Bailey nodded. He folded himself into a chair, pulled a pipe from his shirt pocket and stabbed it unlit into his mouth. "What about this? Do they know who did it?"

"Harry just told me they have two of the men," Bernice said.

"Oh?"

Harry nodded. "Yeah. Jim Perkins and a friend of his caught 'em. You know Jim—Big Jim?"

"Yeah, we met at Bernice's party a while back."

"Well, he said there were three guys. One got away."

"And who are the two men they caught?"

"I don't know. Jim said they looked Japanese but he didn't know who they were. The cops probably do, at least by now."

"Hm." Bailey held the bowl of his pipe, clicking the stem against his teeth. "Any idea who the other man was? The one that got away?"

"I, uh—I'm not sure," Harry said. He glanced at Violet Gray, then down at his hands.

"Any description?" Bailey asked, pressing him. "Bernice told me they were wearing masks, but there must be something."

"Well, Jim did say the guy's mask came down for a second."

"It did? Was he a haole?"

Harry worked his eyebrows. "I guess you'd have to ask him, Tom. Why, you have some ideas about this?"

"Oh, I don't know," Bailey said vaguely, looking at his pipe.

A plump nurse in a white polyester uniform glided into waiting room. In a stern voice she said, "The doctor says you can see Mr. Tate for a short time."

They followed the nurse's wide bottom and whisking white hosed thighs to the end of a corridor, where she held a door open.

Bernice was the first one inside. "Oh, Neal, hon," she cried, "you look awful!"

He was propped up in bed, listing slightly to one side. His face was puffy and dark, the skin raw-looking. His left eyebrow was missing and a row of black stitches angled over the shaved skin like a crude replacement. His ribs were taped up to his armpits and his right arm was encased in a cast from elbow to wrist, with one finger of his protruding hand trapped in a metal and foam splint.

"That's funny," he said in a thick croak, "I feel great." His smile turned into a wince as it pulled his lips.

Bernice moved beside the bed. "Here." She picked up the water glass on the bedside table and helped him drink.

Neal nodded his thanks, wiping his mouth with his good hand. Speaking slowly through his swollen lips he said, "Well, this is like a party. How are you, Violet? How's your leg?"

Violet Gray had hobbled to a chair beside the bed, where she sat with her crutches across her lap. "Not bad," she said. "I can only imagine how you feel, thank goodness."

He smiled with one side of his mouth, keeping his lips together. "With all these drugs in me I feel pretty damn good."

"Why did these people do this Neal?" Bernice asked. "Did they want something? What did they say?"

He laughed delicately. "They didn't say much."

"You know they caught two of 'em, don't you?" Harry said. "Big Jim and your other friend—I forgot his name."

"Kawika. Yeah, I seem to remember that. Well—two out of four, that's not bad."

"Four!" Harry said. "Jim said three."

Neal coughed, wincing again. "One left early," he said. "I should've gone with him."

Tom Bailey spoke up. "Did you get a look at any of these people?"

"No. They had masks on."

"Yeah, I heard. But I mean none of them looked, uh, familiar?"

Neal stared at Bailey for a moment. "Not sure."

Harry was starting to say something when the nurse appeared in the doorway. "I'm sorry but time's up. The doctor said just three minutes."

Violet got to her feet and fit the crutches under her arms. "We'll be back, Neal," she said with a wink. "You can't get rid of us this easily."

Bernice leaned over and patted an unscratched spot on his arm. "And I'll bring you something to eat," she promised. "I know how hospital food is.

"Thanks Bernice," Neal said. "And everybody. I'm glad you came."

Violet Gray and Tom Bailey said goodbye and went out. Bernice followed, giving a last finger-wave at the door.

Harry lingered. When the others were down the hall he went to the door, closed it, and came back to the bed.

"You know who did this, don't you? You know and Tom Bailey knows and Big Jim knows. It was the guy who was with Skip Schaefer. The bodyguard."

"How did you—"

"Big Jim told me about him," Harry said. "The guy's mask came off when they were fighting."

Neal focused his good eye on Harry's face. It seemed different, somehow. Harder. "Harry—I don't want this to get around. I don't want to stir things up. At least not until I know what they plan to do now."

Harry stroked his jaw, tight-lipped. He hadn't shaved and the whisker stubble made a sandy sound under his fingers. "I understand." He suddenly grunted. "Well, I better get my ass out of here before that nurse comes back and gets me in a head lock." He gave Neal's foot a pat. "Take it easy, kid. I'll be back to see you before long."

He was at the door when Neal stopped him. "Harry. Wait."

Harry turned, pushing the door shut behind him.

Neal licked his lips. "Did you say anything to Violet about the rockets? About—" He made a gun with his hand and flicked the thumb.

"As a matter of fact," Harry said, smiling grimly," she already knew. She saw someone on the shore with a rifle during one of the launches and your truck was parked near there—I described it to her a while back. She put two and two together. She's a smart cookie."

"Yeah. I guess Sam Kane is, too."

"Yeah, I guess. Sam paid her a visit a few weeks ago,

but she didn't tell him anything."

Neal let out a ragged sigh. "I appreciate that. What the hell was she doing in that boat anyway?"

"That's what I asked her," Harry said peevishly. "She said she needed some pictures showing where the rocket smoke was going. Something about a pollution lawsuit."

"Oh."

"Well—take it easy, guy." At the door Harry paused with his hand on the knob. "You know, I keep thinking about the things you said on the boat, Neal. And, hell, a rocket's just a damn machine."

*   *   *

A few minutes after Harry departed the nurse peeked into the room. "You *are* awake," she said, almost reproachfully. "Feel like taking a phone call?"

She put the telephone within reach and left. A few moments later it buzzed softly and he picked it up.

"Is this...Sleeping Beauty?"

"Jim. Hey, howzit."

"How am *I*? *I'm* fine, brah."

"Good. Hey, Jim, I don't remember exactly what I said when I woke up the last time. So if I didn't say thanks, I'm saying it now."

"No problem. Don't forget, your buddy Kawika helped."

"I haven't. What's he doing here, anyway?"

"Decided to come back early and...look for a place to stay."

"Oh. That's great. So why the hell were you two at my place?"

"Well, we had a few drinks and...decided to pay you a friendly visit."

"In the middle of the night?"

"It's a long way, and...we drove kinda incredibly slow. Anyway, I never claimed to be eat up with...*etiquette* or anything."

"Lucky for me you're not. Did Kawika get hurt? Maybe I hallucinated that."

"He got a coupla stabs. Just flesh wounds. And he's got lotsa flesh. They sewed him up and...turned him loose."

"He's okay, then?"

"Yep."

"And you're okay?"

"Physically. Maybe not mentally."

"Well, what about—does Kawika know about..."

"Oh. Yeah, sorry, it just slipped out. But I told him if he told anyone else—even Muriela—I was gonna chop him up and use him for...shark bait."

"What did he say about it?"

"Hah! He started laughin' and bangin' on the car. Said he wished *he'd* thought of it."

"Yeah, well, the fact that he didn't shows he's smarter than me."

"Maybe, maybe not," Perkins said. "Hey, you sound kinda washed out. I just called to tell you I'm gonna...pick someone up at the airport this afternoon. A chick you may remember. Name of Susan."

*   *   *

Neal awoke from a light sleep hearing whispers in the hallway. His good eye blinked open. He said, "Hello out there."

Susan put her head in the room timidly. "You're awake?"

"No, I'm talking in my sleep."

381

She came in, followed by Big Jim, and stood across the room looking uncertain. "I didn't want to wake you up," she said apologetically. "Um. How are you feeling? Should we come back later?"

"No, I feel a lot better." He took in her tanned skin, longer hair, new dress. "Boy, you sure look good."

She burst into tears and rushed over to him. "Neal," she said, pressing a wet cheek against his face, "I'm sorry this happened to you. I'm so sorry."

"So it was *you* that sent those guys," he said sternly. She laughed, wiping her face and sniffing. "At least my brain wasn't damaged. It still comes up with the same bad jokes.

"You're not shittin'," Big Jim said from across the room. "You shoulda heard him on the way to the...*hospital.* He kept bleedin' all over my car and...crackin' jokes. It was a goddam relief when he...passed out again." He coughed. "You know, I think I'm gonna get a...Coke or somethin'."

He left, closing the door.

Susan sat beside Neal on the bed, wiping her face again. She reached out and ran a finger lightly over his remaining eyebrow. "They said you had some head injuries. A concussion.

"Yeah, whatever the hell that is. So, how come you're here?"

"Jim called me yesterday and told me you were in the hospital. I got the first flight out."

"Good ol' Jim." Neal rolled his head and looked away for a moment. "I guess he told you what happened," he, said turning back to her.

"Not everything. He said some men wearing masks attacked you up at the house and he and Kawika came by while it was going on. I'm supposed to talk to you if

382

I have any other questions.

"That's about it, really."

"Bullshit. Who were they, Neal?"

He closed his eyes. "Remember Howard Tubbs? The guy that came out to the house that day with Skip Schaefer?"

"Him? You're sure? You saw his face?"

"Jim did. But I knew it was him."

"Why did they do it? He couldn't have been mad at you after all this time."

Neal laughed, a soft hack that hurt. "Well, we sort of ran into each other again."

"What happened, did you have a fight?"

"I guess you could say that. I knocked him out with the butt of a rifle."

"What! What the hell happened, Neal? What were you doing with a rifle?"

"Oh, hell." He sighed again, flinching at a stab of pain. "I'm afraid to tell you. You'll probably get up and fly back to LA."

Susan sat wordlessly. Tears swelled in her eyes. "Does that mean you want me to stay?"

He turned to look at her. "Of course I do. I always did. You know, I...I understand why you wanted to sell the place. I guess I just couldn't accept what was going on. I wanted everything to be the way it was before. Maybe now we can...I don't know, work something out. I really love you, Susan. I missed you."

"Yeah, well I'm glad. Because I love you too." She brushed away more tears and kissed him, then blew her nose on a tissue from the box by the bed. "I figured out something in LA," she said, red-eyed. "You and I may be screwed up, but we're only about ten percent as screwed up as everybody else."

"You think?"

"Yeah. And as far as LA itself goes we may be only, like, *two* percent as screwed up as everybody else."

"It's the pollution," he said. "Bad for the brain."

"You may be right. I was going crazy there. I kept thinking about how...peaceful it was back here."

"Used to be, anyway."

"Well, I—" She suddenly frowned. "Wait a minute. You haven't told me what you were doing with the rifle."

"Oh. That." He gave her a lame smile and shrugged with one shoulder. "Shooting rockets."

Chapter Forty-Two

Skip Schaefer paced angrily across the dense white carpet in Hideo Kamada's office. The carpet felt like wall-to-wall marshmallows under his feet, irritating him and feeding his anger. Right now he wanted something solid to stand on, something that made an unambiguous clack when you walked on it.

"I can't believe you sent those—those *goons* after that guy!" the astronaut said, barely able to refrain from shouting. "Jesus H. *Christ*, Hideo, are you out of your damned mind?"

Across the room, Kamada sat placidly behind his long marble-topped desk, his elbows on the polished surface, his chin resting on clasped hands. He looked to Schaefer like a toad on a sarcophagus.

"I do not think so," Kamada said crisply. He leaned back in his chair and the white leather creaked, filling the electrified silence like high voltage sparks.

"You do not think so! Well I *do* think so! What the hell did you think you were doing? Who the hell are *you* to endanger this company like that? If this gets out CSS is finished!"

"Calm yourself...Laurance," Kamada said. There was a hint of testiness in his words. He disliked Schaefer's uncivilized display of emotion. "Consider this situation rationally and logically. The law could not help us. It was unable to provide our protection. So. We were forced to provide our own insurance against another

385

mishap. It is quite simple."

This time Schaefer did shout. "*Simple!* You seem to think that *shooting* people is the natural way to resolve a conflict. I got a call from that chopper pilot a few days ago."

"Chopper..." Kamada frowned. "I do not—"

"The helicopter pilot, the one we hired when we were trying to trap Tate. He told me you ordered the security man up there with him to *fire* on Tate."

Kamada folded his hands against his chest. One finger moved, a tiny shrug. "It is true."

"It is true." Schaefer closed his eyes. "My god, what if he'd *done* it?"

'If he had done it he would be working for us now."

"What? You mean you *fired* him? For not *shooting*?"

"Of course. I gave him an order and he ignored it."

"You're absolutely *mad*. In the first place he probably didn't have time to shoot, thank god, since the chopper ran out of fuel. In the second place, have you thought about the consequences if Tate *had* been shot?"

"What if he had been shot? Tate was running from his crime. He was trespassing. He harmed the guard dog. He shot the rocket. It would be better if he had been killed."

"Oh, sure!" Schaefer tossed up his hands. "Excellent publicity."

"In the...long run," Kamada said, "the bad publicity would not be nearly as damaging to us as another destroyed rocket. Besides, it would be seen as merely the act of an excited security man. I doubt that he would go to jail."

"Oh, you do? Now you're going to take over the legal department and give us guidance there, is that right?"

Hands folded, Kamada calmly studied Schaefer. "I do not care for the way we are speaking to one another...Laurance."

"Well I don't care for the way you're jeopardizing this company. *Hideo.* What's going to happen when the cops grab your boy Tubbs and he spills his guts to keep from going to prison? They caught his two idiot buddies. One of those fools'll talk. And Tubbs said one of the men at the house got a look at his face, right?"

"That means nothing," Kamada said. "Someone may have seen his face for an instant, but that does not mean that he will be identified. Howard will not be going back to that island for a long time. And if somehow he were to be caught, he would not, as you say, 'spill his guts'. He is...loyal."

Kamada eased himself forward in his chair and laid his hands on his desk. "Skip," he said in a conciliatory tone, "we have been through difficult times in creating this company. We have passed through these times before, and we will pass through them now, as we will in the future. I do not wish for us to fight. Perhaps I am wrong in the things I have done recently. But they are all for the good of Concord Space Services. In time, this recent trouble will be behind us. In a few years, we will perhaps even be amused by certain...aspects, of the events."

Kamada leaned forward and his monotone took on a hint of urgency. "By that time, if we work together as we have done this far, we will have grown into a great and powerful force in space technology. If all goes as I envision, it is very possible that we will become, in Japan, a great force. Such as General Dynamics is in America."

Schaefer's eyebrows knitted. "What do you mean, Japan? And what do you mean, like General Dynamics?"

Kamada floated from his chair. Moving deliberately, he stepped from behind his desk and walked toward the window. "We must open our minds," he said softly. "Skip. Surely you have had dreams about what we can do. Think of it. Japan is more and more assuming responsibility for its own military protection. You are well aware of how the U.S. congress feels about spending money to defend Japan—a country that has taken over many markets held before by American companies.

"Please understand," Kamada continued, giving the air in front of his stomach a little chop with one hand, "I am happy for...my country...that it has been so successful. And I am happy to see Japan...standing up again. Willing to put swords back in their own hands, rather than continuing to hide behind America. After all, Japan is the land of the *samurai*. But I can also see the problem from the American point of view, and I see how it must make people very angry."

Schaefer lowered his head, staring at Kamada from beneath his bushy eyebrows. "Exactly what are you getting at, Hideo?"

"Skip." Kamada said. "Concord Space Systems will one day—*forge*—the new swords for Japan." He had looked that word up especially. "Just as Lockheed, or General Dynamics, or General Electric and other such companies—just as they make rockets and other weapons for America, this is what we will do for Japan. It is an...open field. Before now, only the Japanese government itself has been involved at much depth with rockets, through NASDA. But NASDA is a civilian organ, as is NASA in this country. There will be a limit to their involvement with military matters. But a private corporation such as ours, located out of the country—we will have an advantage if we plan ahead. We will have...our foot in the door. To meet Japan's growing military needs. And the military needs of other countries."

"Their *military* needs?" Schaefer said angrily. "We never—"

"I must tell you," Kamada said, holding up a hand, "I am emphasizing the military because it will grow very quickly in the coming years. And because, I am happy to say, I have many excellent friends in the military of Japan, as well as the government. So—"

"Wait a minute, wait a minute!" Schaefer interrupted hotly. "I thought this was understood a long time ago. We're a civilian aerospace company, not a weapons-maker. Not for America, not for Japan, not for *any*one. The *peaceful* exploitation of space, remember? I'm through with the war business, Hideo. I finished with it when I left the Air Force and I'm *not* getting back in."

Kamada scrutinized him. "You cannot tell me you have not thought about developing rockets for weapons."

"Sure I've thought about it," Schaefer said, leaning toward him. "And I *do not* want to do it. I don't care how much money there is in it. Look, when we started this company the idea was to build ourselves into a great space technology group. Satellite delivery, building and operating space labs, cargo delivery service to other space stations. If we live long enough, delivery to goddam moon stations, maybe even mining on the moon ourselves, or running a space shuttle of some kind."

Kamada flicked a hand impatiently and moved to the windows overlooking Honolulu. "Yes, this is true. This is all fine for the future. For the distant future. But we must be able to reach the future. That is the reason behind our present commercial venture, though you seem to find it...distasteful."

"Are you referring to shooting cremation ashes into orbit? You're right, I never have been too excited about that. It's morbid. And it's unproductive."

"Unproductive. It is the only venture we are involved with that has a chance of quickly producing revenue. That is productive, as I see it." Kamada stepped away from the window abruptly, as though he had seen enough of the outside world. "It is a means of bringing in money, which will allow us to expand. That will be true of weapons, also. Think of the money France earns with only their small war missiles. Before long we will be able to move our manufacturing facilities from California to Japan, which will greatly decrease our costs. We will be extremely competitive in price."

"To hell with that," Schaefer snapped. "I didn't get into this thing to bolster Japan's economy. This is an American chartered corporation and I want to keep it in America. And I want to keep it non-military."

"Laurance. Military contracts will bring us capital. You are aware of how desperately we need this. Especially now, after we have lost all but two of our first production of rockets because of that madman. The capital will enable us to survive. At the expense of governments, we will develop our own technology and experience."

"No," Schaefer said vehemently. "It doesn't work like that. You get hooked into the government thing and that's it. It's like a great big tit. You suck on it until you're a gigantic, drooling, addicted baby. You do anything to keep getting your contract fix. You're out of control, you can't tell where the government stops and you start. That's not what we had in mind for this company! God dammit, I...I had *dreams* for CSS. About a great company looking to the future of man in space. Not about missiles and warheads and killing. Let other people do it, not CSS."

Kamada turned back to the window. "We will discuss this another time. Laurance...you must think about it in a less...emotional way."

Schaefer's voice grew coldly quiet. "I don't feel like being less emotional, Hideo. If you want CSS to get involved in making missiles then you're going to have to buy me out. Because I won't have anything to do with it."

Kamada revolved his head until his obsidian eyes rested on Schaefer. "If that is your wish."

Schaefer glared at Kamada, his face burning. He turned on his heel and walked out of the office, leaving the door open.

Chapter Forty-Three

Idling the engines of the *Suzy Q*, Big Jim Perkins swiveled his seat around and took his bearings. Judging from island landmarks the big sportfisher's position was about a quarter mile öffshore and a quarter mile north of the Concord Space Systems Kona Launch Facility. Just right. He shut down the engines; they would drift some—the water was too deep for an anchor—but that wasn't a concern. What *had* concerned them was the weather, and that had taken care of itself. After a cloudy start the day had turned clear and hot, with the sun's rays now plunging vertically into a gem-blue sea.

Perkins—shirtless, exposing bruises on his back and chest that looked like grape juice stains—shaded his eyes and scanned the sea to the west, where a line of puffy cumulus clouds drifted along the horizon like a herd of albino elephants. No boats; so far so good. He turned his attention to the digits on his wristwatch. "I've got forty-four minutes, exactly," he said loudly, looking upward. "What's the report, Mr. K?"

In the tuna tower above, Kawika Kahooke lowered a big pair of binoculars from his eyes. "I don' see nobody watchin' from da rocket place. Some cahs pocked up on da highway, but too fa to see anyting." He turned and trained the binoculars seaward, careful not to rub against the safety rail or top stanchions. His tee shirt was puffed out by thick gauze bandages on his belly, shoulder, and back. "Oh-oh," he said. "I tink we gon have visitahs."

Big Jim squinted across the water. "Well, we figured they'd give us a look."

Tom Bailey looked up from the rear deck, his teeth clenched on his pipe. "The Coast Guard?"

"None other."

Harry Sturdivant re-lit his own pipe inside the cabin and expelled a puff of sweet-smelling smoke. "We're okay," he growled confidently. "Jim and I went over this boat for three hours yesterday and made sure everything was kosher. If they don't find any violations they can't make us move." He pulled a foil pouch from his Bermuda shorts and held it up. "Hey, Tom, ready to try some of this?"

Bailey caught the pouch. He began cleaning the ashes from pipe bowl, keeping an eye on the approaching Coast Guard vessel.

By the time he had his pipe repacked and lit the red-striped cutter had arrived. It maneuvered to within fifty feet of the *Suzy Q*, engines slowly throbbing, and a man in a blue shirt and dark pants hailed them from the bow through a megaphone.

"Ahoy, folks."

Big Jim held up a hand from the tower and Bailey waved.

"Do you know you're in a possible hazard area?"

"I thought it was okay to...*come* here." Big Jim yelled across the water.

The man with the megaphone conferred with an officer standing beside him, then spoke again. *"It's legal, but we recommend you stay at least a mile to the north or south during the launch. Like all the other boats are doing."*

Tom Bailey pulled out his pipe and cupped his

hands around his mouth. "We're here to get some pictures," he shouted. He pointed to the rear deck, where two tripod-mounted cameras equipped with fat telephoto lenses stood.

Harry laughed hoarsely from the cabin, where he sat on the floor out of sight. "Another lying lawyer."

The Coast Guard officer signaled to the man in the wheelhouse and the cutter's throbbing engines dropped to a murmur. He took the megaphone from the seaman next to him and raised it. *"Please stand by for boarding. We'd like to inspect your vessel."*

Harry grunted from the cabin, "Well, I think I'll just visit the head until they leave. No sense showing my ugly mug to 'em unless they come looking for it." He made his way to the boat's cramped toilet facilities and closed himself in.

The safety inspection was carried out by a seaman and a boyish lieutenant who motored over in a small inflatable boat. They looked around for only a few minutes.

"We don't find you in violation of any regulations, Mr. Perkins," the lieutenant said as the seaman clambered back into the inflatable, "but we still strongly recommend moving farther away from the launch site."

"Thanks for your concern," Big Jim said. "We're out of the flight path, aren't' we?"

"Yes, you are, but—"

"How about if we...move another couple of hundred yards north? Would that be okay? We could still get what we need from there."

Expecting resistance, the lieutenant was visibly mollified by the concession. "Well, that'd be a bit better. But we still recommend the one mile distance."

"So noted," Big Jim said. "Thanks again for...your

concern."

With a brisk nod, the lieutenant climbed down the boarding ladder.

When the inflatable was aboard the Coast Guard cutter again the big vessel cruised in a wide arc around the *Suzy Q*, increased speed, and headed out to sea, slicing through the azure waves.

Tom Bailey watched it depart, puffing his pipe meditatively as the wake rocked the sportfisher. "That worked out just right."

"Sure did," Big Jim said. "I'll move us a little. You can tell Harry it's safe to...come out of the head."

Bailey grinned. "With that crack about lawyers I'm tempted to let him simmer in there a while."

Half an hour later Bailey checked his watch and called down from the tuna tower, where he had replaced Kawika. "I've got T-minus fifteen. How's it going down there?"

The cameras had been moved and the *Suzy Q*'s engine cover taken off. Big Jim, in coveralls, poked his head out of the engine compartment. "Just about got it," he said, wiping sweat from his eyes.

A minute later he passed up a heavy package wrapped in plastic to Kawika, who carried it into the cabin and laid it on the floor.

"Plenty of time," Harry said, unwrapping the plastic.

*   *   *

Hideo Kamada strode with stolid confidence down the middle aisle of the low-ceilinged Concord Space Systems Launch Control Center, pausing occasionally as he moved from one control station to the next to look over a technician's shoulder. Trailing behind Kamada were half a dozen men in suits. Following their host's example the suited men—investors who had accepted an expenses-paid invitation to witness the launch—stopped behind each station in turn, running their eyes over the confusion of lights, buttons and switches.

The technicians manning the consoles seemed oblivious to the VIP inspection tour. Headphones on, they stared at their video screens and digital readouts and murmured terse comments into mouth microphones as the last minutes ticked away.

The muted sound of the warning siren came over the building's speakers, bringing Hideo Kamada to a halt. He turned to face his guests. "Gentlemen," he said, smiling rigidly, "the launch will occur in less than three minutes." He pointed with an open hand. "Therefore, I suggest we move to the viewing area."

Kamada led the troupe of investors back to the center of the building, where the front wall of thick reinforced concrete curved out a few feet to form a long alcove. Set into the wall were small rectangular windows of heavy plastic-laminated glass that provided a direct view of the rocket.

When his visitors were lined up in front of the viewing ports, Kamada returned unhurriedly to the north end of the building, where he seated himself in front of a color television monitor to await the launch.

*   *   *

The hysterical whooping of the warning siren died and a strident beeping blared across the water.

"Two minutes," Tom Bailey cried out from the *Suzy Q*'s tuna tower.

Up in the flying bridge Big Jim manipulated the controls with sweaty concentration, working the throttle and shift levers with one hand and the wheel with the other to keep the boat's stern pointed directly at the CSS launch pad. "Still okay?" he hollered.

Harry's hoarse growl came from the cabin. "Perfect. Now just stop the damn waves."

Kawika was hunched over a camera on the foredeck, watching the rocket's oscillating image through the viewfinder and snapping off a picture every few moments. Bailey fooled with the zoom lens of the other camera, which they had set up next to the gunwale beside the cabin door.

They waited.

Bailey looked at his watch again. "Less than ten seconds now, Harry! You ready?"

"Ready as I'll ever be. I think—"

A flash of light came from the launch pad and a cloud of smoke burst sideways from the exhaust deflector, forming a roiling orange cauliflower as it rose into the air. The thunder of the first stage engine reached the *Suzy Q* just before the support arm fell away from the rocket, and the Independence lifted from the launch pad, sliding upward beside the gantry.

Glued to their posts, Big Jim, Kawika, and Tom Bailey waited for another sound. They flinched when it came: a sharp crack enveloped in a gut-thudding *phoom*. The *Suzy Q*'s cabin seemed to bulge outward as the sound-suppressed .338 caliber rifle was fired twice more.

A wart of flame appeared on the lower stage of the climbing Independence. In less than a second brilliant tendrils spread outward from the wart and the rocket's hull ripped open, disintegrating like a colossal exploding cigar and thrusting the top half of the rocket upward. The solid fuel in the second stage ignited, turning it upside down, and in this position it fell onto the launch tower. A double explosion erupted as the upper stages struck the ground, covering the entire launch pad in a storm of fire.

"God damn *hell!*" Big Jim breathed, awestruck. He tore his eyes from the pyrotechnics. "I think you hit it, Harry."

A flaming meteor suddenly hissed down from the sky and hit the sea not a hundred feet from the *Suzy Q*, throwing up a fountain of spray.

"Kawika!" Tom Bailey shouted from the tower, "Get under cover!"

Kawika made a dash for the cabin. There was another rippling hiss and a suitcase-sized slab of burning solid propellant struck the *Suzy Q* amidships, blowing out a window and spraying smaller chunks of fuel inside the cabin.

Harry let out a curse and jumped to his feet, slapping at a burning patch on his pants. Kawika collided with him as he bolted through the door and both men fell, Kawika screaming in pain as he landed on a small piece of fiery propellant.

There was another crash from above followed by a short scream from Tom Bailey, and Big Jim looked up to see a bowling ball sized hunk of burning propellant roll from the tower. It fell to the foredeck, bounced, and disappeared over the side. Big Jim swung onto the tower ladder and climbed it in three steps.

He found Tom Bailey sprawled on the small tower deck, unconscious. The hair was burned from one side of his scalp and the top of his shoulder showed a red, blistered welt. There was a split in the bimini top where the hunk of propellant had come through.

In the cabin below, Harry pulled Kawika to his feet

and together they beat on the sofa cushions, both sets of which had caught fire.

"The extinguisher!" Harry shouted, coughing from the fumes. Kawika ripped it from the wall and blasted the cushions, sending Harry reeling for the door, choking on the combined smoke and extinguisher powder. He sank to the deck as Kawika emerged from the smoke-billowing cabin.

"I need some help! Tom's hurt!"

Harry pulled himself to his feet and followed Kawika up the ladder to the flying bridge.

"What happened?"

"He got hit by a piece of that stuff," Big Jim said anxiously. "I think he's just knocked out but he has some burns. Let's get him down."

Carefully, they handed Bailey down to the flying bridge and carried him to the rear deck. The lawyer groaned as they laid him down.

Harry knelt beside him and said, "Tom, how do you feel?"

Bailey's eyelids dragged open, blinking. "Like hell," he mumbled. "My shoulder—"

"It's okay. You got burned a little but nothing seems broken. You got hit by a piece of something from the rocket."

"Yeah," Bailey said, coughing. "I saw the stuff coming down."

Big Jim looked toward the smoke and twisted wreckage on shore. "I think we broke their launch pad," he said nervously. "Maybe we oughta...*split*." He climbed up to the flying bridge and put the *Suzy Q* in gear, wheeling the bow north.

Kawika climbed up to join him. "What you tink?" he asked.

"About Tom? He'll be okay."

"No, not Tom." Kawika pointed. Two miles distant the Coast Guard cutter was coming their way with bow spray flying.

"Take the wheel, Kawika. We gotta get that rifle stowed."

Big Jim found Harry squatting in the cabin surrounded by broken glass and charred cushion debris, feverishly breaking down the big test rifle.

"I don't know about this, Harry. That cutter's gonna be here pretty damn quick."

"I know. *Dammit!*" Harry laid down the rifle and blew on his hands, which he had burned while putting out the fire in the cabin. "Hell, we'll never get it back where it was. Got any other hiding places?"

Big Jim shook his head. "None I'd trust." He stepped over to the shattered remains of the port window and looked out. "We've just got a few minutes. I have a feeling they might...*inspect* us again.

Harry remained squatting on the floor. "Well," he said suddenly, "there's a simple solution to our problem."

Chapter Forty-Four

Squatting on their prodigious haunches, Kawika and Muriela Kahooke pulled away the ti leaves covering the imu, a fire pit dug into the beach sand. Clouds of steam rolled upward and filled the evening air with the smells of baked pineapple and pork.

"Dis gone broke da mout', brah," Kawika said, gloating.

Neal, with a beer in one hand and his eyes half closed as he listened to a chirping ukulele, leaned over to breathe in the sweet aroma. "That's fine," he said contentedly. "Another broken part or two won't make any difference."

Kawika's grin was white in the torchlight. He reached out and tapped the cast on Neal's arm. "Ey, how much longer fa dis?"

"A few more days. Any longer and I'd saw the damn thing off myself. It's driving me bonkers."

Big Jim Perkins materialized amid the steam and smoke, a bearded apparition in a Panama hat and banana-print aloha shirt. "Whatever you're talkin' about," he said, "you mean more bonkers." Perkins picked up a stick and helped Muriela rake away the glowing coals. \

"Hey, Neal," he said, waving smoke out of his eyes, "Susan said your...ear was better.

"Yeah. Not a hundred percent, but the loud ringing is gone. I guess those guys beating on my head did

401

something."

Tom Bailey's disembodied voice came from the far side of the pit. "What about the headaches?"

"They're slacking off," Neal said. He located the lawyer beneath a hovering patch of white; Bailey had taken to wearing a Panama hat himself to cover his singed hair while it grew back.

"Ey, Kawika," Muriela squealed impatiently, "stop you droolin' an' hep wi' dis."

Kawika grabbed the wooden skewer running through the roasted pig and together they lifted it from the coals, raising a chorus of oohs and ahhs from the small crowd of onlookers. They set the pig on a bed of fresh ti leaves spread on a table beneath the palms.

Neal found Susan in a group of people scattered around the ukulele player. He knelt down in the sand where she was sitting and said into her ear, "The first pig is done."

"Great!" she whispered. "I'm starving!"

On the way to the table they ran into Harry and Violet Gray walking in the same direction. "Trying to sneak over there ahead of us?" Harry asked accusingly.

"Actually, yeah," Neal said. "But as soon as we ate I was going to come get you, I swear."

Bernice Hollings and Tom Bailey were waiting for them in a line moving past the serving table, where Big Jim and Kawika slashed off slabs of steaming pork and dropped them onto paper plates. "You got here just in time," Bailey said worriedly, looking over his shoulder. "Those guys are being way too generous with my food."

The line moved forward slowly. Neal bumped Susan with his cast. "Would you mind getting me another beer?" he asked. "It's hard to lift the lid and dig through the ice with one hand."

She rolled her eyes at Bernice. "He loves having a broken arm. I get orders all day long."

Neal scowled. "Hey. Just go get the beer—slave."

Paper plates came down the line. As Violet handed the stack to Neal she noticed the lei made of small green leaves around his neck. She lifted one end of it and sniffed. "Maile," she said, recognizing the clove-like scent. "Where did you get it?"

"Kamuela gave it to me. The man I introduced you to."

"With the white hair and cane? How sweet. Any special occasion?"

He laughed. "He said it was from the people in Mokolea. A token of appreciation for not selling my place."

"A well-deserved honor," Bernice said, patting his shoulder.

"Hell," Neal protested, "you deserve all the recognition, you and Tom and Violet. All the GYRO people." He nodded toward a banner stretched between two palm trees and flanked by blazing tiki torches that read MAHALO GYRO—Goodbye ROCKETS!! "That's what this luau's all about."

Susan returned and slipped back in line, trading Neal a dripping beer for two paper plates, which Kawika immediately loaded with slabs of pork and chunks of roasted pineapple.

"You don' finish dat, Susan, save fa me."

"Of course."

"Same fa you, brah."

"Of course."

"Ovah deh nex'," Kawika nodded at the table a few yards away where a second kalua pig lay in state. "Dey gotta big bowl a poi."

Neal nodded. "Thanks for the tip."

Harry waited at the end of the table while Big Jim served Violet. He said, "Why don't you guys take a break and eat with us? Someone else can take over the hacking and slashing."

Kawika eyed Big Jim, then the pig. "Okay."

Two men from the village took over the carving. Big Jim and Kawika carried their beers and sagging plates over to the pile of lava rocks near the water's edge where the others were sitting.

"Where's Muriela?" Susan asked. "Isn't she going to?"

"She tokkin to some frins ovah deh," Kawika said. "Anyway, she on a dite or sumtin crazy."

Conversation lagged as the eating turned serious.

"The just rewards of virtue," Tom Bailey said, smacking his lips. "All the GYRO headaches are finally paying off."

"I'm sure there'll be many more where those came from," Bernice said. She sighed. "You know, sometimes when I look back on everything I can't help wondering how much good GYRO itself really did."

Bailey looked at her. "Are you kidding? It did a lot of good. The most important thing was making people aware and getting them to work together. I know what I'm talking about. Raising the environmental consciousness of the indigenous population is crucial to any serious ecological activism campaign."

Neal raised his beer. "Hell, everybody says that, but I'll drink to it anyway."

"Hear, hear," said Violet Gray. "And I'd like to propose a toast." She lifted her can of beer. "To you lunatic gentlemen," she said, giving each of them a stern look. "May you never do anything so damn fool crazy again." She paused, then added, "On the other hand I can't argue with success. Anyway—here's to you."

"And to getting away with it," Harry said as they lifted their cans.

There was a space of thoughtful silence as they ate.

"Bernice, what did you hear about Kamada?" Susan asked.

"He's still in Japan. According to...uh, one of my sources, he's trying to keep CSS alive in Japan. They want to lease the Japanese government's facilities for launches, or something like that."

"That's it? He just goes away and everything's hunky dory?"

"Have to wait and see," Bernice said. "Tubbs hasn't been formally charged with anything yet. But if he is and he tries to cut a deal by talking they might try to extradite Kamada. But Tom says it'd be hard to get a conviction."

Harry turned to Bailey. "A conviction on what charges?"

"Some kind of conspiracy and assault charge at the least," the lawyer said with a somber glance at Neal. "You could probably throw in conspiracy to violate civil rights and a few other things. I'm not really up on my criminal law."

"But you doubt they'd get any conviction?" Violet asked.

"Not if it comes down to Tubbs' word against Kamada's. Tubbs already has a few minor assault charges on his record so I don't think his word would count for much."

"What about the other men, Tom?" Harry asked.

"The three that helped him?"

Bailey said, "They haven't found the third one yet. The two men that Jim and Kawika caught were hired by someone else, so they never saw Tubbs' face. Which means Jim's ID of Tubbs is the only one that counts."

Perkins glanced around, making sure no one was in ear shot, and then said in a low voice, "What if Tubbs talks about the...rockets being shot?"

"I don't think he will," Bailey said. "First of all there's no point since they can't prove it. The evidence is either at the bottom of the sea or blown to bits. Second, it introduces a strong motive for Kamada to order the attack on Neal—for either revenge or to stop him. Right now the only connection to Kamada is circumstantial—Tubbs was his bodyguard. I think Kamada wants to keep it that way, and I think Tubbs is doing what Kamada tells him to do."

"But that connection could help finish Kamada in Hawaii," Bernice said. "Even if Tubbs is never charged. There's been a lot of bad publicity and probably more on the way. There's rumor of a bribery investigation between CSS and a couple of government people."

Harry grunted. "And what's the deal with Skip Schaefer now, Bernice? Is he completely out of CSS?"

"That's the story." She waved her plastic fork as she spoke. "I talked to my ex, the esteemed rear admiral, the other day. He knows a guy who knows Schaefer, who said Schaefer sold his interest in the company. Supposedly he's trying to buy a ranch in California somewhere."

"Huh. He's still in the clear as far as everything goes?"

"It seems that way."

Neal tossed a gnawed bone onto his plate. "Good,"

he said. "I think Schaefer's wrong-headed but basically not bad guy. I think it was Kamada who went off the deep end."

The two baked pigs lasted less than an hour. With the food dwindling, the luau's center of gravity moved down the beach to a wide section of sand where driftwood and scrap lumber had been stacked into a tall pile. After a liberal application of gasoline the bonfire was ignited with a dull whump and spectacular ball of flame that delighted the mob of children looking on.

Satiated luau-goers scattered along the beach struggled to their feet and wandered toward the blaze. The giant fire threw a flickering orange light on the dozen or so men and women away from the main group who were costuming themselves for a hula dance. The women, including Muriela Kahooke, wore loose cloth skirts, leis made from plumeria blossoms, and fern-leaf headdresses and bracelets. The men were tying on fern anklets and wide loincloths.

Big Jim rolled up his paper plate and stood. "Excuse me, everyone," he said, wiping his mouth on his arm, "but I feel compelled to...check out the fire." He leaned toward Neal with a peeved glower. "My Neanderthal heritage."

"Hang on, Jim," Harry said. He helped Violet up. "We'll go with you."

"I believe I'll accompany you folks, myself," Tom Bailey said, folding his plate and pushing his lanky frame off the rocks. "Ladies?"

"I'll go," Susan said, getting up.

Bernice said, "I'll be along in a minute." She winked at Susan. "Neal may need me to hand-feed him or something, poor thing."

When the others had departed in the direction of

the fire Bernice pulled a pack of cigarettes from a skirt pocket and lit one. She blew out smoke and said, "Kawika, Neal tells me you're looking for a house in Hilo. How's that going?"

"Oh. Nuttin yet. We fine sumtin fo long."

"Didn't you live in Hilo before?"

"Yeah. Mo bettah heah but Hilo okay fa while. Make da money an' buy anuddah place, maybe Kailua. Da main ting, I be fishin' again."

"Big Jim told me you're the best fisherman he knows," Neal said.

"Shoo, das not true," Kawika mumbled. He looked pleased.

Around the bonfire the hula drummers were warming up, their patters, thumps, and wooden clackings reaching through the pungent sea air.

Bernice finished off the last piece of baked pineapple on her plate and dabbed her mouth with a neatly folded paper towel. "I think I'm going to head over there," she said. She stood up. "When I hear drums I think of something Violet's husband wrote. He was an anthropologist, you know, and this was something he wrote in a book about music and culture. Let me see if I can get it right, now...'Even the simple, rhythmic beating of a hand against a hollow log has the power to stir our souls, for it is nothing less than the sound of primitive man's first knocks upon the door of civilization.'" She paused in the firelight, cigarette in hand, a melancholy smile on her lips. "Isn't that wonderful?

"It is," Neal agreed.

"Then again," Bernice said, "look what was behind that door. Oh well. You two coming?"

"I'll be there shortly," Neal said. "Can't let this food

sit around uneaten."

After Bernice had strolled off Kawika said, "Ey, Neal, whass Susan gone do? Stay or go back?"

"She's going to stay. Do some writing. Help me fix up the house."

"Don' like California?"

"She didn't like LA that much, but she met some people that might be good contacts. She's going back in a few weeks to clear up some business. And while she's there she's going to show my paintings to some galleries."

"You trine to fine somebody to buy you stuff now?"

"Yeah. If Susan doesn't have any luck I'm going to Honolulu. Bernice has a friend who owns a gallery there."

"Yeah? Well, good luck wit' dat." Kawika picked up a slice of pork from his plate and bit into it. "Ey," he said, munching thoughtfully, "whass gone happen all da propitty? Da rocket proppity?"

"I'm not really sure, Kawika. As far as I know CSS still owns it. I guess if they need the money they'll sell it. Who knows."

"Huh. I wonder if all dis gonna make a diffrince. Da lan' still b'long to CSS. Dey a'ready mess it up."

"Well, a lot of it's still the same as before," Neal said. "Most of your land is like it was, except for the house. Maybe we'll save it somehow."

Kawika nodded slowly, rolling his beer can between his palms. "I guess I nevah gone git my place back. You know brah," he said dolefully, "I really miss da ol' house. I love dat place."

"Yeah. I know you did."

"Yeah. Well..."

Kawika worked on the sand with his toes for a

moment. A smile creased his face. "At leas' dose bastids got it, ey? Ka-blooom! Dat's one ting make me fee okay."

Harry walked up, a dark blot outlined in orange by the bonfire. "You're going to miss the start of this thing," he warned. "Kawika, I'm delivering a message from Muriela. She says—and I quote—get your butt back there to watch the dance or she's gonna kick it good."

Kawika hoisted himself up. "Yeah, shu, I don' wanna miss. How 'bout you brah?"

"Be there as soon as I finish this beer."

Kawika left. Harry lingered, leaning against a rock.

"You crazy bastards," Neal said, shaking his head. "I still can't believe it. You must've been out of your minds!"

"Look who's talking."

"Good point." Neal drained his beer. "You know, we agreed it'd be better not to talk about this thing, right?"

Harry kicked at the sand a few times. "Well, yeah. No sense knowing things we didn't need to know."

"Right. But it looks like we're in the clear. So I guess we can share our adventures at some point. I'd kinda like to know how yours went."

Half of Harry's mouth lifted in a smile. "Yeah. Likewise."

Neal nodded slowly. "Good thing Kamada shut up to save his own skin." He kicked the sand himself. "You know...I've been thinking. From what you said the day we went fishing, I never would have thought you'd get, uh...involved like this."

Harry pursed his lips, pensive. "I don't know," he said at last. "I thought a lot about what you said. About the islands and all. Then after what happened to Violet and you, it just sort of—cleared up. Who we were dealing with, what the issue is." His disturbed look deepened. He started to speak, but didn't.

"What?"

"I don't know, Neal. Sometimes I have this doubt. I want to think I did the right thing for the right reasons. For the islands, mainly. And then sometimes I think—maybe there was something else in there."

"Something else?"

Harry pulled slowly at his nose. "Kamada," he said, reluctantly. "Kamada's Japanese. Maybe I...maybe I still haven't gotten over the past."

It took a moment before Neal understood. "The war? No, I can't see it, Harry," he said. "That's just not you."

Harry looked at him searchingly, then sighed. "I wish I could be so sure."

"Harry. Even if there was something to what you say, it wouldn't matter. The other reasons are still valid."

Harry nodded heavily. "Yeah. True. After thinking back on everything a hundred times, I'd do it all over again." He studied Neal, his blue eyes pale in the firelight. "Would you?"

There was a long pause before Neal said, "I'm not sure I can really say, Harry. I think that, for me, there wasn't really a choice. The price for not fighting back seemed too high, so—I just did it. Sometimes it seems it wasn't really me who shot the rockets. Like it was...another me."

Harry had listened with an unwavering gaze but now his eyes drifted away. His expression was half sad, half angry. "Things have changed," he said. "They're more complicated." He shook his head. "I had some serious doubts when we were riding out there in Big Jim's boat. I would've called it off if everything hadn't looked right. But the nearest boats were a mile away and an A-bomb wouldn't have fazed the...the control bunker, or whatever the hell it's called."

"Good thing, as it turned out."

"Yeah, good thing," Harry agreed. "Scared the peewaddlin' out of me when the rocket exploded. I wasn't expecting it."

Neal lowered his voice. "Which reminds me of something I keep meaning to ask you. Where'd you hit the thing?"

"Where? Hell, who knows? It was a seven hundred yard shot at a moving target. I just aimed at the fattest part."

"You mean the bottom stage?" Neal pulled in his chin. "That's the solid fuel booster, Harry, it's got a steel casing! What did you shoot it with?"

He made a face. "You can't guess?"

Neal looked perplexed, then the light dawned. "That big-ass rifle."

"You never heard it here. And you didn't hear that I made some special hardened steel bullets with copper tubing swaged around them."

Neal looked awed. "Hell, you really are crazy."

Harry's face was tragic in the torchlight. "I know, I know. But everything's okay so far." He tapped his head with his knuckles. "Knock on wood."

"Wait a minute," Neal said. "Kawika told me the Coast Guard boarded the boat after the rocket blew up. Where the hell did you hide that thing?"

Harry laughed. "I didn't even try. I tossed it overboard along with the leftover cartridges. I'm gonna have to explain things to Jerry but I'll come up with something that ain't a real lie. I couldn't outright lie to him but I could sure omit some details."

"Jesus.

"Yeah. May have tossed it for nothing. They were just worried about the fuel that hit us. After Tom convinced 'em he wasn't seriously hurt they left."

Neal shook his head. "Wow. Well, we all got lucky. The thing is, I still think you're crazy."

"Exactly what Violet said," Harry grumbled. "She told me if I was that nutty I needed someone to look after me," He glanced sideways at Neal. "I guess that's why she agreed to marry me."

"Seriously? You're getting married?"

"We are. Sent out invitations this morning."

"I'll be damned!" Neal stood up and shook Harry's hand, giving him a one-armed hug. "Congratulations! Hell, come on, let's go back and tell Susan."

"All right. And maybe we can find a little more food to stuff in our faces."

They strolled along the beach toward the bonfire. Neal said, "This is funny—Susan said this morning that you and Violet were perfect for each other."

"Yeah?" Harry laughed. "So she thinks I need a keeper too, huh?"

"Exactly. I guess she figured I do too, which is why she came back."

Harry chuckled roughly and draped an arm over Neal's shoulders. "You know, there's a lesson here," he said. "Sometimes it pays to be crazy."

Made in the USA
Middletown, DE
23 March 2023

27501960R00235